D0708908

Dear Target Guest,

If we met for real, in the book aisle, it would probably be my three boisterous toddlers who introduced themselves first. "Hell-o!" They'd croon, with flushed cheeks and starfished hands, trailing Goldfish crackers from our red shopping cart.

And maybe sometime in the seconds after, you and I would smile at each other over the open books in our hands—nothing big, just that small smile of kinship that booklovers sometimes share, a flash of warmth in the eyes that says, So you're looking for it too. Looking for comfort, or amazement, or even a good fright. Looking to better understand the sunburnt strangers flip-flopping past. Or looking for a writer who has lived through some familiar challenge and is now giving testimony, transforming an experience of helplessness and terror into a story of human resilience and strength.

Like Mother, Mother's William Hurst, I've been a book junkie from the first time I managed to read Are You My Mother? on my own. (Funny how P. D. Eastman's book seems significant in retrospect: a baby bird wandering all over town in pursuit of a loving maternal figure.)

Growing up in a dysfunctional family, I quickly learned that an open book could be used like a shield. In a family that disallowed boundaries, "I'm busy reading" was one of the few parameters a young child could set. I read exhaustively, desperate to find a family that behaved like mine, searching for the exact right word that summed up what felt so terribly wrong in a suburban home that looked Pottery Barn—perfect from the outside.

This book isn't a memoir, but in a way, it's a story I've been struggling to tell all my life. In retrospect, I see that I was trying to tell this story back with my first book, Smashed. Only ten years ago, I didn't know that my heavy drinking was a symptom of post-traumatic stress. I hadn't yet realized that putting myself into danger at college keggers was my subconscious mind trying to tell the story of things that happened in my youth—repetitive traumas that seemed too terrifying to fully remember, let alone say, write, or publish.

Mother, Mother is told from two perspectives, but I will always think of it as Violet's story. Violet is the black sheep—a family role I shared and coped with by writing. At Violet's age, I stored my diary and poems in a locked box in my closet (the only place my mother couldn't scrutinize them).

There are times when being a writer still feels like stuffing letters into bottles and lobbing them out to sea with the dim hope of making human contact. And so, it's a blessed joy to have so many bottles come back, so to speak, not only to be Target's book club choice but also to hear from the readers who've so far written to say, "My ex-girlfriend's mother was just like Josephine Hurst," or "My parents divided us siblings into scapegoats and golden children too," or "Mother, Mother was like group therapy . . . it's such a relief to know I'm not alone."

There's a lot of abuse that doesn't leave physical wounds or scars, and it's been a privilege to find solidarity with people who've managed to stay incredibly funny, openhearted, and warm even though they were raised by people who left them psychologically out in the cold.

Thank you, deeply, for reading. I hope you too will share your stories and reading lists with me.

Very best wishes,
Keep in touch,
and as Violet Hurst would say, Namaste.
Koren Zailckas

Praise for
MOTHER, MOTHER

"A stunning debut that is sure to spark debate and cause a stir. . . . Full of wise and witty observations, and a mounting sense of dread . . . brilliant firecracker-like prose, a page-turning plot, and an unmistakable voice."

—*Paramus Post*

"Think *Mommie Dearest* meets *Psycho*. Then just sit back, open the book, and have an absolute ball."

—*Suspense Magazine*

"Mind-blowing . . . Delving deeply into the psyches of a disturbed, vicious woman, an insecure man, and younger, developing minds, [Zailckas] cleverly uncovers the intense ways in which personal interactions affect each member of a family. *Mother, Mother* will certainly make you look at your relationships with your closest relatives in a very different light."

—*Woodbury*

"Grab a copy of this book. . . . her story is riveting. Don't miss it."

—*Hudson Valley News*

"An electrifying debut novel about a family being torn apart by the woman who claims to love them most."

—*Chronogram*

"A creepy thriller [that] starts with an ordinary family and ends in nail-biting suspense. . . . A horrifying and deeply moving look into the dark secrets in a seemingly 'perfect family,' this is a hard-hitting page-turner."

—*Parkersburg News & Sentinel*

"[An] impressive debut novel . . . engaging, well crafted."

—Bustle.com

"Koren Zailckas's *Mother, Mother* is disturbing in the best possible way: believably. The slow, subtle darkness at the core of this book starts as a trickle and grows to a flash flood, and not once does it stop feeling absolutely authentic. Zailckas has written a gut-wrenching exploration of narcissism, dependence, and family. It's an amazing book."

—Kelly Braffet, author of *Josie and Jack* and *Last Seen Leaving*

"Zailckas crafts an intriguing mystery surrounding this family that will keep readers on edge as she slowly peels back layer after layer of deception."

—Booklist

"A riveting fiction debut . . . it's the kind of book that keeps you up at night, featuring a mother to rival Medea or Mrs. Bates. . . . The shocking and violent denouement shows Zailckas to be a consummate storyteller."

—Publishers Weekly

"Richly imagined and bring[s] to mind Susanna Kaysen's *Girl, Interrupted*. . . . An excellent page-turner."

—Library Journal

"A hall of mirrors reflecting chaotic maternal psychological mayhem reminiscent of *Mommie Dearest* or *Push* or *Ordinary People*."

—Kirkus Reviews

MOTHER, MOTHER

Also by the Author

Smashed

KOREN ZAILCKAS

MOTHER, MOTHER

A NOVEL

B\D\W\Y

BROADWAY BOOKS / New York

This is a work of fiction. Names, characters, places, and incidents either are
the product of the author's imagination or are used fictitiously. Any resemblance
to actual persons, living or dead, events, or locales is entirely coincidental.

Copyright © 2013 by Koren Zailckas
Reader's Guide Copyright © 2014 by Random House LLC.
"Extra Libris" and the accompanying colophon are trademarks of Random House LLC.

All rights reserved.
Published in the United States by Broadway Books, an imprint of the
Crown Publishing Group, a division of Random House LLC,
a Penguin Random House Company, New York.
www.crownpublishing.com

BROADWAY BOOKS and its logo, B \ D \ W \ Y, are trademarks of Random House LLC.

Originally published in hardcover by Crown Publishers, an imprint of the
Crown Publishing Group, a division of Random House LLC, New York, in 2013,
and subsequently in paperback by Broadway Books, an imprint of the
Crown Publishing Group, a division of Random House LLC, New York, in 2014.

Library of Congress Cataloging-in-Publication Data
Zailckas, Koren.
    Mother, mother : a novel / Koren Zailckas.—First edition.
        pages cm
    1. Mothers and daughters—Fiction. 2. Narcissists—Family relationships—Fiction.
    3. Domestic fiction. I. Title.
    PS3626.A6254M68 2013
    813'.6—dc23   2013010450

ISBN: 978-0-553-41938-2
eBook ISBN: 978-0-3853-4724-2

PRINTED IN THE UNITED STATES OF AMERICA

Book design by Ellen Cipriano
Cover design by Christopher Brand
Cover photography by Seth Smoot

10   9   8   7   6   5   4   3   2   1

First Paperback Edition

A family is a tyranny ruled over by its weakest member.

—GEORGE BERNARD SHAW

through fog, it is impossible to perceive
fiery eyes
greedy claws
jaws
through fog
one sees only the shimmering of nothingness . . .
were it not for its suffocating weight
and the death it sends down
one would think
it is the hallucination
of a sick imagination
but it exists
for certain it exists

—ZBIGNIEW HERBERT,
"THE MONSTER OF MR. COGITO"

MOTHER, MOTHER

WILLIAM HURST

HER FACE WAS the first thing William Hurst saw when he opened his eyes from his not-so-sweet dreams. His mother, Josephine, was smiling down at him, her blue eyes misty-soft, sunlight streaming through her hair, the same way it did to the happy Jesus in Will's *Storybook Bible*.

On this particular Saturday, *mother* was both a noun and a verb.

Behind her, at the end of Will's bed, was the frog habitat he'd begged for all summer. It had a paddling pond for tadpoles and a rocky ledge where frogs could doze beneath a canopy of green plastic clover.

Will knew he should be jabbering with excitement. There she was, waiting for him to pump his fist and thrash with glee (not that he would *ever* dare jump on the bed). But something was off. The timing didn't add up.

"Is today my birthday?" Will asked. "Did I do something to deserve an extra-special reward?"

"No," Josephine said. "Today isn't your birthday. And *you*, little man, are my extra-special reward."

She reached for the boy's face, as if to give his bandaged chin a playful pinch or tuck his too-long hair behind his earlobe. But then the phone rang and her freshly moisturized hand froze, suspended in the space. She pulled away and padded off in her slippers to answer it, a Velcro roller tumbling out of her hair and sticking, burr-like, in the carpet.

The house should have been quiet now that Will's sixteen-year-old sister Violet had been banished. Oddly, the Hurst family home was louder. Even after his mother hung up her cell phone, her voice remained nervous, her actions rackety. Will followed her downstairs to the kitchen, where the radio was already on, cranked to WRHV. Cupboard doors slammed. Silverware barrel-rolled as she jostled the drawers.

The rotten-egg smell of his father's morning shower wafted down the staircase. The well water was sulfuric. Violet liked to say that hell smells like sulfur. So do places infested with demons. If Will believed his mother—and he had no reason not to—demons were rebels like Violet. They fell from grace when they looked into God's gentle eyes and announced they didn't need him anymore.

At the kitchen table, Josephine asked, "Is a noun a doing word, a describing word, or a naming word?"

"A describing word," Will told her between swallows of oatmeal.

Josephine's smile—a bright sideways sliver of moon—made it impossible for him to know whether he'd answered right or wrong.

"Let me put it this way," she said. "Which word is the noun in this sentence: 'I always know what I am doing.'"

"What."

"I said, which word is the noun in this sentence—"

"No, Mom. I wasn't asking, What? I was trying to tell you 'what' is the *answer*."

"Oh," Josephine said. "Oh, I was expecting you to say 'I.' But I suppose 'what' is right in this instance too."

The portable phone screamed in its cradle. Josephine picked it up and wandered out of the kitchen saying, "No, I told you. I have a twelve-year-old special-needs son. She's a danger to him. I can't have her here."

Will had autistic spectrum disorder with comorbid epilepsy. To him, that always sounded like a good thing—the word *spectrum* being halfway to *spectacular*. But Will knew his differences secretly shamed his family, his father, Douglas, in particular. At Cherries Deli, Will was always aware of his dad's gaze lingering on the youth soccer leagues eating postgame sundaes. Probably, Douglas longed for a sturdier and more social son—a buzz-cut bruiser who could shower and climb stairs unsupervised, without the nagging threat of seizures.

Will's mother tried to put a positive spin on his health conditions. Once when Will was in a wallowing mood, he'd blubbered, "I'm not like normal people!" And Josephine had consoled him by saying, "No, you're not. And thank God for that. Normal people are dim-witted and boring."

Will had received his dual diagnosis nine months ago, and his mother had been homeschooling him ever since. A onetime academic, Josephine was every bit as good as Will's former teachers. Plus, she custom-made his curriculum. She was patient with Will in math, where it took him ages to grasp square roots, and rode him relentlessly in language arts, where she prided herself on the quality of his writing and his ability to read above grade level.

Violet used to tell Will that he was blessed to have autism. She was studying Buddhism, and she said that Will must have been an exceptionally good person in a past life. A patient, selfless, saintly sort of person. So in this life, he'd been rewarded for his past goodness with heightened sensitivities. According to Violet, Will felt things more deeply and understood things most people overlooked, and this made his everyday more like Nirvana.

Josephine didn't appreciate his sister's interest in Eastern religion. She didn't like the humming sound of Violet's Tibetan singing bowl, her woodsy incense, the picture of Geshla in a glitzy gold frame on her bedside table.

The Hursts were Catholic. Whenever Violet sat cross-legged with a strand of mala beads, Josephine told her to put away her "faux rosary." Back in August, Violet had shaved off all her hair with their father's electric beard trimmer. Will remembered Douglas storming into the family room, a long brown wisp threaded through his fingers, shouting, "Violet! What is the meaning of this?!" Without so much as turning her bald head away from her guided-meditation DVD, Violet had said: "Meanings are the illusion of a deluded mind, Dad. Stop trying to squeeze reality into a verbal shape."

Violet would not allow herself to be squeezed into anyone's reality.

"Violet is unpredictable," Josephine liked to say. "Just when a person thinks she's got Violet pegged, she transforms like ice into water."

That was when the trouble started, with one of Violet's transformations. His sister's "extreme personality changes" were one of the reasons Josephine had spent the last forty minutes on the phone, whispering about "crisis wards," "involuntary commitment," and other words Will couldn't find in his *Scholastic Dictionary*.

"Violet is sick," his mom had explained weeks earlier, after Violet had once again made her dissolve into tears. "You know how parts of our bodies get sick sometimes?" she'd added, dabbing at her eyes. "Like, we get stomachaches or sore throats? Well, Violet is sick in the part of her brain that controls her feelings."

Will assumed Violet's brain was sick because she had stopped eating food. Well, not all food. Violet had recently stopped drinking everything except pomegranate juice or milk, and stopped eating everything besides Uncle Ben's instant rice or a stenchy combination of mung beans and sugar.

As her body got smaller, all of Violet's clothes started to look like disguises. She wore long-underwear tops, Douglas's dress shirts, and low-crotched pants that made her look like one of Ali Baba's forty thieves. Their mother said Violet wore a gauzy kerchief because people at school made fun of her bald-headedness. But when Will asked Violet, she told him she was covering her head because she was doing *sallekhana*.

"Is that Buddhist?" Will had asked.

"No," Violet said. "It's Jainist."

"But she is suicidal," Josephine told the person on the phone now. "I've done some research, and this Jainist thing—or however you say it—is a ritual fast to *death*."

Still in her bathrobe, Josephine was hunched on a stool at the kitchen island. The remaining rollers were gone from her Bambi-brown hair, but she'd been too distracted to reach for her comb. Curls corkscrewed from her scalp at bonkers angles. "Presentation counts": that was what she'd always taught Will. Seeing her un-kempt disturbed him more than almost anything else, and that said a lot given the circumstances.

Will hovered by the stove, trying to feel the stitches beneath the surgical tape on his chin. He made no attempt to disguise his eavesdropping.

"I feel like you're asking me to choose between my children," Josephine told the mystery caller. "I love my daughter more than words can express, but I'm terrified of her. She critically injured my son. Uh-huh. Yes. I am afraid for our lives."

Whumpa whumpa whump. Josephine's ballpoint pen was the only sound while the person on the line spoke at length.

"I know we're not the only victims here. Violet suffers the ef-fects of her condition more than anyone. Uh-huh. I agree. We've tried to get her the medical attention she needs, but she flies into a rage at the very suggestion of it." She paused and listened briefly. "That—" Josephine's voice splintered. She jotted down 5150 hold on her notepad and framed it with stars. "That breaks my heart. But if you're telling me this is her best chance at recovery, then I guess I don't have much choice."

Will's chest twanged with pity and helplessness. He wanted to protect his mother every bit as much as she wanted to safeguard him. It was Will who got hurt last night, but their mother was the one Violet really wished dead.

Of all the crazy that had transpired the night before, Will had felt most unsafe when he saw the way his sister eyed his mother across the dining room table. How Violet-like she'd been, glower-ing with her hangdog neck and hooded eyes. Anyone else might have mistaken her for someone meek and self-punishing. But Will knew the truth: Violet thought she was proof of nature over nur-ture. She didn't need their mom's loving care to survive.

Will crossed the kitchen and put a supportive arm around his mother's sashed waist.

Josephine cupped the mouthpiece with her palm and whispered, "Don't worry, sweetie. You're safe now. I promise. I won't ever let her hurt you again."

VIOLET HURST

ON HER FIRST night in the psychiatric ER, Violet found herself curled up on a stretcher in a hallway that smelled like a combination of dirty hair and Lysol. Her brain was still steaming like an engine turned off after revving, but thanks to the liquid charcoal she'd sipped earlier, she felt a little more coherent, a little less like the universe was a big holographic time loop.

On the stretcher opposite Violet was a thickset Hawaiian woman. She was sitting bolt upright, her eyes flitting around wildly.

"I feel a question," the woman said. "Is it okay to be me?"

Violet's first thought was for the woman's privacy. She assumed the woman was praying aloud or having a heart-to-heart with a voice that she alone could hear. She tried hard not to look at her and instead stared down at the disposable foam slippers she'd received when she arrived barefoot.

At this time last week Violet had been registering by phone for the SAT. She'd been writing an English paper and trying to decide if she ought to go to the Halloween dance. All that seemed like it happened in a previous life. Less than three hours ago, Violet had been reincarnated as a mental patient. She'd walked through three sets of locking doors and a metal detector. She'd peed into a series of cups and had blood drawn from both arms. She'd been stripped of her clothes and handed a pair of pajamas that refused to stay snapped at the waist.

The Hawaiian woman continued her eerie chant. "Why can't I be me? What's so unlovable about me?"

"She's talking to *you*, you know?" This came from the young Puerto Rican man on the stretcher to Violet's right. He was lying on his stomach, a supermarket tabloid open between his propped-up elbows. From the looks of it, he was methodically tearing up the pages and Frankensteining the shreds back together in grotesque combinations, pairing Angelina Jolie's mouth with John Travolta's chin and Simon Cowell's nose.

"Me?" Violet asked stupidly. They were the only three people in the hall, save for the constant flux of orderlies and nurses.

"She says she's an intuitive," the man said.

"Oh." Violet didn't want to admit she didn't know what that meant.

"Oahu, over there? She's got the gift. She gets possessed by the people around her. She feels what we're feeling, get it? Like some *Invasion of the Body Snatchers* shit."

Suddenly accusatory, the woman stopped flailing and turned to stare directly at Violet.

"Who's controlling *you*?" she demanded.

Violet thought of Oahu again half an hour later, when the intake nurse asked her, "Do you hear voices or see things other people cannot see or hear?"

While the counselor ran through a series of questions, spitting them out like rapid gunfire, Violet wept convulsively, drawing tissue after tissue from the box balanced between her pajamaed knees.

"Do you have a history of mental health problems?" the counselor asked. "Do you know your clinical diagnosis?"

"No," Violet said. "Neither."

"Are you currently taking any drugs, legal or otherwise?"

"No." She paused. "Well, after school today I ate some seeds a friend gave me. Flower seeds. Morning glories?" According to the Internet drug forum Violet and her best friend, Imogene Field, had consulted, the LSA the seeds contained was a cheap, legal version of LSD. LSA was supposed to bring euphoria, rainbow fractals, and what one user called "an overall feeling of pleasant fuckedness." But what began as a fun afternoon with friends had turned into a train-wreck trip when Violet went home for dinner. Every moment since had been mental cannibalism. A strange thought, but that was exactly how it felt: like Violet's brain had swallowed two-thirds of itself.

"How many seeds did you eat? How did they make you feel?"

"Five, I think? And the water they'd been soaked in. I felt nauseous, mostly. And my thighs cramped up. I guess I also felt giddy and, later, spaced out and trippy. But then my family came after me." Violet felt her eyes fill and run over. "Or maybe I lost it on them?"

After school, she and Imogene had gone to the Fields' house, where Imogene's brother, Finch, and his best friend, Jasper, had shown them a mason jar filled with water, lemon juice, and the ground-up remains of the Heavenly Blue morning glory seeds that they had pulverized in the Fields' coffee grinder. Mr. and Mrs. Field, who preferred to go by Beryl and Rolf, had been away at the studio apartment they kept in Manhattan, where they were meeting with a new oncologist.

Finch assured everyone that the seeds were organic.

Imogene suggested adding ginger, just in case the concoction made them feel nauseated.

Jasper questioned whether extraction was potent enough, so they spooned four or five seeds into each glass like a garnish.

The taste hadn't been sickening. It had reminded Violet of wheatgrass. Jasper insisted it tasted more like very weak hot chocolate. It didn't work at first.

"What happened when you lost it on your family?" the nurse asked.

"I was looking at my mom, and she was a different person. But it was also like she'd always been a different person. Like, at the end of every day, when no one else is around, she unzips her suit of flesh. I know it was just the acid distorting things, but as, like, an analogy it holds." Violet rubbed her eyes. The sockets ached.

"How does your family get along as a whole?"

"We don't."

"Let's go back to what happened tonight. I know you're shaken up, but this is important. Do you think you can tell me more about the assault?"

The word assault made Violet feel turned upside down, kicked in the stomach, and orphaned at the same time. She was in mortal terror of her mother. She felt guilty about Will. She was scared she'd said something she couldn't take back, and committed a crime that would fit her for an orange prison jumpsuit. Even trying to remember what happened felt like a threat to her physical safety.

"Have you ever attempted suicide?" the counselor asked.

"I suppose. Technically." Still, Violet tried to explain that the Jainist fast to death wasn't really suicide. "It's kind of like a peaceful way to give up your body. Not an act of despair, but an act of hope. You're not giving up on life, you're just passing into the next stage of it."

It made sense to Violet, but the counselor looked dubious.

"Do you consider yourself 'eating disordered'?"

"Not really. It's more like a detox gone too far. I just wanted to feel pure, like all the venom's been sucked out of me."

Sallekhana was gradual. First, you fasted one day a week. Then, you ate only on alternate days. Next, you gave up foods one by one: first fruits, then vegetables, then rice, and then juice. After that, you drank only water. Then, you drank it only on alternate days. In the final step, you gave up water too, erased your bad karma, and hoped to shit you weren't reborn into another nightmare.

Violet looked down at her hands. This was a newly acquired nervous tic. A month into fasting, her hands went cold and her fingernails started to turn blue. Ever since, Violet had been hiding them under thick layers of Night Sky, a sparkly navy polish.

Within the hospital's cinder-block walls, it was impossible to know whether it was dusk or dawn. "What time is it?" Violet asked.

"Ten p.m. Let me ask you again. Did you attack your brother with a knife?"

"I don't remember. Everyone keeps asking me that. When are they going to stop asking? I keep saying, I don't know."

"Do you think you need to be admitted to the hospital?"

All the feeling trickled out of Violet's arms. An old childhood fear—claustrophobia—set in.

"Please don't make me stay," Violet whispered.

"I know you're frightened. People come here, and the idea of the hospital is scary. But you're going through some difficult things, and the people here are trained to handle difficult things. You're on a journey. The lights are out right now, but they will come on again. For the moment, I think we should give you a bed and a pill to help you get to sleep."

"I'm afraid to go home," Violet confessed. "But I don't want to stay here."

"I know, honey. But according to what your parents told us, you said and did some things that make you a threat to yourself or others. So we need to keep you here."

The walls of the office seemed to constrict. Violet cast a helpless glance at the Audubon nature calendar that hung on the wall behind the nurse's shoulder. October's photo was a redwood forest—the kind of woodland scene that could make a person feel very awed and alone.

"For how long?" Violet asked.

"The next seventy-two hours."

"There's one more thing I haven't told you."

The counselor crossed her arms and blinked once.

Violet exhaled in a great gush. "I saw my sister last night."

WILLIAM HURST

THEY DIDN'T USUALLY have school on Saturdays, but they'd fallen behind on account of prepping for Will's coming math Regents exam. The state said students with disabilities only had to score fifty-five out of a possible hundred percent in order to pass. But it was important to both Will and his mom that he score at least a seventy-five. That was the grade that indicated "college readiness," and it was Josephine's endgame that Will graduate early and go on to Columbia in four years' time.

"We don't have to push ourselves too hard today," Josephine said. "But a little bit of social studies will take our minds off last night. After that, I have to drive to Violet's hospital and sign some forms. Does that sound okay?"

Will nodded. He adjusted his costume beard over the bruise on his chin. He fashioned his sister's black bowed headband around his neck like a tie.

Ever since the controversy at Stone Ridge Elementary last fall, Will really had come to think of the breakfast nook as his new school. This had required some adjusting, of course. Gone were the familiar sights and smells of learning: pencil shavings, lunchbox rot, the stab-and-drag sound of chalk against a blackboard.

. . .

Sure, Will still nursed a few aching, phantom limbs: recess, book fairs, games of Heads-Up, 7-Up with lazy substitute teachers. When he confessed to missing weekly job assignments like "board eraser" or "math shelf helper," his mom put him in charge of keeping her orchids evenly moist. When he got word of his former classmates' field trip to watch *Othello* at the Rosendale movie theater, Josephine had, in her words, "done one better." She'd driven Will to the city to see the real deal at the Met. She'd even bought him a new brass-buttoned blazer for the occasion.

When Will realized he'd never be in another school play, his mother had the idea to organize a one-man performance of Edgar Allan Poe's "Annabel Lee." He'd recited it in the Hursts' formal sitting room, for an audience of Perrier-sipping ladies, mainly Josephine's various girlfriends and golf partners from the Rondout Country Club. The verse had wormed its way into his long-term memory, and months later, Will still found himself crooning it under his breath:

> *The angels, not half so happy in heaven,*
> *Went envying her and me—*
> *Yes!— that was the reason (as all men know,*
> *In this kingdom by the sea)*
> *That the wind came out of the cloud by night,*
> *Chilling and killing my Annabel Lee.*

"Where's the tea?" Will asked his mother.

Social studies usually began with a game called "Tea at the White House." They would both dress up as famous people from history, and together, in character, they talked about how they grew up, how they died, and what made them famous. There was usually iced tea in a heavy crystal pitcher.

"There's no tea today," Josephine said irritably. "Just pretend."

"Okay." Will rose from the table, trying to make himself six feet, four inches tall. "I grew up in a one-room log cabin in Kentucky . . ." He trailed off. He asked his mother why she wasn't in costume. She was supposed to be dressed like Florence Nightingale.

Josephine didn't seem to hear his question. Her gaze lingered over a patch of condensation on the windowpane.

Will insisted on running upstairs to his parents' bedroom to fetch a lace doily for his mother to wear on her head.

He pushed the door inward to reveal his father sitting on the bed, wearing only a towel. His cell phone was cupped to his ear. His pleading voice was unfamiliar, so very different from the managerial tone that he had used to persuade Will to join the Boy Scouts.

"I made a mistake," Douglas said. "I *need* to see you. When I'm in a place like this I just can't see the light. Are you hearing me? I can't see the fucking light."

Somewhere toward the end of his father's plea, the doorknob hit the closet door with a clatter.

Douglas startled at the sound. His rimless glasses were off and his eyes were tear-swollen.

"Sorry, Dad," Will said, swiping the doily from the top of his mom's mahogany jewelry box and swiftly closing the door behind him.

"Did you know Dad's on the phone?" Will asked his mother when he went back to the kitchen.

"So?"

"So it sounded like a funny conversation, is all."

Josephine's crossed arms and knitted brow put Will on edge.

"What do you mean, funny?"

Will scoured his brain for the right word. He needed something accurate, but also something that was sensitive to his mother's feelings. Words meant a lot to his mother, so they meant a lot to Will. He spent a lot of time trekking through the dictionary. He filled notebooks with long and unusual nouns that might impress her (*rastaquouère: a social climber; widdiful: describes someone who deserves to be hanged*).

"Not funny, ha-ha," he said. "More like funny, strange. Maybe Violet called him?"

"Oh, Will," Josephine said. "You're still really worried about Violet, aren't you? I told you, she can't hurt anyone where she is now. They won't let her call anyone for quite a long while. Now, let's get back to tea at the White House. You were telling me about yourself, Mr. Lincoln?"

Will, as Abe, cut straight to the part he knew his mother would like best. "When I was nine, my mom drank bad milk and puked herself to death," he said. "I used to tell people, 'All that I am, all that I hope to be, I owe to my angel mother.' "

Josephine's eyes went slushy and sad in the corners. She gave a weak smile and touched the hand splint Will got at the ER last night. Then she leaned in and kissed the bandage on his chin. Somehow, it made Will's stitches hurt less.

Will decided to leave a few things out of that morning's tea. He didn't tell his mother about Abe Lincoln's older sister, Sarah, who raised him after his mother died. He also omitted the part about Abe's younger brother, Thomas, who died in his cradle. No one likes to talk about dead babies. And his mom definitely didn't like to speak about older sisters.

Shame and defensiveness hung, like skunk spray, around Josephine whenever someone mentioned Will's oldest sister, Rose. Most people in town wouldn't touch the topic with a ten-foot pole, knowing precisely how much pain it caused the Hursts. But every so often, one of the well-meaning but half-demented old ladies at Saint Peter's Church would ask whether thespian Rose was in the latest production at Ulster Performing Arts Center. Josephine usually responded with something polite and evasive like, "No such luck," and quickly moved on to praise the play's actual female lead. But Will knew she wished the rest of Stone Ridge would get with the program and forget Rose at least half as quickly as she'd forgotten all of them.

A little more than a year ago Rose had run away with her boyfriend and disowned the Hursts. "Just give her space," Violet had said when Josephine told the family about the hateful details of Rose's final phone call. "You all talk about Rose like she's so much younger than she is. She's twenty. When you reach adulthood, 'running away from home' is generally known as 'moving out.'"

Rose was so self-absorbed or cowardly (or both) that she hadn't even told the Hursts she was leaving. Will's parents had reported her missing twenty-four hours after she didn't come home from her morning class at SUNY New Paltz. A week had gone by before Rose could be bothered to call her mother, and the Hursts had been painfully aware of every passing hour and what it said about the chances police would find her alive. Josephine had organized ground searches of the creek. Douglas had created a "Find Rose Hurst" Facebook group. Will had helped his mother post flyers in the storefronts around town; they featured Rose's angelic face beneath the pleading question "Have You Seen This Girl?"

The details read:

Hair: Brown

Eyes: Blue/Gray

Rose was last seen wearing jeans, a peach sweater, and a fur-trimmed white puffer coat. Other identifying characteristics include a mole under her right eye and a dime-sized birthmark behind her left ear.

At the time, Will thought his mother should have given a different photo to the National Center for Missing and Exploited Children.

"Why?" Josephine asked.

"Because Rose's smiling in it," Will had said. "No one will be able to recognize her."

These days, wherever Rose was, she was probably grinning. Whereas Will's mother was the one who wore the frown Will couldn't erase no matter how hard he tried.

These days, monanthous was a word that seemed to apply. It meant having only a single flower. And that was all the Hursts had. One Violet. No Rose.

Now, during tea, Josephine, with a middle part and her doily bonnet in place, was much too convincing as Florence Nightingale. With tired, downcast eyes, she read the words that supposedly proved Flo's bipolar disorder. It was an open letter to God, in which she asked him why she couldn't be happy no matter how hard she tried. "Why can I not be satisfied with the life that satisfies so many people?" Josephine croaked. "Why am I starving, desperate, and diseased on it?"

The real answer, which Will didn't dare say, was Rose. Before Rose ran away, Douglas hadn't worked odd hours. Will hadn't been bullied. Violet hadn't been nearly as vengeful and nuts. Rose had left Will's family with a deficit, and every single day she seemed to drain more out of them. The gap between what the Hursts were and what they'd once been was widening by the day. Will knew the difference pained Josephine most of all. Rose had turned their mother's perfect family into a perfect wreck, and Will couldn't shake the feeling that she wouldn't stop there.

VIOLET HURST

THE NURSE WHEELED Violet into a stark room containing a grated window, metal lockers, and a roommate, a corpse-still back-sleeper who made her cot look more like an autopsy table.

Violet had barely choked down a pink sleeping pill and laid her head on the mattress when a flashlight beamed across her still-teary face. "Check," said the orderly silhouetted in the door. When it happened again fifteen minutes later, it dawned on Violet that she was on the kind of suicide watch she had read about in *Girl, Interrupted*.

For the first time, Violet wondered if she really *was* crazy, not just deliriously hungry and high. Maybe morning glory seeds had brought out some kind of latent schizophrenia. Where acid was concerned, some people—maybe Violet included—left reality and never quite made it back. Was that why she had no recollection of what she'd done to Will? She sometimes had difficulty remembering all the insightful parts of an acid trip, but she'd never had an entire memory slip through her fingers. LSD didn't make people black out. Maybe schizophrenia or some other mental disorder did.

Violet knew, of course, that there was a chance she'd hallucinated Rose. Her sister could have been a trick of the light, a trick of Violet's drugged or possibly diseased mind. Even before morning glory seeds, Violet had been ill-fed and ill-rested. The thinner she got, the more sitting or lying down hurt, so she'd been spending most nights doing walking meditations, pacing around and around her room, trying to drum up some forgiveness for Rose. Sleep-deprived, Violet had been having basic distortions. Colors seemed brighter. She'd been feeling like she had less control over her angry thoughts, which just kept returning to the Hurst who got away.

In the final months before Rose fled the scene, Violet had watched her sister closely. She'd seen Rose say no to drugs, no to dating, no to saying no, and she'd thought, *What if I pick the opposite for myself? Because what's the point of being good when Rose ended up miserable all the same?* Although the Hurst daughters had never been close, their mother had made life equally difficult for them. Violet believed that her sister left because it was the only solution to a long-standing problem. The problem was this: Josephine had made it very clear that no man, woman, or child should be more important to Rose than her family. That was why Rose rarely dated. That was why she was withdrawn. That was why Rose ran off with a mysterious stranger named Damien. *Damien*, like an *Omen* joke. Like the devil's son.

But no one was going to swoop in and help Violet start her independent life. Every day, she had to plow through her controlling household like someone machete-whacking her way through a jungle that grew right back thicker and thornier every night. That was what she'd been thinking in the kitchen as she gesticulated with her mother's chef's knife.

The knife. Violet could remember lots about the knife. She could recall how brilliant the blade looked in her hallucinated gaze. She could remember the feel of it rocking back and forth against the cutting board. She even remembered how empowered she felt, aiming the tapered tip at Josephine. But she could not remember practicing her knife skills on Will. What in the hell had she done? Butterflied his palm like a chicken breast? Grabbed and pared his thumb? Why?

Violet laid still and searched her mind for any reason she might have hurt her brother. Had he tried to intervene on their mother's behalf? Had he said something in defense of Josephine that had pissed Violet off? She couldn't ignore the possibility that she'd hurt Will—odd little yes-man that he was—because she envied the way their mom's love came easily to him.

The longer Violet brainstormed on the subject, the woozier she felt.

Her most lucid memory so far was a premonition—the moment she realized just how bad her trip was going to be:

They'd been sitting, sipping their algae-green cocktails in the casbah comfort of the Fields' vaulted living room. The Fields' house always made Violet feel pleasantly stoned from the moment she walked in the door. Stained-glass lanterns cast fractured rainbows over the leather pouf ottomans. Ceilings were painted lagoon blue or blazing saffron. The air smelled like cedar. Josephine called the Fields "platinum card hippies." Beryl and Rolf had met when they were both enrolled at Bard College, but when they found out they were pregnant with twins, Rolf had shaved his Fu Manchu and swapped his burgeoning art career for one in finance.

Violet was still occasionally starstruck in the presence of her exotic and blasé friends. Imogene's rainbow-dyed hair resembled a Neapolitan cookie. Finch had heavy blond bangs hanging over his horn-rimmed glasses. Jasper was wearing a coonskin cap and a T-shirt that bore a quote by the street artist Banksy: *A lot of parents will do anything for their kids except let them be themselves*. How they hadn't realized they were too cool for Violet was beyond her.

A full hour had gone by with no effect. Finch sat in front of his MacBook, watching a bunch of short, surrealist films by the Czech artist Jan Švankmajer.

"Fuck botany," Jasper said. "Those seeds are worthless."

"Maybe we should have fasted before we ate them," Finch said, and Violet had felt a little trill of excitement. She *had* been fasting, in secret, for reasons she hadn't shared with her friends.

Something happened while Violet was racking her brain for the answer to 40-across ("motherless calf"), and the boys giggled over Švankmajer's *Meat Love*. On-screen, two slabs of beef grunted and thrust against each other on a floured cutting board.

"Ha!" Finch cried. "He de-floured her!"

Jasper laughed. "Gives a whole new meaning to the phrase *slapping your meat*."

The sight of all that rare, glistening steak sent a prickling sensation spreading up Violet's legs. Her empty stomach spasmed. She stood up to go to the bathroom and felt the room jump very close to her, almost as though she had taken five steps forward instead of just one. When she stepped backward, the same effect happened in reverse.

"Are you okay?" Finch asked.

"Hurst looks like she just hit a wall of fucked-up-ness," Jasper said.

"I'll go with you," Imogene told her. "I'm not feeling pitch-perfect either."

Violet felt like she was spinning along a slanted axis. In the bathroom, she lifted the toilet lid to puke and saw a steak, blue-rare and bloody, in the bowl. Hot on the heels of that hallucination came an auditory one. She heard shrieking laughter. Then, her mother's voice whisper-hot in her ear: *It's the food chain, Viola. Shut up and eat it.*

Now she crept across the hospital linoleum (frigid) to the bathroom (unlockable). Inside, she was greeted by a twelve-inch shatterproof mirror. The image reflected back at her was far more Martian than girl. Voluntary starvation had yellowed her skin. Her pupils—although not the full lunar eclipses that they'd been earlier at Imogene's house—hadn't shrunk back down to normal, nonwasted size. She ran her palm, neck to widow's peak, over the hedgehog bristle of her scruffy head. Even in her tolerant locale— the Hursts lived only seventeen miles from Woodstock—Violet's peers regarded her hair and diet as a little extreme.

There had been a couple of love interests back in freshman year, when Violet had sported a loose ponytail (not just stubble). Troy Barnes had given her a Vicks VapoRub massage the first time she took Ecstasy. Finch had kissed her in the Rosendale caves and sent her hilarious text messages for weeks after, things like, *You have soiled my soul. I feel swollen and ashamed.* But after Violet shaved her head, lesbian rumors swirled and those two backed off, along with the rest of the male species. Finch just wanted to be friends. Troy called her *cue ball*, when he called her at all. For all the social troubles that zealotry had caused Violet, she couldn't seem to give up fasting, meditating, or reading books with lotus blossoms or cumulus clouds on the covers. After Rose ran away, Violet had needed something to disappear into too. Religion seemed as good an escape route as any, plus it was conveniently compatible with psychedelics.

After her sister left, Violet discovered that she could no longer pray to their mother's god—the divine bully Josephine had called upon to justify her actions, especially the way she had treated Rose.

Violet had always sensed that Josephine wasn't like other mothers, but in the past year, she'd finally been able to put her finger on the weird behaviors that made her different. Once Rose was gone, Josephine snatched Will and Violet from their places at the back of the family shelf. That was when Violet realized just how much Josephine had seen Rose as her favorite doll: someone to dress up, show off, and manipulate. Violet had always been more resistant to that kind of one-sided play: Violet wore what she wanted, tried to say what she felt, and mostly recognized the differences between herself and the stifling, spoiled woman she called Mom.

Even though Violet could sympathize with Rose now, that was one of the main reasons they didn't get along as sisters: Rose could grin and bear Josephine's demeaning comments, and Violet couldn't. Rose kept censoring what she did and said even when Josephine wasn't around, and Violet swung the other way; Violet developed an almost pathological need to point out whatever the rest of the Hursts wanted to sweep under the rug and parade it around like a skull on a stick.

Unfortunately—as Violet quickly found out—being your own person only increased Josephine's claim on you. Josephine took credit for your good traits with her cream-of-the-crop genes. Your school or social successes were proof of her careful child-rearing. And if you veered the other way—if you became a freak and a flunky, like Violet, if you self-sabotaged so Josephine couldn't use your achievements to build herself up—well then, the matriarch turned hate-riarch and pawned off her own evil qualities on you. She'd say you manipulated people (which she did). She'd say you were vengeful (which she, above all people, was). The game worked because the more Josephine played the victim, the more a person wanted to victimize her. The more she told you you were angry, the more pissed off it made you.

Hazy as Violet still was on the details, she knew her outburst in the kitchen had been a last-ditch effort to tell the truth about her mom to Douglas and Will. She'd never once considered that they might hear her out and still opt to believe that Josephine was just some benign mom, packing lunches and kissing boo-boos. Of course, Violet's delivery might have also played a part. Tripping, she was no stellar speechmaker. Her main points might well have been howls and expletives.

Violet pictured Josephine at home, cracking a bottle of victory champagne. So she'd driven Violet to attack her own brother, proving at long last that she was invincible and Violet had terminal piece-of-shit-itis. All hail Josephine. Josephine had won.

WILLIAM HURST

TEA AT THE White House was drawing to a close. It was time for Will's grand finale. He told Josephine that on April fourteenth, he'd gone to see a play called *Our American Cousin*.

"During intermission, my bodyguard left the playhouse to get trashed with my driver," Will said.

"How do you know that word?"

"What word? *Trashed?* I don't know. Violet says it. It means you've drunk so much alcohol that you spin without moving."

When Josephine didn't approve of something, her eyes went as slitted as Will's old plastic dinosaur toys.

"Anyways, while my driver was drinking alcohol, an actor-slash-spy shot me in the back of the head. Right *here*."

Will staggered to the floor. All tea parties at the White House ended this way: with Will gasping, moaning in unimaginable pain, clutching his wound, and letting his eyelids go fluttery. Like Rose before him, Will relished his acting skills. Usually he could make his mom laugh, no sweat. But this time, Josephine didn't crack a smile or teasingly try to catch him breathing in the grave. No matter how much she claimed she wanted to return to their routine, last night hadn't loosened its hold on her. She might have cleaned up the splattered risotto and mopped the blood off the floors, but the kitchen still had an air of something not quite right.

Will opened his trying-hard-not-to-quiver-because-he-was-dead eyes. "What's wrong?" he asked. "Did I do a bad job?"

"You were fine," Josephine said. "Although you might have placed more emphasis on repealing slavery and the Gettysburg Address. Tea at the White House is a school lesson, remember? It's not an acting exercise. We don't just do this for the drama of it all."

Will was crushed. He let his beard fall to his chest like a hairy necklace. "Sorry, Mom. Maybe I shouldn't die next time?"

"It's all right if you die."

"I don't need to."

"William, I don't have the energy for this today. You can die, okay? It's fine by me. Maybe just don't make such a big to-do about it."

His mom's gaze drifted to the window. Outside, the mailman idled in his doorless truck. He had a third-trimester-sized belly and wore shorts, regardless of season or weather. Will noticed he always left the mailbox ajar.

"People on the Internet say Abe Lincoln used marijuana."

"Marijuana?"

"People said he was a homosexual too."

"Oh Will, don't be ridiculous. I really don't have the time for this today. If we don't get in the car now we'll be late for the hospital."

Ridiculous. A describing word, reserved for people and things you didn't have to take seriously.

What *was* wrong with Will? He thought about that question as he climbed into the backseat of his mother's burnt-red sedan. Ultimately, he came back to his autism, the root of his wrongness. All the Asperger's books his mother left lying around the house said that people like Will lacked empathy. But Will didn't think that was his problem per se. If anything, he picked up too many signals from other people. So much like a crowded radio spectrum, he was, that it was hard to get a clear reading on any one person (including himself). Every human interaction was static-ridden. Each conversation crackled.

In the rearview mirror, Will glanced at Josephine's profile. He studied her hooked lashes and the perfect brushstroke of her nose. It was probably hard for her, faking a distant and controlled expression for the sake of Will's comfort, but he saw her white knuckles on the steering wheel.

She sighed as she reversed past the mailbox. "So he *did* leave it open again. Will, will you jump out and grab the mail for me?"

The stack of mail in hand, Will noticed a seal on the back of an envelope for Violet that caught his attention. There was a musical symbol—a *treble clef*, he knew from his mother's piano instruction—pressed into the dark pink wax. There was little else on the envelope, except for Violet's name, the Hursts' address at Old Stone Way, and a nameless New York address in the upper left-hand corner: 130 Seventh Avenue, #123.

When she slowed for the tollbooth at the Poughkeepsie bridge, Will glanced at the passenger seat, where the mail stuck out of his mother's boxy ostrich-skin purse. It suddenly became clear to Will why the envelope looked so familiar: *Missing* could be either an adjective or a verb. And the New Yorker Violet knew was his lost sister, Rose, who used to put a wax kiss on everything.

Violet Hurst

The next morning, when the head nurse (even this seemed like a double entendre) appeared in the doorway, Violet asked her a series of questions:

"Is it possible to get a toothbrush? Am I allowed to use the phone? Have you heard anything from my family?"

"Later," the nurse said. "Right now, I need you to come with me. There are some officers here who'd like to speak with you."

Violet trailed her down the hallway to the visitors' lounge, where two uniformed police officers were drinking black coffee.

So this was the moment of truth. Violet imagined the sound of handcuffs clinking around her wrists.

The two men stood as she approached. They looked like linebackers.

It was hard for Violet to remember a time when she'd ever associated police with safety. Faced with a blue uniform, Josephine would fall all over herself, offering to buy policemen gas-station coffee and asking them how to organize a neighborhood watch. But Violet's fear of authority ran deep. Even when she didn't have red-wine lips or a one-hitter pipe in her pocket, the sight of a badge made her blood run cold.

"I have Viola for you," the nurse told the officers.

Viola was her real name, after the wild yellow variety *Viola pubescens*. But she'd insisted on going by *Violet* since kindergarten. "I don't know why you'd possibly want to be a shy little Violet," Josephine said. "That's as bad as being a common Rose." This dig was directed at her sister, whose Christian name was Rosette.

Violet held her pajama pants closed with one hand and tried not to look mental. She was so nervous she barely heard the cops' introductions. Their names went in one ear and out the other without so much as a whistle, leaving her to think of them as one beast with two heads and two guns. They were Tweedle Dee and Tweedle Dum, only armed.

"I should begin by saying you're not being charged with anything at this time," Tweedle Dee said. "I understand you're an unemancipated minor, is that right?"

Violet must have given a zombie stare because the other cop translated. "You're under eighteen?"

"Uh-huh."

"And your parents are still your legal guardians?"

"Yeah."

Officer Dee crossed his rib-roast arms. "You see, Viola, we're here in response to a domestic violence complaint. Your brother arrived last night at Kingston Hospital with serious damage to his right hand. There were other minor injuries too. Injuries your mother said he sustained from you."

"I've *never* hurt Will!" Violet cringed at her own ugly adolescent whine. She took a jagged breath and tried with mixed success to mellow out her tone. "I didn't try to stab anyone. I can't remember everything, but I know that for sure. If it's her word against mine—"

"You're talking about your mother?" asked Officer Dee.

"*Yes*, my mother." Secretly, Violet preferred the term *womb-*

donor. Convinced as she was that her mom was lying, she still wasn't sure if she could trust her own mind's version of events. Most of what had happened in the kitchen felt like some strange half-reality. The drugs had fragmented things and forced them back together in ways that didn't entirely fit. Violet's memory had kaleidoscoped. Every time she tried to examine the details, the whole scene shattered. She wanted to say something about Rose, but every time she brought up her sister's name it seemed to get her in more trouble. When she'd mentioned Rose back in the kitchen, her family had turned against her. When she'd mentioned Rose during her intake, she'd come off like someone grasping at straws.

"Look," said Officer Dum. He was the one with the rounder face, the softer eyes. "We weren't there. We didn't see whether this was an assault or what. We've given your mother a notice of her rights, and she's trying to decide whether to press criminal charges. Your mom did say she was going to pursue a protective order unless you agree to admit yourself here."

"Like, a restraining order?" Again, Violet hated herself for sounding so young.

Dum cast a look at the head nurse, who had been hovering in the corner like a Crocs-clad warden. "Your mother says you're a threat to yourself and your family. It's in everyone's best interest if you stay here."

She gritted her teeth, but figured she'd rather be in the hospital than at home. And so, without knowing her clinical diagnosis, Violet Hurst voluntarily committed herself to a facility that treated serious mental disorders with the help of psychotropic meds.

Back in the intake office, the counselor on duty read her the riot act: "You can go home if and when the doctors agree to discharge you. If you insist on being discharged, you can write a three-day letter asking for your release from the hospital. The hospital has three working days—Monday through Friday, weekends and holidays excluded—to give you a decision. We will either release you or we will file an affidavit and you will receive a court hearing. Do you understand all that?"

"I think so."

"Sign here, please."

Her heart pounded. The pen felt too thick in her cold fingers. The name Violet scrawled on the line began with a headstrong *V* but soon after collapsed into a mousy grade-school script. Her last name, *Hurst*, looked like a blight on her first, which, by this point, it was.

After she signed away what precious little agency a sixteen-year-old girl has, Violet took her first shower in days. She had to sign out a showerhead at the front desk—a strange procedure, born of the fact that past patients liked to unscrew them and throw them at the staff. After drying off with a rough white towel and stepping into a fresh set of the standard-issue pajamas, she wandered into the dayroom. As she walked down the hallway, Violet felt her distended stomach flip. For the first time since intake, she felt like a detainee. She had no ID, no cell phone, no clothes, no escape. A terrifying thought cut through her façade of couldn't-care-less. *What if I never get released?* Relieved as she was to get away from her mother, she wasn't eager to spend her teens and twenties in lockup. What if they gave her drugs? The antipsychotic kind that left her slurry and diabetic, grimacing at walls?

In the dayroom, two girls brawled for control of the channel button. They looked roughly the same age as Rose. One had a tumble of dyed red hair and thin, eyeliner-drawn brows. The other was tall and angular with eyes that were almost aggressively blue, piercing through the overgrown bangs of her Mick Jagger haircut. A fresh-looking scar, pink and terrifying, curved from her earlobe to her voice box. Violet couldn't help thinking the girl had a sad majesty. She was scrappy-beautiful. A beam of sunlight picked up the rusty highlights in her otherwise clove-brown hair.

After the nurse broke up the squabble, the screen was smeared with fingerprints. Violet grabbed a tissue from the box on top and gave it a quick buff.

"Thanks," the brunette said. "And sorry. I'm Edie. This is Corinna."

Corinna eyed Violet like a target, then aimed her sniper gaze back toward the TV.

"Violet."

"Did you just get here?"

Violet tensed and nodded. "Last night," she said.

"Was it pills?" Edie asked.

It took Violet a few beats to catch her drift. By then the girl was already elaborating.

"Suicide attempt? It's okay. You don't have to be embarrassed. I mean, come on"—Edie gestured to her scar—"Have you ever seen anything more embarrassing than this?"

Later, Violet would find out Edie had strung herself to a curtain rod with a length of electrical wiring. Instead of killing her, the rod had snapped and the wiring had gashed a four-inch wound in her neck. Her Vassar roommate had found her, bleeding nearly to death, making a second attempt with a plastic shopping bag over her head. One hundred stitches and a six-pint transfusion later, Edie ended up at Fallkill Psychiatric. This was her second stay in two years.

"Psychedelic crisis." For simplicity's sake, Violet added, "LSD."

"Wow," Edie said. "You look all right, considering. Was it bad?"

Was it bad? High on seeds, Violet had joined Imogene in front of the mirror and been surprised by the size of her own widened pupils. They looked like dark holes in a Violet-featured, rubber Halloween mask.

"Do you feel really heavy?" Imogene had asked. "I feel like gravity is working triple-time."

Violet hadn't felt heavy. Just the opposite. She was having a bad trip, and after hearing her mother's voice, she felt weightless, like not even her friends could ground her in the moment. Some invisible current was already pulling her back across town to the very last place she wanted to be: her parents' house, where her mother was destined to ambush her with another accusation. *Damn it, Violet! Just admit it! You were angry with us and you broke the window! Your friends keyed your father's car! You came home drunk again and tipped over the trash!* Violet could defend herself all she wanted, but no one ever believed her. Not with her mother in the other corner, spinning stories like rows of knitting and crying on demand. Violet couldn't explain these freak events, but she knew they weren't her fault.

She couldn't take it anymore. That was the reason she'd taken the seeds to begin with. Her mother had come into her room Friday morning and (falsely, homophobically) accused her and Imogene of being lesbian lovers, to the tune of, "I'm not some clueless mother, Viola! You with your buzz cut! And that little dyke with her rainbow hair!" It might have been comical, were it not for her mother's lecture about dressing like a "sloppy lesbian" and the mention of some gay-be-gone camp in Sullivan County. When Violet had screamed at Josephine to get her bigoted ass out of her room, her mother had laid into her harder than she ever had: "You are sick, Violet! I wish other people could see this anger you reserve just for me! You're so superficial! So false, with those big cow eyes you lay on your father! And the phony compassion you lavish on Will! I feel sorry for you, you know that? All the natural fibers in the world can't hide how artificial you are. Keep doing your Buddhist chants all day long, little girl. They won't hide the fact that you're a selfish bitch. You're ugly, Viola. You're ugly *inside*."

That was the speech that had sent Violet seeking out oblivion one last time. Seeds crunching between her molars, she'd been thinking she just wanted to melt her face off. She'd needed Love, Salvation, Deliverance. LSD, for short. Violet thought, under the circumstances, she deserved at least that.

William Hurst

"Mom?" Will asked, as the car shot under the tollbooth's rising yellow arm.

"What?" she said, with an undisguised tone of annoyance.

"You know that letter that came for Violet?"

"What about it?"

"It has that thing on the back. The same thing Rose used to use."

"You mean a wax seal. You need to call things by their proper names, Will. How many times do I need to tell you that thing isn't descriptive? Neither is stuff, by the way. Or neat, or cool, or amazing."

"Sorry. The wax seal. Rose loved those."

"Yes, she did. You've always been such an observant boy." Her eyes in the rearview mirror crinkled with sad warmth. "Even when you were a baby. When you were eighteen months old, you'd walk into a room and immediately home in on what was different. You'd fixate on it. Even if it was just the smallest detail: someone wearing a new brooch, or a book someone had moved onto a high shelf."

"I did?"

"You did. You're like me that way. We have an eye for detail.

If you apply yourself, that kind of watchfulness could make you a very famous writer one day."

"You really think so?"

"Of course. You're so observant. That's why I know you already know what I'm going to tell you . . ." The wiper blades did a screeching arch, and her shoulders started shaking. She sobbed gutturally and choked on the words: "Your father is cheating on me."

Will hesitated. Even from the backseat, he could see tears pouring down her face in the mirror. "I didn't know-know," he said.

The car swerved the slightest bit as she groped inside the door pocket for a tissue. "But you suspected."

"Well, he went into *work* on a Saturday. Plus, I heard him talking on the phone."

"Your father and that goddamn phone! He thinks nobody notices him whispering in the dark, pouring his heart out." She took one hand off the wheel and sarcastically clutched her chest, as if the contents of Douglas's heart couldn't fill a teaspoon.

"Have you checked his call history?"

"Yes! He wipes it clean! The man is so devious." The line of traffic in front of them slowed for construction, and it took Josephine a few terrifying seconds to notice and brake.

Will made a supportive but vague sound. The dashboard heater was cranked too high, but this was not the time to ask whether she could turn it down.

"Maybe I should have kept all this to myself. But it affects you too. Your dad uses *you* too. On the one hand, he likes how we reflect on him. We're the perfect family he never had growing up. But he also hates the way we restrict him. He hates sitting down to dinner when he could be off somewhere, talking programming with other megabrains."

Below them, the Hudson River was the same slate-gray color as the overcast sky. It made Will feel disconnected, like he was flying or falling. His skin crawled inside his sweaty sweater.

"What are you going to do?" He wondered if he ought to brace himself for divorce. His head swam with the idea of a joint-custody agreement. He couldn't handle spending half the week away from his mom.

"I don't know," she said, audibly wiping her nose. "Before I can even think about that, I need him to admit it. As if I don't have enough going on with your sister going off the deep end."

Will leaned forward to crack his window and had a full-body pins-and-needles sensation. An upward jolt shot through him, tailbone to head, and the dreaded tightening returned to his chest. *Recumbentibus: a knockout punch.* That was the word Will had copied into his unusual-word notebook a few months ago. In Will's experience that was how epilepsy felt: like getting hit by an opponent much bigger and more depraved than him. Every time—every single flipping time—was a filthy sucker punch to the head.

He came to in a fast-food parking lot, where his mom had pulled into a handicapped space. The handicapped plates on her car were new—another weak upshot of Will's health conditions.

The neurons in Will's brain were still firing every which way, mostly in directions he sensed they really shouldn't. His head was cradled in his mother's lap. After pulling over, she'd moved into the backseat, unbelted him, and rolled him onto his side. She'd also balled up her cashmere coat and put it under his head. The fur collar tickled his ear. The smell of her Shalimar perfume brought the world roaring back to him.

"Are you okay?" Josephine asked.

Will responded with a groan.

"Oh honey, I shouldn't have stressed you out," she said.

When Will was teetering on the edge of a mini-seizure, a big dose of worry could cause him to seize. Now that he was awake, he felt more stressed out than ever. Every seizure was a reminder that he'd lost the ability to lead a normal life, and it usually took Will a day or two to pull himself out of the downward spiral of frustration and shame.

"It's not your fault," Will said. If anyone had stressed him out, it was his dad.

Josephine draped her watch over her wrist and redid the clasp. Presumably, she'd taken it off to time his seizure.

"Did it last long?" Will asked.

"Objectively, no. Subjectively, God yes."

When Will first started having seizures, he was desperate to know what he looked like in their midst. He'd imagined all the terrifying eppy clichés: flopping around like a fish, his tongue gyrating around his gaping mouth. But Will's fits were what his doctor called "absence seizures." During them, his mom said he just stared at her as though she were a stranger. It sounded pretty underwhelming, and the doctor said Will ought to be seizure-free by the time he was eighteen, but each attack still scared Josephine and physically drained Will.

Things had barely come back into focus before Will conked back out in a drooling crash-nap.

Will woke up starving, his exhausted brain craving nourishment.

"Are there any snacks in the car?" he croaked.

She passed him half a roll of Life Savers from the glove compartment. They wouldn't do a thing to kill the gnawing pain in his stomach. He was so hungry he could eat a city block and still have room for a footlong sandwich.

"Any water?"

She shook her head and killed the ignition.

Will's head rang as he righted himself. The car was idling in front of a brick building with arched windows and fortressy turrets. It looked as sad and complicated as the people Will imagined pacing its halls.

Josephine reached across the seat for her purse. "Wait in the car," she said. "I just need to go inside and sign those forms."

Will slipped one arm through his coat. "I'll come with you," he said. He didn't want to be alone. Seizures were like earthquakes; sometimes there were aftershocks.

"I'll be in and out. I promise. I don't want you to be involved in this any further. It's bad enough what Violet did, but the stress, setting off your seizures—No. Just stay still and I'll be right back."

The horn beeped twice and Will realized she'd hit the lock button on her keychain.

He returned his cheek to the seat fabric. His mind flitted back to the letter in his mother's purse. He wished he'd had the good sense to copy down the return address before she took the envelope away. He wondered if his mother was thinking the same. Why had she delivered it to Violet without opening it first?

His mother's cell phone interrupted his train of thought. It was vibrating between the two front seats, smacking its silver head against the plastic cup holder, the whirring sound threefold. Will reached over and inspected the screen. DOUG, read the caller ID. Maybe Will should have pressed Ignore. Instead, his thumb wandered to the green Talk button.

"Dad?" he said.

On the other end of the line was the swishing sound of a pocket call. There was a loud, social din. A restaurant, maybe. His father's lunch hour?

A woman's giggle cut through the racket like a clinking teaspoon. It was followed by the unmistakable sound of his father's voice. "You're a remarkable woman," Douglas said. "A few of us are heading down to the Bull and Buddha. Any interest in joining us?"

As the call cut out, Will made a vow to himself: if he could not help his mother by bringing Rose home to apologize for the hurt she'd caused them, he would save her by finding out the whos and whys of his father's indiscretions.

"See? That didn't take long, did it?" Josephine said later, sliding behind the steering wheel and slinging her purse onto the passenger seat. "And now we're safe. We really don't have to worry. There won't be a big, Violet-shaped cloud hanging over us any longer."

Will glanced up at the spiky-looking building with its too-dark windows. "What's it like inside?"

"Don't worry about her, Will. It's one of the nicest hospitals money can buy. The Roosevelts once owned all this land. And these buildings—they're called high Gothics, by the way—are a national landmark." She said it in the same tone he'd heard her use to help sell his sisters on colleges she liked.

Will felt a pang of guilt when he realized Violet might fall behind in school and not get into her first-choice college, Bard, now.

His mother seemed to read his mind. "Will, either she'll get better or she won't. It doesn't have anything to do with us now."

. . .

Will was still starving when they arrived at home and found a car idling in the driveway at Old Stone Way. He expected his father, but the car in question didn't belong to Douglas. It was as compact and green as a lime. At the rear dash, a scrum of stuffed animals begged for rescue.

At the Hursts' front door, a wide woman in a trench coat looked casually up from her clipboard.

"Can I help you?" Josephine asked, opening the driver's-side door.

The woman hobbled over on a bad hip and thrust out her hand. "Mrs. Hurst?"

His mother nodded. "And you are?"

"My name is Trina Williams. I'm from Child Protective Services."

Violet Hurst

It was barely lunchtime, and Violet was already tired of being cooped up all morning. She'd always felt sanest in the great outdoors, especially when there was compost in her cuticles and maple pods in the ends of her long-ago hair.

Even during Violet's bad trip, her mood had instantly improved after her friends brought her outside. The Fields' eco-contemporary sat on ten enchanted acres, the Mohonk mountains guarding it from the south side like a high garden wall. The wind pulled the leaves across the lawn in crested waves. Violet saw vortexes and patterns in the hellfire sunset. This, she decided, was all she ever needed or wanted in life. She wanted only to wrap herself up in the misty red-gold dead of autumn. She wanted to make these three enchanted creatures—Imogene, Finch, and Jasper—her permanent family.

Imogene rode Finch's BMX bike around the driveway while Violet stood on the rear pegs. Finch smiled beatifically behind the twirling flames of the copper fire pit. His face bloomed red and gold with reflected flashes.

"Hurst, you remind me of that Inuit story about the Stone Child," he'd said.

"What?" Violet had asked. By that time, she had been lying on her back, her cheek in the overgrown grass, doing a slow improvised backstroke through a pile of dead leaves.

"So there was this orphan, right? And his mom and dad died in a bear attack. He lived by himself, angry and starving to death. All he had was a rock the same size as he was. He wrapped his arms and legs around it and refused to let go."

Violet had a thought that it sounded like her parents' relationship: doting Douglas clinging to an ice-cold hunk of rock.

"That's how he got the nickname the Stone Child," Finch continued. "The villagers thought he was out of his fucking mind. But that bat-shit little boy didn't let go. He just kept clinging to the thing, until one day, the big rock broke in two. And inside was the most perfect girl he could ever ask for. She gave the Stone Child bows and arrows and a harpoon. They got married and had kids."

"What the fuck does that even mean?!" Jasper cried.

"And what does that have to do with Violet?" Imogene asked, shrieking with laughter.

"I was just trying to say Violet is intuitive. She reminds me of some of the great healers."

Violet felt all her organs flush hot and pulse.

Her cell phone had squirmed uncomfortably in her pocket. It was a text message from Josephine:

WE NEED YOU AT HOME. YOUR FATHER AND I HAVE DIVORCE ON THE TABLE.

After passing her phone around the group—Violet had to make sure she wasn't tripping hard enough to imagine that—she texted the wary response: WHAT??? ARE YOU OKAY?

"It's about time," she'd told her friends. Her parents' relationship wasn't like Beryl and Rolf's, or anyone else's she knew. It was like a business arrangement, where her father provided the capital and her mother funneled money out the back. The only "business" they were in was denying reality and their true natures, and business had been failing ever since Rose ran away.

Violet's phone buzzed with Josephine's reply: YES, I'M OK. DINNER. I MEANT *WE HAVE DINNER ON THE TABLE. MY PHONE CHANGES MY WORDS. COME HOME NOW.*

They'd practically pissed themselves laughing. Violet rode her bike home via the town rail trail. The clouds on the horizon had darkened, and the bent trees looked a bit like they were clawing for her.

As Violet pedaled, she'd hatched a plan to fake a migraine and duck out on family dinner. She rehearsed everything she was going to say under her breath. She thought of the mantra for peace of mind—*asato ma sadgamaya*—which meant roughly, "lead us from darkness to the light / from knowledge of the unreal to the real." Maybe she'd been having auditory hallucinations, but the bike's spinning wheels had sounded like a sitar.

High on seeds, Violet would have much rather slept on the rail trail if she'd had her choice. Climbing off her bike, she found the front door locked. The more she tapped the brass door knocker (nobody answered), the more she began to feel like a stranger. Pacing back and forth on the personalized doormat (HURSTS, it read in severe, serifed letters), she'd started to feel like a home intruder.

Finally, knowing full well that her mother hated the sound, Violet hit the doorbell and listened to the dissonant electric sound of "When the Saints Go Marching In."

The door had snapped inward, and Josephine's grimacing face popped out.

"Why did you ring the doorbell?" she asked. "I hate that sound. That's no exaggeration. I hate it. Douglas! Haven't I told you to reprogram that thing?! It's not your fault, Violet. It's that father of yours."

Violet had stepped into the foyer, where the chandelier seemed to bloom open like a crystal chrysanthemum, and felt like she'd crossed a psychic threshold that could never be uncrossed. Violet had wanted to retreat to her bedroom, but she couldn't seem to vocalize anything. "It's locked," she finally said, tapping her temple with one finger.

"Let me smell you," Josephine said, backing Violet against the door. "Have you been smoking cigarettes? You're eating tonight. You're eating something. Do you understand me? I hope you're hungry, little girl."

Now, in the hospital, Violet really did feel like a little girl. She felt as utterly aimless as she did during summer vacations when her mother used to confiscate her books as punishment for fighting with Rose. Since she was no good at sitting still to begin with, Violet decided to walk every inch of the resident area. She perused a cart of books donated by a ladies' auxiliary (it was mostly graphic horror and super-inappropriate "throbbing manhood" smut). She scanned the patient art that had been stuck to the bulletin boards with packing tape (presumably tacks could be swallowed or used to self-harm). A handprint collage returned her thoughts, for the billionth time, to Will. For all the times people had questioned her about him, no one had told her how he was doing. She wondered whether he was home from the hospital. She hoped he wasn't in pain.

After she'd done the full tour, Violet headed down the long hallway toward her room. She was nearly there when a nurse headed her off.

"Violet, right?" the woman asked. "Your mom dropped this at reception when she came in for paperwork."

Violet felt a rush of blood as she reached out for the envelope.

Any letter her mother left was sure to enumerate all of Violet's faults. Or else, allude to the punishment she should expect when she got home. Violet's anxiety turned to utter disbelief when she saw the perfectionistic print and the return address. When she noticed the sealing wax, she knew without a shadow of a doubt it was from Rose. Pyro Rose, who would melt down anything from crayons to Babybel cheese cases and stamp it with a peacoat button.

Violet shivered as she recalled the image of Rose standing in the foyer on the night of her intake. Her throat felt tight as she slit the envelope with one blue fingernail. Inside was Rose's stickman handwriting, all perfectly round circles and precision-straight lines, the pressure slightly too hard. Their mother was always appalled that no one of their generation used cursive.

> Dear Vivi,
>
> Greetings from corporate hell. I'm in acting class most nights, so I only have time to write when I'm at my day job. From what I can see, office life is like this big theater exercise where everybody just shuffles papers and acts really busy. I'm playing along, pretending like I'm taking the minutes for a meeting and really taking the opportunity to write you with a year's worth of questions like . . .
>
> How is Stone Ridge High these days?
>
> Do you have your license?
>
> Do you have a boyfriend?
>
> Are you still thinking about art school? I hope so. I know I didn't always "get" your art in the past, but you're good. You should go for it. Whatever you do, don't end up an office slave like me. Every second of the day is soo boring. Half the people I work for don't even bother to ask my name, and the rest are too filthy rich to remember what it's like to be young and broke. "How broke?" you might ask. This morning I bought coffee filters on credit!

Does it sound too stupid and optimistic to say I think I might catch a break soon? I'm auditioning again and I have a callback I'm crossing my fingers about.

My new acting teacher is the best I've ever had. The other day, he was like, "Rose, you're a young twenty-something and the pool is pretty full of your type. You need to think about who responds to you best in real life. What kind of strangers smile at you before they even get to know you? Figure it out, and then audition for commercials for products that those people buy." For me, it's old people and little kids. According to this teacher, I'm the good girl, but not the leading lady. I'm more of the cute office clerk or the supportive older sister type. So ironic, isn't it? I'm only typecast at parts I suck at in real life!

Which brings me to why I'm writing . . . I'm sorry I lumped you in with the rest of the family. I know we've both always done our own things, but I see now I should have let you in on my plan. I just didn't want to be criticized, and I really didn't want anyone to talk me into staying. Damien asked me to move in with him, and there's no way Mom and Dad would have let that happen. You know how it would have gone . . . Dad inviting him over for dinner, Mom ribbing him about "living in sin." I thought hopping on a train was the best way to spare everyone!

I'm really hoping you'll play pen pal with me, and also that you'll keep my address secret? That is, if Mom hasn't already seen this and put two and two together! I'm just not ready to have the whole family banging down my door. I'm sure you understand why I'd rather visit them on my own terms.

I miss you!

Rose

It came as no surprise to Violet that her sister was alive and well, nor that she was living in the city. The police had said as much when they closed her short-lived missing-person investigation last year. It all ended with relief and embarrassment when

Rose's car was towed away from the Poughkeepsie MetroNorth station. Its metered parking ticket had expired, and the police found her Dear John letter to the Hursts placed prominently on the front seat. CCTV at the station had shown Rose buying a one-way ticket to Grand Central—a charge that matched the credit card the company confirmed she still used. It all proved what Violet had secretly suspected: the whole "case" was really just a five-alarm overreaction on her mother's part, not to mention a waste of public sympathy and taxpayer money.

After her disappearance was deemed voluntary, other emotions whooshed in to fill the family vacuum Rose's absence had created. Violet's parents had been able to deal (just barely) with their panic over Rose's so-called abduction, but they were totally unequipped to handle the fact that their golden child hated them enough to cut them out of her life. Douglas, even in his self-contained way, had seemed dejected for months. Josephine was rip-shit at being ignored. Will was angry too, in allegiance to their mom. And Violet . . . Once Violet was a hundred percent sure Rose was safe, she was overcome by sickening envy. She wanted the freedom her sister had. Of course she did. But Violet was most jealous of the subversive means by which Rose had broken free. Rose had escaped by doing exactly what Josephine asked of her, waiting until just the right moment to rebel. By comparison, Violet's small, daily rebellions put her mother on guard around her. The harder Violet fought back, the more controlling Josephine became; she was in a choke chain of her own making.

Violet's parents hadn't been exaggerating to the police; it really was unlike Rose to take off for days without telling anyone. But they'd also failed to mention all the ways Rose had been acting out of character and causing tension for months—dropping her theater major and taking long walks alone, supposedly, on the town rail trail.

Only Violet and her mom had known the reason for Rose's sudden bitchy pensiveness. Rose had come down with the kind of sickness that gets cured by either (a) a two-hour appointment at Planned Parenthood or (b) eighteen to twenty years of servitude. Rose had picked the former: A for abortion. If Violet had figured it all out sooner, she would have applauded Rose for not just going ahead and having Damien's kid, simply for the ego trip (genes, lineage, legacy). She would have told Rose that she had lots of time to push around a mini-person who shared her last name. Violet knew in her gut that Josephine was the major reason Rose had done what she'd done. With a mom like theirs, it was impossible not to equate becoming a mother with becoming a monster.

William Hurst

"Can we ask what this is in reference to?"

Will stood up straight and crossed his arms, mimicking his mother's offense.

"I need to ask you a few questions about your daughter Viola. Your family was entered into our system when your older daughter"—Trina Williams's gaze fell to her notes—"Rosette ran away. It's a formality. Going forward, anytime you have a domestic disturbance, Child Protective Services is required to investigate. It won't take very long."

"Fine," Josephine said. "Just let me get Will into bed and I'll be happy to discuss the matter with you."

"I'm afraid I need to speak to your son as well."

"In that case, you'll have to come back another time," Josephine said. "I don't know if this is in your files, but in the year since Rose ran away, my son was diagnosed with epilepsy. He's had a difficult week. I need to let him rest, have his fluids, and give him more Keppra." Again, she lifted Will's arm, pulled back his sleeve, and rattled the sterling bracelet. It was Will's good hand. He instinctively turtled his other hand—the one with the brace—up into the sleeve of his orange down coat.

"I'm sorry to hear that." Trina's tone didn't exactly ooze sympathy. "I'll make a note in your file. Here's my card. Do you think I could come by tomorrow?"

Josephine leaned Will's head against her hip and stroked his forehead as if checking for a fever.

"Possibly. It really depends on William."

"I understand." Trina nodded. "Well, we'll be in touch."

Will watched from the front steps as her neon car reversed out past the gaping mailbox.

When they returned to the kitchen, Josephine gave him a bowl of Stewart's ice cream—the flavor, Death by Chocolate, seemed grave and momentous—and sat opposite him in the breakfast nook, while he ate it in slow, measured spoonfuls.

"We need to talk about the night Violet went away," she said. "I need to make sure you can synthesize your thoughts about what happened. That woman who came by is going to make you explain it to her. If she can't keep up with you, or if you don't explain yourself well, there could be big consequences. You don't want to confuse her, or give her the impression you don't know what you're talking about."

"Okay." They did this sometimes. She helped him role-play scenarios when she worried his Asperger's was going to get in the way.

"So go on . . . Tell me what you remember."

"You and Dad and Violet were fighting."

She nodded. "That's right. Only we were *arguing*, not fighting. 'Fighting' can sometimes mean hitting. And we weren't hitting. We were just having an argument."

"You were arguing," Will corrected himself. "Because Violet had made a mess in the dishwasher."

There was her approving nod again. She was proud that he'd remembered that detail.

"I'd made a special vegetarian dinner for her, hadn't I?"

Will hesitated. "Yes."

"And Violet wouldn't eat it."

"No."

"So then what happened? What happened in the kitchen?"

"Violet started pointing the knife at you."

"And what was that like?"

"Scary."

"You were really frightened, weren't you?"

"Yes." Will *had* been frightened. The thought of someone, any-one, hurting his mother was more than he could bear.

"Remember to tell the woman that. That's the kind of thing she'll want to hear."

"I was scared. I'll tell her."

"What happened next?"

Will stared into the skid marks his spoon made in the ice cream bowl. "Violet said she saw Rose in the foyer."

When he looked up, a shadow had fallen across his mother's cheek, and the whites showed in the bottommost part of her eyes.

"No," she said. "You're confusing things. Do you have any idea what would happen if you said that to this Trina person?"

He knew. Of course, he knew. Will's chin did a Jell-O-mold quiver.

"Stop it. Will you? You're overreacting."

Will wiped his teary face on his sleeve.

"Use a tissue!"

She asked him to start the story from the beginning.

"You and Dad and Violet were arguing in the kitchen. And I was really frightened."

His mother nodded. "Yes, but probably not as frightened as you were when Violet turned the knife on you."

"When she turned the knife on me . . ." Will's voice went soft the way it always did when he was anxious. It was one of those Aspie language quirks that made him hate himself.

"You could have cowered when Violet came at you with that knife, but you didn't, did you? You aimed your hand right for that blade and tried to snatch it away."

Will paused and tried to absorb the heroism she was ascribing to him. Then he asked the only question that really mattered to him: "Were you proud of me?"

"Are you kidding? I was so proud of you. You saved me. You saved us all."

Will touched the splint on his hand. He remembered the bloody dishrag that she'd wound around his hand before they drove to the hospital.

"How did it feel?" his mom asked now.

"When I took the knife away from Violet?"

She nodded.

He knew this was another detail she wanted him to tell Trina. But emotions were not his forte. He could only guess.

"I felt brave," he said.

"Yes, it was a very heroic and brave thing to do. But you know, even heroes feel scared in the heat of the moment. Don't you think you were a little bit frightened?"

"Yes," Will said. "I was frightened."

"And how did it feel when the knife pierced your skin?"

Will winced. *When the knife pierced his skin.* It was too horrible to remember. "It hurt," he said.

She had a finger in her mouth. There was a dreamy, unfocused look in her eyes. "Yes," she said, her cuticle in her teeth. "Your sister really hurt you."

Even after his father came home from work, Will's stomach remained knotted.

Douglas, for his part, went straight for the kitchen cupboard and removed what Will knew was his favorite cup. It was a cheap, blue plastic tumbler—tall and opaque, so a person could only guess what he was sipping.

On this particular night, Will watched his father fill it with hissing cherry-flavored seltzer. Douglas drank about a case of twelve liter-sized bottles of sparkling water per week. Lately, every time he opened one, it exploded as though someone had been shaking them.

After they'd rehearsed their version of events, Will's mother had called Trina and arranged a meeting. Now, watching his father, Will couldn't stop thinking about the reminder his mother had scrawled on the family calendar. *Trina visit, 2 p.m.*, it read. Would his mother mention it over dinner? Would Douglas, in his postcoital daze, even pretend to care?

As they silently chewed their dinner, Will followed his father's gaze to the roman numerals on the dining room clock. The little hand was on the VII. Another few minutes, and his father would vanish to his home office, sports highlights blaring behind the locked door.

Will remembered his father's pocket call. *You're a remarkable woman.* He remembered the daring he'd heard in Douglas's voice; it was so unlike the feeble, measured tones his dad used at home.

"Does anyone mind if I excuse myself?" Douglas said, pushing back his chair right on cue.

Josephine looked at Will with a pinched mouth and hurt eyes.

"We don't mind," Will answered. "Where are you going?"

"Where?" Douglas echoed. In his hand, his plate of food was only half-finished.

Josephine raised her eyebrows.

"I'm just going down the hall, to answer some e-mails." Before Douglas retreated to his office, he sponged down the granite countertops with aggressive, excessive force. He scrubbed the sauté pans with a martyred expression that rivaled Christ on the cross.

Will was serious about investigating his dad's double life. His father couldn't just betray his mother like that. He just couldn't take Will and the rest of the Hursts for fools. Had Douglas really thought the rest of them wouldn't notice the way the past few months had changed him, looks- and attitude-wise? Had he really thought no one would notice the twinkle in his eye? Or the way he had been hitting the gym like he was competing for gold in the next summer Olympics? Will was determined to get to the bottom of things. He felt certain he had most of the qualities that made for a good PI. No, he couldn't drink straight scotch or fire a gun, but he was mature for his age and alert to details. He believed in the importance of law and order and protecting the innocent. It was just going to be a matter of opportunity. His challenge, as he saw it, was twofold: it was going to be hard enough to slip away from his eagle-eyed mother, but latching onto his antisocial father would require real skill.

Watching TV with Josephine later, Will sensed an opportunity. The show was a workplace comedy, and the episode revolved around Take Your Kid to Work Day.

"Mom?" Will asked. "When is Take Your Child to Work Day?"

"I don't remember. Maybe sometime in spring."

Dang, thought Will. It was October.

He knew he shouldn't push his luck, but this might be his only chance, and time was of the essence. "It just feels like another thing I'm missing out on since I'm not in a regular school anymore."

His mother's blue eyes narrowed. Will tried a different approach. "It's just—I remember Tyler McCastle saying how cool it was going to his dad's office in the city. His dad has two secretaries and an office with a sofa in it. His office looked right out over Radio City." Tyler McCastle was an old friend from Stone Ridge Elementary. Will hadn't seen or talked to him since June.

"Tyler McCastle's father sells print *ads*," Josephine sneered. "And magazines are dying. I wonder if he'll be able to see Radio City from the unemployment line."

"Tyler says his dad is a genius."

Josephine's eyes rolled. "Your dad is a genius. Your dad holds five patents. Your dad knows everything there is to know about computer science, engineering, programming. Tyler McCastle's dad is a *salesman*. He doesn't make anything. He doesn't contribute to society in any way. He just profits off other people's contributions."

"So I can't go to work with Dad?"

"You really want to spend a whole day at your father's office? Can you say, *boring*? Do you have any idea what your father's work colleagues are like? Do you really want to spend a whole day around smug little men in smudged glasses, talking about platforms and interfaces when you could be here with *moi*?"

Will held his breath. He didn't want to say yes.

Josephine's face changed. She looked thoughtful for a moment. "All right," she said. "I'll have a talk with your father."

Later at bedtime, she changed Will's sheets. She gave him his nightly bath, the water near scalding, and the bath puff foaming with the peppermint soap that didn't so much clean the skin he had but stripped it away to reveal a redder, subaqueous layer. Next came the part where Will lay faceup, across her lap, in his hooded bath towel. From that angle, she brushed and meticulously flossed his teeth.

After that, they were nearly there. Will's night-light was in sight, and he got to sink the lower half of his body under those bulldozer sheets. His head swam with exhaustion, but he knew he still needed to take his final round of pills—vitamins and bedtime medication—which Josephine lined up in an ant trail across his nightstand. She sang little songs of encouragement as he struggled to gulp them down in order of size and color. "Take the big ones first," she always said. "Everything after will feel like Easy Street."

But tonight nothing felt like Easy Street. Will couldn't shut his brain off. He could not stop thinking about his appointment with Trina the social worker. *Wednesday*, 2 p.m. He was destined to come off too emotionally flat. The very cold, logical way Will presented himself caused enough megadisasters with normal people, let alone a people person like Trina, someone who presumably went into social work because she considered herself a warm, caring, demonstrative lady. She was bound to think Will was detached to an unhealthy degree.

And there was so much he and his mother hadn't rehearsed. Was he or was he not supposed to tell Trina about the way Violet had been talking in circles when she left—saying the same things over and over and making the same strange, jerking series of gestures? Whooping. Flapping her hands. Saying, "Boom! Agh. Okay. Okay. Okay. Okay."

At the very least, he knew he wasn't supposed to talk about Rose. He wouldn't say a word about the moment Violet had widened her eyes and announced: "Look! Rose is here! Did you see her? I *saw* her!"

Violet Hurst

In the hospital cafeteria, Violet cracked open her sandwich and let the pink flesh curl out onto her tray. But it was too late. The meat had sweated and sogged the bread, exactly like a living creature would.

Violet's stomach spasmed. Friday night's dinner had been mushroom risotto.

"Especially for my Violet," Josephine said, slopping a ladleful into Violet's bowl.

From Violet's stoned perspective, the dome of rice swarmed like a maggot colony. Each grain seemed to move, burrowing inward or climbing onto the twitching backs of others. Violet had known her mom made it with Fleisher's beef stock because she hadn't bothered hiding the empty carton, and because the rice was as dark as gravy.

"Oh dear, I wasn't thinking," she said when Violet called her out on it. "Beef stock was just what the recipe called for. What's the big deal anyway? It's just broth, not meat."

Eating had been beyond Violet's comprehension. She marveled at the way her family moved their jaws, and all the while she couldn't remember how consumption actually worked, couldn't picture the mechanics of it, the tongue-smacking up-down of it all, couldn't remember what *chewing* was called.

Everyone was staring at her.

"Mom," Will said. "Violet's not eating her food. Does that mean I don't have to eat my food?"

Josephine threw down her fork with a clatter. "Violet *is* eating her food. Aren't you, Violet? Because I'm not making two separate meals every night. One for the Dalai Lama and one for everyone else."

"Now, Josephine. Josephine," Douglas said. Violet had long ago figured out why he repeated himself so much during dinner—it was so he'd have a second chance to repeat what had slurred the first time around. In this case, his first stab at *Josephine* had sounded more like "Juicy-fiend."

"Has it ever occurred to you this is just a sage?"

Josephine sighed. She spoke in the gritted voice of someone who imagined she had a lot of patience. "You mean a *stage*, Douglas?"

"She's just doing it for attention. It's just a fasting phase." Possibly, he had meant "a passing phase." His head wobbled at an unnatural angle.

Violet had glanced at Rose's empty seat and wondered why, in her unaltered life, she let herself get so upset about her family. It didn't matter how much stress, fear, or even enlightenment Violet brought to the table—it didn't even matter if she took off just like Rose—the Hursts would continue their long downward spiral, and everyone would remain exactly as they were. Violet had stood up without a word. She carried her untouched plate to the dishwasher and put it in, risotto and all.

Josephine appeared behind her screaming something at the top of her lungs, but in Violet's ears, her voice was like an infomercial playing in a far-off room: distant, agenda-ed, predictable. In any other company, this audio hallucination—selective

deafness—would have been unsettling, but given the circumstances, it was bliss. Nirvana on earth.

Even though Violet still hadn't been able to bear the idea of
eating, she'd flung open the refrigerator door and its related plastic drawers and begun pulling out every piece of produce she
could find: a jalapeño, a flaccid cucumber, a quartered onion in a
ziplock bag, a lacy bunch of kale, a bruised apple, half a lime. She
dumped it all out on Josephine's epicurean cutting board, grabbed
the biggest conceivable knife from the slotted block, and set to
work making her own goddamn dinner.

She looked up just in time to see Edie's red tray hit the table. Sitting down opposite Violet, she twisted what little hair she had at
the base of her long neck. The blue pen she stuck through her bun
was printed with the word ZOLOFT.

"In group this morning, didn't you say you have a sister who
ran away? Do you think she'd let you go and crash at her place?"

"I don't know." Violet paused and considered. "I don't know if
I'd even want to."

"You don't like her? Your sister?"

Edie had been a foster kid. CPS had moved her out of her
drug-addicted mother's house and placed her in a home with
belching, acne-scarred, pedo foster brothers and a woman who
branded her tongue with a heated spoon. Probably, she idealized
sisterhood.

"I don't know," Violet said. "I honestly don't know her very
well. When we were little, Rose was like this cleverly arranged
slide show, projecting whatever my mother wanted her to be.
And I don't mean typical good-girl stuff, like try to be polite, try
to be kind. My mom really wanted Rose to be a child actress. She
was always taking her to acting coaches so she could perfect her

fake Cockney accent or dyeing her hair different colors for cast-
ings: Irish red, California blond." Violet had a brief but vivid
flashback of her mother bent over the bathtub, hosing bleach out
of her nine-year-old sister's hair. How envious she had been at the
time. In retrospect, the whole business horrified her. Later, she'd
seen Rose crying about her burned scalp. Violet rubbed her palm
across her mouth and shivered. "Even in everyday life, Rose
seemed to be reading from a script. It wasn't till last year that she
finally broke character."

"Did she wild out?"

"Sort of. She dropped her major in theater arts and went un-
decided. I think she was looking to transfer into something in
the science department. Rose didn't want to live at home anymore. She started screaming her head off about wanting a student room in New Paltz, probably so she could be closer to her
boyfriend. No way she was gonna bring him home. My parents
have all sorts of rules about 'no shut doors' and 'no boys allowed
upstairs.'"

"Is he right for her? Her boyfriend . . . what's his name?"

"Damien."

"How very dark . . . and French. I know a Damien at Vassar.
What's his last name?"

"Koch."

"So is he? Right for her, I mean?"

"Dunno. Probably. It sounds like he got her back into theater
or whatever. Personally, I never met him. Rose always kept her
relationships top secret. She didn't talk about them. She never
once brought a guy home to meet my parents."

"Maybe she's not into guys? That's the reason most people
hide who they're dating."

Violet shook her head. No way Rose was sapphically inclined.

"I think it was more like she knows no one will ever be good enough for her in my mother's eyes. Besides, I always got the sense Rose was an undercover freak. A few months before she left home, I was giving her a hard time about being the Virgin Mary, and she looked at me with this filthy smile and said, 'If you only knew what I've been up to.' After she was gone, when the cops were searching her room, they found this little vibrator hidden behind the smiling side of her comedy/tragedy masks. My mom looked furious. My dad almost died of embarrassment."

"Cops?" Edie asked with interest.

"Yeah. It was scary for a few days. My super-considerate sister moved out without any warning. My parents reported her missing. Turns out she'd only run away. It didn't take the cops long to find CCTV from the MetroNorth station. The footage showed Rose buying a one-way ticket to Grand Central. She'd been alone, pulling a suitcase. She didn't look the least bit distressed."

How was it possible to hate someone straight down to their marrow and still miss them? Violet missed Rose. Desperately. She had never let herself think that before, not one time in all the months since the first responding officer had pulled her aside and pointedly asked, "What do you think happened to your sister?" Even when Josephine started obnoxiously doting on Will and when Douglas—a marginal figure to begin with—fell clean off the pages of the family history.

Sure, there was a time not too long ago when Violet was crying nightly and throwing things at her wall, and she took Rose's absence as further proof that everyone would discard her in the end. But as the year progressed, Violet had found blotter paper, THC, and transcendence. She'd learned to turn her brain inside out and leave her emotions behind.

But ever since Rose's letter had arrived, Violet had been feeling like she'd stepped in the same shit again. Her feelings had roared back at high volume. She felt light-headed, off-center. Her shoulders were clenched so tight it hurt to turn her head.

Edie was wearing a look she'd probably borrowed from one of the many shrinks she'd seen over the years. "Was it some kind of cry for attention? You think your sister is BPD?"

"I don't know what that is."

"Sorry. Borderline personality disordered. It's like, an *I-love-you-I-hate-you-Don't-leave-me* kinda thing. Emotional roller-coaster shit. Do you think she ran away hoping you all would come hunting her down?"

"Maybe. When we were kids, Rose's favorite game was hide-and-seek," Violet said. "She loved hiding at the bottom of the laundry basket, knowing everyone was pulling their hair out trying to find her."

After lunch Violet borrowed Edie's phone card. Clutching the greasy yellow receiver, her back to the booth's closed accordion door, Violet was faced with a first-world problem. She could not remember her best friend's phone number, which she'd always dialed from the saved entry on her cell phone.

She had three misdials.

She thought for a second and admired the graffiti that still showed through a janitor's efforts to scrub it off (*Is it solipsistic in here, or is it just me?*). Then it occurred to her to call 411. Thankfully, Imogene's parents had a landline.

Two conflicting voices said hello. The frazzled one belonged to Imogene's mother. The kind of endearingly monotone one was Finch. "I got it, Mom," he said.

Violet felt as though her tongue had been cut out. "Finch," she said. Violet's desperation—she was dying to talk to Imogene—gave her voice a breathy, stalkerette quality.

"Yeah. Is that Violet?"

For the past few months, she'd been trying to put the way she felt about Finch out of her mind. She wouldn't allow herself to call it a crush. Crushes weren't a precursor to love, they were a precursor to having your heart chewed up like Shark Week.

"Yeah, it's me," Violet said. "Listen, is Imogene there?"

"She's in the shower. What's up? Where have you been?"

"Is there any way you could get her? I don't really know when I'll be able to call again."

"Man, Hurst. Are you in the clink or something? Is this your one phone call? Do you need me to call a lawyer for you?"

"I'm not in jail. Just get Imogene, okay? I'm calling on a phone card and I don't know how much money's on it."

After Violet spent a few more minutes perusing the phone booth graffiti, Imogene finally picked up.

"Violet? Are you okay? Finch said you got busted for those seeds. That's outrageous! They're legal! For fuck's sake, we bought them in the gardening section of Gordon's Fairtrade Farm!"

"I didn't get arrested. It's a long story. My mom's lying about me, I think. Saying I'm abusive to Will. My dad brought me to Fallkill."

"Wait. What? The mental hospital?! What are you doing there? Do you need us to come get you?"

"You can come visit me. I can't leave until they say it's okay."

"Which 'they'? The doctors or your parents?"

"The doctors."

"How is she saying you abused Will?"

"I don't know. Something happened to his hand. A knife or something. I'm afraid I might be in serious trouble. My mom is trying to decide whether she's going to press charges."

"You're fucking kidding, right? This is serious, Violet. You have to get the fuck out of there. My parents will get you out of there. My mom's right here."

"No. Imogene, don't trouble your mom with this. She's dealing with enough—"

"Violet? Are you all right?"

Violet thought of magnanimous, huggy Beryl Field as the mother she always wished she had. It had been Beryl who'd taught Violet how to parallel park; who explained to her how to put on eyeliner ("Tilt your head back and close your eye about halfway. Think Marilyn Monroe"). On the night of the spring chorale concert, Beryl had gently suggested Violet take off the reinforced-toe pantyhose Josephine had earlier insisted she wear. ("There! That's better, don't you think?" Beryl had said, once the hose were balled in Violet's pocket. "You looked beautiful before, too. But now, there's nothing detracting from your pretty peep-toe espadrilles.") Beryl asked the open-ended questions that Josephine didn't: where Violet wanted to travel, what qualities Violet found attractive in boys, how she felt about applying for college. Naturally, Josephine thought Beryl was spineless and overindulgent; she liked to poke fun at the way Beryl was raising Imogene like she was a "precious little snowflake" when, in her estimation, what Imogene really needed was a mom with the courage and conviction to "rip the piercings out of her face."

"I'm okay," Violet said, fighting back tears.

"Imogene says you're at Fallkill Psych? What happened, honey?"

Violet couldn't help registering the hoarse, tired tones in Beryl's voice. She sounded so unlike the vivacious woman who used to find time to make giant abstract sculptures out of PVC pipes and teach a hula-hoop dance class at the Stone Ridge Community Center.

Violet wanted to ask for help, but she wasn't yet ready to fully fight her mother's accusations. She needed more information. She needed time to build her defense case. Whatever had happened to Will, it was Violet's word against Josephine's, at least or until she was clear on whether Rose had really been there.

The only words she managed to get out were the understatement of the century: "Nothing happened. I had a fight with my mom and then a panic attack. Or maybe it was the other way around."

Violet had a sudden picture—a flip book, really—of her mom's face that night in the kitchen: She saw her mother's eyes shrink, then widen, then narrow as though she were taking aim. She had a flashback of Josephine's mouth: first contracting nervously, then opening in a scream of horror, then snarling, her upper lip curling past her eyeteeth. What the hell had Violet said that had propelled her mother's face—which was usually restricted to sadistic smirks and phony smiles—through such a range of expression?

It still didn't make sense, the way Violet's freak-out had incited her mom to have one of her own. Hanging up with Beryl, Violet couldn't shake Josephine's good-bye face as she left for the hospital. Her mother's eyes had held Violet with a looks-could-kill glare. It was a face that carried a vindictive warning. A face that told Violet, *Just you wait* . . .

WILLIAM HURST

"Can I get you a Coke?" Douglas asked without looking at Will directly. They were at his office, and he was powering up one of three desktop computers, the login screen prompting him for a password.

Will flinched, then tried to cover his shock. Josephine had always forbidden him soda, and as a result, he'd never developed a taste for it. Everything about Coca-Cola—the smell, the excrement color, the carbonated hiss—made vomit rise in Will's throat.

"No, thanks," Will said. "I'm not thirsty."

Will tried to peer over the desk and track his dad's fingers as he typed his password. But Douglas was fast. Too fast. In less than a second, he was logged in. The striped IBM logo glowed bright on his monitors.

Will couldn't help noticing that his dad was different at work. He seemed to be witnessing a complete personality transplant. Before, Will had worried that his father had a parallel life, but the reality was something even more disturbing: his father seemed to have a parallel identity.

The Douglas of Old Stone Way—the evasive guy who had spent

all day Sunday glumly going through the motions of church and an IHOP breakfast until he could slip away to the "gym" for close to five hours—was gone. He'd been replaced by the Douglas Hurst of IBM, the kind of chummy blowhard who made people flash squeamish smiles and avert their eyes. He wasn't confident, exactly, but he had a fine-tuned schtick, composed of business-management-speak and comedic timing.

Will briefly wondered which persona was real, and decided on neither. For a moment, he tried to look at his father from an outsider's perspective—to see him as Douglas instead of Dad—but all he saw was an aging nerd with thick graying hair and his work shirt buttoned too high on his Adam's apple. Will didn't have the first inkling who his father was beyond the surface of his faintly smudged glasses.

Maybe Douglas felt shy and awkward in Will's presence too. He started rambling abruptly, out of nowhere. "Years ago, we had this PA who never liked to wear the same thing twice. . . . She was obsessive about it. So you know what I did? I built her a program that would help her track her outfits. She'd just input whatever she wanted to wear—polka-dot blouse with a tan blazer, you name it—and the computer would go ballistic and tell her she'd worn the same thing back on the fifth of December." Douglas laughed and took a slug from his travel mug. "Will, don't ever let anyone tell you that tech geeks don't know a thing about women. We're not all social pariah types. Well . . . with the exception of Don, here, of course."

Don, the co-worker who'd been leaning in the doorway, laughed a little too heartily and walked away clutching his chest as though he'd been shot.

Women. That one word hit Will like a glass of ice water in the face. It brought him back to his real objective. Officially, the ringed notebook in his lap was for taking notes (his mother expected him to write a report about "Multinational Technology and Consulting and What It Means to Me"), but, unofficially, Will was using it to log his father's interactions with the opposite sex. At 8:49 a.m., Douglas had held the elevator door open for a blond woman (Cindy) who was reasonably pretty, despite her wake-me-when-we-get-there eyes. Ten minutes later he had stopped mid-hallway to chat with another female (Marnie) who had a sagging, anxious face and curly gingersnap-colored hair that made Will imagine her in Ronald McDonald's yellow jumpsuit.

Yesterday, when Josephine had slipped away to the bathroom during a MathBusters computer lesson, Will had sneakily used the Internet to image-search the word *mistress*. He'd wanted to acquaint himself, in case he was looking for a certain type of woman, in case all home-wreckers looked the same. The results (Will had only ever seen cleavage, not actual unabashed breasts) gave him a guilty feeling in his stomach. But they also made him think he was looking for a very particular sort of cat-eyed woman encased in black latex. He had spent nearly every moment since trying to suppress visions of his father naked and shackled, licking some snarling woman's feet.

The phone on his father's desk trilled.

Douglas answered it with a jab of the speaker button. "Yes?"

It was strange to hear the voice of his father's secretary in stereo, coming at once through the phone and through the open office door. "Carrie's on the line," she said.

For a fraction of a second, his father flushed.

Carrie. The familiarity of that statement was not lost on Will. The fact that the secretary hadn't used a last name meant this was a frequent caller. He scribbled the name, very discreetly, in his notebook and marked it with a star.

Holding the receiver in one hand, Douglas fished in the pocket of his khakis with the other. "Here," he said, opening his wallet and thrusting some singles at Will. "Take a walk to the vending machines and get yourself a snack."

"I just ate breakfast. And I'm supposed to shadow you for the *whole* day. I have a report to write. What's Mom going to say when I tell her that you wouldn't let me do my work?"

Douglas's cheeks were pinkening. He looked flustered.

"Your need to observe my work doesn't trump my responsibility to *do* my work." Douglas paused for a second and softened his approach. "Just give me a few minutes. *Please*. I'd really appreciate it. When you get back you can sit in on a very important meeting."

Will gave a grunting sigh. As soon as he'd rounded his father's door, he stuffed the small wad of cash into his pocket and bent to "retie" his firmly knotted shoelace, wary of anyone who might catch him eavesdropping.

"Carrie," his father said in a voice that gave little away. "No. I *am* glad to hear from you. I've been worried you might not call me back . . ."

There was an agonizing pause. A pair of goateed men strode past and eyed Will with interest. The secret to being a good private investigator was blending in—not exactly Will's forte, but he stood and flipped through his notebook in a way that he hoped looked purposeful.

"I can't tell you how much I want to," Douglas said. "But I've got my kid here today. I was gonna take him out to lunch. Yes, I know. Well, that makes me a very sick man. Yes, I'll call you later. I swear. I will. I won't ever stand you up like that again. I *do* appreciate you. I know you worry."

Will's ears roared. His horror was like an earthquake. The

hallway walls around him swayed and liquefied. He felt the pol-
ished office floor swell beneath his Top-Siders, and he worried he
was on the verge of a seizure.

There was a woman in the world—even closer, in the state,
the county, even—who felt close enough to Will's dad to worry
about him. Triumphant as Will was that his detective skills had
paid off, he felt a crushing wave of anger and heartbreak for his
mother. His father's affair didn't sound like a fling. It sounded
powerful and devastating, like something destined to blow their
whole lives apart.

Later, Douglas went to a meeting, leaving Will to watch a video.
The video was on YouTube, meaning Will really could have
watched from the comfort of his mother's kitchen desk. It said
nothing about his father's business associates. It gave little insight
into the extroverted work persona Douglas appeared to slip on
each morning along with his wrinkle-resistant dress shirt.

On the upside, the video gave Will forty untroubled minutes
to scroll through his father's computer files.

Will was no tech prodigy. His mother wasn't exactly pepper-
ing his school curriculum with HTML lessons. Heck, she still
thought WordPerfect was the industry standard.

Still, Will managed to search his father's hard drive for any
documents that might mention *sex, Carrie, affair,* or *love.* When those
resulted in no hits—aside from a PowerPoint presentation titled
"Eight Reasons You'll Love Using Lotus Notes"—Will dug into his
burgeoning mental gutter. He searched for *hotel* (this only brought
up a few ancient itineraries for his father's work conventions). He
hunted for *divorce, lawyer,* and even *custody,* before zeroing in on his
father's open e-mail.

I've got my kid here today. Whoever Carrie was, she knew about Douglas's family. Will decided to start with Rose. *Eigne,* a naming word, meaning "firstborn." An in-box search of Rose's name brought up dozens of e-mails.

The most recent was a series of e-mail messages to a man his dad appeared to be considering hiring to sniff out Rose's address. At least according to his signature box, this man worked at a "bonded and insured private investigations firm servicing greater New York City." Will felt a touch competitive, knowing he wasn't the only PI on the case. He couldn't help imagining the man he was up against. Did he have real spy tools: voice changers and night-vision goggles? Did he turn up the collar on his black leather trench coat?

In the first message, written a few months earlier, Douglas wrote that he "just wanted to verify" that his runaway daughter wasn't stalking or harassing his wife and remaining children. There had been some incidents, he said. His wife was feeling jumpy.

What kinds of incidents? the PI had written.

Nothing conclusive, Douglas wrote. *My car was keyed. A few personal items have gone missing. There were some defaced photos in the family album, although my younger daughter might have done that.*

"Are you hanging in there?" When Will looked up, his father's secretary was standing in the doorway, smiling the kind of exaggerated smile that made the tendons stand out in her neck.

It took Will a second to figure out what she was talking about. He felt like he had chewed gum in his ears. "Uh-huh," he said, and turned up the volume on the IBM school-spirit video.

The assistant—Peggy was her name—nodded vigorously. A woman on the brink of retirement, she had large dangling pieces of jewelry and pictures of grandchildren on her desk. In the name of thoroughness, Will had added her name to his list of potential mistresses anyway.

"Okay," Peggy said. "You're awful self-reliant, aren't you? You're just like your dad. Okay . . . If you need anything, give me a holler."

Will bit his lip. His ears were buzzing, and his fingers had turned so inexplicably cold that he had trouble moving the cursor across the computer screen.

The defaced photos, things stolen . . . it was all news to Will. But he had felt something strange in the air over the past couple of weeks, even beyond Violet's usual weirdness. Twice, bears had battered the garbage cans and made trash salad all over the garage floor (no Hurst would cop to leaving the door open). Once, he'd found his mother in her master bathroom, crying over the shards and puddles of her favorite perfume bottle.

He did, of course, remember his father's keyed car. He'd heard his parents fighting about it through their closed bedroom door:

"You pissed *someone* off, Douglas!" his mother had wailed. "Just admit it! You cut someone off! Or you blocked a bike lane! Or you, I don't know . . . You stole a parking space someone else was waiting for!"

And his father: "It happened here, Josephine! In our garage!"

"Well, it serves you right for leaving the garage door open!"

"Could Violet have done this? Or one of her friends?"

It went on and on and on.

Also, there was the incident a few nights before Violet flipped her biscuits. It was a humid night, unseasonably sweaty. Will's windows were open, and his striped blue drapes twitched in the barely there wind. He'd been waking every thirty minutes, playing WrestleMania with his sheets. His hair was drenched and his pillowcase was damp with perspiration. But when he reached a hand underneath to flip his pillow to the cooler side, his fingers had tripped over a sharp metal point. By the glow of his ancient Noah's Ark night-light, Will had pulled out eight gleaming inches of his mother's sewing scissors. He'd turned the orange handle over in his hand and thought of various reasons why they might have ended up one down-filled inch away from his face: *Some chance Violet was playing a joke? Maybe his mother, midway through making Will's bed, had left them there by mistake?* Eventually, Will got up and returned them to the sewing box on his mother's desk. When he woke up the next morning, he didn't breathe a word about the scissors to anyone. He'd chalked it up to a very vivid dream.

The last e-mail from his father's potential PI was dated just one week before Violet's breakdown. *I feel very confident I can find your daughter. To begin with, I will need some information from you, including Rose's birth date, a recent photograph, driver's license number, social security number, a list of alternative names she might be using, as well as information on her electronic communication devices, such as known cell phone numbers and e-mail addresses.* As far as Will could see, either his father hadn't responded or, covering his tracks, he'd deleted that message and every one that came after.

Will stared up the web of scribbles on his father's whiteboard. He tried to will his brain into the same kind of organized algorithm, every arrow leading him from one logical thought to the next.

There was no end of explanations, but only two immediately jumped out. One was that Douglas had changed his mind. Maybe he'd found another culprit for the hacked-up family photos and the car. Like his father said, it was fully possible that these were just a few more items in Violet's à la carte rebellion. The other possibility was that Douglas had gone ahead and hired the investigator. In that case, he'd either spent the past few weeks talking to the PI exclusively on the phone, or else he'd begun deleting every trace of what he'd found.

. . .

Will's train of thought was broken by the sound of Peggy transferring a call to Douglas's voice mail. Will looked down at the red message light blinking on his father's phone and felt a cold suspicion crash over him. Maybe, just maybe, his father had started being careful with his e-mail because the PI who'd gone looking for Rose had found her. There was a small chance that his father's late nights and sly phone calls weren't romantic at all. Sex, no. A secret connection with Rose, yes. After Rose ran away, Will's father had been far more hopeful and forgiving than his mother. But then, he wasn't the one Rose had called for one final F.U. once she got to the city. Rose and Damien had called Josephine, and Josephine couldn't forgive the things they had said to her. "She told me we were dead to her, Douglas. She told me if I contacted her, she'd make me pay. She said we were toxic."

Will opened his notebook to his ongoing list of women's names. Across the margin, in double-sized letters, he wrote ROSE.

Violet Hurst

Violet's boss, Mrs. D, was beyond understanding when Violet called to apologize about missing her shift at Dekker's Farm Stand. Work was winding down there anyway. In less than a month, they'd be closed for the season.

"Take all the time you need, honey. The leaf-peepers are gone, and there's not much work here anyway. The rest of the kids are out back doing popcorn shelling. I'll tell them you called." Violet smiled despite herself at the thought of her co-workers.

"Listen, when you're feeling better, drop by and visit me," Mrs. D continued. "I've got your paycheck, plus a stack of pear tarts I want you to take off my hands. For some reason, the city-its aren't buying them this year. They must all be on the same Sugar Busters diet. No one gave me the memo."

Violet had been working at Dekker's for well over a year. It was fun, varied work: manning the cash register, helping plan the corn maze, arranging clumps of annuals in hanging baskets. Violet had been on staff there, literally, since the first moment she was allowed to work legally. Mrs. Dekker was the only person on the planet who could raise Violet's appetite, no death threats involved. It wasn't just that Mrs. D enjoyed feeding people; it was that she enjoyed *people*, all walks, enough to want to feed them. Any time of day, you could peek between the shelves of the baked-goods case—past the hand-punched donuts and oozing blueberry scones—and see Mrs. D laughing and bustling around in her apron, a lard smear on one lens of her glasses.

One day in the later stages of *sallekhana*, when Violet was supposed to be sipping little more than clear broth or celery juice, she'd succumbed to the siren song of Mrs. D's warm, thrumming kitchen. The smells of fresh-baked bread and apple butter had hooked Violet around the neck like an old-fashioned vaudeville cane, and she'd stuffed her sallow face with all of the above. It was the equivalent of a food bender—a gastronomical blackout. She had glanced up halfway through a bowl of Mrs. D's black bean chili and didn't remember ladling it.

The Dekker's gang referred to themselves as the box of broken toys. They were rejects, dropouts, freaks . . . and proud of it. Facial piercings twinkling, sorting new potatoes with bloodshot eyes, Violet and her co-workers knew how they must look to the Audi- and Beemer-driving crowd who took a wrong turn on the way to Dutchess County. One girl in the Dekker's gang—a twenty-year-old single mother named Trilby—had the word *Dickavore* prominently tattooed on the inner slope of her thumb, and Mrs. D still let her work the register, even though customers were bound to see it as she counted their twenties.

Violet imagined that Mrs. D had been a teenage wildebeest herself. The twinkle in her eye whenever she overheard someone talking about hitchhiking to Burning Man betrayed her tacit approval. Once, when someone asked Mrs. D what she majored in at SUNY, she'd winked and replied, "It was the seventies. I majored in peace."

After Violet had called Imogene and Dekker's—the friends she considered family—there was the question of phoning her actual family. But what would she say?

The question of Will was freaking her out. Actually, it was spacing her out, making it impossible to focus on the therapists who were trying to tease epiphanies from her tangled-up brain. Violet worried that her brother was badly injured. She felt guilty, not only for whatever she'd allegedly done to hurt him, but for leaving him all alone at home with their mother.

Violet kept imagining an ER in the dead of night: Will's shoulders raised to his ears, his teeth gritted and his nostrils flared, his brow knitted in suppressed pain. *Serious damage to his right hand.* That was the phrase the police officer had used, a phrase that made it impossible to gauge how badly he was hurt. Had things (fingers or parts of them) been severed and reattached? Would he be able to play the piano again? Violet visualized a round, white surgical light illuminating the space between Will and the doctor. She couldn't bring herself to picture Will's hand itself. Even the thought of blood—dripping from a tattered wound—made Violet's throat constrict and her vision go shimmery. Her fear of blood went beyond your typical shut-your-eyes-during-a-horror-movie aversion. She'd had it ever since she'd seen the picture on her mother's desk a few weeks before Rose ran away.

At the time, Rose and Violet had been seated in the breakfast nook, where they sometimes did their homework in silence, sitting at opposite ends of the table as though competing in a head-to-head competition. On the other side of the room, Josephine had been browning stew beef while Satie's *Gymnopédies* played on the stereo in the background. Violet had been memorizing a series of Spanish flash cards. *Hermana. Madre. Amiga. Conocida.* (The unit was "People and Family.") Rose had been working on something for her human biology class at SUNY. Her assignment was to draw a picture of the brain and label where the three different kinds of human memory were stored.

Like Josephine, Rose was a gifted artist. It was one of few bonds they shared and one that made Violet jealous as hell, especially on the afternoons when they'd take their canvases to the Poet's Walk in Rhinebeck and, presumably, spend the whole day in side-by-side conversation as they painted the mountain-framed Hudson River. No matter how hard Violet tried, she couldn't seem to infiltrate their discussions about painting terms and techniques— endless communions about "scumbling," "wet-on-wet," or the color phthalo blue. Josephine claimed Violet's landscapes lacked richness and her earnest portraits looked like carnival caricatures. (Eventually, Violet started playing to this. Although she'd never shown the drawings to anyone, she'd done a horrifically ugly charcoal series of the Hursts as a three-ring circus. In them, her mother was the ringmaster, and Rose was the kind of trained animal who jumps through hoops.)

Anyway, Rose had been doing just fine sketching out the brain with black ballpoint pen. It was for science class, after all. Not the National Art Honor Society. But the very second Josephine saw, she'd insisted Rose draw her brain in colored pencil.

"No, Mom," Rose had said. "It's fine like this, really. I still have an anthropology paper to write."

But Josephine had made the most monumental deal about the colored pencils that she had upstairs on the desk in her office. "But they're a seventy-two-color set of Prismacolors! I just bought them yesterday at Catskill Art Supply!" Josephine's eyes danced with glee while she said it. Her mouth had been corkscrewed into such a strange expression, like she was desperate to suppress a smile.

Rose had finally trudged upstairs, muttering something about how her forthcoming masterpiece was going to be lost on her professor, Mr. Cadaver-Travers.

She wasn't gone long. Not more than thirty seconds passed before Rose came whooshing down the stairs like a flying ghoul. Her face was a mask of melted eye makeup and tears.

"That's why you wanted me to go up there?!" Rose screamed, her voice breaking in the middle. "You are sick! You know that?!"

"Oh, Rose, you're too sensitive! It was an accident! I forgot it was there!" their mom shouted back, dropping her knife on the chopping board beside a piece of sinew.

"Like hell you did!" Rose cried. "How much longer are you going to torture me? For the rest of college? For the rest of my life?"

"I'm the one who's tortured! I mourn that baby!"

"In that case, you put that paper baby in a box and you bury it!" Rose thrust her finger at Josephine, at which point Violet had seen that her sister was shaking clear up to her shoulder.

Violet had never seen Rose so wild with emotion. But while a part of Violet had wanted to peel her fourteen-year-old butt off the bay window cushion and go put an arm around her sister, another part felt like her spine was made of concrete. Violet had sat, frozen in place, naïve and baffled by the source of the argument.

In fact, Violet had only been able to mobilize after her sister stormed out the front door, Josephine trailing behind her, screaming: "Every day I have to face the knowledge of who you are and what you've done! You are lost, Rose! You are morally and academically out to lunch! There's no point to living the way you do it!"

Violet could still remember what she was thinking as she'd mounted the stairs. She'd been secretly and unforgivably thrilled that someone other than herself was in trouble.

Josephine's office was a little room at the top of the stairs. Inside, there was a drawing desk, a goosenecked lamp, and at least a dozen yards of bookmarked art books. Much as the style bored Violet, even she couldn't deny that Josephine knew her stuff. Her mother had always been most in her element when she was talking about the X-shaped composition of *The Martyrdom of Saint Bartholomew* or the fact that Murillo's *Two Women at a Window* were really common prostitutes.

That said, what Violet had seen upon approaching Josephine's desk was no Francisco de Zurbarán or Jusepe de Ribera. It was a color photocopy of a dead and possibly dismembered baby, its neck wrenched at a broken angle, as though someone had angled its slashed and bloodied face toward the camera lens on purpose. Its bloated umbilical cord (still attached) was slung on the other end over a bucket that was three inches deep with blood. In fact, blood was what Josephine might have called the "major theme of the composition": It was smeared across the table. It was the viscous red shadow on the towel under and around the dead baby. It was the sheen on the instrument almost out of the frame—the one that looked like an oversized pair of tongs. The caption read: *What a proud society we are: killing the defenseless in the name of a woman's right to choose.* In the upper right-hand corner was a friendly message from the sponsor: *The Mid-Hudson Pro-Life Coalition invites you to stop the abortion agenda.*

That photo was the main reason Violet had gone vegetarian. Anytime she smelled beef, anytime she saw a bloody cut of meat, she saw that picture of the late-term abortion. As for the incident, Violet had never mentioned it to anyone. She'd let it sit—or rot, really—in the part of her mind that Rose had labeled the amygdala in her drawing of the human brain. Violet never again set foot in her mother's office, and she actively avoided thinking about what she'd seen there—what it meant *about* her mother, who'd seemed to delight in the pain she'd caused, and what it meant *to* Rose, who'd gotten the hell out of Dodge because she couldn't stand to have her personal struggles batted around for sadistic sport anymore.

· · ·

Violet leaned her head against the phone box, and when the faintness passed, she dialed 411 for the number of Kingston Hospital. The woman on the switchboard said there was no one by Will's name in the system and explained that he'd probably already been treated and released.

So Will had no complications. It should have been a huge relief, but Violet wasn't sure exactly what to make of it. Did it mean her mother had just blown a small thing out of proportion? It felt ominous—yet not entirely surprising—that everyone was purposefully leaving her in the dark.

Violet pictured her brother at home on the couch in his girlish nightgown, their mother feeding him ice chips from the palm of her hand. The image was disturbing in more ways than one. Because as much as Violet resented pampered Will, she also wanted badly to protect him from the light of his life. It seemed like only a matter of time before Josephine betrayed him the same way she had betrayed Rose, in a way that was designed to seem "accidental" and utterly deniable.

Violet thought Will would one day self-fulfill his mother's prophecy exactly the way the rest of the Hursts had. Josephine said Rose was "lost" and Rose had gotten lost. Josephine liked to accuse Violet of being "crazy," and out of nowhere, Violet had flipped her shit. Josephine treated Will like he was an extension of herself, and it seemed only a matter of time before he started treating people the same way she did. He was a good boy, but there was no way he'd grow into a good man with their mother bearing down on him, teaching him how to punish and manipulate.

Violet had read about a deity who came to Buddha and asked, "Who is the best friend one has at home?" Buddha had answered: "*Mata mittam sake ghave*" ("Mother is the best friend one has at home"). But a shitty mother made either criminals or lifelong victims. The only real question, in Violet's mind, was which one would Will become?

After phone time, Violet and Edie were sprawled on the floor of the dayroom, playing a game of bingo that the ladies' auxiliary had recently donated.

"O twenty-four," Edie said. "So what are you gonna do about Rose?" During afternoon group therapy, Violet had discussed Rose's great escape and bizarre resurgence.

"Bingo!" Violet was too dignified for victory dances. "Ignore her, maybe. I'm not sure I trust Rose. It feels like she's only doing this because she wants something."

"Your turn to call . . . ," Edie told Violet. "So you're not gonna write her back?"

"Have you noticed some of the numbers are worn off these balls? This set has to be fifty years old. How much do you think we'd make if we listed it on eBay?" Her attempt at a diversion didn't work. There was a loaded silence; the other girls were staring slantwise at Violet while they stacked their bingo markers. "Pissed off as I was about the way Rose left, I was glad she got away. I always thought she was too. There's something creepy about Rose coming back, especially now, at the height—the fucking zenith—of Hurst hysteria—"

"Hold up," Corinna said, using her bingo card to form a T for time-out. "Do you think your sister is living under a fake identity?" She didn't give Violet a chance to say she didn't know before she added: "That shit is hard. I've tried that. Making up names and addresses. Always worrying someone's gonna recognize you while you're pumping gas and call out your name."

"Why'd you run away?" Edie asked.

Corinna shrugged. "Don't know. I like the idea of clean slates."

Maybe it was Violet's imagination, but everyone in the room seemed to exhale at once. Anyone who'd taken a whack at suicide knew that was a blank slate too.

In a way, Violet's *sallekhana* wasn't all that different from Rose's decision to take off. Fasting to death was the only way Violet could think of to put space between herself and her mom. It was the only way she could conceive of ditching her post as beloathed daughter and beloved scapegoat.

Corinna wistfully twiddled her ID bracelet. "Seriously, though. Write that bitch Rose and ask her how she ran away without anyone catching on. After I leave here, I have to go back to sharing a trailer with my three-hundred-pound mother and her maggot-infested dogs. I need to know the methods of big sister's magic. Please? I'll even lend you a stamp."

Violet still had no idea what *she* was going to do when she got discharged. She refused to go home, yet the idea of cutting herself loose made her feel guilty and terrified. Guilty . . . because wasn't it heartless to disown your own mom? Terrified . . . because TV or, maybe, society at large had taught her a person couldn't succeed in life without a loving, supportive family. But if life hadn't handed you great role models or lessons, weren't you obligated to go out and seek some for yourself?

Corinna had a point, though: How *did* a person do it? If it were summer, Violet could take a tent and live at campsites. But winter was coming, and Violet's next-to-nothing savings wouldn't cover a camper. She could hitch or take a bus south to warmer weather, but then what? Ironically, the only person who could teach Violet how to disappear completely was the same person she felt all too conflicted about. Very suddenly, all roads led to Rose.

William Hurst

Will's father drove him ten minutes north of Poughkeepsie for lunch.

Douglas pored over each wordy dish on the menu like there'd be a pop quiz later. For his part, Will didn't know whether it would be ruder to ask the waitress to hold the truffle spread on the grilled cheese or to go with the macaroni and try to substitute cheddar for Gruyère.

After Douglas ordered braised short ribs and iced tea, Will felt his shoulders relax. He'd been worried that his dad was going to order scotch.

At the table beside them, a waiter was reading the specials with the gusto of a celebrity chef. Watching him, Will's father leaned back in his chair. "Sometimes I wish I'd gone to culinary school," Douglas said. "I love food. There's just not much point in making it anymore. Your mother's such a superior cook."

Will didn't know what to say. He tried to imagine his father whipping up dishes instead of computer code. He'd never seen him so much as boil an egg.

On second thought, Will seemed to remember, years ago, his father going on an ice-cream-making kick. One summer, before

Rose left, Douglas had made giant batches of challenging flavors—white wine sorbet and jalapeño gelato. But in mid-August, his beloved ice cream maker accidentally found its way into the display at a Hurst family yard sale. If Will remembered right, it was sold for fifteen dollars and was never replaced.

"You know, we met in a kitchen." Douglas looked down at his stemmed water glass. He started spinning the liquid into a fury the way Will often saw him swish and whirlpool red wine.

"You and Mom?"

His father nodded. "We both had jobs at the same steakhouse. We were working our way through school. My mom had just died. Jo's mom had thrown her out." Douglas cast a sad look at the plate of heart-shaped garlic butter. "When I met your mother, she was so flirtatious, so enthusiastic. She was a waitress, I was a busboy. She wore this red lipstick; you never saw her without it. She used to be a nude model for life drawing at her art college."

"You took life drawing?"

"No, she told me about it."

His father was opening up—this was rare—so Will didn't want to break the spell by letting on that his mother had also told him about her modeling before. Perhaps other mothers would conceal the fact that they had once sprawled naked before a wolf circle of strangers, but Will's mom was unique. Josephine had said it was a powerful thing, having all those eyes on her. It was a chance to "show her stuff" without being sexual. Even then, she said, she was being an educator—teaching one-day Raphaels about the human form.

"So you were boyfriend and girlfriend when you worked at the restaurant?" It occurred to Will that any inside scoops about his parents' romantic life could be helpful to his investigation.

Douglas sighed. "It took at least six months to convince your mother to go out with me. She didn't say yes until her boyfriend broke up with her. *Clyde.*" The face he made told Will he would still murder Clyde if given the chance. "Your mother was devastated. I found her crying in the walk-in refrigerator one day, and she told me all about how this guy had just packed up and told her she'd changed. And I said, 'No, Jo. You haven't changed. That guy just didn't know you, that's all.' We were so young. Now that I'm older, I think both things can be simultaneously true."

"I don't know what you're talking about, Dad."

"No one changes quicker than a person you never knew to begin with." His eyes dropped to the napkin in his lap. His voice sounded sad, but his expression said he lacked energy to carry the emotion through.

Will nodded like he had a vague idea what Douglas meant. He didn't. In fact, the whole conversation made him feel off-kilter.

Will's father rarely waxed philosophical. And he certainly never did it without a supersized bottle of wine at hand. For a second it occurred to Will that his father might have been drinking at work, but then Douglas didn't have any of the other telltale signs. No red cheeks, no hairline sweat.

Will acted interested. A spy's acting skills were his number one weapon. "So you cooked in the restaurant?"

"Only for a little while. I had just been promoted to line and prep cook when I quit. I used to love making soup. You can always tell how much work someone's put into a good soup. You have to use bone stock. Gives it depth of flavor. My potato leek soup was like nothing you've ever tasted."

"Why'd you stop working there?"

"The manager had some kind of problem with your mother. When he fired her, I left too."

Douglas remained lost in thought as the waiter set the plates down with fussy precision.

Will had a flash of his mother as a big-eyed, leggy waitress with a tinkling laugh and a clever comeback for everything. His dad was a fool to think he'd find anyone—Carrie included—who was better than her. Carrie was a *nupson*. Carrie was a *nothington*.

"I'm glad I decided on grilled cheese," Will said. In his few days of wearing a hand splint, he'd gotten better at manipulating a fork with his left hand. But he still wasn't good. He wasn't *restaurant*-ready.

His father was salting his food before tasting it—a nervous tic. "Oh yeah?" he said, trancelike. "Good, is it?"

"I meant I only need one hand to eat it."

Douglas looked up from his side of butternut squash. "Oh," he said with a small exhale. "Oh of course, your hand. I keep forgetting how disruptive that must be."

To Will, his hand splint had become a near-constant reminder about the upcoming meeting with Trina. It was less than two days away. Somewhere, in the farthest recesses of his mind, a digital clock was counting those fifty hours down to the half second.

But instead of mentioning this to Douglas, Will continued: "I'm glad I only have to wear the splint for a couple more weeks. It makes my hand look like the metal claw in one of those arcade games."

"I used to try to teach Rose how to beat those games. Skill has nothing to do with it, you know." Typical Douglas, cutting straight to diversion. Straight to science. "The machines are programmed to allow someone to win every number of games. You just have to watch for a while, and count the number of losers in between two winners. But Rose never had the patience for it."

"Maybe she wanted to earn her prize."

"Maybe. Or maybe Rose was just used to being showered with the things she wanted. No work required. You know Rose."

No, Will thought. He wasn't entirely sure he knew Rose. There was a ten-year age difference between him and his oldest sister. If the Hurst family was like a troupe of actors, then, in her time, Rose had been the star. The rest of the family hushed in respect when Rose entered a room. They stole glances. They followed her cues and avoided troubling her with mundane questions like, how was she feeling and what was new in her life? But no matter how much they paid attention, who Rose was on the inside remained a mystery.

Since they were already talking about Rose, Will decided to begin his interrogation in earnest. Unfortunately, he didn't have the authority of a bona fide cop. Will was going to have to use the fact that someone had already talked. That was what investigators were always doing on TV police shows.

Will put down his sandwich. "The night I got hurt, Violet said Rose was there."

Douglas's head jerked back slightly. He stopped chewing.

"Don't you remember?" Will continued. When it came to controlling his emotions, Douglas was a Jedi. Will thought his dad looked taken aback but wouldn't bet his life on it. He was going to have to apply some pressure, hint at Douglas's drinking. "I mean, I know it was after work and you were groggy—"

"Will, Violet wasn't in her right frame of mind. She'd taken drugs. You're old enough to know that. She took the kind of dangerous, illegal drugs that make people imagine things. Some people see snakes or flying monkeys. Violet thought she saw Rose."

A tingle ran up the back of Will's arms. He couldn't remember the last time he'd done something to upset his dad. In truth, he'd never really thought it was possible.

Douglas flexed his jaw. The flicker in his eyes was almost anger. His gray eyes looked hard and dark as asphalt; they pinned Will to the curlicued back of his café chair. "Rose had nothing to do with that night, Will. And I won't let you or anyone else try to bring her into this. I won't stand by and let her become a conve-

nient scapegoat. Are we clear, here? *Are we?* I need an answer."
Will nodded, his eyes downcast. "Excellent. Now excuse me
while I make a phone call." Douglas's water glass jittered as he
slammed down his fisted napkin. He strode out the restaurant
door, bumping into people as he dialed his cell phone.

"How is everything?" the waiter asked with impeccable
timing.

"Exceptional," Will said, because it was the kind of answer his
mother usually gave.

"Well . . . great." The waiter looked a little stunned. Will had
a talent for bringing out the awkward in people. His mother told
him it was because people found his intellect intimidating.

Through the window, Will could see his father pacing the
parking lot. His collar was turned up against the wet wind and his
phone was pressed to his head, cowlicking the hair above his ear.
Whoever was on the other end of the line seemed to be doing a
decent job of calming him down. Douglas's shoulders had
slumped back, and he seemed to be primarily listening, opening
his mouth only to make short, desperate blurts that could be either questions or complaints.

Will touched his splinted hand. Carrie or not, he knew, just
knew, in his Gruyère-filled guts, that his father was protecting
Rose. Rose was the one person who could hurt Will's mother, and
thus him, the most.

Violet Hurst

For the past two days, Violet had been pining for Internet access, but now that it was finally time for computer lab, she was stuck with the rather unsympathetic problem of having eight billion websites and no place to click. She was hardly going to be changing her Facebook location to "psych ward" or tweeting I'm sitting next to a woman who ripped off her ears because she thought there were bugs in her head. In fact, she couldn't think of anything to do besides draft a reply to her sister.

"Violet?" Edie leaned back in her Velveeta-colored plastic chair. "What are you doing over there? It sounds like a swarm of cicadas."

Violet hadn't been fully aware of the way she was nervousticishly abusing the computer mouse, highlighting what little she'd written over and over. "Sorry. I was trying to think of something to say to Rose."

"You're e-mailing her?"

"No, just typing a letter. I'm not sure she checks the e-mail address I have. She's never answered any of the messages me or my parents send her there."

"You think she put blocks on your e-mail addresses?"

"That's what my dad thinks. There's no real way of knowing."

"I don't get it. Don't the messages bounce back to you?"

"No. Dad says if Rose blocked us, her e-mail just deletes them automatically. Anyway, why do you care so much if I make up with my sister?"

Edie shrugged. "I just thought it might be good for you to have someone you can go to when you get out of here."

Farther down the row of monitors, Corinna groaned. "Glad to know I'm not missing out on much out there in the *sane* world. Abby has 'some serious eighties hair going right now.' 'Crystal just joined the group YES, I'M A GIRL AND I DON'T LIKE PINK.' Oh, well done! You fucking imbeciles. I hate Facebook. It's just a bunch of stupid asses jumping up and down saying, 'Look at me! Look what I've done!' "

Violet laughed. "Wow. And how many times have you been defriended today?"

"More like how many people have I defriended."

"No, she's right," Edie said. "Ever since social networks, the number of people with narcissistic personality disorder has doubled. There are way more narcissists than there used to be."

"I can always tell a narcissist," Corinna said. "She's the one who puts up pictures of herself in her new bikini. She's the one posting Marilyn Monroe quotes and saying most guys are intimidated by her."

"That's just teenage exhibitionism," the monitoring nurse said, hovering over them. "Girls of your generation with your low self-esteem. Flashing your privates because you need validation."

The phrase *flashing your privates* gave them all a moment's pause.

"I don't even wanna know what sites you're looking at." Corinna turned her attention back to Edie. "Narcissists are always posting about how they learned to looove themselves."

"No, narcissism's different from exhibitionism," Edie said, a dead serious look on her face. She was an autodidact of abnormal psych, given she'd spent so much time in the ward. "And narcissists don't love themselves. They hardly have any selves to begin with. They put all their energy into the fake image that they wear like a mask. Only there's nothing but dead space behind it."

"Like sociopaths." Corinna's eyes were bloodshot behind her raccoon liner, and her hair looked like it needed washing.

Edie made a wishy-washy motion with one hand. "Eh, they're like halfway to sociopaths. Sociopaths have no conscience. Narcissists have no empathy. Neither one thinks other people are real. Narcissists think other people are just ego food, tools or extensions of themselves. So like, to a narcissist, you're either the steak, or the steak knife, or the hand that cuts the meat."

Violet's stomach did a little somersault at Edie's choice of analogy.

"Either way, narcissists aren't seeing Corinna," Edie said. "Instead of seeing you, they're seeing what they can get out of you. Sometimes it's attention. Sometimes it's someone they can order around. Sometimes, if they can't control you, they'll just make you fear them. It's like a drug to them."

"P.S.," Corinna said. "I just sent a friend request to both of you."

"Is Rose on Facebook?" Edie asked suddenly.

"Last time I checked. Unless she's deleted it. My parents used to check it every day and try to see if she'd posted anything they could use to find her. But I don't think she uses that account anymore."

"Maybe she set up a Facebook account only her close friends know about," Edie said. "You know, fake name. No picture. Set to private. That's what I did."

"Your real name isn't Edie?" Corinna asked.

"Well, it is now. I changed it when I turned eighteen. Let's see Rose," Edie said. "Pull up her old profile?"

After all this time, it was strange to see Rose's online version of herself. The pictures weren't recent, but Violet had only ever glanced at them in passing. For instance, she'd never noticed the photo of Rose at some kind of garden party, dressed in blue gingham and one of Josephine's wide-brimmed hats. The family resemblance was so eerie, Violet had to look twice. At first glance, she'd actually thought it was their mother hugging Rose's friend Amelia. It was all Violet could do to keep from shuddering.

"She's mad pretty," Corinna said.

"But kind of avoidant, huh?" Edie added.

"What makes you say that?"

"The comments in her timeline. When did she move away?"

"A year ago. Give or take."

"Well, look. Even before that, her friends were posting things about how much they missed her."

Edie was right. The general theme was: *Miss you* or *Call me sometime, we need to catch up.* One guy—his name was J.C. and his picture showed him cuddling a French bulldog—had even written *Lovely Lady . . . Where are you living right now? Wish I wasn't missing out on all the big parts of your life!*

"It's hard to tell who her close friends are," Edie said.

"There . . . Amelia. Other than her, I don't know." According to Rose's relationship status, she was "in a relationship," but Damien Koch wasn't listed among her Facebook friends. "Rose was one of those people with lots of acquaintances, but not many really close friends. She could be a social butterfly, or she could just as easily drop off the face of the earth. You know, stay in her room for days. With Rose, there was no in between."

Violet scrolled through the pictures again. Each one had a strange, posed quality. In every shot, Rose's head sat at the same leftward sixty-degree slant, as though she'd decided that was her only lovable angle. Also, there was something incongruent about her face. Her features never seemed to meld into one coherent mood. Even when she was smiling over a birthday candle, her blue-gray eyes seemed vacant and the popped vein in her fore-head showed strain. The emotional disconnect was even more obvious in Rose's "silly," "spontaneous"-style photos, wearing a turquoise wig or striking a disco pose; her eyes were deer-in-headlights and her smile looked gritted in anticipation of pain.

"*Dogs never bite me, just humans,*" Corinna said, reading Rose's very last post aloud. There was a small, uncomfortable silence. It was a quote from Marilyn Monroe.

Later, in the dayroom, Violet sat in the windowsill and resumed her stalled letter.

This time, she was writing with Edie's sketchpad and a purple colored pencil. Colored pencils were one of the few writing im-plements that weren't forbidden as a kill-yourself tool, and pur-ple seemed less aggressive than red. The official color etched down the pencil's side was "Violet." "Here you go," Edie had joked, pulling it from the pack. "This one has your name written all over it."

Violet went through the various things she knew about her sister. Rose was living in Manhattan with Damien, who had likely knocked her up. Their mother had known about said pregnancy, and probably the termination of it, based on what Violet had wit-nessed when she confronted Rose. A year after disowning her family, Rose had returned to acting. Maybe it was an attempt to regain her mother's approval, but to Violet's knowledge, Rose wasn't in contact with the rest of the family.

Unless, of course, her sister really *had* been lurking on the night Violet swerved into the mental-breakdown lane.

• • •

Violet had been in the kitchen, preparing her own makeshift dinner, something that didn't include beef stock. The flashing knife left tracers in the air above the chopping block. Wheels of cucumber rolled off the counter.

When Violet looked up, her father had joined the commotion her mother was making about the mess in the dishwasher. He and Josephine were wildly pointing their fingers at each other, each one looking like a maestro conducting the orchestra of the other's anger.

Then, between and behind her parents, down the darkened hallway, in the foyer, Violet distinctly saw her sister. Rose looked a year older, or maybe just far more serious, with her hair half obscuring her face. Her eyes were unreachable, her mouth set in a determined line. She padded past on quiet dancer's feet, not looking at any of them—neither Violet nor her oblivious parents— and ascended the steps to the second-floor bedrooms.

The fact that her sister had come home, at that moment of all times, hit Violet in a wave of dizzying confusion and heat. "Rose!" She'd gestured toward the foyer. "Rose is here! Rose!"

High out of her megamind, it felt like the single most exciting experience of Violet's life. She'd wanted to shout about it in the streets like Paul Revere. She wanted to call every person in her phone's address book. She wanted to interrupt the news broadcast and let everyone know their prodigal daughter had returned. The sensation that followed felt like reliving the past Rose-less year through a telescope of thirty seconds over and over again, until she heard the piercing sound of her mother screaming.

I'm sure you understand why I'd rather visit them on my own terms.

In her letter, Rose had never definitively said that she *wasn't* in contact with their mother. But for all Violet knew, Josephine was meeting up with Rose in private, helping her run her lines like old times. That would also explain why their usually snoopy mother had delivered Rose's envelope unopened.

Violet rubbed her temples, as though this might massage her tense brain. Fuck it. She began to write.

> Rose,
>
> Glad you're well. I am not, as you can see by my return address.
>
> I don't really blame you for getting lost. I used to keep a book of Post-it notes, counting down the number of days until I turned eighteen. I used to tear one off every day. I finally threw it away because Mom interrogated me about it constantly. It pissed her off because she couldn't figure out what it was for.
>
> Bit confused about a few things in your letter:
>
> A) Are you in touch with Mom? Dad?
>
> B) What are you doing for work?
>
> C) Have you been back to Old Stone Way since you left?
>
> Also . . .
>
> D) About Damien? Are you living with him? I've spent a full calendar year thinking of a sensitive way to put this, but there really doesn't seem to be any way aside from straight-up prying . . . I'm assuming you were pregnant for a short time last year? And that Mom (who, regardless of whatever she has to say is not "pro-life" but pro-whatever-causes-other-people-maximum-misery) became a one-woman abortion protest after the fact? Is this the reason why you left?
>
> E) Why did you decide to get back in touch now?

Then she origamied an envelope out of another sheet of art paper, borrowed the stamp Corinna had promised, and dropped the letter at the nurses' station.

William Hurst

WILL OVERSLEPT AND was two hours late for home school—one sign that his mother was still peeved that he'd chosen his home-grown Take Your Kid to Work Day over her.

Another was the fact that she hadn't been in to lay out his clothes for the day. He walked to his closet and tried to imagine what she'd want for him based on the weather. Stumped, he picked an outfit much like he'd worn the day before: belted gray pants and a collared sweater that toggled around the neck.

In the kitchen, his mother was at the stove, flipping pancakes with a delighted look on her face.

"Good morning, sweetheart," she said, bending down to kiss the gap where his forehead peeked through his bed-headed bangs. "My word, what are you wearing?"

Will glanced down, wondering if he was overdressed or under.

She turned up the radio at the precise moment he started to apologize for sleeping late.

"I said I'm sorry I overslept," Will repeated over a loud, brassy overture.

"It's fine," she said. "You didn't oversleep. I let you sleep. I have a surprise for you today."

Will's stomach pretzeled. The vanilla extract hanging in the air brought a vomity taste to the back of his throat. After the week he'd had, he couldn't handle any more surprises.

"Do me a favor and don't look so nervous. Really, Will, I don't know where I went wrong with you. You have no spontaneity. You're such a killjoy." She sifted confectioner's sugar over a smeary chocolate stack.

He took the plate she passed him. It was so heavy in his hand, he imagined it hitting his chest like a wrecking ball.

Josephine leaned over and began cutting Will's pancakes into small bites. "So aren't you curious about your surprise?" she asked. "It's a big one."

The scene at the Rosendale Community Center was babies with rabies. The decor was childish—pre-K, really. There were train tables and hobbit-sized basketball hoops. The toy boxes over-flowed with decades' worth of Happy Meal toys, most of which "transformed" into robots or Hot Wheels cars, all of which looked like they had been infected with three decades' worth of norovi-rus and whooping cough.

Yep, this was the surprise: a "play group" for homeschooled children. Perhaps Josephine was preparing for the CPS investiga-tion, or bolstering her case against Douglas-like arguments that Will was too "isolated." Or maybe she really did want him to make new friends. Or she was punishing him for going to work with Douglas, like he thought.

The mothers—it was mostly mothers, with the exception of one bald dad sporting a wind-energy T-shirt and hairy, bare feet in flip-flops—were gathered around a snack table. They were munching raw Brazil nuts, dehydrated green beans, and other virtuous fare from the local food co-op.

It was the kind of nouveau-hippie crowd that usually drove Will's mother crazy. She smiled politely and made efforts to break through the cliquish conversation.

"When Will was in public school," Josephine said, "I noticed there were two types of teachers. The first were idiots who didn't care. The second were decent teachers who seemed to know that most parents are idiots."

Will ached to sit beside his mother, but whenever he went near her, she nudged him off with an instruction to "go play." Then she'd turn to whatever alpaca-sweatered woman she was mingling with and explain how her autistic son had terrible separation anxiety: "At this point, even if I wanted to send him back to public school, he wouldn't stand for it. I swear, he barely lets me go to the bathroom alone."

So instead Will watched his mother from afar, trying to make at least some show of "meeting new people." He knew he should find someone—some other kid—to latch onto before he embarrassed or disappointed her, but he could barely remember how to talk to kids his own age. But he owed it to Josephine to try.

He carefully approached two blond boys with shoulder-length hair—brothers from the looks of it. They were eyeing each other, through their long bangs, over a game of Battleship.

"Hi." Then, remembering to lead with an open-ended question, Will asked, "Do you like home school?"

"We're not homeschooled, we're no-schooled," one boy said, sinking a submarine.

"You mean, you don't have to do any lessons? Is that even allowed?"

The other boy sighed, blowing a lock of hair out of his eyes. "The term is unschooling. It was established in the late seventies by John Holt. The curriculum is child-led. If we wake up and feel like doing art, we do art. If we want to watch a shark documentary, we do. If we want to bake peanut butter granola and call it home ec, Mom preheats the oven."

"What about grades?" Will asked.

"There are no grades."

"Tests?"

"Nope."

"Books?"

"No set books. No curriculum." He groaned, "Hit."

"Yes!" his brother gloated, sticking a red pin in his board. "We go at our own pace. We learn through our natural life experiences."

"But how is that preparing you for the real world?"

"Let me guess," the boy said. "Your mom is your teacher, your gym teacher, your school nurse, your lunch lady, and your principal."

Will nodded, his embarrassment widening to include Josephine.

"Then, I could ask you the same thing. How well are *you* prepared? Isn't *real life* self-directed?"

So apparently all homeschooled kids spoke like pretentious, liberal arts college students. Maybe Will should have been relieved knowing he wasn't an original freak, but the criticism burned, and it hurt even more that these boys—they looked like long-haired Jesuses—seemed smarter than Will himself.

Will knew God said to rejoice when other people did well, but these boys' intelligence seemed to take something away from him. These boys and their parents, even the play group as a whole, somehow made Will and his mother less special. He'd always thought their curriculum was challenging, groundbreaking, the homeschool equivalent of Harvard. The truth was: they were conventional, even below average.

Will found himself slowly circling the room's perimeter,

dragging one shoulder along the wall as he went. He was suddenly starving despite his heavy breakfast, but the thought of eating in front of strangers made him anxious. He could be out of public school a million years, and yet he'd never forget the horrors of the cafeteria, never break the emotional association between embarrassment and public consumption.

He took the coward's way out: through his bladder. He ducked out the door in search of the bathroom.

Compared to the awkwardness taking place in the rec room, the bathroom was a beautiful space for self-imposed exile. The locking stall was cool, white, and soundless like the Fortress of Solitude. Will sat on the toilet lid with his Ugg boots tucked under him and imagined he was Superman, writing his memoirs in a giant steel diary with a touchpad that instantly recorded his thoughts.

Will didn't like to talk about the trouble at his old school. He much preferred it when his mother blamed his dropping out on his epilepsy. She'd tell strangers that Will was photosensitive to the fluorescent lights. Or she'd explain that the school didn't have enough carpets or soft places to protect a seizure victim. The truth was: the trouble had started in English class, long before Will's first seizure. His teacher at the time, Mr. Razz (short, somehow, for Randall) was one of the "cool" teachers. Razz was fresh out of teaching college, in novelty ties and limited-edition sneakers, and his classroom became ground zero for Will's degradation.

It started with vocabulary quizzes. Mr. Razz had a system whereby the students would pass their quizzes to the person at the desk in front of them, and on up the row until they landed in the ironically titled "To Do or Not to Do" box on his desk.

Will's last name planted him firmly in the very last seat of the second row. There were five kids in front of him, including golden boy Jake Greenberg and jerky Daniel Harrison, and at least once a week, Jake or Daniel would draw a massive penis on Will's quiz as it made its way to the front of the room. Sometimes the organ was flaccid, sometimes fully erect, sometimes there'd be more than one, but every single time, Mr. Razz would dock Will five points off his overall score for his "immature" and "inappropriate" works of art.

The first time Will contested this—privately, after the bell—Mr. Razz told him, "I can only go by what's in front of me, and your name is printed at the top of the page."

The second time, Will made the mistake of saying something *during* class, which only made his classmates convulse with laughter. Will implicated Jake Greenberg, but Greenberg had diverted the blame with a quip about how penis drawings harked back to Neolithic times: "Carved penises were used like arrows to point men to prostitutes. My dad and me saw it on the History Channel." Mr. Razz had agreed, not even bothering to correct Jake's grammar and adding a story of his own about how he'd seen a raised cobblestone penis outside the site of an ancient brothel in Pompeii.

The third time, again after class, Will had accused Jake and Daniel outright, demanding that Mr. Razz dock points from them. "Will," Mr. Razz had said, "I'm gonna level with you. Jake and Daniel might be jerks, but they're easy to like. They smile. They laugh. You, on the other hand . . . You're a tattletale. You provoke boys like them because you're phony. I'd love to help you out with that, but I get the feeling you don't really want help. You want to be annoying, and then have me tell you that any time someone gets annoyed with you, it's their fault."

It was the worst thing anyone had ever said to Will, and when he went home and told his mother about it (confiding also, for the first time, about the dick situation), she immediately typed an e-mail to Mr. Razz, the principal, and various school board members. Josephine referenced Will by the last four digits of his student number, cited school policy that said no teacher should be alone in a classroom with a student without the presence of a third-party witness, and demanded Mr. Razz's resignation if he continued to enable classroom bullies.

The following Monday, Mr. Razz begrudgingly unveiled his new policy for test collection, whereby anyone who finished raised their hand so he could personally collect their paper. "That's right, gang," Razz had said. "I now have a we-pick-you-up policy. Look at me, I'm Enterprise car rental." He laughed weakly, but everyone glared at Will.

But there was no going back once Will had confided in his mother. As the weeks went on, she filed more misconduct reports, which led to Mr. Razz directing more thinly veiled classroom sermons at Will. Still, Josephine must have felt she was losing the fight. Will remembered her many dinnertime rants about how "underwhelmed" she was by the principal's response, how the so-called disciplinary action against Mr. Razz was a joke. "They have no idea who they're dealing with," she'd say, while she slammed mashed potatoes onto Will's and Violet's plates. "I'm not some clueless mother. I'm an educator. I know how the system is supposed to work."

It was around that time that Will became acquainted with child psychologists' offices. His mother had read a best-seller about Asperger's syndrome (or possibly just a review of it) and thought Will showed some of the symptoms: his social anxiety, his fear of loud noises, his almost physical need to look away when someone looked him deep in the eye. The first shrink thought Will was too empathetic to be Aspie; she said she could see that Will carefully filtered his words with regard to other people's feelings. The second shrink didn't agree with Josephine either; he thought Will was anxiety disordered. When Josephine brought Will to the third shrink, she took along the unusual-word journal she encouraged him to keep in an effort to expand his vocabulary. That kind of obsessive interest was what sealed it. Will got his autism diagnosis that day and burst into tears. "Oh, Will," his mom had sighed. "Stop acting like it's the end of the world. Everybody's equally odd, some people are just more aware of it than others. Besides, you heard what the doctor said . . . . Asperger's is on the lowest end of the autistic spectrum."

Once a doctor had confirmed Josephine's Internet diagnosis, she yanked Will out of therapy and her master plan became clear. Diagnosis in hand, Will was not just any misfit, he was a (quickly the) disabled kid the school system had picked on. Josephine wrote an op-ed for the *Blue Stone Press* titled "The Biggest Bullies: Meet the Teachers and Administrators Who Pick on Autistic Students."

After Josephine threatened the school board with a discrimination lawsuit, they put Mr. Razz on administrative leave and Will's peer problems worsened. The student body wore black armbands and printed T-shirts that said, *Don't Razz the Razz*. People sneaked open ketchup packets onto Will's chair when he got up to use the bathroom. They rubbed the metal edges of wooden rulers against their shoe soles and pressed them against Will's neck once they were hot enough to burn his skin.

Still, Will's social rock bottom happened when sweet Chloe Cho, who Will later learned had been counting on Mr. Razz to write her a recommendation for boarding school, filled her palm with hand sanitizer and rubbed it in Will's eyes. He went home that same day and begged his mother to homeschool him instead. Tears in his stinging eyes, he'd pleaded, "Why should I be there, when you're a teacher? You're a way better teacher than any of them!"

Will had never once regretted making the switch to home school.

But crouched in the stall of the Rosendale rec center, staring at the streamers of toilet paper on the floor and wishing he could vaporize—not kill himself, exactly, just suddenly cease to exist—it was hard for Will to imagine he had even one redeeming quality. He could barely talk to kids three grades younger than him without getting so anxious that his words rushed out all at once, tossed and choppy. He couldn't imagine how, in four years' time, he'd muster up the confidence to walk into one of the local farm stands and apply for a job the way Violet had. And forget about finding the swagger to one day interview for college or kiss a girl.

Just as he was feeling a genuine urge to pee, the bathroom door opened and stopped Will midstream. The stall door juddered as someone tried the handle.

"Just a second," Will gasped as he shoved his wee william back in his husky-sized briefs.

"Open the door, Will."

Without thinking, he did.

"I thought you'd abandoned me," Josephine said, as she zipped up Will's fly and took extra care buttoning his pants. "Oh honey, I know this is hard for you. I saw the way the other kids left you out."

Will swallowed a lump of self-hatred.

"But this group has been good for me," Josephine continued. "I've been much too isolated lately. I'm so lonely."

"You've got me."

"I know, but there are days when I wonder whether leaving the art department was the right thing to do. I've given my life for you. I've sacrificed it all."

"It means a lot to me."

"I know. You love me, right? Tell me you think I'm a good mom and a good teacher. Tell me you don't hate me as much as Rose and Violet do. It's you and me against everyone, Will, and there can't be any secrets between us."

Violet Hurst

On the fourth day, a nurse announced, "A pipe has burst in the Spacken Center, so those of you who have twelve-step meetings to attend tonight will be bused to an off-campus facility."

Edie gave Violet a gentle poke in the ribs. "Looks like you're going on a field trip."

The meeting was already in progress when the Fallkill crew tumbled into the last row of folding chairs, coffee cups sloshing, hospital ID bracelets discreetly tucked into their sweatshirt sleeves. Violet had borrowed some leggings and a dress shirt from Edie, although both were a good half a foot too long and the former did a saggy elephant-wrinkle around her ankles and knees. She'd borrowed a peacoat and black beanie too; even through the double-glazed hospital windows, she could tell the weather had turned from cold to freezing.

"Mmm-mmm," Corinna whispered. "Some of the guys here have poh-tential. Three o'clock, in the leather jacket. I only wish I didn't have this crap in my hair."

It was the first time Corinna mentioned the greasy, clumped

quality to her head. Violet had noticed it, though. It had a familiar scent that she couldn't quite place.

"What is it?" It was the first time Violet felt comfortable asking.

"Vaseline. The nurses put it in. It's a trichster thing. So I can't start pulling when I feel stressed."

"Trich-ster?"

"Trichotillomania. God, I hate that word. Try saying it five times fast after four tequilas."

At the front of the room, a leprechaun-tiny woman was reading through the twelve steps and vouching for how well they work if "you work them."

It was hard to see herself sticking with meetings after her hospital stay was over, but even so, Violet didn't mind the twelve-step scene. You didn't know tedium till you sat through a high school chemistry lecture, and Violet would much rather giggle along through an addict's Freudian slips ("We sought help through prayer and *medication*") than slump in the back of some classroom, jotting notes about ionic compounds.

There was also something weirdly refreshing about meetings. Violet had never witnessed such depths of empathy or confession. The people at meetings spoke a whole different language than the one Violet had grown up with.

Violet barely heard the next speaker get introduced. In her right ear, Corinna was still prattling away about the guy in the leather jacket. "I'd let him thirteenth-step *me*. Do you think he's an NCF?"

Violet pressed one index finger to her lips. "I don't know what that stands for," she whispered. "National Cancer Foundation?"

"A newcomer fucker."

Burnt coffee slid down the wrong pipe, and Violet fought off laughter with a small coughing fit. A few old-timers cast annoyed looks over their shoulders.

As she composed herself, Violet became aware of the voice at the front of the room. It disoriented her. After a four-day hiatus, the voice snapped her back into survival mode. "I'm glad to be here today. I'm always glad to be here."

Time seemed to slow and Violet's vision tunneled. In the rows ahead of her, heads parted, and there he was: Douglas, standing behind the scarred wooden lectern. He was a nervous public speaker—eyes downcast, hand jingling the loose change in his pocket. The words were coming out of him fast and monotone, and the whole room seemed to draw closer in silent support.

"I didn't get here by accident. I'm a real alcoholic. I'm a drunk—the kind the Book talks about. Allergy of the body, obsession of the mind."

Violet was stunned. So stunned that she wondered for at least the second time that week if she was losing her mind or having an acid flashback. It was impossible to reconcile her father's voice with the recovery quotes she was coming to know too well.

Part of her wanted to leave the room out of loyalty to him; he was about to violate at least two of the Hurst family commandments: thou shalt feign perfection and thou shalt not air the family laundry. But she was curious. She had never once, in sixteen years, heard her father open up about his feelings or his childhood. The few times she'd been brave enough to ask, he'd made a joke of it, smiling glibly and saying only, "Ah, you want to know about the man with no past."

"I think I was an alcoholic from birth. I was five or six when I sneaked my first sips of wine. But there was something wrong with me even before then. I didn't like myself. Not one single thing. I hated wearing glasses. Hated that I was fat. Hated that I couldn't play second base like Joe Morgan. I would've traded places with any other kid on the planet. Any kid in the world had to have it better than me. The only thing that made me feel better was building old crystal radios with razor blade tuners."

Violet remembered the dinner before she'd come to Fallkill. Her father had clearly been drinking that night, hadn't he? Distress, plus head-mashing chemicals, still blearied her memory, but she was almost positive: her father had been drunk. He'd stuck to his seven p.m. vodka time. She cupped her hand around Corinna's ear. "How long do you have to be sober before they let you give these speeches?"

Corinna shrugged.

"Do they let you talk if you've relapsed?"

Another shrug. Corinna stuck her bottom lip out and shook her head. "Dunno."

As Douglas talked, his eyes slid away to the floor or the clock in the back of the room, anything to keep from holding the audience's gaze. Violet was thankful for Edie's hat. She ducked a little anytime her father's gaze veered her way.

"I grew up in dreary Erie, Pennsylvania. The Mistake on the Lake. My old man was an angry drunk. Of course, nobody talked about *alcoholism* then. Back then, you weren't an alcoholic, you were a tough guy. My dad didn't even qualify as that. He was only hitting me with a belt. Back in the day, my best friend's father liked to hit him with a two-by-four. By comparison, I had it pretty good."

Violet had a flash of her late grandpa Earl, catching houseflies in his hands and releasing them outside. She'd always thought he was, literally, too gentle to hurt a fly. The fact that he was all fists and whiskey was sad—devastating, really—but Douglas laughed ruefully, so other people did too. Some of the men nodded their understanding.

The tension seemed to ease out of Douglas's neck. He took a deep, jagged breath.

"Only two things ever worked for me, and helped me forget: alcohol and a woman. Given what I've told you, you probably won't be surprised to hear that I wasn't a social drinker. I know many of you had a lot of party years and good times. But me, I was never interested in feeling good. I was a thermos drinker. A few-slugs-in-the-bathroom-stall drinker. I wanted to be one of those tough guys like my father. I wanted know what it felt like to be the big man on campus, the guy who got the traffic-stopper . . . And then I met my wife."

Violet swallowed, hard.

"Josephine reminded me of a fifties screen goddess. A real woman. I'm talking silk dresses and Liz Taylor eyes. Wit like a razor blade and all the charm I was missing. She was studying art at Mercyhurst. Way too good for the likes of me. So I figured out what was important to her and I *became* that. Before I met her, if somebody asked me what I liked in a piece of art, I would've said I like it to hang straight on the wall. Suddenly, I'm wearing checkered scarves and hair grease, trying to keep up with conversations about Rothko and the *human drama*."

Laughter rippled across the room like a wave.

"I know . . . We could teach those art school kids about the human drama, couldn't we?"

Someone spit-whistled. Again, laughter bounced off the cinder-block walls.

"In the beginning with her—my wife—I didn't even need to drink. Booze stopped me feeling bad, but Josie did me one better. She made me feel special because *she* was so special. A perfect ten like her would *never* go out with a guy who wasn't up to snuff.

"But I couldn't keep it up, of course. After the wedding, my artsy-guy mask started to slip, and Jo saw the real nerd she'd married. I tried to make up for it by spoiling her. Taking care of her the way I used to look after my mom. I got myself a decent IT job. Tried to take Josie on vacations, buy her jewelry, rub her feet, paint her toenails. I've always said if I get canned from IBM, I'll make a damned good pedicurist. I even push back the cuticles."

This round of chuckles was tinged with embarrassment.

"Eww," Corinna whispered. "I'd never date a guy who knows his way around a pumice stone."

Violet grimaced.

"Anyway, nothing worked. Josie started backing away. Maybe because I was too demanding—I've never really figured it out. Anyway, the change was immediate. She stopped telling me she loved me. You name it, she hated it: the way I eat, dress, drive, floss my teeth, answer the phone. On the surface, everything was fine. We had a baby. Then, two more . . ."

Violet slouched lower in her seat. She prayed her father wouldn't mention her by name.

"I kept hoping with each one that things would get better. Don't get me wrong. I love my kids. I do. But I don't know them very well. Josie used to stare daggers at me if I tried to pick one of our crying babies up. If I tried to bring my son outside for a game of catch, Josie would act jealous or say something about how I couldn't catch a ball if it was smothered in Gorilla Glue."

Violet remembered that dig. Her mother often pointed out her father's lack of man skills. She also liked to say Douglas couldn't light a fire if you handed him a burning match; he couldn't tie a knot even with a troop of Boy Scouts there to show him the way.

"I guess you could say I backed off being a father to my kids. Booze helped there." He gave a slow whistle. "Alcohol gave me a break from the voices in my head. And I don't mean schizophrenic voices. I'm talking, my father's voice and my wife's voice were singing this duet in my head, and the lyrics went: 'Douglas, you're useless. Douglas, you're a shit.'

"I can't say for sure when I started blacking out. I don't remember a lot. I was blacked out at my oldest daughter's choral concert. I was blacked out the night my youngest daughter had a psychotic episode. I don't remember most of Christmas Day, 2006. I woke up the next day, and it was like Christmas all over again. I was going, 'Oh, look at this. I got an iPod. Someone gave me *The Sopranos* on DVD.'"

People hee-hawed. Douglas had obviously written his speech to include sitcom timing, jokes at regular intervals. But Violet wasn't laughing. *She* was the one who'd given him that DVD. And that mention of the "psychotic episode" confirmed it: her father *had* been hammered.

Violet thought back on the car ride to Fallkill. She remembered sitting in the passenger side of her father's car while he swerved around the southbound curves of Mohonk Road. The radio had sounded, at least to Violet, like a combination of untuned violins and fingernails on chalkboards. Fog shrouded the hood. If they'd talked during the ride, Violet couldn't remember it. She had no gauge for how drunk he'd been when he dropped her at the psych emergency room.

Corinna noticed Violet's wet eyes. *Are you okay?* she mouthed.

Violet nodded.

"Wow," Corinna whispered. "This is really getting to you, huh? He just needs to dump her, hit the gym, and lawyer up."

Violet felt a soft hand grip her shoulder. When she turned around, she saw the Fallkill counselor with a warning finger to her lips.

"At a certain point, I was drinking to stop the guilt too. Because sometime during that period, Josie eased up on me and started going a little Joan Crawford with the kids. I could have done something. Interceded the time Jo slapped my youngest daughter across the face."

Violet remembered that slap; later her mother had called it a "love tap," as if to further confuse love with pain.

"I came to AA after my pal, and now sponsor, Kerry, saw me spiking my coffee with a ziplock bag filled with whiskey. . . . Yes, the ziplock bag is what they call the poor man's flask. It's also the sneaky drunk's flask of choice." The alcoholic-addicts did their laugh-track thing. "Anyway, Kerry told me, 'I'm still kind of new to this recovery game and they've told me I can't diagnose anyone else's disease but my own. But in your case, Doug, I'm gonna make an exception.' Kerry said, 'If you don't find yourself a program and take the advice those people suggest, then something major's gonna happen to you in six months or less. You're going to lose your job or your kids. You're going to smash your car into the side of the Poughkeepsie bridge.'

"Three weeks after that, an incredible thing happened. My daughter ran away." Douglas shrugged. His voice wavered.

The crowd murmured in sympathy.

Violet's eyes wouldn't focus. She took a swig of her coffee, but it tasted charred and the cracked foam cup fully split, scalding her thighs and splattering Edie's white shirt. "Give me your cigarettes," she hissed, and Corinna handed over her pack with a look halfway between amusement and shock.

Violet heard her father continue his stream of self-confession as she turtled her head into the collar of her peacoat. She half-skittered, half-staggered out the door.

"After my daughter left, the only person I hated more than my wife or my dead father was myself. I hated myself enough to come with Kerry to a meeting like this one. And when the time came, I raised my hand and told the people there about my poor baby Rose . . ."

. . .

Violet sparked her lighter. She was beginning to understand why people liked smoking cigarettes; they were an available source of comfort, always at the ready, even if they did leave you feeling fragile and dependent as a newborn baby.

"Violet Hurst!"

Part of her expected to whip around and see her father. But it was only the angular, bug-eyed face of Fallkill's resident addiction counselor. "Where do you think you're going?"

"Nowhere. Sorry. I just needed some air."

"Do I look like a chump?" The counselor snatched the cigarette from Violet's fingers and stamped it out with her age-inappropriate Doc Martens boot.

"No." The counselor's questions were never rhetorical.

"I've been in your shoes, remember? You think I never tried to slip out of a meeting and thumb a ride?"

"I wasn't gonna leave."

"Suuure," the counselor said, incredulous. "I'm going to report this, obviously. But for the moment, I suggest you get your ass back in your chair. Willingness is the key."

Back in the basement, the official proceedings were finished. Still, the room hadn't cleared. It felt tinier now that people were standing. Alcoholics and addicts were milling around, hugging, confiding things to each other as they slammed more coffee and chewed on crumbly bakery cookies. Violet spied Corinna in the corner with her biker boy and gave them a wave.

"Not so fast," the counselor said, hooking two fingers into Violet's coat pocket. "There's the meeting before the meeting; the meeting; and the meeting after the meeting. I expect you to attend all three."

Violet's heart was hammering. Across the room, a small huddle of people were commending her father on his "beautiful message." "I've got seventeen months," a boy not much older than Violet told Douglas. "I felt like you were telling my life story."

Douglas asked him if he had a sponsor. He added, "A bunch of us are going to the Bull and Buddha. Come along if you like."

The more Violet heard, the angrier she got. It was more paternal than anything she'd seen of Douglas in years.

"You'll always be an outsider unless you start interacting and sharing at meetings," the counselor told her. "It's like your hair." She reached up and snatched Violet's hat like a high school bully. "Anyone who looked at you would think, *Now there's a girl who knows how to make herself vulnerable*, but in reality, you're more closed off than Cuba . . ."

It was too late. Douglas glanced over from the person he was talking to and spotted her buzz cut.

Violet grabbed the beanie back, but the damage was done. Pulling it over her forehead, she looked up and saw her father standing directly in front of her. His cheeks flushed red, almost as though he'd been slapped.

"Dad," Violet said. Her heart was speeding. She could feel the barometric pressure around them changing, getting sucked out the way it does before a damaging storm.

WILLIAM HURST

ON WEDNESDAY MORNING, Will woke to his mother arranging an outfit. A drift of clothes was piling up at the foot of his bed: flannel slacks, sweater vests, button-down shirts in seasonal orange plaid. There was the *screech-scratch* sound of his mother moving hangers in the crowded closet.

"I can't decide what we ought to wear," she said. "I worry that if we dress the way we normally dress, this Trina woman will think we've scrubbed ourselves up and gone out of our way to impress her. But then, if we dress the way *normal* people dress, especially the kinds of people *she* tends to see . . . Well, I don't even think we own anything like that." She laughed to herself. "I'm letting a civil servant on a power trip send me to pieces."

A few moments later, she stepped toward Will holding an (obviously) fake letterman's sweater and a pair of wide-wale corduroys with tiny Scottie dogs embroidered all over the cuffs.

"Are you sure?"

"Will, please do as you're told. Do I really need to remind you about the gravity of the situation we're in? Do you really want someone to rip you out of your crying mother's arms?"

Will stepped into the corduroys, suddenly wishing Violet

were home. He realized that without her, he had no idea when their mother was being dramatic.

"Right," Josephine said. "That brings us to hair. Not your hair. Mine."

He followed her down the hall to the master bathroom and watched her unloop her curlers in the "hers" side of the his-and-hers antique mirrors.

For a fraction of a second, she stopped fluffing her hair and looked sharply at him. "That thing I told you in the car the other day? About your father?" She didn't turn away from the mirror. She was addressing Will's reflection.

"Yeah?" Will felt his stomach drop away like the floor on his least favorite carnival ride.

"I probably don't need to tell you not to mention that today."

His mother was always scariest when she spoke in double negatives. "No," Will said. "You don't need to tell me."

"That's what I thought." Her voice was hardening. She screwed her face into a look of sham bewilderment, brows pinched, scratching her head with the blunt edge of her lipstick pencil. "And can I ask what you took away from your father's office the other day?"

"What do you mean?" *Took away.* He was thrown by her word choice. Had she sent him there hoping he would walk off with some tangible evidence?

"I *mean* did you find out anything new? About your father's business?"

Will still couldn't decide whether the words were specific or offhanded. Did his mom mean Douglas's profession? Or his personal *business*?

Will knew this was the perfect moment to tell his mother about the suspicious calls from Carrie and to ask her if she knew about the private investigator. But he wanted his final reveal to be big. He didn't want to go to her until he knew more about Carrie's identity and Rose's resurgence. As they said on the cop shows, he had to find that one crucial piece of information that would blow both cases wide open.

"Dad's work is fine. For him, I mean. They're building cool programs. Trying to make a computer that speaks like humans instead of in zeroes and ones. I wrote all about it in the worksheet you gave me." It occurred to Will to wonder if she'd read his so-called assignment. "I still don't think I'd want to work there."

That quirk of a smile. She was pleased with his answer. "Why not?"

The dread was building in him. "I'd rather be a writer or an artist like you."

"Anyone can work in a place like Dad's work. It takes someone very special to see the world with an artist's eye."

He was speaking her language. He was the star pupil quoting the teacher to the teacher herself. But, even as he said it, he didn't buy it. The words were gluey in his mouth. Josephine was still considering Will's reflection. Something—a look of boredom in her depthless eyes—said she didn't believe him either.

He asked about the day's science lesson to change the subject.

"Oh, Will," she sighed, "I think we have bigger concerns to-day. Don't you?" She grabbed a tissue from the shimmery gold tissue box cover and set to work cleaning an invisible smudge on the mirror.

He said, "The house looks nice."

She snorted suddenly. "It ought to. I spent all day yesterday on it. I cleaned so hard I broke the mop handle. I want those CPS people to come in here and be wowed. No, intimidated. Remember this, Will. Social workers are just as mean as lawyers. They're jeal-ous of families like us. They want to believe that everyone grows up in the kind of abusive households they did. They want to be-lieve every mother is a monster and every child is a punching bag, boo-hoo. It makes them feel better about themselves."

Will's mother had grown up in an abusive household. He didn't know the details because they were too horrible; his mom said her childhood was so gory she couldn't remember most of it. Will knew only that Josephine's mother had kicked her out of the house when she was eighteen for reasons unspecified and promptly died six months later.

Josephine huffed with annoyance as she yanked the last tissue in the box. "Will, honey. Pass me some toilet paper, will you?"

And then he noticed it: a small but undeniable thing. The toi-let paper roll was on backward. His mother was very vocal about her preference for the "over" orientation (it was the manufactur-er's intent, she argued; the pattern was printed on that side). For reasons Will couldn't quite explain, seeing its tail brush the wall made his blood run cold. Would Rose change things around the house just enough to make them feel disoriented and slightly nuts? Was Rose trying to send them a message? Or did confusing them just make them easier to manipulate? *Lochetic.* That was yet another word Will had copied into his unusual-word notebook. A describing word, meaning "waiting in ambush," it reminded him of Rose.

"Hello, Trina. I wish I could say it's a pleasure to see you. But I'm not one for false pleasantries. Am I, Will?"

"I applaud your honesty." Even when Trina laughed, her face seemed built for pity. Her eyes were too wet and her big, fleshy cheeks tugged downward. "This is my colleague, Mr. Flores."

Mr. Flores. It was strange to hear him introduced so formally, given he was just a few years older than Rose. He was a slight Hispanic man with a buzzed head and a tie that looked extra wide against his slender chest. He flashed his ID card.

"For heaven's sake," Josephine said, waving his badge away. "I have neighbors, you know."

Mr. Flores's frown said he was already forming opinions.

"May we come in?" Trina asked.

"There you go again . . . Acting like I have a choice in the matter." Josephine's deep, theatrical laugh conveyed anything but joy. "Come right this way. I have Martha's scones in the oven."

"Martha?" Trina's eyes fell to her clipboard, as if scanning for a third Hurst daughter.

"*Stewart?*" Josephine said. Her nose crinkled. Her half-smile was the one she reserved for top-shelf idiots. "Please leave your shoes by the door."

In the middle of the kitchen table—right alongside the linen napkins and tiered serving tray—was a conspicuously placed computer printout about state and federal laws as they pertained to child protective services. The top page read: KNOW YOUR RIGHTS! Will was suddenly fearful for Trina and Flores. *Turn and run,* he wanted to say. *Run and don't stop running until you get to a place that serves strong drinks. After my mom's done with you, you're gonna need one.*

"This is all very generous," Trina said. "But we should probably just get down to business so you can get on with the rest of your day."

"I thought you might say that." Another flash of that fangy smile. "In that case, Will, could you please start the video camera for me? I'm hopeless with electronics."

Will started. Sure enough, sitting directly next to the bowl of clotted cream, was his father's digital camera. He felt Trina's horror as he picked up the cold hunk of metal and opened the shutter.

"That's my boy. Just press Record and set it over there on the china cabinet."

"Mrs. Hurst." Trina's voice rippled with hesitation. "I want to assure you we are on your side."

"Right. I'm sure that's exactly why you're here. To prove there are two sides to every story." Josephine smoothed the darts on the front of her dress. "I think we both know you're here to build a case *against* us, not for us. And I have every right to protect myself. To document every move you make and ensure that you won't twist my words to suit your quota."

Trina and Mr. Flores eyed each other over the steaming teapot. For the first time, it occurred to Will that they were a well-oiled machine, like police partners. Will could practically read their thoughts: *We've got a live one. Hostile. Adversarial.*

Trina changed her mind and dropped a scone onto her plate. "Right, well . . . As I mentioned when I saw you last, the hospital notified CPS after Will's recent hospital visit. The doctor who treated him had some concerns about the nature of his injury."

"As well he should. Given my son was stabbed by his sister."

"Yes, we've been told. But before we get to the night of Will's injury, I hoped you might be able to give me a tour? All standard procedure. Just one of many silly things we're required to do." At last, Trina seemed to be speaking his mother's language. The knot in Will's chest loosened a millimeter. Soon this would be over. Soon he could get back to his investigations.

Mr. Flores grunted in agreement. "We just need to see the things Will eats. And make sure he has his own bed."

"His own bed!" Josephine trilled. "Will has his own *playroom*. He has his own *bathroom*." Her voice bristled with condescension. The look she gave Mr. Flores was like a backhanded slap.

Will trailed the three of them through the house, nodding in agreement—though no one was looking at him—because he thought someone ought to appear cooperative.

"Cool construction mural. Did you paint it yourself?" Mr. Flores asked when they got to Will's room.

Will glanced at the wall's cranes and bulldozers. He shook his head.

"I painted it," Josephine said.

"Very cool," Flores repeated. "So I was thinking, maybe Will and I can hang out here and have a chat while you show Trina the rest of the house?"

"It would be *my pleasure* to let you talk to Will privately when you come back here with a court order." Josephine smiled. "But until then, Will has a legal right to be accompanied by me or an attorney."

They did the final loop of the tour.

Mr. Flores continued to watch Will with prowling cat eyes. "So, buddy . . . Why don't you and I sit right here at the table and talk, man-to-man, for a few minutes? Don't worry, your mom's gonna stay in the kitchen. She'll be right over there by the stove with Trina."

Trina smiled and waved from her place between his mother and the breadbox. Will had a feeling that Trina would put her hand out if Josephine tried to step toward him, the same way, in the car, his mother sometimes threw her arm across the passenger seat if she braked short at a light.

Mr. Flores reached into his leather backpack. He took out a notebook and pack of crayons that made Will feel as patronized as he did in restaurants where the waitress brought him a sippy cup and a word search puzzle. "So Will . . . Does anyone in your family smoke?"

Will wasn't prepared for this line of questioning. He ached to glance over at his mother. Instead, he found himself studying Mr. Flores for clues to whatever answer he expected. "Just Violet."

"Your sister," Mr. Flores said. "Why don't you use these crayons and draw me a picture of what Violet smokes?"

Will's stomach clenched. He had no idea if he could render what he'd once caught Violet hiding in one of the basement armoires his mother used for storage. *Please don't tell,* Violet had pleaded. *No one will find it here. Mom rifles through other people's stuff, but she's totally unwilling to look at her own baggage.*

Will had never told. But now he picked up the green crayon and drew a few crinkly green turds in the bottom of an old caper jar. *Marijuana.* Somehow he'd just known. *Your stoner sister.* That was what Will's old public school tormentors used to call Violet.

His mother was looking at him sidelong. Will wasn't sure which Josephine would hate more: the fact that Will had besmirched their fine, upstanding family or the fact that—even after all the contouring lessons she'd given him—his drawing techniques hadn't much improved. The crayon went oily in his fat, clumsy fingers.

"You okay there, buddy?"

Will realized he was jittering his foot hard. On the table, the teaspoons were vibrating. "I'm okay."

Mr. Flores poured himself a cup of tea but didn't take a sip. "So let's talk about when you left school—"

"The school wasn't carpeted," Josephine butted in. "In the event of a seizure, we didn't want Will to hit his head on those hard floors."

"That's understandable," Mr. Flores said, writing.

"Plus, with the Asperger's . . . Public school was too stimulating. Will doesn't do well in crowded, noisy places."

"The thing is, Mrs. Hurst, I'd rather Will tell me these things himself." Flores leaned in an inch. "Tell me how you feel in crowds, buddy?"

"I don't do well in crowded places," Will said. *Echolalia: a echo-like repetition of another's words.* His mother's voice brought him back: "Honey, you need to look Mr. Flores in the eye when you speak to him."

"I don't mind," Flores said, but by then, Will was holding his gaze.

This time, it was Mr. Flores who looked away first. He seemed as unnerved as most people Will looked in the eye for more than a few seconds. That tension was the real reason Will avoided focusing intently on anyone. Eye contact didn't disturb Will, but it seemed to disturb other people; it was easier for everyone when Will kept his gaze below sea level.

Flores said: "I gotta say, the homeschool thing has always struck me as pretty lonely. Do you get a chance to hang out with kids your own age?"

"Oh, yeah. All the time," Will said automatically. His pulse was thumping. He hoped the lie didn't show on his face.

"Where?" Mr. Flores asked.

"Where do I hang out with other kids?"

"Yeah."

"Play group," he said loudly. "At the Rosendale rec center."

His mother did nothing to disguise her approval.

Mr. Flores had a pitying look on his face. He ran his palm over his New York Jets tie. Will thought it was a fashion choice that must have endeared him to other (sporty, *normal*) twelve-year-old boys. "Let's talk about your epilepsy for a minute," Flores said. "That must stink. Getting dragged around to all those doctor's appointments."

Will shrugged. "Lots of people have it worse. When my mom

was little, she had such bad asthma she could barely walk up the stairs."

"What does it feel like? A seizure, I mean?"

"I feel it in my chest, first. Not pain. It's just kind of hard to breathe. Then, nothing until I wake up, and I can't remember anything, and I feel like I've been hit with a frying pan. Sometimes there's a little blood if I've bitten my tongue or the insides of my cheek."

"Do you have seizures often?"

Later, thinking of his mistake, Will would blame the fact that he was on autopilot. He'd gone through the same spiel, so many times before, with so many different doctors.

"I have a seizure about every two or three months. I had two this month, which was"—Will almost said *aberrant*, a word his mother would use, but then he remembered himself, the fact that he should come off like an ordinary twelve-year-old runt— "freaky."

"You had two seizures this month?"

"Yeah. One in the car the other day and one the night Violet went away." Will's heart clanged the second he said it. The seizure was not in the version of events he and his mother had rehearsed.

Mr. Flores twitched like a sleeping dog. He turned to look at Trina, but midrubberneck, he caught himself. "Can you tell me a little bit about the night Violet went to the hospital?" There was a softness in his eyes and a delicacy in his manner that scared Will more than anything.

"Um, sure." Will, scrounging for ways to backpedal, realized there were none. All he could do was recite, word for word, the version he and his mother had practiced, and pray Mr. Flores forgot the small detail of the seizure. "Violet was pointing the knife at my mom. My mom called her sick, and Violet started charging at her. I put myself between them, and I snatched the blade away. She cut me a few times in the process, but I got it in the end." Will looked away. There was a sickening feeling in his stomach when he remembered the way it seemed like the bleeding would never stop. He'd bled all over the tiles, all over a dropped oven mitt, all over his best khaki pants.

Mr. Flores scratched one tapered sideburn. "So, I'm a little confused here. Explain it to me like I'm a kindergartener. Did you have your seizure before or after you grabbed the knife away from your sister?"

Will's vision tunneled. A cold numbness swept down his arms, and he wondered if everyone could see his heart squirming beneath his sweater vest. "After," he said. Very suddenly he remembered the jagged pain in his hand and his mother's angry face as she applied pressure to the wound. She couldn't stand it when he hurt himself, even if he *was* only trying to help.

"You're sure about that? Even though these seizures make it hard to remember many minutes before and after?"

"Uh-huh," Will lied. "I remember it all really vividly."

Will couldn't help it. He turned and glanced to his mother for reassurance. It was an old habit, inevitable as drawing his next breath. Only her lipsticked mouth—lips pulled together like a little, red fist—foretold her disappointment and the classical punishment she had in store for him.

Misodoctakleidist: someone who hates practicing the piano.

Violet Hurst

Violet's therapist, Sara, was an intimidating-looking woman, with her Eleanor Roosevelt hairdo. Like a master hunter or fisherman, she seemed to be able to sit still for hours without breathing audibly or adjusting the cross of her legs. Her pursed lips and squinted eyes blatantly warned Violet, *I am judging you. I'm determining your future.*

"I'd like to discuss the truth for a moment," Sara-pist said.

"The truth," Violet repeated, and for a moment she felt as though a weight had been lifted from her. At last, someone was at least *considering* the idea that Josephine wasn't telling the truth about Friday night.

"Yes, the truth. Your parents seem to think you have a problem being honest. Do you find the truth makes you feel too vulnerable? Does it cause you some irrational fear?"

"No," Violet snapped. She loved truth. She craved truth. If anything, being the family truth-teller was what got her in so much trouble.

"Let's talk about lying, then. How do you feel when you're doing it? Do you ever feel like you want to stop lying, but you can't?"

"I don't lie! Is that what my parents told you? That I'm some kind of pathological liar?!"

"The clinical term is *pseudologia fantastica*."

"My mom is the liar!"

"Sounds like you're projecting," Sara-pist said. "Instead of seeing bad in yourself, you perceive it in others. It's a defense mechanism. One that allows people to go on believing they're perfect." Her desk chair gave a little squeal as she leaned back in it. "Is that it, Violet? Do you think you're perfect?"

"Of course not! And my mom is the one who does the projecting. Calling me crazy, when she's the one who's insane . . ."

"True. By sending you here, your mother made you what we call the 'identified patient.' Maybe you're the person who shows the most symptoms, even if other people in your family have mental health issues too."

"So why am I here and my parents aren't?" It was such a whiny, teenage, it's-not-fair-type question. Violet hated herself for having to ask it.

"You're here, Violet, because you're a violent offender. I can't help you, and I definitely won't release you, until we get to the heart of your lying, your violent tantrums, the ways you hurt your brother."

"You're not going to release me?" Strange the way Violet was both disappointed and relieved. She wanted to get home to Imogene and her farm stand friends, but she still hadn't made an escape plan. She wanted to hear from Rose, and she needed to get to the heart of what had happened the night of Will's injury.

"I can't. I got a memo saying you've been named an elopement risk. Did you try to run away during last night's recovery meeting?"

"I took a five-minute break. Without permission, yeah. But I needed some air. Did your memo say my dad was the guest of honor?"

Violet watched her meaning slowly register in Sara-pist's expression. "Your father was the speaker?"

"Ask him yourself. He's coming to visiting hours today." It had been, hands down, the most awkward exchange Violet had ever had. Even worse, it had happened in front of a small audience of reverent addicts, all of whom were commending Douglas on his "emotional honesty." In a totally Hurst fashion, they'd both pretended, however stiltedly, that nothing was wrong. Douglas faked like he'd invited her, and Violet didn't breathe a word about his recent relapse.

Sara-pist took off her glasses and cleaned the lenses in the folds of the bland, expensive-looking blouse she wore under her white coat. "I'd love to see your dad while he's here. I'll alert the front desk to send him to me before he comes to you. Did you know he was in recovery before last night?"

"I knew he slurs like a Bowery bum. That wasn't hard to miss. But I didn't know he'd quit drinking. He said he was blacked out the night he brought me here. How did everyone here miss that?"

"*You* missed it."

"I was tripping my face off."

"Exactly. There's addiction in your family. On the one hand, that's a painful thing to accept. But there's an opportunity for connection. You and your father have something in common."

Violet shook her head vehemently. "My dad was too drunk to stand up for me and say I didn't hurt my brother. *That's* the painful thing to accept."

"Listen to me, Violet. If you think you've been set up, then that's a *big* setup. No one made you take drugs. No one forced you to pick up that knife. I think your main priority needs to be you. Not your mother, not your dad. I want you to take deep breaths and focus on the things you can do something about." She glanced at her watch. "Sorry to cut this short, but it's time to go."

Sara-pist was right. It really *was* time to go. Violet needed to buckle down and make a two-year plan for herself. Homeless shelter. Storage unit. McJob. Whatever. She would get away from her cruel mother by whatever means necessary. It was time to stop panicking and start planning.

WILLIAM HURST

AFTER TRINA AND Mr. Flores left, Will sat at the piano keys, wondering how the heck he was going to play DeBenedetti's "Arctic Nights" with just one hand.

"A real musician is someone who can create true and original music with every performance." Josephine was lounging on the silk fainting couch that always made Will imagine a gang of shirtless men hoisting it up onto their flexing shoulders.

Josephine's pantyhose whispered as she rubbed her feet together. "Real musicians play under all kinds of conditions," she continued. "They play through tinnitus and arthritis. If you weren't using your hand as an excuse, you'd be using your autism or your epilepsy. Stop making excuses for yourself, little boy." Her tone was joking, but it had a hard edge.

"Are you angry?" After Trina and Flores left, Josephine had just stood behind the stove, pressing her palms against the unlit burners as though in a trance. When she'd snapped out of it, she'd gone directly to the sheet music. She'd actually lifted Will onto the piano bench as though he were a much smaller child.

"I said *play*. If you make me ask again, you'll regret it."

He tried to play only the left hand, but that was the melancholy bit and it was not the same without the loud, fierce trillings of the right.

Josephine's smile was prickly. "Funny, I don't remember asking for half of a song. That's like ordering a hamburger and getting only the bun. I need sirloin."

But how? There must be some way to play the song with a splint on his hand. He was certain of it, or else his mother wouldn't be demanding it. Will's ears were buzzing. He felt out of sorts, unsteady on the bench. Will tried playing the right-handed parts with his left. It was still only half a song, and even choppier than the first time around. *Rhadamanthine*, a describing word. *Like a stern judge.*

"Enough," she finally said. "It's obvious to me that you haven't been practicing. Get up."

"No, Mom . . ." How dumb he'd been to think piano time was his punishment. What she had in mind was much worse.

"Don't 'No, Mom,' me. I am the mother and you are the *child*."

Will reluctantly followed her to her second-floor office. The smell inside was the same as always: hand lotion and expensive art paper. The curtains were drawn. Josephine flicked on the desk lamp, and Will went directly to the spot on the back of the closed door that no one but the two of them knew about. He seemed to find himself there, for one reason or another, at least once a week.

She pulled open her desk drawer and took out a sheaf of reward stickers—the ones she bought at Kingston's Parent Teacher Store. Will watched her peel off a red apple giving the thumbs-up. *Great Work!* the sticker read. It was so strange to be punished with praise. He felt certain it would hurt less if she gave him emotionally honest stickers: ones that said *Bad Job!* or *Boo!* or *So disappointing!* But then, no company printed put-down stickers, did they?

Will watched his mother thumb the apple sticker high onto the back of the door. *Too* high. He wasn't even sure he could bring his nose to reach it, let alone hold it there for an hour or more.

"I thought I did a good thing!" Will pleaded, as she nudged him toward it. "It was good, wasn't it? Telling them about what Violet smokes? I thought you'd be happy." Tears were dripping down his cheeks.

"Be quiet, William," she shushed. Her face was pursed in disgust, a harsh downward crease where the sides of her nose met her liberally rouged cheekbones. She sat back in her white linen chair, waiting.

Will rose high up on his tiptoes and brought his nose to meet the *Great Work!* sticker. After what felt like thirty minutes, his calves started to cramp. His thighs quivered. His loafers creased and cut into the tops of his feet. Each passing minute, the sticker seemed to get higher, but Will knew it was really his will failing him. Gravity was relentless. The pain was spider-crawling up the back of his knees.

What made it even more humiliating was the view she had of his butt crack, the way his pants always began to slip at what felt like the forty-minute mark, and still he couldn't move to pull them up. *Steatopygic*, a describing word, reserved for someone with a sofa-sized ass.

As he stood there, his mother had her open Bible in her lap. She sounded calm for the first time since Trina and Flores had left, her voice no longer breathlessly high and unnatural. She was reading Timothy 3 aloud: "For people who be lovers of self . . . proud, arrogant, abusive, disobedient to their parents . . ." Josephine was never more devout than when her children transgressed.

After an hour or more, when Will's ankle finally gave out, he half-hoped, as always, that his mother would physically punish him—smack the back of his neck, maybe, pinch his bicep, what-ever. But physical brutality was beneath Josephine.

Or maybe she'd conditioned Will to do the job for her. Still on the floor where he'd fallen, he started crying again, banging his head against the door in frustration. She kept on reading: "un-grateful, unholy, heartless, unappeasable, slanderous, without self-control . . ." Will's vision curled black at the periphery, and at this his forehead budded lumps like a buck growing antlers.

Pedicle, he thought. *The bony protrusion of the skull from which an antler grows.* And then he smacked his head once more.

They ate frosted wheat squares that evening after Douglas called to say he was staying late at work. This was something they al-ways did whenever they were alone for supper. When Violet and Douglas were home, dinner was a many-coursed, fancy-named thing—*angel hair* something and *soy-glazed* whatnot. But when Will and his mom were alone, dinner was Froot-Looped and Cocoa-Krisped.

It was the kind of guilty pleasure that made him feel closer to her, even though she left him alone at the table to eat it by him-self. After the lengthy punishment in her office, Josephine had slammed a bowl and a carton on the kitchen table, then carried her own portion upstairs.

Alone at the table, Will smelled rose hips and sulfur in the air. He heard the water running in the master bath, and he knew his mother was eating her cereal in her claw-footed tub, mirror steaming, bath salts crunching under her thighs.

Will dragged his spoon through the sugar-slick mush, won-dering what time his father would come home. Was he with Car-rie? Will knew how sex worked. When he was five his mother had given him a very descriptive "intercourse" talk (her right pointer finger "erect," plunging into the "okay" sign she made with her left hand). It was still weirdly horrible to imagine any man doing it to any woman, let alone his father doing it to Carrie.

Bible passages were still ringing in Will's ears, and he couldn't eat, not when he was thinking these bad thoughts, knowing that God thought him *treacherous, reckless, swollen with conceit.*

He got up from the table and listened for a few minutes at the foot of the stairs. There were no footsteps, no opening and closing of dresser drawers. Will knew, intuitively, that his mother hadn't toweled off yet.

He crept to the living room, his least favorite room in the house. Probably because his parents only summoned him to it when they needed a place to give him bad news: "Rose has run away" or "We've decided you're not suited for public school." Maybe they chose the space for their bad-news talks because they thought its big dripping curtains and throned chairs had gravitas. Or maybe they wanted to keep bad talks and bad memories confined to a part of the house that they rarely visited.

The room was pristine and grand, but Will knew the chaos that awaited him. He pulled open one door of the soaring built-in cabinet and saw an infestation of mess. There were toppled vases, tangles of Christmas ribbon, mouse droppings, oyster plates, gravy boats (plural), and big-eyed porcelain doohickeys. *Antiques,* his mother would say. They'd seemed to multiply, especially over the past year. Toward the back, Will uncovered the leather-bound photo albums.

It was true. The Hurst family album was littered with blanks, exactly like Douglas had told the PI. It was exactly the kind of betrayal his mother had described to the person on the phone: "She's tearing our house apart. Destroying our possessions." All but a few of Rose's baby pictures were gone, and in the few that remained, her cherubic face was obscured. In one photo, Rose was just a lump of pink blanket in Josephine's hospital bed. In another, Rose was just a bald skull peeking out over the top of the baby carrier their father wore strapped to his chest.

In later family shots, Rose had simply been torn or scissored out. There were jagged holes in the middle of their Christmases, their school graduations, their vacations to Lake George and Cape Cod. There was a slight tremor to Will's hand as he turned the plastic pages.

He dumped the albums back in the cluttered cabinet. He stopped again at the bottom of the steps to listen for signs of life upstairs. It was still quiet as a tomb, no sound of the tub draining.

He thought again about the e-mail his father had sent the private investigator: *a few personal items have gone missing.* What else had Rose come back to take? She was so much older than Will—ten unbridgeable years—he had no idea what mattered to her. When she left, she'd taken her computer, her phone, and a good-sized chunk of her wardrobe. Surely, that was all a twenty-year-old would need.

Unless she'd come back for money. But to Will's knowledge, his parents weren't the type who hid dollar bills in cookie jars. Heck, his parents hardly even *used* cash.

Will searched his TV references, his only window into the logistics of the crime. Reality law-enforcement shows always showed people stealing jewelry in order to pawn it for cash, but surely Will would have heard all about it if one of his mother's tennis bracelets had gone missing. 20/20 always ran specials about young people swiping their parents' prescriptions, but Will knew the meager contents of his parents' medicine cabinet; there was little inside beside the basic aspirins, laxatives, and fish oil supplements, plus, of course, his epilepsy drugs.

For a minute, Will considered going upstairs and clawing around in Rose's desk drawers. But then he remembered Violet and her caper jar: *Mom rifles through other people's stuff, but she's totally unwilling to look at her own baggage.* Had the same thing occurred to Rose? Maybe she, too, had used their mother's storage for safe-keeping. Maybe the basement was the place where things had gone missing?

The basement smelled of dampness and the kitty litter his mother sprinkled around to absorb the humidity, and it was shadowy no matter how many bare bulbs his father hung from the ceiling. Will began with the scarred oak armoire. Violet's caper jar was still in the side pocket of his mother's sable coat (half full), along with sixty dollars cash and a little metal pipe that looked menacing. But the rest of his mother's coats, capes, and blazers turned up empty.

He moved on to the next wardrobe. He was worried about the time, whether his mother was upstairs looking for him. There were too many garment bags to unzip, too many little satin-lined pockets to finger. Violet was right. It was a shocking ton of clothes, much of it unworn, the price tags dribbling out of the cuffed sleeves. Will was about to give up when he spotted the hat boxes beneath a long dress cloaked in dry cleaner's plastic.

Idiot, he told himself when he flipped open the top and found, merely, a globular fur hat. It looked Russian, reminiscent of a Bond villainess. Will couldn't help but pick it up. The silvered fur felt so *alive* beneath his fingers. He half-expected it to pant and growl as he petted it. The hat was halfway to Will's head before he looked down and saw the book that someone had hidden beneath it: *Waiting for Baby: A Nine-Month Journal*.

Will perked his ears for any sounds of footsteps upstairs. His breath suddenly felt like he was back in real-school gym class. Each pinched inhale burned, and his legs cramped under him. Tiny reindeer bells jingled as he repositioned himself, and it took him half a second and a near heart attack to realize he'd grazed the side of a Tupperware container marked X-mas.

He lifted the book carefully, by the edges of its lavender cover. He was hoping it belonged to his mother, even as he knew it was too new. Its corners were uncurled and the spine was barely creased. And right there on the first page, on the dotted line designating *mother's name*, his sister's rigid hand had penned *Rose Hurst*.

It was painful to read. The writing was so emotional—such blurty stuff, full of expectant joy—that it drew a sharp line under the fact that Rose had documented it for someone other than Will. The first few weeks were Rose's fragmented biography. On the line marked *favorite pastime(s)*, Rose had written: *Hiking, camping. Also, cooking. Although I can only do it when visiting friends at college. At home, Mom complains about the mess and me using her spices.* When the book had called for *three words to describe me*, Rose had answered: *Rose-colored glasses!*

Evidently Rose's "earliest memory" was *Playing bank at a neighbor's house. Pennies and fake bills everywhere! A bigger mess than my mom would ever let me make at home!* She'd added: *I *swear* to tolerate normal-kid messes. So bring this book to me anytime I am being unfair. I don't mind if you are mouthy and messy and a little bit savage. Much more fun than being like me, who acted like my mom's best employee!*

Will shuddered a little on the last word. Did he act like he worked for his mother? He consoled himself with the thought that he'd never had Gerber-baby looks. Even now, he wasn't cute enough to score model management in the manner of grade-school Rose.

And that was something. With the exception of the veiled employee comment, the journal made zero mention of Rose's acting, singing, or modeling. Will had always thought these were the things that defined his oldest sister. But now he wondered whether he'd confused her with the sound bite his parents gave their friends.

Her baby's father was suspiciously absent from the journal. Unlike the "family tree" section of the book—where Rose had left blanks after headlines like *fond memories of my parents* and *favorite family vacation*—she had written something, however vague, in the space marked *qualities I love about your father*: *If you're reading this, I hope we've had lots of talks about your dad and you don't have any unresolved questions! I wish so hard that I could give you a dad who could be there for you!*

The son or daughter in Rose's journal seemed so real, like a flesh-and-blood relative Will ought to be able to play Blokus and Uno with on Thanksgiving. The baby even had a name! Well, Rose had scrawled a few possibilities—*Sophia, Audrey, Oliver*—into a section titled *baby names I've always liked*.

Suddenly, it occurred to Will that he could be an uncle. Uncle William. It had a nice ring to it: not the kind of uncle who could teach you gun safety or how to pour beer from a keg, but the kind who could teach you etymologies and show you how to make a present look professionally wrapped.

Will kept flipping through the pages.

I first suspected I was pregnant because . . . . I threw up in my lap while driving on I-87!

I found out for sure on . . . April 25, 2006.

My reaction was . . . . Brief terror followed by joy!

At the nine-week mark, Rose had pasted a murky ultrasound photo following a visit to the doctor—*Your heartbeat looked just like a firefly!*—and spilled the beans to their mother:

When I told my family I was pregnant, their reaction was . . . Told Mom today because I had to . . . Somehow, she knew I'd been to Planned Parenthood. She probably scrolled through the outgoing numbers on my phone. Well, baby, she thinks

I am ruining her life. Not my life, mind you. Not yours. HERS. She trapped me for hours in her office, trying to make me tell her about your father (I wouldn't) and pressuring me to terminate. Holy shit, I must really be losing my mind . . . What am I doing writing "shit" and "terminate" in your baby book? I'm not terminating. You're a part of me. Yes, Mom is right, you will be needy, expensive, and all-consuming (that's your job). You will poop and cry 'round the clock, and IF I was ever #1 in my life (I'm not sure I even was!), that will certainly not be the case once you're born. You're gonna be a life-changer. But I like that! At this point, any change is good. P.S.—Don't worry, I WILL NOT raise you in my mother's house!

It got worse.

What role do you see your family playing in your baby's life? At this point, next to none. Mom's threatened to kick me out of the house (fine) and stop paying my tuition (problem!). She keeps giving me printouts of studies about how single mothers have poor health later in life. I was in sociology the other day, and an article titled "Why Pedophiles Love Single Moms" fell out of my notebook. Mom had obviously tucked it where she knew I would find it. Thank God I saw it before I mistakenly turned it in along with my research paper!

That was the last entry. Weeks eleven, twelve, and thirteen were blank.

Will decided to go and get his mother. He'd already forgiven her for the afternoon's punishment (he had been slacking on piano) and he was on her side where it came to the child protective people. (Trina and her partner did, in Josephine's words, seem like zombie clones trained to "steal children" and "eat up federal funding.")

Josephine, at the very least, needed to know that Rose had it in for her.

Will climbed the stairs with the heart of a lion. His whole body had tightened. His brain was hardened with some emotion he didn't often feel, maybe rage.

Now, he wanted more than anything for Rose to come back. Will wanted to catch her red-handed in the midst of slashing the tires, or Saran-wrapping the toilet seats, or whatever prank she had in mind next.

It was more than just outrage, this shimmer of a feeling that made Will's teeth grind and his jaw chatter. There was uneasiness there too. He was afraid. How far would Rose go to get back at them? Would she rub their toothbrushes with raw meat? Rub their sheets with poison ivy? Cut the brake lines in their mother's car? In Will's mind, there was no end of terrifying revenge scenarios.

Will wasn't sure which scared him more: Rose's revenge or the idea that she might drop the pranks and prowling and come back to live with the Hursts in a real way. If Rose came home, would their mother forgive her? If Rose came home, would she replace Will as their mother's favorite? He couldn't live with his demon sister. He couldn't go back to breathing shallowly in some corner. Will felt a whip of despair, and beyond that a boy prince's desire to defend his kingdom. The basement, make that the whole house, was motionless, but for the circling, overhead threat of rogue Rose.

Violet Hurst

"Violet," barked the scrubs-clad figure in the doorway. Violet, painting her nails with Edie, expected a quiet-down warning, but instead the nurse said, "Mail call." She dropped the letter face-down on the bed, and Violet's eyes fell to the dusty-mauve seal.

She felt oddly exhilarated. Maybe because she really was warming to the idea of living with Rose.

Edie urged, "Open it."

> Dearest Vivi,
> I'm so sorry to hear about the asylum . . .

"Asylum?" Edie said. "Is this, like, *Valley of the Dolls* and you're the Patty Duke character? Or does she think you've sought political asylum?"

Violet rolled her eyes so hard they nearly fell out of her face. She read on.

> . . . Thank you so much for understanding!
> I love your questions to me! You must be studying for the SATs if you're thinking in multiple choice. I can remember what that was like. For, like,

six months I could only think in analogies. Vindictive : Revenge as Dishonest is to _____. Yuck, I would not trade places with you!

Anyway, let's see.

A) I am definitely not in formal touch with Mom and Dad. Although I am curious about them! Do you hate them as much as I did when I was living there?

B) I'm doing temp work. I move between a lot of different offices, all of them boring. Acting is my real work. Or maybe, I should say <u>trying</u> to get acting work is my real work! I've been really trying to change my approach to auditioning. I make bolder choices than I used to. A director may not like what I'm doing. He may think, "That's all wrong," but he sure won't say, "This Rose girl isn't <u>doing</u> anything!" I'd rather they hate me than forget me.

C) Yep, Damien and I are living together. Sometimes I still worry that cohabitation is a "relationship killer" the way Mom always said. But we plan to get married eventually. You'll have to meet him and tell me if you approve! What about you? Do you have a boyfriend? You didn't answer in your last letter!

D) You know about that picture, huh? It's okay now. I've made peace with everything . . . . Do you believe that? Nah, sometimes I don't know if I believe it either.

So how is Will? He was such an innocent little boy when I left, but that's probably not the case anymore.

Fill me in. I need details!

Still missing you,

Rose

P.S. Write me at the below address. Damien's father has some health issues, so we're staying at his parents' country house for a little while. You heard me, I'm back in the Hudson Valley!

· · ·

"Are you as disturbed as I am by that revenge analogy?" Violet asked.

"Hmmm," Edie said, blowing contemplatively on her wet nails. "Maybe it was a coincidence that she picked that one?"

"I thought Freud said there are no coincidences."

"It's a touch passive-aggressive," Edie agreed.

"Who's passive-aggressive?" Corinna strode in and plopped herself down on Violet's bed. "Fill me in. I've been talking on the phone with Leatherboy. He's at MARC sober house, so he has unlimited phone privileges and all day to describe his thick, throbbing—"

"Aggghhh, phone sex." Edie gagged and covered her ears. "I ca-an't hear you. La la la la la la."

"Just be careful he doesn't give you hearing AIDS," Violet said.

Corinna laughed. "That joke took me a second," she said, and proceeded to read Rose's letter. When she finished, she said, "See, I was right. A *country house*, la-di-da. Big sis found herself a Daddy Starbucks."

"A Daddy *Warbucks*," Edie corrected.

"I got Starbucks on the brain," Corinna said. "I'd kill for one of those caramel apple cider drinks. When it's cold out and you're stoned, it tastes like apple pie. So what's the address on big sis's stately country home?"

Violet tossed her the envelope. "Newburgh."

Corinna lifted her chin, put her pinky in the air. "No, dahling, not the old burg. The *neeew* burg."

Edie grabbed the envelope. "We'll Street View it. Next computer lab."

"Why do we even have that?" Violet asked. "Computer lab, I mean. I can't figure it out."

"It's so we can keep up our studies," Edie said. "Online courses. GEDs."

"It sucks, right?" Corinna added. "The last hospital I went to had Wi-Fi. *And* they didn't confiscate cell phones."

The most unsettling thing about the letter was the part about Rose being back in the Hudson Valley. Violet appreciated the buffer the city put between them, at least while she tried to figure out Rose's intentions. Now Rose had halved the distance between herself and the rest of the Hursts. It was like the games of Red Light, Green Light they used to play when they were little. Now that Violet's back was turned—now that Violet was locked away—Rose was inching closer and closer, trying to tag her, trying to reset the whole game, whether Violet was feeling ready or not.

Violet's stomach fell when she felt an authoritative hand on her elbow. "You've got a visitor," the nurse said.

Violet was tempted to say, *I know.* She was expecting her father. She was expecting a long, frustrating talk about their "shared substance abuse issues."

But the man at the table wasn't Douglas. He was young, Latino, and, at least in Violet's approximation, retina-searingly good-looking. *Boyish,* she thought. The man's eyes reflected light like dark leather, and Violet was stupidly glad she was still in the sweater dress Edie insisted she borrow.

"Viola Hurst?" the young man asked. He banged his knee as he pushed out his chair and awkwardly rose to his feet, giving Violet the impression that she wasn't the person he was expecting either. She'd let Corinna conceal her dark circles and line her eyes in soft gray. The result was surprisingly un-mental-patient.

She shook his hand. "Most people call me Violet."

"Nicholas Flores. I'm from Child Protective Services. Sorry—" he stammered. "It's just—We have the same haircut. It's kind of tripping me out."

"Oh." Violet reached, self-consciously, for her scalp.

"Did you play the soundtrack for *V for Vendetta* while you shaved it? I did."

"No," Violet laughed. "I did donate it to Locks of Love. I'm sorry, did you say you were from social services?"

Nicholas nodded and slid Violet his business card.

She felt her face flush from the bottom up, a sensation like she'd been pushed out of her depth and could feel herself going under. "Someone else hurt my brother. Not me. Does that answer your question?"

"No. I'm not—" He paused and looked out the window. The sky was cornflower blue. "I'm actually more interested in your family as a whole, and your sister Rose. I went to Old Stone Way earlier today."

"You went to my house?"

Nicholas nodded. "I met Will and your mother."

"Mom," Violet repeated. The shock of it was enough to make her pull out a chair and sit down.

"She's a tough customer, huh?"

A flood of breath rolled out of Violet, like she'd been kicked in the stomach. "You don't know the half of it. I'm sure you got Mom at her most presentable. All oven mitts and cookies from scratch."

Nicholas met her eyes and laughed. "Scones, actually. Yeah, I can see how she could be convincing, how she might come off real put together to someone she looks up to. Me? I think I'm probably an inferior being, so she made it pretty clear she'd rather have a conversation with the dirt on my shoe. Besides, I've been doing this long enough to be suspicious of people who play at being perfect."

Nicholas was studying her with his deep black eyes that weren't unkind. "I could be totally off-base, and I hope you'll tell me if I am. But I left your house feeling weird . . . disoriented. It's my experience that dangerous people make you feel off-balance."

Violet wanted to be distrustful of this kindness, but it felt too good. Her hair-trigger tear ducts were ready to go.

"I can see I'm upsetting you." He looked genuinely apologetic. "Maybe you can just start by telling me about your sister? She's the real reason I'm here. When she ran away, your family got entered into our system. This matter with your brother was more like . . ." He struggled with the word.

"Strike two?" Violet offered.

"Not quite. I just wouldn't be doing my job if I treated them as unrelated incidents."

"Well, like, what do you want to know about Rose? Her personality, or hobbies, or what?"

Nicholas shrugged. "Anything that gives me a better sense of her state of mind when she ran away."

The more Violet tried to describe Rose—and she seemed to be doing it a lot lately—the more she felt like she was objectifying her, pinning her down as a musical theater girl, the kind of person who sipped Throat Coat tea and asked questions like "Does my voice sound *pitchy* to you?" The sad truth was: her sister was a *really* good actress, but Violet was starting to realize that she had no idea what lurked beneath the public persona Rose was so skilled at putting on.

"I don't know. Rose lived at home, but we were never really that close. Anything I have to say, well, you've probably heard the same thing from Mom and Will. Rose did a lot of school plays. She owned character shoes. She didn't drink milk before big shows. My mom was always buying her shirts that said things like *Drama Queen* and *Broadway Bound*. And some days Rose would sit around for hours doing diction exercises, like *You know New York, you need New York, you know you need unique New York.*"

Nicholas surprised her by laughing. It was a contagious laugh, twinkling and sincere.

Violet went on. "Anyway, halfway through college, she had a kind of quarter-life crisis, dropped her theater major, decided she'd be happier sampling rocks, being some kind of scientist. I guess she's changed her mind since. She's back to vying for a Tony."

"So you two still keep in touch?"

"That's overstating it. It's only a few letters. And she only just started writing me." Nicholas was the first kind and helpful person she'd interacted with since checking herself in. She didn't want to blow it just yet by telling him about seeing Rose. She couldn't stand him thinking she was a hallucinating schizo-person. "It's weird, I feel like her presence has been with me for the past few weeks, and then suddenly she gets in touch now that I'm in the wacky ward."

"Any chance I can get her contact info from you?"

Violet shrugged. "Didn't my mother give it to you?"

"She said she figured the letter she brought you was from Rose, but she didn't copy the address down. She's been trying to give your sister space. She said that's what the police advised her to do."

"Sure, I can give you her addresses. I don't have her phone number."

"That would be great. So do you mind taking me back to the weeks and months before she left? Was Rose fighting with your parents? Anything going on at home that would explain why she'd run away?"

Nicholas must have noticed her sudden squirrel-in-the-road posture. "You can tell me," he said.

"I'm pretty sure Rose got pregnant the spring before she left. I think she had an abortion, and Mom went a little Rick Santorum on her."

"How do you know that?"

He kept his eyes steady as Violet told him about the photo on the desk, but she could tell it wasn't the kind of thing he was expecting. "Cruel and unusual?" she asked.

Nicholas rubbed the back of his neck. "Hard to say. Is your mom especially religious?"

"Only when it's convenient."

"Have you told anyone about this? Your dad? Did you mention it to the police after Rose ran away?"

Violet shook her head. "I should have. I know that. But it's one thing to call bullshit to your family and another thing to call bullshit on them. I didn't want everyone knowing what weirdos we are. Then they found Rose anyway. And I figured she'd been through enough without having to rehash it all over again."

"How did they find her?"

"She'd left a pretty obvious paper trail: cleaned out her bank account a week before she left, filed a leave-of-absence form with SUNY, applied for a couple of new credit cards. She'd left a note for my parents on the seat of her car."

"What did the note say?"

"I don't remember exactly. Something about how she was tired of chasing the carrot on the stick."

"Any idea what she meant by that?"

"I used to think she was tired of playing the game. You know, sick of college. Done with auditions and rehearsals. But after the week I've had, I think the carrot was something else."

"Like what?"

"Love." Violet reddened. "My mom's love is a pretty conditional thing. Rose had spent years trying to earn it. It led her in circles."

"She was disoriented."

"Yeah. Anyway, Rose called my mom up a few weeks later and

told her she was finished with the bunch of us. Her boyfriend, Damien, got on the phone too and told Mom to fuck off. Told her there'd be hell to pay if my mom ever got in touch with them. Not that they even left her a way to do it."

"So, Rose found the love she was looking for in a guy?"

"Guess that's a pretty old story, huh?"

"Can you tell me about Damien?"

"Never met him. You'll have to ask Rose yourself."

Violet found herself wondering, for the first time, whether the abortion was hard on them as a couple.

"Do you remember the name of the investigator you spoke to when you thought Rose was missing?"

"Unh-uh. Sorry."

"No worries. I'll see what I can find out." He looked so sad, Violet knew the question he was going to ask next. "So the night Will was hurt—"

"I told you already. I didn't do it to him."

Nicholas put both hands up. His dark eyelashes beat once. "Will you just listen to me for a second? That's not what I was going to say."

Violet folded her arms, self-protective but resigned.

"I was going to ask if you knew your brother had a seizure that night."

Violet gave a quick shake of her head. "He didn't have one while I was there."

"I've read seizures affect memory."

"I've asked Will what they're like, if he feels any pain. He says they don't hurt. I think it's just lights-out, like going under anesthesia." She paused for a stunned second, and the meaning of this new information sank in. "I think he usually has a hard time remembering the minutes that lead up to the seizure. Even afterward, he's groggy and confused for a while."

"So I'm wondering, did anyone else see the incident? Your dad, maybe?"

"He was drunk. Blacked out, actually. He said so last night at Christ Episcopal Church. There were a roomful of witnesses. Only it's a support group and they have a confidentiality thing. They're not supposed to repeat anything they hear there." Violet glanced down at her yellow bracelet and saw that her hands were trembling. She felt as trapped as she had on the night of her intake.

"Hey." Nicholas's fingertips fell soft on her elbow. "I believe you. That's why I'm here. But right now it's your mom's word against yours. I just wanted to ask if there was somebody else who could come forward and back you up."

"Rose," Violet said suddenly. "I don't know for a fact. But I thought—I don't know, I thought she was there that night. If you're planning to get in touch, you can ask her."

Nicholas nodded. "I'll ask Rose."

Violet saw the compassionate glimmer in Nicholas's eyes and finally saw the real reason she wanted to get out of the hospital, out of her parents' house. There were honest people out there, reasonable people who cared and wanted to help. Not everyone bought into her mother's make-believe. Not everyone thought Violet was on the fast track to bag-ladydom, shrieking gibberish and shaking her fist at vapors. Josephine *was* dangerous. Hers weren't victimless crimes. Just the opposite: Violet's mother made crime-free victims. Other people sensed it too, people like Nicholas, who knew the proof was in the feeling she gave him.

Fresh from her conversation with Nicholas, Violet spent the next forty minutes scrawling another letter to her sister. She was ready to spring and run, to find any escape route, even one that included Rose. Also, Nicholas reminded her of Rose's boyfriend query. She kept coming back to the feeling he'd given her—a warm, rare, decadent feeling that stayed with her, melting like stolen chocolate in her pocket.

Nope, she scrawled with her self-titled colored pencil. *I've never had a boyfriend, officially, and I think it will be a while before I do. What's it like? Are you happier? Is your life more complicated? I can't think of you cohabitating without imagining you roasting Cornish game hens in a black garter, but surely men have feelings beyond, "rawrr sex and food." What was it about Damien that made you run off like a character in a Grimm fairy tale?*

She thought for a minute and added:

You asked about Will. He's definitely not a little boy anymore. And probably not so innocent either, thanks to Mom. It's pretty horrifying, actually, the way Mom treats him like her little husband. Sometimes she calls him "stud." I've even seen her pinch Will's ass. If something doesn't change soon, I'm sure he'll be joining me in here soon. Maybe he'll be treated for depression. More likely he'll come for starting fires or choking the Wildomars' dog.

And do I hate our parents? Yes, I hate our parents. And not for typical teenage reasons either. I hate them for mature reasons. Well-founded reasons. Mom is not "difficult," she's abusive. She's not "different," she's mentally fucking ill. Being here only makes me more dead sure of it.

William Hurst

Will's mother didn't answer when he knocked on the door. He tried the knob. Locked.

"Mom?" he called.

Will had grown up in a house where females outnumbered men, and still he had little idea what women did when they were alone with their lotions, pink razors, and cotton balls. The closest he'd come to finding out was the time that he'd walked in on Violet, then thirteen, screaming that Josephine wouldn't allow her to shave her legs or wear deodorant. Ironically, as the years passed, Violet had just embraced fuzzy shins and organic stinks anyway.

"Mom!" Will called again, louder this time. "I don't want to bother you . . ."

"Then don't!" Her tone was joking, but her laugh had a serrated edge.

When it became clear she wasn't going to open the door, Will wandered down the hall to Rose's room.

He couldn't remember the last time he'd been inside. Before Rose disappeared, the little room with its canopy bed and Holly Golightly posters had seemed adult and off-limits. Afterward, it was like a war zone; police had taken apart Rose's paper lanterns and unpinned all her snapshots from the clothesline where she had them displayed.

Now, Rose's room was more childish than Will remembered. There were still teddy bears lined up on one bookshelf. There was still an old Girl Scout sash in plain sight.

Will was looking for something to bolster his case against Rose. Something that definitely proved that she'd been back to stalk and shake up his family. Sure, Rose was pink macaroons and Violet was hemp seed crackers—Violet was macrame and Rose was rhinestones—but once you got past the surface, the younger female Hursts were one and the same. As far as Will was concerned, *both* his sisters were sick in the brain.

He rifled through wire baskets. Hair-straightening balms oozed into nests of Velcro curlers that were just like his mom's. And what was that about, anyway? Why did girls have to straighten their hair *before* they curled it? Will rattled through about fifty bottles of pink nail polish (if there were subtleties of shade they were lost on him—they all looked *pink*). All the brushes, and compacts, and hair dryer attachments.

Will moved on to the dresser. He had almost forgotten the way his sister dressed. Everything that remained was bright, stretchy as second skin, low-cut in the back, front, or both. Still, the drawers seemed sparse to his eye. Will wasn't sure how much Rose had packed when she ran away, but there seemed like a decent chance she'd sneaked back for more clothes.

The police had done a thorough job stripping the desk. Not that Rose had left behind anything truly telling. She'd made off with all the electronic goodies her parents had bought for her freshman year at SUNY: laptop, memory sticks, external hard drive, and cell phone. Only a few college textbooks remained. As he was leafing through them, a page fluttered out onto the cabbage-rose rug. It was a folded piece of paper, a copy of Rose's schedule from the spring before she ran away, likely printed off before she committed it to memory. Courses like ENG393 and GLG293 meant nothing to him, but he folded it into the pocket of his Scottie dog pants anyway.

He sat on Rose's bed and opened the journal again. Will flipped through the pages, slower this time, scouring for any tidbits he might have missed the first time. When he didn't find anything, he flipped through the pages from the back.

His heart screeched to a momentary halt. There, at week twenty-four, Rose had resumed her diary entries.

At week twenty-four, I am feeling . . . Defeated. Also, trapped and too tired to find a way out. Thought I was fine about everything . . . memories of that giant maxi pad fading. Feel played, but there was no other choice if I wanted to finish school. Even if I transferred to community college and tried to pay myself, Mom still would have refused to fill out my financial aid forms. Of course, there's no such thing as a forced abortion. The counselor asks, "Is anyone forcing you to do this?" And if you say "Yes," they toss you back out on the street with the protesters. I did tell my counselor about the tuition issue. She told me financial strain is the number one reason women terminate, and then handed me a hospital gown.

Feticide, Will thought. A naming word. *The killing of a fetus.*

Will knew what an abortion was, thanks to the time he watched *Dirty Dancing* with Violet. But he never imagined Rose had anything in common with Penny, except for the fact that they both wore lots of leotards and did insanely flexible things with their legs.

Nothing written on weeks twenty-five through twenty-six. Then out of the clear blue, on week twenty-seven, Rose got caps-y. Her straight-up-and-down handwriting started to slant.

Picture on Mom's desk is PROOF, clear-cut PROOF that it doesn't matter what I do. ANY choice is the wrong one! Not because the course of action is wrong, but because, in her eyes, I am WRONG! I'm crumbling. I can't shake the past, and there's nothing to look forward to in the future now that the baby is gone. Opened up my sock drawer and found a pair of pink crocheted baby booties (mine? Violet's?) on top. Evil bitch Mom claims she's "never seen them before." Opened my laptop and found some photographer's online portfolio of newborn portraits. When I went to bed last night, my pillowcase smelled like baby powder. I've got to get out of here. I can't live like this anymore.

The sound of a motorcycle passing the house made Will jump a yard.

It didn't make sense. Will wouldn't let himself believe Rose for a moment. Will's mother had a certain set of expectations, high standards, but she was a mentor, not a tormentor. She was a prime example of the Mark Twain quote she'd taught him: "Really great people make you feel that you, too, can be great."

Bottom line: Rose was wrong. She was mad, and regretful, and making stuff up.

The journal *did* seem to explain why Rose would come back to steal or play tricks on the family.

It was nearing eight p.m. by Rose's alarm clock. Feeling pleased with his detective skills and shocked by his findings, Will went downstairs to resume his nighttime routine.

Doing it without his mom filled him with a sick, growing sense of anxiety. Was he allowed dessert? He skipped it just in case. Would Josephine be angry if he watched the digitally recorded *Dancing with the Stars* without her? To be safe, he watched a reality show about an animal behavior expert who went into people's homes and went sarcastic on them: "Golly gee, owning a pit bull sure does make you more manly." Or "A critter who survives on a bugs and plants in the wild doesn't do so hot when you feed him a diet of Tater Tots. I wonder, why is that?"

Come bedtime, Will was faced with another fraught round of

decision making. Should he run a bath for himself? There was a huge likelihood he'd make a mess in the process, forget a damp towel on the floor, or drip water where he shouldn't.

Will took a chance and skipped the bath, but otherwise he followed his mom's procedure to a T. The childproof caps on his prescription bottles didn't even prove to be a struggle. He flossed meticulously, massaged baby oil into his shoulders and thighs, and white-knuckled it through a few pages of *Anne of Green Gables*.

Why was his mother ignoring him? She never did that unless she was giving him time to reflect on his own bad behavior.

One time, when he was eight or so, Josephine had given him the silent treatment for almost a week. They'd been eating apples together, and he'd made some thoughtless joke like, "Mom, seems like with your big teeth you could take really giant bites." She'd frozen and then immediately left the room. In fact, after that, she left every room the second he walked into it. She'd talk to him in public, but the second they walked through the front door, her cold shoulder returned. Grocery store: chatter. Home: silent as a stone. Car pool: running at the mouth. Home: mum (and not in the way that was mom's synonym). It had taken Will days to figure out the pattern, and by that time he'd literally had his arms wrapped around her ankles. He'd been sobbing, begging for her to acknowledge him in even the smallest way, even if it was only to trip over him.

But it was different now. Now, Will had epilepsy. Now, leaving him alone meant he could have a seizure, bang his head, and bleed out before anyone was the wiser. Exhausted as he was, he found that his eyes stayed pinned open and his brain didn't punch out for the day. Even after the punishment, was his mother *still* mad that he'd botched his CPS interview? He could hear occasional toilet flushings and the chatter of her bedroom TV—he knew she hadn't slipped while getting out of the tub—but he still couldn't shake a feeling like he'd lost her forever.

He decided to rip a blank sheet out of his vocabulary note-book. He wrote his mom a long, vague letter saying he was sorry. He told her she was the most special person in his life. Slipping it under her locked door, he returned to bed.

Will awoke to the sound of his mother's loud, wrenching sobs in the upstairs hallway. He threw off his blanket and was about to run to her when he heard footsteps and his father's tenor echoing. He couldn't tell if his parents were arguing or if Douglas was try-ing to talk Josephine down.

"Please, *please* be a man, for once," his mother was begging. "I can't do *everything*. It's the *least* you can do. Especially after you've been out God-knows-where, with your phone turned off for hours. You don't see me demanding explanations, asking you if the sex was worth it."

Will's father was speaking more softly, but Will could hear him mumble something about how his mother's mind always went to cheating because that was the kind of thing *she* would do.

"What is *wrong* with you?! Really, what is your problem? Do you think you'd feel better after a drink, Douglas? Is *that* it? Why don't we go downstairs? I'll mix you a martini and you can have a good cry. Then maybe you can open your ears and listen to me."

"I don't want a drink, Jo." It was the only time in the conver-sation that his father's voice sounded loud and firm. "And I'm trying to listen to you. Tell me again what happened? And what exactly you want me to do about it?"

Will heard his parents' bedroom door shut as they drifted back inside. His stomach burned.

Was it hours or minutes later that Will's father shook him awake? The bedside lamp backlit its ugly plaid shade. Douglas was crouched on the floor, holding something in his lap. When Will's eyes focused, he realized it was a piece of paper.

"I know it's late, but we really need to talk about this, buddy." Douglas spun the paper around and Will recognized his own handwriting. It was the apology letter he'd written his mother before he went to sleep.

"Oh, that," Will said, trying to force down a yawn. "Mom was upset with me. I wanted to say *sorry*."

"Well, at least you knew enough to apologize. But this is one of those times when saying *sorry* doesn't automatically make things better."

The wave of shame started at the crown of Will's head. It dripped down onto his sagging shoulders. He felt disgusting and disgusted by himself, even though he wasn't sure why.

"Will? Will. Don't cry. It's all right. But we need to talk about that word. What it means, and where you learned it."

Was he talking about the interview—Violet's drugs? Did his dad mean *marijuana*? As far as Will remembered, he hadn't even said the word aloud. He'd only drawn it best he could on a piece of paper.

"Violet taught me," he told his dad. "The word, I mean. Because I walked in and saw hers by mistake."

His dad's expression changed suddenly at the mention of Violet. Douglas's eyes flashed from bafflement to horror before settling on a look of protective, papa-bear rage.

"Leave your sister out of this. That word is a slur, especially when someone without one says it to someone who has one. It's derogatory. That means it takes something away from the person you say it to."

Will wanted to say he knew what *derogatory* meant.

As if reading Will's mind, his dad went on to say: "I shouldn't have to tell you this, buddy. Aren't you the guy whose tests showed he was gifted in reading and vocabulary? You're a very smart boy, Will. I think you know that. And I know socializing is hard for you."

Will had his quilt balled in his fist. Why did someone who had never taken any interest in Will's conditions get to wake him up in the middle of the night to tell him to hurry up and get over them?

He opted for Violet-esque sarcasm: "Thanks, *Dad*. Good talk. Next time I'll remember not to use the word *marijuana* unless I've smoked some."

"What?" Douglas's face had paled. The little lamp brought out the tired grooves in his forehead. "You think I'm here to talk to you about the word *marijuana*?"

Will shrugged.

"Will, I was talking about the word *cunt*. During your piano lesson, you called your mother a cunt."

Will's breath caught. He was looking at Douglas without seeing him. He rewound back to that afternoon's lesson. He saw his dumb hand prodding the keys. He saw his mother on the fainting couch, her feet massaging each other in sensual, satisfied motions.

Will had never dared *think* the word his father was accusing him of speaking, but maybe there was a chance he'd called his mother something? Some name she'd misheard?

"Will?" His father had him by the shoulders now. "Your mother told me you called her a cunt. I'm going to ask you again, did you call your mother . . . that name?"

Will began to nod, but he was a second too late.

"Right," Douglas said, strangling one bedpost as he rose to his feet. The doorknob slammed against the wall as he flung Will's bedroom door open. He froze for a second at the threshold but didn't glance back at Will. Instead he barked, "Go to sleep."

VIOLET HURST

VIOLET HANDED IN her stamped envelope to Rose at the nurses' station, and the nurse handed her a slip of paper back.

"What's this? A receipt?" Violet joked, but the woman's sagging face didn't shift.

"Phone message."

Violet unhalved the pink paper and quickly realized the call had been logged because it was a message from CPS. Beneath the *While You Were Out* heading a nurse had printed Nicholas's name and checked the box that instructed Violet to *Please call*. The nurse's handwriting was anally legible, possibly a reaction to years of dealing with doctors' pretentious chicken scratches. In the space for notes, she had penned: FYI, *both addresses you submitted were not residences. They are UPS stores. Rose must keep P.O. boxes there.*

At a quarter to dinnertime, Violet was resting her head on the gray table in the visitors' lounge, waiting for her father to finish his progress report with her therapist.

Under the soupy fluorescent glare, Violet unfolded Rose's letters and examined them again. Rose must have known Violet would assume she was writing from her home addresses. It was so unfair for Rose to pass her UPS address off as her home, keeping herself firmly in the shadows herself, beyond consequences and out of Violet's reach.

"Hi," Douglas said suddenly, just as Violet was refolding the letters and stuffing them in the ankle of Edie's borrowed boots.

"Hey," she replied, choosing not to go in for a hug.

After they took their chairs, the room filled with an eerie, underwater hush. "Are you going to a meeting tonight?" Violet said, just to say *something.*

"I think I'll try to make the seven thirty at Saint John the Divine."

"That's my favorite thing about meetings—the way people talk about them like movie times."

"Your therapist says you've been attending them every day."

As usual, her dad turned formal, almost lawyerly whenever he dealt with her, especially in a crisis. She would have much rather he cursed and screamed.

Violet nodded. "Five meetings in five days."

"Do you find them beneficial?"

"I appreciate the honesty people show there," she said pointedly. "Your speech was really honest. But harder to appreciate, obviously, because it made me feel lied to. I didn't know you were trying to"—she had to fight the sarcastic tic on the coming word—"recover."

"No," he said. "No, I haven't told anyone."

"Why not?"

"It seems to me everyone in this family has secrets. Some of your secrets have come to light this week."

It was a very subtle, Hurst-like shifting of blame, and Violet felt her face harden in spite of itself.

"Also," Douglas said, "I didn't want anyone to sabotage my efforts."

"You mean Mom."

"I mean, *anyone*."

"But you were"—Violet couldn't bring herself to use the word *wasted*—"drinking the night you brought me here. Who sabotaged you, then?"

"Oh, Violet, people slip. That night was a stumble, not a fall. Addiction is a chronic, relapsing disease. It's not easy. In order to succeed, I have to put sobriety in front of everything else in my life."

Violet was not in the mood for a canned recovery-speak answer. "Is that so? You have to put sobriety in front of your kids? Even if one of them's in the hospital? And the other one's stuck at home all day with no friends and no one to talk to? It seems to me you've been putting yourself first for a long time. And how honest are you really—when you got blackout drunk less than a week before your rousing speech?" Violet's hands were shaking. She was finding it difficult to keep her voice down.

"I know what I did," Douglas said. "I'm not sugarcoating it. My sponsor, Kerry—"

"Kerry." Violet had failed to make the connection during the meeting. Over the past few months, she'd heard him taking lots of calls from Kerry, but it had sounded like a woman's name. Carrie.

"Yes, Kerry. I know him from the Sterling Forest office. We've been examining what I was doing and thinking prior to me taking that first drink. That way I can get better at spotting the warning signs and avoiding future slips."

"The *warning signs*?" Violet was livid. "How's this for a warning sign? Our family is so miserable that my sister *ran away*. Ran away because our mother was *terrorizing* her. Want another warning sign? You let everyone think that I slashed up my brother, when you were too slaughtered to remember how it happened. How's this for a red flag? Child Protective Services came to our house to investigate the welfare of my brother, your son."

Douglas's eyes were bloodshot, blazing with rebuff. He shook his head. "No, they didn't."

"*Yes*, they *did*."

The color drained from Douglas's cheeks, and for a moment he looked like a statue from one of Violet's childhood story books—a villager turned to stone. "When? When did CPS come?"

"I don't know! You're the one who's been home! I've been here. I only know because the guy—the caseworker—came to see me."

Douglas raked his fingers down his six-o'clock shadow. "What did he want to know?"

"Why Rose ran away, mostly."

"You told him about Damien?"

"I told him what I should have told the police to begin with. I said Mom and Rose were fighting like rabid squirrels over Rose's abortion."

Douglas's half-mast shoulders slumped even further. "I didn't know you knew about that. Yes, your mother worried that having a baby so young would ruin Rose's life. Jo didn't want Rose to have to sacrifice everything she'd worked so hard for."

Violet was about to ask whether he meant Rose or her mother had worked hard, but then his deeper meaning sank in.

"Wait," she said, hearing the strange echo her voice made in the small, empty room. "You think Mom pressured Rose to have an abortion?"

"*Pressured* is a strong word. She thought it was the right course of action."

"Mom *tortured* Rose for having an abortion. She showed Rose a hideous photo of a dead baby. I saw it with my own eyes. She called Rose a murderer. She said she was going to hell."

"Violet, I'm not calling you a liar, but that just doesn't make sense. Why would your mother give Rose a hard time before *and* after she had an abortion?"

Looking at Douglas, it occurred to Violet that he didn't know true from wrong, real from utter fantasy. He looked so boyishly small and confused—his overcoat too big for his computer-geek frame. Violet thought again of the way Nicholas said dangerous people try to keep you off-balance and constantly questioning yourself.

Violet felt for her father in his confusion, she really did, because she was beginning to understand why it had once felt so good to be thinner than the skeleton in her science classroom. Those old symptoms—that twisting pain in her stomach, the migraine headaches, the heart palpitations, the dizzy feeling that made the whole world look like it was positioned on a slant—had been comforting because she'd known exactly what caused them: lack of food. By comparison, life before starvation was agony without logic, bafflement without any identifiable cause.

"I know how your mother can be. And I know tensions are running high between the two of you. Were you able to talk it out when she came to see you?"

"See me *here*? Mom told you she *visited*? She never visited. She won't even return my therapist's phone calls. She lies, Dad, she can't control it. What's it going to take for you to stop believing her? Didn't it ever occur to you to stand up for me? To help me get released? You think everything's about you! You and your sobriety! You're as self-obsessed as she is!"

Douglas raised his chin defensively. "That's not fair, Violet! I'm doing my best!"

"Well then, your best is epically shitty! She's a psycho, Dad. She can't control that! But you have a choice! You could do the right thing, but you don't!"

"I am *RECOVERING*, Violet!"

Douglas's roaring voice brought a nurse to the door, but Violet didn't care. She'd had enough.

"Great! You're recovering, while the rest of us are SUFFERING!"

"Visiting hours are over," the nurse said.

"I am not an abusive parent," Douglas said, standing, dead-eyed, flailing his arms into his overcoat.

"No, you're not, Dad. You're a bystander. And if you ask me, that's even worse."

Violet's heart pounded as she watched Douglas thunder out the door with a broken expression that didn't match his puffed-up posture. She felt as sick-stomached and sorry as she ever did when she lost her temper at home. She felt guilty for raging against a man who couldn't do better, and stupid for confiding every feeling and resentment to someone who had no basic ability to hear or understand them. But once she got past the self-punishing voice—*You took the bait again*, it said, *you stirred up the family drama*—Violet took some small comfort in the fact that she'd been honest. She'd been real. She'd finally told him how she felt. She wasn't acting as vacant as Douglas, or Will, or the old blank Rose before she ran away. And maybe that was a sign that her mom hadn't driven her crazy yet. Now, if only Rose felt the same, they could join forces, help each other in the fight not to become like the people who'd raised them and let the rest of the Hurst family go to hell.

Dinner was intestine-y pasta slathered in ectoplasmic pesto. The definition of "food" in the hospital was incredibly loose. Still, Violet wolfed as much of it as she could manage. *Sallekhana* was officially a thing of the past. Even if Violet lived the rest of her life in misery and substance dependency, she was going to keep living if only to spite her parents. She was going to stop trying to forgive her mother, and get to work on outliving her. She hustled to the phone booths to return Nicholas's call before her evening meeting.

"Violet Femme," he said. "Sorry, stupid joke. I'm glad you got my message. I sent snail mail to both addresses you gave me. Made me feel like I was back in 1994. Do you know how to reach Rose by phone?"

Violet felt protective of her sister, and the feeling surprised her. Violet didn't want anyone else speaking to her before she got the chance, especially not their parents. "Nope. Rose only wants to play pen pal for now."

"Ramblin' Rose," he whistled. "Sorry, I only pun when I've been at my desk too long. At least she's in contact with you. I spoke to Detective Donnelly at the Kingston Police Department—he inherited the case after the last investigator transferred departments—and it looks like Rose was declared voluntarily missing on account of her financials and the fact that she's over the age of majority. The law recognizes her right to remain out of contact with your folks, but Donnelly said he'd review the file anyway, just so we can talk to her and make sure she didn't sustain any abuse while she was living at home."

"No point," Violet said. "There was no physical abuse. Only emotional stuff."

"Hey," he said softly. "Abuse is abuse. If you ask me, the emotional stuff is some of the worst. I guarantee pretty much every battered woman I see was an emotionally abused kid, especially the ones who come in talking about how it's their fault, how they just can't seem to stop provoking him."

"Yeah, well. The way the girls in here talk, I doubt many family court judges share your concern."

"Things are changing," he said. "A jury in Florida found a

mother guilty of child abuse in the case of her teenage daughter's suicide. She'd never laid a hand on her. But she'd forced her to work as a dancer and lived off her tips."

"My sister was pretty sheltered before she ran away. The only pole Rose ever touched was a fishing pole. On second thought, I'm not even sure she's done that."

Nicholas's exhale sent a ripple through the receiver and down Violet's spine. "Well, I'd feel a whole lot better if I could talk to her. I can see if she has any insights on this Will situation, and while I'm at it, I can make sure this Damien is an okay guy."

"Nicholas?"

"Yeah?"

Violet wanted to ask if it was okay to call him Nicholas, and also why he was confiding so much in her. But she wasn't sure she could handle the rejection if he said it was purely a matter of pro-tocol. Some vicious, paranoid inner voice—Josephine's echo—was already piping up to tell her Nicholas was just pumping her for information he could use against her. Instead she asked, "How hard is it to get emancipated?"

"Depends. You'd have to wait a year, until you're seventeen. You'd have to move away from your parents, refuse any financial support from them, and get a job."

Violet allowed herself a moment of wondering whether Mrs. Dekker would hire her full-time, but then it hit her like a ton of bricks: if she divorced her parents, she couldn't possibly stay in Stone Ridge. In a town of less than twelve hundred people, she'd be sure to bump into her parents at the Rite-Aid or the bank, and all the while, her mother would be spreading Lord knows what kind of gossip about Violet to her friends from the historical soci-ety and Saint Peter's Church. Josephine was too powerful. She'd already had Violet locked up for almost a week; who knew how much damage she could do if Violet was living just a couple of blocks away? No, Violet would have to move to a city with good public transportation and a slew of barista and retail jobs. If not New York City, then Hudson, at least. Beryl was an option, but Beryl was sick and Violet would be an imposition. What's more, the Fields' house was apt to be the first place her mom looked for her.

"You'd probably qualify for Medicaid and student loans," Nicholas said. "You could finish out high school at a community college, where your credits could be applied to your undergrad too. But emancipation isn't always the clean break you think it will be. You might still need your parents' permission to get your driver's license or routine healthcare. But I'll help you file all the forms, if that's what you decide to do."

Violet was taken aback at his willingness to help. "Thanks. I'm just feeling out my options."

"No problem. Hey, can I ask you one more question? Do you remember how old Will was when he got his autism diagnosis?"

"It was last year," Violet said. "So he would have been eleven. I'm assuming you have his medical records."

"Not yet. If it comes to it, I can try to subpoena them. Anyway, I just wondered. Eleven is a little late for the onset of autism."

"I think Mom probably watched some nightly news special about high-functioning autism, and got it in her head that Will fit the bill. The first doctor wasn't so sure, so she dragged him around for second and third opinions."

"Do you remember what the other diagnoses were?"

"Mom never said."

"Do you think Will would know?"

"I doubt she told him either."

"Do you worry about your brother? You think he's okay?"

"Inside our family, he's more okay than any of us. Outside our family, well . . ."

"Violet, can you think of any reason that your mom would want to hurt Will?"

It was impossible to ascribe normal human motives to her mother, but she couldn't actually imagine Josephine going that far.

"I don't know," Violet said, honestly. "It might just be that Will's so close to becoming a teenager. Mom takes puberty personally. She gets weird about it." Each normal teen milestone had been a fight. Their mother had made Rose wear a Hanes sweatsuit to her first dance. She consistently left Violet's makeup bag on the bathroom radiator "by accident," causing everything inside to melt.

"Look, I probably shouldn't be telling you this, but I've been working for eleven hours straight and I drank some kind of energy drink that I thought was grapefruit juice. When I said would your mom hurt Will, I meant would she really hurt him? She's said from the beginning that Will grabbed the knife from your hand, but the doctor at the hospital had concerns . . ."

"Concerns like what?"

"Well, it wasn't a very clean wound. It was cut in a few places. *Shredded*, that's the word the doctor used."

WILLIAM HURST

ANXIETY GNAWED AT Will's stomach as he dressed for the day and rehearsed ways to apologize to his mother for that horrendous word.

Will hadn't said it, he was (pretty) firm about that. But *something* he'd said had twisted like a game of telephone before it reached Josephine's ears. Only, not many words sounded like the offending one. *Blunt? Grunt? Up front?* Few were his style. Even fewer fit the context of the piano lesson.

Still, Will crept downstairs feeling remorseful.

Josephine was sitting on the couch, watching *The View* over a steaming mug of hot chocolate. She fixed one for him too because he'd never confided that the smell made him nauseated. He breathed through his mouth and held the cup very far away from him, where he couldn't see the mini-marshmallows doing the dead man's float.

"Mom, I just want to say, I'm really sorry—"

His apology was drowned out by the sound of the studio audience clapping.

"I said I'm really sorry about what I said during my piano lesson."

"Ugh, Will." Josephine sighed. Her face was unadulterated disgust. "Please don't even mention it."

Will wondered if now was the right time to bring up Rose's journal, and decided to risk it. "I want you to know I know about Rose," he said.

His mother hit the Mute button on the remote. "What are you jabbering about now, Will?" she said, spinning to look him dead in the eyes.

Heat rose to Will's face and he felt the words jamming in his throat. He realized he'd made a terrible miscalculation. Mentioning Rose now was far more likely to annoy her than impress her with his fine detective skills.

"*What*, Will? What about Rose?"

"Nothing . . ." Will rubbed his cheek, self-consciously.

Her voice flared. "How many times do I have to tell you to keep your hands off your face?! It's no wonder you're practically polka-dotted. I swear, Will . . . Twelve is just too young for acne. It's too young. You're so handsome, Will, but you need to keep your skin in check."

Papuliferous: pimply.

"I've been using the soap you gave me," he said. "I'll keep my hands off my face. I just wondered if Rose is coming back to get us because she's mad at you."

Josephine sighed heavily. "There is a chance that your sister is"—she seemed to fish for a word—"*resurfacing*. Apparently she thinks I destroyed her life, and she's taking revenge on our family as a whole. She sees all of you as an extension of me."

Will didn't know what to say.

She gave him an encouraging half-smile. "Don't worry about it too much. There's nothing to be afraid of. If Rose wants to get to you, she'll have to get through me first. I have it taken care of. I won't let anything happen to you."

Will felt his stomach settling. There was nothing to worry about. His mother loved him. She lived for him.

"We should take a walk on the rail trail soon," Josephine said over a commercial. "We could hunt for some frogs for that habitat I got you."

Will tried not to show his surprise. "I think it's too late for that," he said. He was hoping it didn't sound like criticism.

"What do you mean?" Josephine asked. She seemed dreamy and half-listening, closing her eyes and running her fingers through her hair.

"It's just—They're probably hibernating already. Burying themselves in the mud. Going way down into the bottom of the creek beds."

"Oh, do frogs hibernate?"

Will was scared to say more. His mother hated know-it-alls.

"Will, you're such an observant boy," she turned to him and said, for the second time that week. "There's no getting anything past you. So I'm just going to be honest with you."

The blood slowed in Will's veins. He pulled his legs even closer to his chest.

"After Rose ran away, she didn't do very well on her own. When I found her, she was living in abhorrent conditions, and the things she was doing for money . . . well, they were things no one like Rose should have to resort to."

Will wondered if she meant dancing? *Ecdysiast*, a naming word for a striptease performer. Prostitution? Singing on subway platforms? With his mother, there was no way to be sure.

"So I set her up with a decent apartment under the strict conditions that she dump that boyfriend, get a good day job, and return to acting. And for a while she did. She did very well. She restored our trust and we were so proud of her."

We—Will shoved his instinctive jealousy aside and realized that his father must have hired that investigator after all. The PI had located Rose, but for some reason, Will's parents didn't want her to be found by anyone else. But why? It was like Rose was being quarantined, like her defiance could infect the rest of the family.

"Why can't me and Violet talk to her?"

"Why can't *Violet and I* talk to her? Anyway, we wanted to let you. But we thought it best to give Rose a trial period. She was so unstable. I didn't want her upsetting you." Josephine didn't even try to fight back her tears. "Oh, Will, if you had any idea how your sister used to treat me. The *anger*. You've never seen anything like it."

"She was mad at you because she wanted a baby."

She looked stunned for a minute. Even so, she didn't ask how Will knew, and so he didn't bring up the journal.

"Your sister didn't really want a baby. She didn't know *what* she wanted. Everything with that pregnancy, it was all just an excuse to cut me off. For months, I could feel her planning it, looking for ways to justify abandoning me—us. Anyway, the trial period didn't last." She laughed bitterly. "Rose's true colors came shining through."

"What happened?"

"She went back to that Damien character, who turned her against us even worse. I think he blames us for the decision Rose made."

"The decision not to have the baby?"

His mother nodded. "We've only ever talked on the phone that once. But I don't have to meet him to know he doesn't really care about Rose. He's just using her."

"For what?"

"What else? Her youth. Her beauty. The fact that she's bound to be famous one day. If it weren't for him, she'd probably be famous already. Who knows what ambition Rose has left, now that she's channeling all her energy into destroying us."

"*Destroying us?*"

There was his mother's almost-grin. Frightened as Josephine may have been, Will could feel her low-level excitement. Despite everything she was saying, she seemed glad to be back on Rose's radar. Being hated by Rose was still an improvement over being ignored by her.

The sick feeling grew in Will's stomach. "What's Rose going to do to us?"

"I honestly have no idea," Josephine said. "If someone had come to us two years ago and said Rose would be keying our car and tearing up our family photos, I'd have told them they were crazy. I would have said, Rose would never dream of doing anything like that. Will, she's tried to *steal* from us. I could see her trying to commit fraud or destroy our credit. But mostly, I'm worried she might try to come between us. I fear she might turn you kids against me."

Will was outraged. "Rose could never turn me against you."

"Thank you for saying that," she said, muffing his ears with her palms and kissing him on the brow. Her hands slipped to Will's cheeks. "Even so, I want you to promise you'll come to me if your sisters say anything—and I mean, *anything*—about me. That way, I can dispel any falsehoods they tell you. I won't have them spreading lies that could destroy me and this family."

"Mom?" Will said. He felt so disoriented, so divorced from himself and his fear, like he was being sucked backward through a tunnel.

"What?" Her hands abruptly fell from Will's face.

"That letter you brought Violet—the one with the wax seal?"

"Yes?"

"That was from Rose, wasn't it?"

"I assume so," she said sadly.

"Should we be worried that Rose is telling lies to Violet?"

"Probably." She gave a glib little shrug. "And probably Violet will believe her. But what am I supposed to do about it? Your sister's a big girl, and she's already made up her mind. She expects me—and the rest of this family—to be perfect. She just can't take me as I am. There's just no winning with her."

"Violet's just so miserable she hates it when anyone else is happy," Will said confidently.

Josephine reached out and took his hand in hers. "Thank you for saying that. I thank God every day that one of my children is normal."

It felt good to hear her call him that. Although there were times when these reclassifications—"disabled" to "gifted," "gifted" to "normal"—gave Will whiplash.

She squeezed his fingers a notch harder. "You're going to be an influential writer, Will. One for the ages. You're so gifted, I can barely keep up with you. I've been thinking, how would you like to go to prep school? Maybe even in England? Be among other mature, intellectual boys—your equals?"

Will's stomach collapsed in on itself. "But my—"

"Epilepsy? Autism? I'm worried that we've been wrong to let them hold you back."

"I'd be too homesick. I'd miss you."

"We'll go with you. Or I will, at least. Your father and Violet can stay here. Anyway, it's food for thought. Let it percolate. Tell me . . . In an ideal world, if you could do anything this afternoon, anything at all, what would it be?"

"Language arts," he said. "Homophones." That was where they'd left off a week ago, when they stopped his schoolwork.

Josephine's smile was tinged with pity. Probably she'd been

expecting an answer like go-carts or the Six Flags amusement park. "Right," she said. "Homophones. Can you name me one?"

"*Rose*," Will blurted, as if possessed. "It can mean either the flower, or the past tense of *rise*." He knew it displeased her, but he couldn't help it. It was the first and only word that came to mind.

Violet Hurst

Corinna picked up the phone, as she had made the scarred telephone booths her second room. She stood there for hours, talking to Leatherboy, despite repeated warnings from the nurse on call ("Corinna, girl, you should be charging by the hour"). "Violet!" she called, holding up the receiver. "Papa bear!"

Violet felt her stomach turn over as she walked to the phone booth. She couldn't stand the thought of a repeat of the conversation they'd had at visiting hours. "Hello?"

"Violet."

"Yeah, Dad. What's up?"

"I was hoping—" He took a deep sip of something, hopefully something whose strength wasn't measured by volume. "I need you to tell me more about this CPS investigation."

"I'll give you Nick Flores's number. But I've already told you everything I know."

"You haven't told me much of anything."

"I don't know anything! I am begging you, talk to Mom directly! I can't be your go-between!" Violet tried to steady herself with one of the deep, nasal breaths from her meditation DVDs. "I'm in a locked ward, Dad. I can't go anywhere. Unless you're going to finally get me out of here."

There was silence on the line.

"Dad? Are you going to help me get out of here or not?"

"I'm trying, Violet. But I don't know how you expect me to help you when you're withholding information from me."

"Mom is the one withholding information. You need to stand up to her."

"You and I are very different people, Violet. I don't see that rocking the boat is going to help matters much."

"It's not rocking the boat, Dad. It's called communication. You're allowed to ask questions. Other people do it all the time. Other people don't live in fear of someone else's reactions. They don't relentlessly stress out about getting into trouble."

Smoking her first cigarette of the day, Violet worried that she'd been too harsh with her dad. Still, she was floored by his repeated failures to acknowledge her predicament. What little they'd spoken to each other since Violet's intake had been about either Rose or him, namely his sobriety or failures at it.

When was Douglas going to ask *her* how she felt about staying in a place that used four-point restraints? Among some patients who were public masturbators and others who "spoke" fluent jabberwocky? When was he going to apologize for drunk-driving to the hospital? Or ask what *she* remembered about Friday night? She'd been evicted from her life and—shitty as her life had been, willing as she had been to throw it away—that still sucked. Hospital life didn't feel like living. It felt like an airport, some dehumanizing, transitional space where the flights were delayed and most people treated each other with less care than they gave their luggage.

Violet was listening to the morning birdsong and wondering why the hospital staff didn't consider smoking "suicidal behavior," when she heard the *fwip* of Edie's Zippo springing open.

"Morning, sunshine."

"Violet? That *is* you, isn't it?" Edie's eyes were the glassiest Violet had ever seen them, and the pillow marks on her cheek gave her skin a texture that called to mind tenderized meat.

"It's me. Are you all right?"

"Yeah, I really need to quit these things." Edie waved her cigarette. "I'm so addicted, I'm having my morning smoke before I've even put in my contacts."

"Have you ever quit before?"

"Once. It wasn't that bad. I only really missed the morning cigarette. And the one after meals." She exhaled woefully. "Plus the after-sex one. And the really bored one. Also the ones when I was studying, and when I was driving."

"Sounds like quitting's a breeze."

"Aside from going no contact with my mother, it was the hardest thing I've ever done. Why is it so hard to say good-bye to something even when you know it's a slow-growing cancer?"

It was unlike Edie to miss sarcasm.

"You're sure you're okay?" Violet asked. "Did they change your meds again?"

Edie shook her head. "No. I'm fine. Sorry. It seems I'm only capable of two moods lately: depressed or pissed off."

"I'm with you there," Violet said, stubbing out her cigarette on the underside of her chair. She'd already made the mistake of trying to stamp one out with her hospital slipper, singeing an angry circle in the sole.

"Why? What's going on?"

"Nothing. Just my dad keeps calling to ask me about the stuff that concerns everyone but me." She explained about Douglas and CPS.

"Triangulation," Edie said sadly, fanning the smoke away from her face. "It's how fucked-up families communicate. Instead of talking to each other directly, everything goes through a third party. If one person controls all the information, they can lie or pit people against each other. Let me guess, your mom usually plays the role of the family interpreter?"

Violet nodded. She never stopped being surprised by how well Edie instinctively understood the Hursts.

"Your dad's probably just coming to you because he's afraid to set her off."

Violet had never really thought about the way Josephine inserted herself firmly in the middle of everyone else's relationships. Their mother hadn't just fostered competition between Violet and Rose, she'd also made it next to impossible for Violet to get to know Will.

"Some mothers *cannot* love," Edie said, her voice a touch too aggressive and loud. "Ask any farmer, they'll tell you some moms just aren't naturals. Having a baby doesn't make you a mother any more than buying a piano makes you fucking Beethoven."

Later, in computer lab, Violet watched Edie out of the corner of her eye, thinking how hollowed-out her friend looked. Edie's lips were raw and cracked. There was a knackered slump to her shoulders, and even her Tahitian-blue eyes seemed muddled and flat. Edie didn't even look up from her computer screen when one of their favorite schizophrenics started coaxing her desktop as if it were a horse, saying, "You'd better be good, or I won't give you an apple when we get home."

Violet went to Facebook and pulled up Rose's friend Amelia. According to Amelia's profile, she was a corps dancer at the Rochester City Ballet. Violet knew how to pronounce *corps*, but the word always made her think of *corpse*. And indeed, there was something distinctly corpselike about Amelia's profile picture. It was a headshot, and Amelia was long-nosed, long-haired, and unsmiling in it—her head tilted backward over her shoulder as if someone out of frame were pulling her down by the ends of her lusterless low ponytail.

Violet had met Amelia only once or twice, both times after school plays, when Amelia and Rose were still flushed and sweating through their pancake makeup, awkwardly juggling cellophane-wrapped bouquets while they air-kissed their castmates.

Now Violet could see how Rose and this girl once made an unapproachable pair. Amelia and Rose both looked courtly and weight-conscious. Both seemed stingy with smiles.

Violet wrote Amelia with the number of the hospital pay phone, asking her to call when she could. It was a desperate move, but Violet was trying all possible options. She needed her sister's help to get out. If Rose had been at Old Stone Way, Violet needed her to help clear her of the possible charges against Will. If she waited for her dad to step up to the plate, she'd be waiting forever.

At the computer beside her, Corinna slammed one excited palm on the table. "Fucking Edie!" Corinna shouted. "You never said today was your fucking birthday!"

Edie just looked up with the same haunted face she'd been wearing all day. "Huh?" she said. "How did you know?"

"It's right here on your Facebook timeline. You sneaky, sneaky bitch . . ."

The woman who'd been speaking to her computer as though it were a pony began to sing "Happy Birthday" to the tune of what sounded like Céline Dion's "My Heart Will Go On." It was at that point that Edie finally broke down and cried, big roaring tears that did not stop until she ripped out the keyboard, noosed the cord around her neck, and got herself escorted to the "quiet room."

William Hurst

When Will's father got home from work, he pulled the family calendar from the wall and proceeded to pore over it in the breakfast nook.

"Who is Trina?" Douglas asked, underlining her name with his pointer finger.

"You've met Trina." Will's mother took off her new hat and set it down on the kitchen island. "From the historical society. She came by to discuss next year's stone house tour. There's some kind of controversy brewing already. The Allerton House won't participate if the Fletcher House is. The Fletchers have exposed the beams in their living room, and it's no longer historically accurate."

The tightness returned to Will's chest. He had a strong urge to leave the room, but he felt like he was caught in invisible gunfire.

There was a small chainsawing sound as Josephine used the electric opener on the bottle they'd bought at the artisan wine shop. She poured a big glass and set it down on the table in front of Will's dad.

Douglas spun the glass once and then nudged it away. "Jo, has Child Protective Services been here?"

Josephine froze, and Will felt the air pressure change in the room. She didn't seem guilty, exactly, but for a split second he could feel her mounting shame. Just as quickly, it was gone, replaced by pure, accusatory rage.

"I told you that yesterday, Douglas. What is *wrong* with you? Do you have early-onset Alzheimer's or something?"

"Jo, I think I'd remember something as important as—"

"No! I'm sorry, Douglas. That's bullshit. You do a very good *impression* of someone who's listening, but unless something pertains to you directly—"

"I'd say a government agency trying to take my children away pertains to me—"

"Listen to yourself! You are so cold. So self-absorbed! You make us feel bad about ourselves sixty percent of the time. You shame us for trying to be close to you. Ask your son. Go on, Douglas. Ask him if he's terrified of you. Will feels like you only take an interest in him if you need something. He feels like you don't even know him. Look at Take Your Kid to Work Day. You left him alone in your office all day. You left him alone at the table when you took him out to lunch."

Spirate, a describing word meaning "voiceless."

Tears were sliding down Will's face, so something she'd said rang true.

When he finally found the courage to look up, his father had left the room, maybe even the house. His mother was sitting in the bay window, drinking Douglas's glass of wine and leafing through a Lands' End catalog. "So, cereal for dinner?" she asked, barely glancing up from the luggage page.

When Will didn't answer, she looked up with a consoling smile and opened her arms for a bear hug. "Oh, darling, don't you worry about him. Your father takes great pleasure in making other people feel crazy." She licked one fingertip and turned the page while Will curled into her lap. "Really, William. All these tears . . . It's *okay*. You don't have anything to worry about. I won't ever let your father do the kinds of things to you that he did to Rose. Now tell me, what do you think about this wheeled duffel bag? I've been thinking . . . if we start applying to boarding schools, you're really going to need a monogrammed suitcase."

Violet Hurst

When the nurse said there was a friend who wanted to see her, Violet's thoughts instantly went to Edie.

The seclusion room, or "quiet room," was the stuff of movies, bare of everything except a wafer-thin mattress. Watching Edie get escorted there by her elbow, Violet had feared her friend would be treated to leather straps and benzo-filled syringes. But Sara-pist explained that the quiet room was just a place to "escape painful stimuli" or "experience strong emotions." The door to the quiet room even stood ajar, although Violet and the rest of the patients were forbidden from peeking inside.

But it wasn't Edie who was asking for Violet. It was Imogene, sitting in the visitors' lounge with Violet's school books and a box of sweets from Krause's Chocolates in Saugerties.

Imogene looked more out of place than ever. She was twiddling her silver ear cuff. Her rainbow-tipped hair fanned over the back of her chair. The notice she was eyeing read: VISITORS PLEASE WASH HANDS BEFORE AND AFTER EACH VISIT WITH PATIENTS. Violet and her friends called it the DON'T FEED THE ANIMALS sign.

"Holy shit." Imogene's Indian bangles jingled as she opened

her arms and gave Violet a hug. "Are you okay? This place is creepy. I always imagined these hospitals being like the heaven scenes in movies. You know, all clean and white. But this place . . . I think it's already given me asbestos poisoning."

Violet felt like she didn't have time to laugh. Her mind was already jumping ahead to all the questions she wanted to ask. "How did you get here?"

"Finch drove. He said to tell you sorry. He just couldn't come in." Violet's heart sank. Imogene puffed her cheeks and exhaled. "He has, you know . . . this thing about hospitals."

"I know. How is she?" Violet couldn't bring herself to say Beryl's name, as if doing so made her diagnosis more real.

"Same."

"How are you?"

"I'm honestly not that sad anymore. It's life. I've tried to stop worrying about Mom dying. We just kinda hang out. When she's feeling low, I comfort her. When I'm feeling low, she comforts me. At least she's got a new oncologist. He says she's the healthiest sick person he's ever met."

Violet's gut warmed at the thought of Beryl. She was absolutely the first person she wanted to see when she left Fallkill. If she ever left Fallkill.

"How's Dekker's?"

"Weird. Finch said cops turned up last night after close. Lots of them. Mrs. D won't say why." Imogene took the lid off the chocolate box and revealed an assortment of their favorite chocolate-covered lemon peels and sea-salt caramels. Violet shook her head *no thanks*. "So I still don't get what happened," Imogene said. "Jasper's brother's wife said she saw your mom and Will at the play group in Rosendale, and your mom was downplaying, telling everyone Will's hand was just a kitchen accident."

"Do you know any of them by name? Does Jasper know them?

Could they vouch for me? You know I didn't do it, right? You believe me? I can't get anyone to take me seriously about this."

"Obviously . . . You couldn't hurt a fly, even if you were tripping your face off."

Violet took a breath. "There are three options the way I see it. Will hurt himself; Mom hurt him; or Rose did it."

"*Rose?*" Imogene's eyebrow stud twinkled.

"I thought I saw her there, in the house that night."

"Violet, we were on *seeds*. I thought I saw God, and he looked like Bill Murray. Why would Rose come back?"

"Because she's angry. Or because she wants something. Or because she's the one who's responsible for all the creepy shit that's been happening at home. At first I thought it was Mom, trying to sabotage me, but the timing of it all . . . I'm starting to think Rose is the one who keyed the car and tore herself out of our photos." Violet unfolded the envelopes she was carrying in her jeans pocket.

"Is this Rose's address in the city?"

"It's a UPS store. Rose bought a box there."

"Maybe she doesn't have a doorman?" Imogene offered.

"Maybe she wants the kind of arm's-length relationship where she can reach us, but we can't reach her."

"But why? I mean, why would anybody do that? It doesn't make sense." Imogene was studying her. The glittery magenta shadow on her eyelids did nothing to lessen the intensity of her stare. "Your mom called my mom yesterday and said you're a pathological liar. She said that's how the hospital diagnosed you. She said we should be careful of you—that you'll come clean when it suits your purpose and go back to lying when it fits your agenda."

Violet's ears roared. It was like someone had opened up the cabin door midflight—like she'd been sucked outside of herself.

"Violet? She said you do things to Will."

"Things like what?"

"She said you're jealous of him. That back when Will was in school, you used to feed bullies information to tease him with. She said you pinch him when no one's around, so hard it leaves bruises."

"I've never *touched* Will!"

"Violet, your mom said the best thing we could do was stay clear of you—to let your condition be your downfall instead of ours." Imogene's chin dimpled. There were tears in her eyes. "I don't know what to believe. I said you've never lied to me. At least as far as I know . . ."

"That's genius." Violet stood up too abruptly, too angrily, but she needed to restore feeling to her legs. "Because if I'm such a stellar *liar* then you wouldn't even suspect there was anything wrong with me. And the reality is: there isn't anything wrong with me!" Violet knew her anger was working against her. Each time her voice jumped an octave, she could feel herself losing Imogene even more. She was about to apologize when Corinna stuck her head in the room.

"Violet," Corinna said, eyeing Imogene suspiciously. "There's someone named Amelia on the phone?"

"I want to talk this out—"

"I do too." Imogene nodded.

"—But I can't do it now. I have to get that. It's Rose's old friend Amelia. She might know Rose's phone number. I need Rose to get me out of here."

Imogene looked baffled. "But you just said Rose is the one stalking you. All that stuff with the trash cans—"

"Rose isn't after me. She's after my parents. And judging by what my mom's done to me, I'd say they probably deserve it." Violet hugged Imogene, who stood, awkwardly, with her hands at her sides. "Thanks for the chocolates. Please know, I have never *ever* lied to you. Give your mom a hug for me. Finch too."

Her mother had to be lying. How would she know Violet's diagnosis if she'd stopped returning Sara-pist's phone calls? Still, some small but treacherous part of Violet made her momentarily doubt herself. Could *she* lie, compulsively, without realizing it? Sara-pist seemed to think so. Imogene was almost sold. Violet *had* been doing a lot of MDMA lately, and her memory wasn't exactly what it used to be. Maybe her brain had been Swiss-cheesed. Maybe she lost snippets of facts and conversations. But she wasn't violent. To date, the only person who believed her on that point was Nicholas Flores, and even so, he couldn't do anything to save her. Not without a witness. Not without Rose.

The phone booth still smelled of the musky moisturizer Corinna rubbed into her shins. The receiver was still hot with Corinna's breath when Violet picked it up.

"Amelia?" Violet hoped she didn't sound as strung out and hysterical as she felt.

"Violet. I'm so sorry. I only have a few minutes before I have to be back in rehearsal." Amelia's voice was surprisingly deep and flat, with a Valley Girl twist at the end that made every sentence sound wishy-washy.

"That's okay. It won't take long. I just wondered if you're still in touch with Rose. She wrote me recently—"

"Rose wrote to *you*?" Maybe it was just that deflated voice that made it sound like a dig.

"Yeah. Have you heard from her?"

"Not in a year."

"Do you know anything about Damien?"

"Who's Damien?"

"Her boyfriend. The one Rose is living with."

Violet heard a swooshing sound like Amelia had switched her phone from one ear to the other. There was the sound of a door closing. Then the din of chattering ballerinas and tuning violins fell away.

"I don't know anyone named Damien. I only knew her last boyfriend, and there's no way she'd ever live with him." Amelia's voice sounded severe and much clearer. She must have ducked outside the echoing theater.

"How do you know that if you haven't talked to her?"

There was silence. Then the click of a cigarette lighter. A sucking inhale.

"Amelia? Are you still there? I said how do you know she's not living with him?"

"Because he's married, all right? Her last boyfriend was married."

There was the sound of the door again, followed by another humorless female voice. "I know," Amelia told someone. "*Yes, thank you. I'll be there in a minute.*"

Violet was stunned. "Who? How long ago was that?"

Amelia took another noisy inhale. "Her old professor"—exhale—"on structural geology or something. His name was Matt. Mister metamorphic rocks. I'm surprised they're back together actually. After the breakup, Rose was so crushed she couldn't even say his name. She started calling him The Volcano. Or, sometimes, The Earthquake. You know, after all those natural disasters he was such an expert on."

"He was married or he is married?" Violet asked.

"He was married, then. Now, I don't know. *Two more minutes,*" Amelia hissed to the person on the periphery of their conversation.

"Did you tell this to the police when we thought Rose was missing?" Violet hoped her voice wasn't too harsh, too judgmental. She couldn't afford to scare this woman away.

"No. I should have. I know what you must think of me. I know I should have told them. But you have to understand, Rose *swore* me to silence. She was so in love. Even after the way he acted, she was worried their affair would get him fired. Can you imagine? I was, like, *screw him*. He *deserves* to lose his job after everything he's done to you. But Rose didn't care. You know Rose."

"I know Rose," Violet lied.

"Then you know the way Rose forgets herself when she's into someone. She gets so wrapped up in guys' interests, it's like she forgets who she is."

"So Rose chose science over theater because she was trying to be more like her married boyfriend?"

"The Rose I knew didn't give two shits about faults, or deformed rock bodies, or whatever the hell she was suddenly obsessed with. I begged her to stay. There were rumors we were doing *Anything Goes* the next year, and Rose was a shoo-in for Reno Sweeney."

Violet made a small, knowing sound. In fact, she only knew enough musicals to know she hated them with every fiber of her being.

Amelia's cough seemed to rattle her rib cage. "I know Relationship Rose loves love. In love, Rose thinks she's being really devoted and selfless or whatever. But she's not. I tried to tell her that once. I said, 'Rose, you latch onto people because a part of you *likes* feeling used.'"

Violet made another small, knowing sound. This time she meant it.

"I told her she liked playing the victim. 'Rose,' I said, 'you like feeling like you're constantly unappreciated. All this has nothing to do with Mr. Geology, it's you're addicted to the highs and lows he gives *you*.' I tried to tell her the way she loved the professor was just as selfish as the way your mom loved her."

"You compared Rose to our *mom*?"

"Not a good move, I know. I think that's the reason Rose stopped talking to me." The person spurring Amelia to hang up returned. "Violet, I should really go. I have a costume fitting."

"One last thing? Did you know Rose had an abortion?"

Amelia gave the sigh of someone who was emotionally drained. "Know? I drove her to the clinic. She didn't want to do it. Your mom was pressuring her. Calling Rose a two-bit whore. Saying she wouldn't lift a finger to help if Rose went through with having the baby; she was just going to laugh and say 'I told you so' while a kid made Rose fat, broke, and bored."

"How supportive."

"It wasn't pretty. Your mom *harassed* her. But—and believe me, I never said this to Rose—I think it was probably for the best that Rose didn't have that baby."

"Because the professor wouldn't leave his wife?"

Amelia's laugh was almost bitter. "No. Rose was fine with being a single mom. I mean, I think she *wanted* to be a single mom. I thought it was for the best because Rose would have smothered that baby. She would have used it the same way she used everyone else in her life—to make her feel better about herself. Even if Mr. Earthquake had left his wife, I think Rose would have wanted that kid to love only *her*. It was the same way in our friendship. Rose got really upset if I had other friends, or if I went out alone with the theater crew. I didn't realize how isolated I'd gotten until she stopped talking to me."

"Rose was that possessive?"

"It was all those years of competing with you and Will. Rose never felt she could live up to you."

"Live up to me?"

"Yeah. She always talked about the way your mom would go on about how smart Will was and how you were the naturally pretty one while Rose had to work for it. Why do you think it took Rose two hours to get ready to go anywhere? She'd go, like, paralyzed with fear anytime it was time to pick out an outfit. If her curling iron broke, her whole day was ruined."

Violet didn't know which was more shocking: the idea that Rose had been envious of her, or the idea that Rose had wanted a baby and their mother had coerced her out of it. She kept trying to make sense of that gruesome fetus picture—how did that fit into this version of the story?

"Amelia, how long was it between when you drove Rose to the clinic and when she stopped talking to you?"

"A few days, maybe? I figured she was just grieving or whatever. It went on longer than I ever expected. She'd already switched majors, so it wasn't like we had to see each other in class every day. I should have called her up and apologized. But I needed a break. Rose needed so much attention and reassurance. She was like a little girl. I felt . . . worn out."

"And then she ran away."

"Yeah. That shocked me, but I thought it was a positive change. I think even you can agree Rose needed to put some space between herself and your parents." A door slammed. The sound of the string instruments returned.

"I'm really sorry, Violet. They're calling everyone for the act two coda. I've gotta go."

"Amelia? One last thing?"

"What?"

"Have you ever seen Rose get violent? Do you think she's got it in her?"

"I don't know. Personally, I think it's a matter of breaking point. Anybody can be pushed to violence. And your mom pushed her hard."

Violet thought about that for a second, and then Amelia added: "Rose's acting was always so seamless. I don't think she'd ever do something wrong unless she *wanted* to be caught."

WILLIAM HURST

WILL WOKE TO an unfamiliar presence in his room. He heard his bedside light snap on. He rolled over, completely unprepared for what he saw: his father standing awkwardly in his day-off clothes. His face was unshaven and he had a pair of haggard slippers on his feet.

"Is all your medication in the bathroom cabinet?" Douglas asked.

Will pulled the covers to his chin and nodded.

"And what about your schoolwork?"

"*What* about my schoolwork?"

"Where is it?"

"All over. Some on the computer. Some in the books in Mom's office. Some in our heads." Will was annoyed by the thought of his dad interfering with his schoolwork, not to mention hijacking his quality time with his mom. "Where is Mom?"

"I told her to take the day off."

Douglas sounded so authoritarian when he said it, and yet Will couldn't imagine his mom taking orders from his dad. "Where did she go?"

"I don't know. There was some talk about a day spa. She might catch the train to the city. She said something about an exhibit at the Guggenheim."

Will despaired at the thought of his mother looking at art without him. She always said she liked the way Will made her feel like a professor again. She loved explaining things, like the way early Romans were wild about orchids until they turned Christian, when the flowers vanished from their art because they suddenly seemed too sexually symbolic—the scientific name *orchis* deriving from a Greek word for *testes*.

"Are you and Mom still fighting?" Will asked.

"Who said we were fighting? Get dressed, please. Then come downstairs for breakfast."

"What should I wear?" Will yawned, expecting his father to go to the closet and select what his mother liked to call Will's "ensemble du jour."

"Something warm," Douglas said. "It's expected to reach freezing today." He turned stiffly and strode downstairs, where Will heard the pinging sounds of O-shaped cereal hitting two bowls.

Dinner for breakfast, Will thought and then caught himself, knowing it should have been the other way around.

Will couldn't help gawking at the angry scribbles on the side of his father's car. The scratches in the paint looked even deeper up close, as though someone had made them with a knife as opposed to a key. The fact that his father had inspired that kind of fury in someone wasn't all that hard to believe. The real question was which sister was responsible for it? Druggy, unhinged Violet? Or calculating, vengeful Rose?

I won't ever let your father do the kinds of things to you that he did to Rose. Those were the words his mother had said the night before. Was there temper lurking beneath his dad's spaciness? Will's mother sometimes alluded to Douglas's "hotheaded youth." Watching him reverse out of the garage, it occurred to Will that his father was like someone who was revved up and frozen at the same time; like, emotionally speaking, he had one foot on the brake and the other on the gas pedal. One stress too many and Douglas could easily be the kind of homicidal doormat people described with the words *He just snapped*.

"Where are we going?" Will asked.

"To the doctor."

"My doctor? Dr. Salomon?"

"A different doctor," Douglas said. "A new one. Dr. Martin. He's a friend of a friend. I've spent half the night looking through your medical records, and there seems to be a lot missing."

Did his dad think he was stupid? Dragging him out to a new doctor, trying to get his diagnoses reversed behind his mother's back? Will was furious. "Like *what*?"

"What?"

"I asked you *what* is missing from my medical records. I don't need to waste time at another doctor! I know what's wrong with me!"

Will could tell Douglas had mentally gone offline.

"Dad!" Will shouted, leaning forward and straining his seat belt. "My autism is none of your business! You can't just mess with my school and my life just to get back at Mom! I'm not going to let you use me just because you feel like a ridgeling!"

"I don't know what that means," Douglas said flatly.

"It's a half-castrated animal," Will spat.

Douglas grunted in a way that said the dig hurt. He kept the windshield wipers screeching for a full five miles before he realized it was no longer raining.

. . .

Dr. Martin was a child psychologist, and it was unclear whether Martin was his first name or his last.

Will felt defensive and a little jaded. Over the course of the past year, he had languished in at least three other offices exactly like the one he was in, and he didn't trust this guy for a second. In the words of Will's mother, most therapists were "whiny abuse victims" out to convince themselves that everyone in the world should "stop trying and wallow" the way they did themselves.

"Where did you go, Will?" Doc Martin asked. "It's like you're here in body, but not spirit. What am I missing?"

Will stared at the zany orange-striped sock peeking out of Doc Martin's pant leg. It reminded him of Nicholas Flores's chummy Jets tie. Did adults really think dressing like clowns endeared them to kids? *You don't "get" me,* Will thought. *I'm more grown-up than that.*

"You're not missing anything," Will said, maybe a little too glibly. "There's just no reason for me to be here. I've done all this before. I'm not sick like my sister. Not sick in my emotions, I mean . . ."

"You're sick in some other respect?" Doc Martin was fishing, grasping at straws, and Will despised him for it.

"Not sick, exactly. Just different. The autism . . ."

"Yes, your father mentioned your autism. We'll get to that in a few minutes. Because the things we experience sometimes affect our health, I need to ask you the same questions I ask all of my patients. Is that okay with you?"

Will had no intention of being this man's patient, but he was physically incapable of being rude. Will's passive, honor-adults side took over, and he shook his head to say yes, it was okay.

"Are there things going on in your life that cause you concern?"

Will's response came so hard and fast he surprised even himself. "No." Floating on the periphery of his thoughts—like helium balloons grazing the ceiling—were Rose's revenge schemes. Also, his father's possible affair. But they didn't really cause him *concern* per se. They were happening, and no amount of worrying on his part could undo them. Far better to put his energy into being the child no one had to worry about.

"Your father said your sister was admitted to a psychiatric hospital last week. You're not concerned about her?"

Will shrugged. "If she's sick or whatever, then she was born that way. Nothing in our family caused it."

The doc seemed startled for a second before his poker face returned. "You're twelve going on forty, anyone ever tell you that? You're very protective of your parents, aren't you?" Will wondered whether he was trying to make him angry. When he failed to react, Doc Martin went on. "Sometimes the very loved ones who seem to be causing all our problems are just calling attention to deeper issues the rest of the family would rather ignore. Maybe Violet has a harder time pretending things are okay."

"No one's acting. Things *are* okay." Will was beginning to think his mother was right. The man in front of him with his Saint Nick beard and "understanding" eyes was already convinced that he knew the Hursts' story; he didn't give a frick what Will had to say.

Doc Martin aimed his ballpoint pen at Will's splint. "Your father said your sister might have hurt you. That must have been frightening. I imagine it made you feel pretty helpless."

"She's where she needs to be now. She won't hurt anyone again."

The shrink looked down at his notepad. "Your father also said your epilepsy has been pretty disruptive. That you can't go to school because of it? I've never experienced a seizure myself. What do they feel like?"

Will relaxed a bit. He was far more comfortable discussing

health problems than family problems. He described the ice-cold sweats to Martin. He talked about the combined tightening/tingling he felt in his chest—the way that, during an attack, he forgot how to breathe. Will had described it all so many times, the words had lost their meaning. Describing a seizure was like reciting a piece of poetry or performing his one-man Edgar Allan Poe show.

Quite suddenly, Doc Martin leaned over and stabbed his pencil into the sharpener on the side table.

The grinding sound made Will flinch. He curled the fingers of his good hand around the leather seam of the couch.

"I'm sorry for the noise," Doc Martin said. "I can see that really rattled you. Do you find that kind of thing happens a lot? Are you startled easily?"

The rest of the session was more of the same. The questions, which bled into one another, set Will on edge: "Do you have trouble sleeping?" "Do you feel detached from other people?" "Do you find you don't feel pain or joy—just a constant sense of unease?"

By the end of the session, Will had a bad feeling he'd qualified for whatever mental defect Doc Martin had been screening him for—a suspicion that only grew when the shrink asked Will to "hang out" in the waiting room while he had a few words with Will's dad.

Will tried not stare at or judge the only two other people in the waiting room: a morose woman who stank of cigarettes and her buzz-cut son who had an air of aggression and ADD. Will sat and read. He eschewed the *Scholastic* magazines and sat in the corner leafing through *Psychology Today*. Inside was an article about how vegetarians like Violet have overall worse mental health than meat eaters. When no one was looking, he brought the magazine to the bathroom and tore out the page, folding and pocketing it to show his mother later.

During the drive home, Will's father turned off at a roadside hot dog truck. Will looked at Douglas skeptically as he returned to the car with a mustard-slathered schlong in each hand.

"Mom and I don't eat hot dogs," Will said.

"Well, Mom's not here," Douglas said with an edge in his voice.

"They're as unhealthy as cigarettes. We read that. They cause genetic mutations."

His father sighed and balanced the second hot dog on the emergency brake between them. He'd insisted Will ride in the passenger seat, even though Will argued he was still a year too young (the department of motor vehicles said you had to be thirteen).

Douglas napkin-dabbed the mustard from the corner of his mouth. "Will, what are your feelings about going back to public school?"

Will's *feelings* on the matter were a lot like the feelings he'd have if he were trapped under the axle of a seventy-ton truck. A crushing weight settled onto his chest, and the air in the car seemed too thick to breathe.

"That's impossible," Will said with a croak of anger in his voice. "My epilepsy—" And he tried his damnedest to list all of the reasons his mother always named about the school's fluorescent lights and lack of carpeting.

"Well, Dr. Martin isn't entirely sure about your epilepsy. And your other doctors aren't either. The fact that your EKGs are normal and you're *still* having attacks even though you're on seizure medication mean something else might be going on."

"Something like what?"

"An anxiety disorder, for one. Panic attacks." Douglas reached into his jacket pocket and pulled out a photocopied article about something called psychogenic nonepileptic seizures (PNES).

"This says it happens to war veterans and mothers in custody battles. Overworked *adults.*"

"Unh-uh, read it to the end." His father pointed to the part in the article that talked about how PNES happened when people with "poor coping mechanisms" faced "unstable relationships" or "stressful life events." Douglas added, "Fifty-four percent of people with these anxiety attacks are misdiagnosed as epileptics."

"I'm not going back to Stone Ridge Elementary! I *am* epileptic!" He tried to calm himself with the possibility of boarding school. He reminded himself that he and his mother already had a plan in mind.

"I'm not saying I don't believe you. It's just that I've never seen you have a seizure, so I can't confirm what I haven't seen."

"My memory goes funny. Like the last time—"

"Dr. Martin thinks something else might explain that."

"What?"

"Turn to the second sheet."

Will tossed aside the handout on PNES and was confronted with a fact sheet titled *TRAUMA AND DISSOCIATION*. It talked about the way some people disconnect from their bodies, feelings, memories, and awareness during times of extreme stress. It was a coping mechanism, the author wrote, a way to split ourselves off from things we don't feel equipped to deal with. Some people, like rape victims, experienced trauma as if they were watching themselves from fifty feet off the ground. Others failed to remember whole days at a time, even as they worked, shopped, and socialized, going about their lives like automatons.

"That doctor told you I have *this*? This is for, like, army men returning from war. Or kids who've lost their families in tsunamis."

"Dr. Martin said it's much more common in people who've been traumatized by someone they know and trust. I have to take this seriously," Will's dad said, balling his napkin in one fist. "This is the second time this week a psychologist has talked to me about post-traumatic stress disorder."

Will's mind went to all the doctors he'd been to before his autism diagnosis. "One of my old doctors said I had it too?" he asked, brain-stunned and fighting tears.

"No," Douglas said, sucking air. "No. I meant Violet's therapist. She thought Violet's Buddhist meditations—pacing around her room all night—were just an attempt to shut off extreme anxiety."

"But who was it who was meant to have traumatized us?" The words had barely left Will's mouth before his mind went to Rose. Had she abused him and Violet? And had their clever, self-preserving psyches changed the channel in an effort to block it out?

Douglas cast a spooked, guilty look in his direction.

Will comforted himself with the reminder that nothing too terrible could have happened to him. His mother had been there. Josephine had always been with Will, and perhaps that was why. Maybe, just maybe, Will's mother had turned overbearing in re-action to something. Maybe she was sheltering Will against a very real storm.

Violet Hurst

Violet was careful on the approach when she caught sight of Sara-pist strolling down the hall. She was walking with a colleague the patients called Dr. Shrink Wrap, on account of the bad Botox that had given his face a strange, shiny film. Much as she wanted to, Violet was not going to charge up, loud and emphatic, demanding to know whether the woman thought she was a compulsive liar.

"Sorry to interrupt," Violet said. "I just wanted to thank you for making me stay. This has been such a big week for me. Everyone in the twelve-step program says it's just the pink-cloud stage, but I've had a lot of insights."

Sara-pist looked surprised, but willing. "Come. Walk," she motioned. Very next thing, Violet was in her supremely depressing office, sitting on her melancholy-colored microsuede couch.

"So you mentioned before that my mother stopped returning your calls?"

"That's right."

"But you saw my dad yesterday, when he came to visit?"

A wary look crept into Sara-pist's face. "Yes. Your father and I spoke a lot about his alcoholism. He feels a certain amount of responsibility for your drug use. He expressed worry that you'd inherited his disease, and that his own addiction put blinders on him. He said he wished he'd been more aware of your problems."

"I know genetics can play a part in addiction. I get that. But I'm the reason I take substances. I take them because I feel like I need to numb out who I really am and be who my mother wants me to be."

"And who does your mom want you to be?"

"The bad seed. Someone she can point her finger at when she falls down on the job. But I don't have to be the bad one. Playing that part isn't making my family any better. It's just making it worse."

"Ummm."

Violet couldn't get a read on Sara-pist. She meant everything she said, but still she didn't know if she was strengthening or weakening her case for her mental health.

"Being here has taught me that I can't pick and choose emotions. When I stop feeling fucking terrified, I stop feeling glad too. I've been numb for so long. I think I wanted to die because I wanted my insides and outsides to match. I tried suicide because I already felt dead."

A smile crept across Sara-pist's face. "That does sound like an insight. And has this new awareness brought you to a place where you feel ready to let go of some of these behaviors?"

Violet nodded. "I can see now that I was identifying with my"—she struggled for a calm, but accurate word—"aggressor. One of my friends here, Edie . . . She helped me see that I was torturing myself by the same methods someone else used to torture me."

"And who would that someone else be?"

"My mother. Edie thinks she sounds like a narcissist."

"I can't speak to the mental health of anyone without meeting them. And I can't diagnose anyone who doesn't come to me, willing to change and actively seeking my help."

"Ethics." Violet nodded. "I understand."

"I will say, it is more or less common wisdom that having a narcissistic mother is one of the worst things that can happen to a kid. Her inability to empathize, her persistent misreading of her child's inarticulate but urgent social cues, her tendency to feel criticized by her child's discomfort, her desperate need to come off like a good mother, at the risk of actually being one . . . all these things severely disrupt a child's development. Children of narcissists tend to feel guilty and dangerous even if they've never stood up for themselves, never committed a crime."

Now was the time to bring up the knife. "I didn't commit that crime against my brother. I'm willing to take responsibility for a lot of things, but not that. I'm not in the business of julienning anyone's fucking hands. But I *do* feel guilty to an extent. Because even though I didn't hurt Will, I've stood by for years, watching him get hurt."

"Hurt how?"

"Hurt, isolated. Hurt, smothered. Hurt, used to prop my mother up and make her feel special."

"Did it ever occur to you to intervene?"

"No. By all appearances, it *looked* like affection. I mean, I was even jealous of Will. Time was, I was jealous of Rose. Both of them seemed to get more attention and approval than I ever got."

"But was it love, really?"

"Of course not. It was exploitation. It was abuse tarted up like love."

"Maybe that's why you're afraid to be seen. That's why you're so afraid of having a real relationship with your sister. You're scared because intimacy *feels* like terror. Because, at least where your mother's concerned, terror is the only kind of closeness you've known."

"So, you don't think I'm a compulsive liar?"

Sara-pist's face remained neutral. "It doesn't matter what I think. Is lying something you're ready to admit you struggle with?"

"I don't think so, but I want to know if that's my diagnosis. I found out from some friends that my mom called them. She said I'd been diagnosed as a compulsive liar."

"Violet, I haven't spoken to your mother since your intake."

Yes, she was glad she was asking questions. Before, Violet might have just accepted her own supposed "lying" as fact and slunk off to some corner with a shit-ton of self-loathing, a dime bag, and a stack of Buddhist self-help books about truth in speech. She might have accepted that drugs had given her some neurological deficit. Now, she was prepared to find out exactly what Rose and, possibly, her parents were hiding. Josephine wanted honesty; she was about to get it. Her little girl was not so little now.

"Here's my three-day letter," Violet said, standing to pass Sara-pist the sheet of art paper it was written on. "I want to be released or I want my court hearing." She needed to get back to her friends before Josephine fixed things so she didn't have a single friend left in the world.

WILLIAM HURST

WILL AND HIS dad returned from Dr. Martin's office to an empty house. His mother hadn't returned from whatever field trip she'd taken alone, and without the Hurst women, Old Stone Way was as impressive and eerie-cold as a mausoleum.

Will watched his father switch on lowbrow talk radio and flick on all the downstairs lights. Still, the light and sound did nothing to lessen the awkwardness that hung around the kitchen the way the smell of old fry oil might.

"So," Will's dad said. "Should we get on with your school lessons?"

Will was floored by the idea of his dad playing at being his teacher. "It's pointless to do it without Mom," he said. "I'd rather start fresh tomorrow."

"Will, if you're home, you need to be studying and keeping school hours. This is serious business. Especially given CPS has been here. We need to be able to account for your academics—"

Will's anger flared. The tension that had been building all day reached Will's mental brim and he simply boiled over. "Look, Dad"—he said his father's name with acid on his tongue—"you are not a teacher the way Mom is a teacher. You don't have her patience. You don't have her enthusiasm or her intellectual curiosity. And you definitely don't have her knowledge of the subject matter."

"I don't know how your mother's managed to convince you she's teacher of the year."

"She's an *academic*."

"Not since I last checked. Not since she was fired."

"Mom left SUNY. She left so she could teach me."

"Is that what she told you?" Douglas's jaw went tight. "Will, your mother got fired for having a fake degree. She got her PhD from some kind of diploma mill. It was good enough for her. She never considered it might not work for her students or her employer."

Tarradiddle: lie; falsehood; nonsense.

"That's not true! I held Mom while she cried over the decision to quit her job. She kept going back and forth, she couldn't decide what to do."

"The decision to leave SUNY wasn't hers to make."

Will wouldn't stand for it. He refused to stand there and let his father, who'd done nothing for Will, talk slander about his mother, who'd done everything for him.

"Fine. I'll do schoolwork," Will huffed. "Today's the day for music class." (It wasn't.)

Will stormed to the piano and pounded out a one-handed Shostakovich waltz for close to an hour. The keys were literally a safe instrument for Will's sudden, Russian-esque angst. Plus, as long as Will's hand kept moving, his father couldn't talk to him about public school or his so-called hidden traumas. Will didn't need to hear any more about Doc Martin's bogus diagnosis. It didn't matter if his father accepted his Asperger's. He was getting away from his dad. Success was the best revenge of all, and soon enough Will was going to be at a pretentious—make that *prestigious*—prep school. He'd be studying economics and hanging out with boys who "summered" instead of "vacationed." One day he'd go to Oxford or the Sorbonne. His dad could kiss his Top-Siders. His dad could eat his number-two pencil dust.

When Will finally tired and gave up the piano, he looked out the window and saw his father on a ladder, cleaning clogged gutters in the rain. Beneath the hood of his slicker, Douglas's face flashed through a strange montage of anguish, shame, and determination. *Too little, too late,* Will thought, watching. The home maintenance, the delayed concern with CPS, the sudden interest in Will's schoolwork and Will's health. It was all too little, too late. The storm had already struck. The downspout was already clogged. The effects of the neglect were already cascading down on them, pouring straight into the Hursts' foundation.

Will wandered into the kitchen, where the talk-radio show droned on.

The DJ's voice was guttural and cheesy: *What personal item do women say they can't live without? I'm guessing it's cotton balls. Tell me, what do you ladies do with all those cotton balls?*

Will was headed for his mother's secret stash of truffles when he noticed his father's cell phone buzzing on the counter. The phone's high volume, combined with the DJ's faux-deep voice, made Will so feel so emotionally flooded, so irrationally angry, that he picked up the phone in a left-handed death grip.

KERRY, read the caller ID.

Classy. The home-wrecker spelled her name with a K.

Will wasn't sure what he was thinking when he answered the call. More likely, he wasn't thinking. He was in the midst of an emotional emergency—a five-alarm fire—and he was simply responding to the bell.

"Stop calling here!" Will screamed. "My dad is *married*! You should be ashamed of yourself!"

He didn't wait for the trollop to respond. He didn't need to hear her justifications any more than he needed to hear her voice.

Will had barely stabbed the End Call button before the phone began to ring again. It continued ringing as he took the box of Lindor truffles off the shelf and ate three without tasting a thing.

Will's eyes flashed daggers when Douglas hustled across the kitchen to answer the third or fourth missed call ("Kerry, hi. I've been up to my neck in clogged gutters"). He wandered out of the room, jacket dripping all over the clean floors, with an expression that was meant to look relaxed or, at the very least, not guilty. But Will knew better. Will knew his father was a cheater and a lush.

Fourth Lindor truffle. Will popped it in his mouth all at once and felt a line of chocolate-infused drool roll down the center of his chin.

Will remembered his mother's words: *Do you think you'd feel better after a drink, Douglas? Is that it?* And he wondered, deviously, whether a glass of wine would help his father ease up on the CPS/PTSD/public school stuff. He used the kitchen step stool to take down a crystal glass. The bottle he and his mother had bought the day before still sat, half-full and corked on the counter. Will eased the cork out and sloshed the ravishing-red liquid to the brim of the glass. He left it on the counter like a wordless invitation to his dad.

More sexist chatter on the radio. Phone-in listeners called in to report they "couldn't live without" their bronzers, ChapSticks, and eyelash curlers.

When Douglas returned, his eyes went directly to the full glass on the counter.

Ebrious: Inclined to drink to excess. Or in Douglas's case, a hiccupping, pants-pissing, word-slurring, lose-all-mental-capacity kind of drunk.

Douglas's mouth bent in a frown. "Will," he said. "Are you all right? You're not acting like yourself."

"What am I acting like?"

"To be honest? It's like watching you impersonate your mother."

His father's words were like an ice cube down the back of the shirt.

"The person you just spoke to on the phone. His name is Kerry. He's my sponsor. Do you know what that means?"

Will shook his head.

"That means that I am an alcoholic. It means that I'm trying to quit drinking and lead a sober life, and Kerry is my role model, my teacher, and my bullshit detector. No one gave me an ultimatum or forced me to go to a recovery group. I've been going because I want to better myself and my relationship with you kids . . ."

All at once, Will stopped listening to what his father was saying. Douglas's voice receded into the background as the radio DJ revealed the answer to the poll:

"The correct answer is . . . can I have a drumroll please? Thank you. A new study reveals the vast majority of women report they can't live without . . . their hair dryers! What is it with you ladies and those things? My ex-wife almost set our hotel room on fire when she used one to blow-dry her panties."

Douglas was still trying to explain the ins and outs of his crippling alcoholism as he trailed Will up the stairs to Rose's room.

"Alcoholism hijacks the circuits of your brain that are responsible for decision making," Will's dad said, bending to sit down on Rose's ruffled pink comforter. "This runs in your family, Will. That's something you should know as you get older. Just a little bit of underage drinking and you might literally reprogram your brain to associate 'alcohol' with 'the only thing in the world worth doing.'"

Much as Will would have liked to tell his dad that (a) it was bad form to lecture someone else when you were trying to "hold yourself accountable" and (b) booze was about as appetizing as cat food (thanks in large part to the memories of it on Douglas's own breath), he had something far more pressing on his mind.

Will went directly to Rose's vanity and pulled out one of the wire baskets he had scrounged through days earlier.

"*Look,*" he told his dad, holding up Rose's Conair 225R.

"Look at what? The hair dryer?" Douglas snapped out of his own fugue. He seemed aware for the first time that they were in his estranged daughter's room.

"*Yes.* Didn't you hear what they just said on the radio? Most women say they can't live without their *hair dryers.*"

Will studied his dad, waiting patiently as he could for Douglas to catch his drift. Someone as image-obsessed as Rose would never run off without her favorite battered old blow dryer. Damien must have made her leave more quickly than she wanted. He'd hurried her, or else he'd lured her away. Maybe they'd had to leap at some opportunity that wouldn't come again.

Will waited for his father to do something. Respond. Move a muscle. Let some emotion twitch across his middle-aged features. He wasn't expecting Douglas's (over?)reaction when it finally came. Will's father pitched forward and thrust his head between his chinoed knees. He cupped his ears with his palms, revealing the damp half-moons of his armpit stains. His shoulder blades shook violently. It took Will many minutes to figure out whether his stoic father was crying or dry-heaving.

VIOLET HURST

NOW THAT VIOLET had a plan, she was determined to find out everything there was to know about Rose and the circumstances of her disappearance. In three days, hopefully, she'd be out of Fallkill. In the meantime, she needed to know more about the boyfriend her sister had pinned every hope on.

Violet managed another visit to the computer lab—two in one day—by claiming she wanted to check her midterm scores. That was top-shelf bullshit and the very act of fibbing made her feel like her mother was winning, but time was of the essence. It seemed pretty clear that Matt was "Damien," and she needed to do a little background on him before the Kingston Police Department came calling, as Nicholas had assured her they would.

There was a photo of Rose's professor, Matt, on the geology department website. He was handsome, undeniably so. But his face had the kind of fine-drawn symmetry that makes men self-loathing and apologetic, especially in the Catskills, where people tended to value social responsibility over sex appeal—or at the very least, pretended to.

Professor Metamorphic Rock—actually, he was an assistant

professor—had downplayed his lantern jaw with sideburns reminiscent of pubic hair. His long hair looked greasy under his Indiana Jones hat. His blue-steel eyes were framed with unfashionably round glasses. But there was a certain contagious joy in his smile as he stood, pointing out something on the side of a crag. Violet didn't trust him, but his enthusiasm leapt off the screen, and she understood how Rose could be drawn to him.

Violet plunged deeper into Google stalking. Matt had a low-budget, low-content website, which listed various field guides he'd written, as well as a page of geology-centered dirty jokes: "What are three reasons life is more fun as a geologist? Thrusting, cleavage, and overturned beds." Matt had assessed earthquake hazards in Morocco. He'd studied faults in the Andes. He was goofy, accomplished, well traveled, and, of course, married.

Matt and his possibly ex-wife, Francesca, had tied the knot five years earlier. The ceremony was in their backyard beneath a homemade hops trellis. Violet knew because she found Matt's old wedding website. Actually, it was more like a blog, and for a full year leading up to the nuptials, Francesca had obsessively detailed everything from her "conflict" about serving cupcakes instead of an old-fashioned wedding cake ("What will we do for the 'cutting' tradition? Do we even *care* about tradition?") to her hunt for a wedding theme ("I'm throwing caution to the wind with a three-color combination of brown, pink, and blue!"). Violet scrolled through the couple's Williams-Sonoma registry and winced when she saw they'd registered for the same Wüsthof knife she'd pointed at her mother. She read the story of their engagement, which began with the sad and delusory words: *Throughout their entire relationship, Matt and Francesca have always been very open with each other.*

An image search for Francesca showed pictures of a dimpled,

toothy blonde, sunglasses on her head, cleavage that looked like it could damn near smother her. She was very pretty, even if it was a paint-by-numbers kind of beauty. Violet could only imagine how a woman like that would take the news of Matt's infidelity. A philandering husband and his knocked-up girlfriend did not factor into princess fantasies, and Francesca had worn a bona fide tiara on her wedding day.

And what about Rose? Violet wondered if her sister felt unique. Did it feel good to know that, even with his Barbie-doll wife, Matt had singled her out?

Violet took a deep breath and sent Francesca a Facebook request so she could snoop a little deeper and find out whether Matt had left her. Then she scrawled Matt's phone number and office hours into her sketch pad, and e-mailed him at his dot-edu address:

> Hi Matt,
> I just wanted to formally introduce myself. I'm Rose's sister Violet. I just
> wanted to thank you for taking such good care of my sister, and helping her
> get out of my parents' house. I'm really looking forward to meeting you.
> Hope we can make it happen soon!

It was forward, but she consoled herself by thinking about what Sara-pist had said about working on her fear of intimacy, trying to be more open and assuming even a little better of people. Also, she remembered what Nicholas from CPS had said: It was worth looking into Matt, taking precautions to make sure he was an okay guy (not a sex fiend, not a serial killer).

If Matt was a decent guy who'd left his wife for Rose, then he might want to know a little more of Rose's family. Violet included her phone number at Fallkill and told him to call if he was ever in Poughkeepsie.

. . .

After computer lab, Violet and Corinna found Edie in the day-room. She was sitting, stone-faced, on the love seat beside the dead palm tree no one on staff thought to either water or remove. The day nurse sat beside her, eating the Krause's chocolates out of the open box in Edie's lap.

"Like takin' candy from a baby," Corinna scoffed, lifting the box out of Edie's hands. "Proud of yourself, boss lady?" This was what she called all the nurses.

The nurse licked a splodge of caramel off her thumb. "She didn't want them."

"It was really nice of you, Violet. But my stomach is knotted. She's welcome to share," Edie said. Her blue eyes still had that haunted look, and Violet sat down and put a soft hand on her shoulder.

Corinna picked up a chocolate-covered cherry, considered it, and dropped it back in the box. "Edie, hon? You okay? We've been worried, Violet and me. Well, everyone's worried, really. You know what it's like around here. Dominoes and shit. One person has a bad day and we all fall down."

"It's true," Violet said. "Jocelyn's been curled in the fetal position ever since computer lab."

"The Tourette's lady has gone racist," Corinna added. "She's going around calling all the doctors street Arabs."

Edie had a look like sustaining eye contact required conscious effort. "I'm okay," she said. "Today is always hard for me. I always feel really vulnerable, like something bad is going to happen. Like I'm going to be targeted. I just try to get through it."

"You're trying to get through your birthday?" Violet asked.

Edie gave a mortified nod.

Corinna shook her head in disbelief. "We should be exploiting this to your advantage. Extra cigarette breaks. More snack room visits. I could have persuaded Dr. Shrink Wrap to go buy us pizza."

"It's her choice," Violet whispered. "If she doesn't want to celebrate—"

"It's stupid," Edie said. "It's just a trigger. Being the center of attention . . . *Birthdays* . . . When I was a kid, my mom always used them as a way to guilt-trip or embarrass me. Sometimes she'd pick a screeching fight with the party magician. She'd mope around, pretending to be sick, or she'd scowl in all the party photos."

Edie's eyes had lost their focus again, and it occurred to Violet for the first time that talking about her mother wasn't a conscious choice Edie made. The childhood confessions were like hemorrhages she couldn't stop. Edie's scar was healing, but she was still bleeding out.

They left Edie in the dayroom in front of a marathon of *House Hunters International*; Corinna swore it was just the right combination of catty and cathartic without the emotional triggers of other guilty-pleasure TV like *Law & Order*.

Violet and Corinna raided the art room's supply of markers, glitter, and Scotch tape. The party "theme" (Violet was still thinking of Francesca) was a trifecta of festivity, insanity, and irony. They were loopy, stringing banners out of toilet paper squares. *HAPPY BIRTHDAY!* they wrote, and *WE LOVE EDIE!* They made their friend a "cake" out of curly ribbon and tiers of generic lemonade cans; they were Edie's favorite beverage from the vending machine and said *ZERO PERCENT JUICE* in big letters down the side. Corinna scrounged up money from who knows where, and Dr.

Shrink Wrap shoved it into the front pocket of his scrubs, promising pizza and hot wings from Gino's.

Violet was hole-punching "confetti" when a nearly mute girl the ward called Helen Keller stuck her head in the door.

"Violet, there's someone on the phone for you."

Corinna, who had never heard Helen speak before, glanced up, aghast. "Another phone call. Damn, girl," she told Violet. "I don't know where you get off calling yourself an introvert. You get visited more than John Edward."

"The politician?"

"No dummy. The psychic."

"I would have returned your messages, regardless. You didn't need to go and friend my wife."

Matt's was not the authoritative teacher voice Violet was expecting. There was a whiny bite to it, like a little dog yipping.

Violet fought a stammer. Confrontation found her more than most people, and yet she hated it, deep down.

"I'm asking you if you've contacted my wife."

"No. I just friended her. I didn't send her a message."

"You're the last thing Francesca needs right now. We're just beginning to get back on track. Everything that happened with Rose . . ." Her name was long and drawn-out on his tongue, a special treat he allowed himself. "It wasn't fair. It wasn't perfect, but it didn't mean that I don't love my wife."

Violet felt confused, then protective. So Matt hadn't left Francesca for Rose.

The line went dead, and Violet realized she was shivering like a wet dog. She hadn't been prepared for an argument. She'd expected to find a boyfriend who was glad to make her acquaintance—a boyfriend who, perhaps, wouldn't mind if Violet came to stay with him and Rose until she landed on her feet.

Violet had barely placed the phone on the receiver before it rang again.

"Sorry," Matt said. "It's just that, whatever lecture you're hoping to give me . . . I can guarantee you I've heard it a million times over. I've spent the past year staring, point-blank, down the barrel of divorce. Do you honestly think I don't feel guilty?"

"I don't care what you feel." It wasn't bad-ass the way Violet said it. She was still confused, embarrassed.

"Fair enough. I was selfish and greedy and weak. But you're all those things and worse if you think you're going to blackmail me. I need my job. I *need* my health insurance. My wife has lymphoma."

Violet thought of Beryl and softened. "I'm not blackmailing you. I just thought you and Rose were still together."

"We're *not!*"

There again was that toddlerish note of complaint. It was clear enough why Matt (who was thirty-three, according to his wedding blog) had started an affair with twenty-year-old Rose: even on the phone, he was a study in arrested development. Before, Violet had guessed Matt appealed to Rose as a father figure to make up for their own withdrawn dad. Now, just the opposite seemed true. Maybe Rose had wanted a man she could baby and reassure, someone more like needy Josephine. Even Violet felt mature by comparison to Matt.

"So you don't go and visit Rose in the city?"

"New York City?"

"Yes, New York City."

"No." For a split second, it seemed like he was going to say more.

"Are you lying?"

"No! It's just—I'm surprised, that's all. Rose told me she liked living by the mountains. She always said they give a person perspective. Whenever you're feeling too full of yourself, you only have to look out the window to see how little you really are."

Violet couldn't help noticing the way he spoke about Rose in the past tense. "Did you and Rose ever visit the city together?"

She could feel him hesitate. "Fran and I have a place there. A little rent-controlled studio in the West Village."

Not so far from the Chelsea UPS store, then.

"So the last time you spoke to Rose—"

"I ended it. It was a relief to both of us, I think."

He thought. Violet exhaled sharply. "I'm sure it was a great relief, huge, when Rose had an abortion. Yet you didn't even bother to go to the appointment with her."

"Rose didn't want me there! She didn't want help paying for it. She said she didn't want anything from me, and I believed her. If it was some head game—some test—then that's not my fault. I'm not a mind reader. I can only go off what people tell me."

"Can I ask you one more thing? And then, I'll get lost . . . How did it start?"

"What? Me and Rose?"

"Obviously, you and Rose."

"Well, we met for a tutoring session before a research paper."

"And?"

"And at the end of it, I asked her, 'Anything else?' I remember she swung her foot onto the table, rolled up her pant leg, and said, 'Look at my new socks!' They were Darn Tough wool trekking socks, not her style at all, but I'd been raving about mine during class. It was flattering that Rose remembered."

Violet tried to remember if Rose's personal style had changed following her switch from theater to science. There might have been a few months where Rose toyed with fleece and flannel, but hers was a fake ruggedness. There might have been mud on her boots, but there was still hair product in her ponytail. "Then what?" Violet asked.

"Then, one night on the school chat page, Rose messaged me to say hi. We ended up staying on there for about three hours, just talking."

"And then what?" Pulling teeth. Violet really resented the way he was making her guide him through a story that was his to tell.

"Then, one day I saw Rose on Church Street. I was still kind of new to the area. I asked her for directions to a certain coffee shop and she said, 'Why don't I just show you?' So we walked over, ordered coffee to go, and drank it while we walked the rail trail. At that point, we were clearly blurring the lines. But I've always had kind of soft boundaries with women. I've realized that since my wife and I started counseling."

Violet pitied the counselor who had to regularly listen to Matt for ten minutes shy of an hour. "So when did it get serious?"

"If you're asking what I think you're asking, we didn't kiss until a month before the semester was over. And we didn't have sex until after finals week."

Maybe all academics measured their year by the same land-marks, but on Matt's lips, it seemed particularly stunted.

"When did your wife find out?"

"Unh-uh," Matt said, half-teasing. "You already had your last question. Now, stand by your word and get lost."

"So you *really* don't talk to Rose at all?"

"Not at all," he said, firmly.

Violet hoped he was a gifted liar. If he wasn't, who was Damien? Who had run off with Rose?

Detective Donnelly tilted a creamer into his tea and blew on the steaming surface. He fidgeted. He clicked the pen in his pocket, as though he were ashamed to cut straight to business. "Nick Flores said you had some new information about your sister?"

Violet nodded. She was still reeling from her conversation with Matt. On some base level, his anger seemed like proof that anyone she opened up to would attack her. She couldn't trust anyone.

She really didn't know where to begin. If she started with Rose's letters, Detective Donnelly would probably say they supported the idea that Rose hadn't been home. "Rose has started writing to me, but I don't want to show you the letters yet."

Detective Donnelly looked surprised, but not annoyed. That was good.

"You can begin the story wherever you're comfortable."

"Well, when she ran away, the police interviewing me kept asking, 'What do you think happened to Rose?'"

"I've read the file." Donnelly nodded. "If I recall, you told police you thought she ran away with her boyfriend. You said Rose was secretive about her relationships. There was lots to indicate that your mother was strict and overprotective. Your mom told the department she didn't approve of sex before marriage, let alone living together. If a girl like your sister wanted to move in with a fellow, she'd all but have to elope in the night."

"My mom is strict, which is why I left something out."

Donnelly scratched his cheek with his pen, then slowly scratched at his notepad while Violet told him the story of Rose's abortion and the photo on Josephine's desk.

"So I'm hoping you'll ask me that question again . . . You know, 'What do you think happened to Rose?'"

The detective rocked forward and put an elbow on the table. "Well, what do you think happened to your sister?"

"It's only a theory . . ." Violet took a quick breath and prayed what she was about to say wouldn't sound crazy. In the visiting room with its barred windows and DON'T FEED THE ANIMALS sign, it was hard to say anything that sounded sane.

"Of course," he said. "It's your job to have the hunches. It's my job to look into them."

"Well, Rose's ex—"

"This is Matt?"

"Yes, Matt. His wife, Francesca, has cancer."

"Okay," Donnelly's expression was dubious.

"Well, my best friend's mother has breast cancer. She's had chemotherapy, radiation, the whole ordeal. And I know all those treatments can damage fertility. Beryl always says if she'd known she was going to get cancer, she'd have spared herself the headache of having her tubes tied."

"Okay."

"Okay, so it seems to me that a man who's just found out he might never have kids with his wife might not be devastated to find out his girlfriend was pregnant. Maybe he was thinking he'd leave his wife and settle down with Rose. By the time the baby was born, Rose would have been just a few months from graduation."

"Is this guy really that selfish?"

"I don't know," Violet shrugged. "I only talked to him the once. But he's immature. Childish."

"Listen to you," Donnelly smirked. "You're all of what? Eighteen?"

"Sixteen," Violet laughed, the joke backfiring on him.

"But hold on now, your sister terminated that pregnancy."

"She did. But that doesn't mean that she wanted to. My mom made Rose's life hell. If Matt—who was coming to terms with the idea that he'd never have a baby—suddenly had the chance to be a dad . . . And if Rose took that chance away from him on account of pressure from my mother . . . Well, it seems to me that Matt might have a huge ax to grind with my mom and our family at large. Maybe he'd even manage to turn Rose against us—to come after us for revenge."

"So you think Matt was lying when he told you he hadn't spoken to Rose since he ended their affair?"

Violet cringed inwardly; the word *affair* called to mind the soap operas some of the older patients watched—melodramas that featured lots of bitch-slaps and gauche close-ups. "I can admit I never knew my sister well. But the timing of these letters is weird."

"So your theory is Matt and Rose want to make your mother pay for the baby they think she took away. But how?"

"By hurting my mother's baby—Will."

While Violet was talking to Donnelly, someone had decided Edie's party would have a talent component. Slap-dash rehearsals were under way. Jocelyn was going to play a bluesy version of Amy Winehouse's "Rehab" on acoustic guitar. Corinna was going to unwrap a Starburst candy using only her tongue. Helen Keller continued to shock with plans to recite a Charles Bukowski poem.

"What's your special gift, Hurst?" Corinna asked.

"Is slacking off a talent?" Violet asked.

"Yes. But for the record, real slackers don't bother asking. How did it go with the cop?"

Violet shrugged and unwrapped a pink Starburst. "I told him what I know. He said when Rose first disappeared, the law respected her right to be a voluntary missing person. But now, because of everything that happened to Will, there's at least some possibility Rose is involved in foul play."

"Does her taste in men count as foul?"

"Said the pot to the kettle," Violet laughed. "I'm trying to say, the police can check up on Rose again. Donnelly also said it's worth making sure Rose didn't disappear last year *because* she did something criminal."

It was beginning to seem like Corinna was one of the few people at Fallkill who didn't think Violet's fear of intimacy was making her overreact. She nodded knowingly. "Like she and the prof pulled some Bonnie and Clyde shit."

"It's hard to picture geology geeks on a killing spree."

Jocelyn was in full-out Joni Mitchell posture, barefooted and cross-legged in the corner, flashing her turquoise rings as she did chords. She butted in to say, "Everyone is capable of murder. In the wild, it's called nature. When governments do it, it's called war."

"Besides," Corinna said, pausing to pull an empty candy wrapper off her tongue. "Geology geeks probably know the best places to bury people."

The fact that her sister had come home, at that of all times, hit Violet in a wave of dizzying confusion and heat. "Rose!" She'd gestured toward the foyer. "Rose is here! Rose!"

"That's not funny!" Josephine screamed. "Douglas, do something! Now! Make her stop!" And then, to Violet: "Your sister has disowned us. You need to come to terms with that. She doesn't want anything to do with me or you, or you, or you!" She directed the last two *yous* at Douglas and Will. Violet's father was pale, trembling. Will's face was slick with tears.

Violet had felt white light coursing out of her chest.

Several seemingly profound insights had come to her that evening—for instance, that "reality" is just made up of layers upon layers of hallucinations—but few drug-induced revelations seemed as probable as this one: every atom in Violet's body was borrowed from something else, whether it was oxygen, or sunlight, or food straight off Dekker's farm. As a fetus, she'd been part of her sickly twisted mother, who had absorbed only the darkest, most rotten parts of her own environment.

Whatever was wrong with Josephine, it was in Violet too. A very clear acid vision of her DNA whirled in front of her, and Violet saw the dark, diseased half of her personality helixed around the bright, joyous part. The two were impossible to separate. She couldn't take one and leave the other, and yet she had a moral obligation to end her grotesque legacy. There was only one way to break the cycle:

"Suicide," she'd said. Violet had been amazed by the ease and joy with which the statement slipped out, simply coasted away on its own accord like it was filled with helium. It was the lightest word she'd spoken all night.

She hadn't stopped there. She'd said it three or four more times as she worked out the details. *Suicide, suicide.* It occurred to her with crushing disappointment that not even *sallekhana* would break the cycle because even if Violet killed herself, her atoms would just be fed back into a closed system of struggle and pain. There was no end. There was no way out. History would just keep right on repeating.

Reality came screaming back at high volume.

"Guys! GUYS!" Will was pleading.

Douglas was slurring, "Now, Violent. Violet."

Violet looked down and realized that she still held the Wüsthof knife in her fist. She had all eight gleaming inches of it pointed at her mother.

"You are so sick!" Josephine wailed in a voice like a battle cry.

The word *sick* had made Violet uncontrollably sad, thinking of Beryl. Violet had given herself a consoling hug, and as she did, she noticed a total absence of feeling. Violet couldn't feel her body.

Her throat was gone when she clutched it with her hand. Ditto her eyes when she tried to rub them.

Violet might have followed through with her original thought—suicide, the old-fashioned kind; Violet might have been one of those acid freaks who carved up their arms or swan-dived out of open windows—were it not for the fact that she thought she was already dead. Her consciousness had been void. She hadn't been aware of herself breathing. She'd worried that she would wake up in a hell that was even worse than the one she was trying to escape from. The time on the microwave oven looked like currency. It read $7.42.

"Poughkeepsie!" her mom was shouting. "Not Kingston! Are you hearing me, Douglas? Violet needs to go to the hospital in *Poughkeepsie.*"

Kingston was closer, but Poughkeepsie had an in-patient psychiatric hospital.

When Violet and her father left for the hospital, the knife had been lying on the cutting board. Will had been standing by their mother's side in silent support. He'd been wide-eyed and watching, overdressed in a cardigan and a clip-on tie. No blood. No tears. No seizures. No expression in his eyes. There hadn't been a single mark on him.

William Hurst

Will hoisted himself onto the frilly bed and put a soothing hand on Douglas's shoulder.

Probably it should have been terrifying to see his robotic father's long, intent stream of tears. But Will was grateful, even relieved. This was a role he knew how to play.

"Shhh, Dad," Will cooed. The gentle hand Douglas put on Will's elbow urged *stop*.

"You don't need to rescue me, son," Douglas said. "It's my job to protect you. Not the other way around. Besides, as Kerry likes to say, if you try to help a butterfly out of its cocoon, it might die. The butterfly needs the struggle in order to be strong."

Douglas moved around the room, leafing through Rose's yellowed *Playbills*, tearing down the few remaining snapshots that were Blu-Tacked above her desk. He went to Rose's rack of handbags and chucked each one down onto the cabbage-rose rug. He tossed Will a pink striped beach bag. "Go through the pockets," he instructed.

Will ran his hands over the canvas. It was still sandy from Rose's last trip to North-South Lake. He pulled out a pair of pink-lensed sunglasses. "The police already did this," he said.

"There must be something they missed. I've missed something. I've spent the past year ignoring the obvious. I didn't want to give up the promise. I wanted so badly for it to be true."

Will nodded knowingly. "You wanted to think Rose left because *she* wanted to leave."

Douglas nodded. "It was all because of that fucking guy," he muttered under his breath. So Will wasn't overreacting. The hair dryer was proof that Rose's no-good boyfriend hadn't given her much warning or choice. For all the Hursts knew, he might have practically kidnapped her.

Will decided it was time to bring his dad his best find: Rose's pregnancy journal. He wanted to save it for his mother, but the last time he'd tried to show her, she'd refused him and then punished him. What use was super-sleuthing if there was no one around to appreciate your work? Sherlock had Watson. Frank Hardy had Joe.

If his dad was impressed with Will's fact-finding, he didn't show it. Douglas only turned the pages delicately with the Ralph Lauren handkerchief he always carried in his front pocket. Will and Josephine gave him a near-identical one every Father's Day. They were always silk, always tartan. "Who else has seen this?" he asked.

"Just me, I think. There's not much in there about her boyfriend. Even so, he doesn't sound like a very nice guy."

"No. No, he doesn't," Douglas said. The sleepwalker quality had returned to his face. He was blank and unblinking, a million light-years away. After he'd read each page two or three times, he wrapped the journal in the plastic bag that had been sitting empty in Rose's wastebasket.

"What are you going to do with it?" Will asked.

"Nothing yet."

"Where are you taking it? *Dad?*"

But Douglas just wandered out of the room. "Meet me in my office," he called back, in a tone so grave it made Will gasp for air.

VIOLET HURST

IT WAS NEARING lights-out when Violet got a phone call.

"You've got five minutes! Literally! Five!" a nurse shouted as Violet sidled into the booth.

Violet nodded as she picked up the phone.

"Violet? Detective Donnelly."

The nurse was still hovering. "I need verbal confirmation."

"I hear you, five minutes." Violet waved the woman away. "Sorry about that," she said, cringing.

"No need for apologies," Donnelly said, and there was a certain closed-off tone in his voice that hadn't been there last time. "I just wanted to let you know I've had a word with Matt and Francesca."

"Both of them?"

"Yes. Matt insisted he hasn't seen Rose since he ended his relationship with her eighteen months ago."

Farther down the hall, nurses were laughing, likely at someone else's expense. "Couldn't he be lying?"

"He didn't give me that impression. And Francesca said she didn't have any reason to suspect Matt had resumed the affair."

Of course these two—who paid property taxes and had

matching simple gold bands—would have more clout with the police than a teenage mental patient. "But Matt wouldn't exactly tell his wife if he was seeing my sister again."

The line rustled with wind, and Violet realized Donnelly was talking on his cell phone. "Both of them were very sorry to hear about your brother," he said. "They're eager to cooperate and put everything that happened with Rose behind them."

I bet they are, Violet thought.

There was a brushing sound like Donnelly switched the phone to the other ear or rubbed his wearied cheek with his palm. "For that reason, they agreed to open their New York apartment to us. The landlord let one of my men in, and Rose wasn't there."

"She's not there right *now*. Rose said in her letters that she splits her time between there and upstate."

"Violet, there's nothing to indicate she's *ever* been here. My guy spoke to the neighbors. Only one of them thought he'd *maybe* seen Rose, and if so, it was well over a year ago."

"But it's Manhattan! They say nobody in Manhattan knows their neighbors!"

The nurse was back at Violet's shoulder, aggression coming off her like heat and body odor. "Five minutes is up," she barked.

"Look, Violet. Nothing in those letters sounds threatening from what you've described. Nothing in here qualifies as stalking or harassment. They seemed pretty friendly to me. And if your sister is writing to you, well then, she's not a missing person either."

The nurse pressed in behind Violet. "Last warning."

"Count of three before I hang up for you," the nurse said. "One, two . . ."

Violet felt her pulse surge. "But I've been thinking . . . Maybe Rose came back to extort my parents for money. Last year, she didn't clean out her bank account 'cause she was planning to run away. She cleaned it out to pay for her abor—"

The nurse plunged her fingers into the cradle and the line went dead.

—tion. Violet's shoulders fell.

She spun around grimacing, and the nurse oh-so-sweetly said, "Three."

WILLIAM HURST

WHEREAS EVERYTHING IN Josephine's cozy, type-A office was organized into baskets, binders, and bins, Douglas's was ice cold right down to its tile floor and cramped, in what the house's previous owners had used as a laundry room. The nature of the small space meant Will had to stand uncomfortably close to his dad's ergonomic chair. Will felt claustrophobic. Everywhere he looked there were computer cables, CD towers, and pollen-tinged dust.

Much like in his father's IBM office, there were no personal touches anywhere: no sentimental-value paperweight, not a single frame on the wall. What did his father *like*? Will had no idea. He could have written volumes about his mother's preferences, but he didn't know a thing about his dad's.

Douglas was powering on his computer.

"So what do you need my help with?" Will asked.

But his father, taking a sip of his (hopefully virgin) seltzer, already seemed too lost in concentration to answer. He steered his web browser to Rose's e-mail provider and quickly entered her address from memory.

"You know Rose's password?" Will asked as the cursor leapt into the next blank box.

"Not yet. You're going to help me figure it out."

"Me? *You're* the computer person. Don't you have, like, some program that can hack into e-mail accounts?"

"No. But most passwords are social in nature. People use passwords that are easy to remember. Or they reuse passwords. I'm saying they can be guessed." His fingers tap-danced over the keys.

"So what are you guessing?"

"Figured I'd try the most common passwords to start with."

That password is incorrect, the site blipped back in red.

"Like what?"

"Oh, you know . . . *12345. Jesus. Princess. Love. Letmein.* A lot of people use the word *password* itself."

Will didn't know. But he was shocked by his own interest in the subject. It was an aspect of language he'd never thought of. Computer language. The wording of privacy. Even to Will, who bludgeoned everything with vocabulary, it seemed dangerous to put words to something secret. Once he and his dad cracked his sister's password—once they figured out, definitively, what was going on with Rose—they might be obliged to act. That was the thing about words: they were the stakes that pinned down reality. Occasionally, Will feared language even as he skewered things with it.

"There are also leet-speak passwords," Douglas continued. "Those are the ones where numbers are substituted for letters. Like if I type *Rose*, but I enter a zero in place of the O."

That password is incorrect.

Douglas drummed his fingers on the edge of the desk. "Okay," he said. "Okay. This is good."

"Good?" Will echoed.

"Yes. I would have been disappointed if Rose were foolish enough to use any of those. And if *you're* using any of those passwords, you might as well go out and hand your wallet over to the first person you see on the street."

Will was ashamed to think he and his mother had come up with the password *ChristLove* for his own e-mail account.

You have too many incorrect answers, Rose's e-mail said, locking them out.

"So what do we do now?" Will asked.

"Let's use an anonymous IP address and try again. Grab those *Playbills*," Douglas said, pointing to the stack at Will's feet. "We're going to try every production Rose has ever been in. Plus the name of every character Rose has ever played."

Will did as he was told. Rose's plays came charging back at him in no particular order: *Camelot*; *Act a Lady*; *Into the Woods*; *Pygmalion*; *Dracula*; *Shakespeare's Pericles*. He and his father tried not only *SandraDee* and *Maria* as passwords, but also *SummerNights*, *GreasedLightnin'*, *VonTrapp*, and *RainDropsOnRoses*.

"Dad?" Will asked.

"Uh-huh."

"Why didn't you ever do this before?"

"Because, unlike your mother, I don't enjoy going through my children's things. But this is an emergency. Anyway, I think we need to change tracks. Go back up to Rose's room and bring down any books and CDs you find. Also, take a look in her closet. Take this notepad and write down her favorite clothing brands."

When Will returned they punched in the names of all Rose's perfumes and clothing labels, but it all felt too frivolous and shallow to be right. What private thing did girls guard most closely? Boys. Relationships. Will knew as much from the puppy loves Violet professed in the journal their mom read. Whatever Rose's password was, it had to do with her boyfriend. Will felt sure of that.

"You didn't find any CDs?" his father asked.

Will shook his head. "Rose listened to music files on her laptop. She took them all with her."

Douglas blew out his lips. "No way to know her favorite songs, then."

"Rose is into different stuff now," Will said, thinking of the pregnancy journal. "Maybe you should try the name of a campsite or a hiking trail."

They pored over Internet maps of Minnewaska State Park and the Mohonk Preserve. Neither of them acknowledged aloud how many years it had been since they'd hiked any of the looping trails.

"Try EchoRock," Will said.

Douglas made the sound of a game-show fail. "Waa waa."

"What about CastlePoint?"

"No such luck."

It went on that way, miss after miss.

"Remind me," Douglas said. "What was Rose's favorite class? What had she changed her major to?"

"Something in the science department." Will flushed again. Why hadn't any of them been listening that first night when Rose came back giddy, ponytail swinging, from the registrar's office? Because they had immediately started in on the reasons Rose needed to return to theater. Will still remembered his mother's mid-dinner speech: *It's just plain selfish, Rosette, to throw away the opportunities you have. You can go around talking about how it's your life and your choice. But a lot of people—professors, agents—have gone out of their way for you. You're letting them down too. It's a slap in the face.*

Just then, Will remembered the class schedule he'd swiped from Rose's room.

He ran to the upstairs clothes hamper, praying that his mother hadn't yet washed his corduroy pants. They were still there, under a few days worth of tighty-whities and stale argyle socks. School-work wasn't the only thing his mother had neglected thanks to the Violet crisis. Will snatched the course list from the pocket and hurried back to the office, where his father was subtly swiveling his chair and biting the inside of his cheek.

"Class schedule. It doesn't say her major. Just what she was taking. Here," Will said, thrusting the sheet at his dad.

"Hold on to it and read them out to me. I'll look each class up on SUNY's website."

"ENG393."

"That'd be an English class. Is there anything on there that looks like science?"

"BIO220?"

"Good, that's biology. Doesn't look like *Biology* is her password, though. Anything else?"

"GLG293?"

"Geology. Selected Topics. That was Rose's new major. I re-member now."

Will suddenly remembered too. *Forgive me, Rose,* his mother had said, laughing. *I just don't see it. I really don't. You want to work for, what? The petroleum industry? You do know they could send you to Niger or something—some primitive, oily place five thousand miles from your beloved Clinique counter?*

"Ha! I'm in!" Douglas cried, slamming a triumphant palm on the desk.

"*Geology* was the password?" It seemed all wrong to Will.

"No. It was that course number you gave me: GLG293."

"*Really?*" Will frowned. Moments earlier, he'd been ready to bet his life that Rose's password had sentimental value. At the end of the day, a favorite class was still a class. Surely, people didn't use passwords that reminded them of deadlines and work to be done; they chose a person, a place, a sweetheart's birthday—some ar-row that struck their memories at the core.

Cingulomania: a strong desire to hold a person in your arms.

"Oh no," Douglas moaned. "Oh no, no, no, no."

Will's scalp crawled. His arms fell asleep at the shoulders. He knew what was wrong the moment he glanced at the screen. There were pages of boldface unopened e-mails. Hundreds of e-mails. Thousands, maybe. Everything from personal messages to spam reminders that there were Facebook friend requests awaiting Rose's next login.

"How far back do they go?" Will asked.

But he knew the answer. They dated back over a year, to when Rose "ran away." Will was going to have to think about it that way now—in ironic quotations. The English book he and his mom used had a special name for them: scare quotes. It had always seemed a strange term to Will, but there in the ice-cold chaos of his father's office, he finally got it. There was nothing, absolutely nothing more chilling than a term you needed to put between bars and distance yourself from.

VIOLET HURST

VIOLET HEARD THE predawn commotion and assumed a new intake was to blame. Patients had been rolling in steadily over the past few days. Maybe it was a full moon. More likely, everyone had eaten the same bad batch of dirty, unpredictable stimulants. Whatever the cause, people kept coming in either so catatonic that they had to be spoon-fed and sponge-bathed or so manic and dangerously sleep-deprived that they thought they were being hunted for sport. Violet heard the stampede of clogs and assumed the crisis probably involved some thwarted med-seeker. She buried her face in her mattress and her ears in her palms. It wasn't until morning that the sickening news reached her.

Jocelyn, Corinna, and Helen were huddled around the same table with trays of the silver dollar pancakes everyone called "sand-cakes" on account of the texture. It didn't help that the maple syrup they were served with tasted more like soy sauce. Violet swung her leg over the bench seat and joined them.

"Did you hear?" Corinna asked.

Violet took a swig of pale, lukewarm coffee and shook her head.

Jocelyn's eyes widened. She stopped sucking the ends of her hair. "Edie tried to kill herself."

Violet's stomach spasmed and shrank. Possibly, she asked, *What?*

"I was sleeping," Helen said. "But Edie tore the spiral out of her notebook and sliced a huge gash down her arm with the sharp end of it. She used so much pressure that it even cut part of a vein. When I woke up, there was blood *everywhere.*"

Violet's eyes fell to Jocelyn's cup of tomato juice, which suddenly smelled too strong and looked much too gory. "Is she okay?" she asked.

Helen shrugged and hugged herself. "That's what they keep saying."

"She's not on the ward?" Violet's words were quivery around the consonants. She heard herself and realized she was trying not to cry.

Jocelyn's Tinker Bell eyes were wide. "We think she's somewhere getting stitched up."

Violet felt irrationally angry. She cared about Edie, but she suddenly felt she couldn't relate to her. For everything they seemed to have in common, suicidal tendencies weren't one of them. Violet had been drawn to drugs and *sallekhana* because they seemed like the only way to end her mom's cruelty. Away from Josephine, life seemed possible, exciting even. Violet *wanted* to live. That was what made her an anomaly at Fallkill. She cared about Edie and Corinna, but she didn't belong among them. She needed to get out.

Violet went to therapy and demanded to know the status of her three-day request.

"I just need to clear your file with a few of my colleagues," Sara-pist said.

Violet fought hard not to roll her eyes at the mention of the file. Everything went into the file: what she ate, what she said, how she looked, who she talked to. People watched her all day and scribbled.

"But I'm better!" Violet insisted. "No acid flashbacks. No urge to hurt myself. To my knowledge, no one's pressing charges about Will."

"I hear you," Sara-pist said. "But you need to sit tight through the paperwork. Do you think you can do that?"

Violet nodded.

"And you're sure you're not too vulnerable to go home? Your friend attempted suicide last night, Violet. You came in here angry and crying."

"Please don't hold that against me when you make your decision. I wouldn't be human, would I, if I weren't upset for my friends?"

"No," Sara-pist said. "You're right. Of course you're upset for them. You're dealing with real emotions and real life. I take that as a good sign. You're connecting with people—honestly, no lying—even if there's no guarantee that things will work out. That's how real intimacy works."

"You've got mail," the nurse said when she saw Violet walking back to her room with bleary, red eyes. The joke was twenty years lame, and Violet couldn't drum up even a polite half-smile.

The seal. That damn, prissy seal. Today, Violet, who was drained already, felt almost offended by the treble clef. It was such a bold declaration, such a call to duty, and Violet wasn't sure she was willing to answer it.

. . .

God, Violet craved a little chemical help. How badly she wanted to light something, *anything*, hit after hit after hit after hit. She needed to flood her bloodstream, change her brain filter, recalibrate, send herself tumbling into far-off oblivion.

Under these circumstances, cigarettes would have to do. Violet tucked the letter inside her waistband and went outside with a pack Edie had given her from her never-ending carton. She took two quick, deep puffs and immediately felt worse. She watched the smoke coil and turned the letter over and over, wishing she could simply touch a match to it and watch a lifetime of dysfunction brown and curl to ashes.

In the end, she felt a tug of misplaced loyalty and clumsily slit the envelope with her finger.

She saw the bright blue ink and Rose's ruler-straight handwriting. *Dear Violet*, it read. *Damien and I have been talking . . . If you need a place to crash, you're welcome here!*

WILLIAM HURST

"Maybe she just changed her e-mail address?" Will asked. He realized it was his nervous tic, saying things that were upbeat and consoling. But it wasn't totally and completely out of the question.

Will's father shook his head and sat up taller in his office chair. "Even so, she would have at least read some of these. She would have written to *somebody* on her contact list and given them her new address. Her outgoing e-mails stop last October too."

"What are you going to do?"

Douglas pushed himself away from his desk and leaned forward with his hands on his knees. "It's time to go to the police again," he said, rocking rhythmically, a sick look on his face. "I almost hired a private investigator a few months ago. But everyone kept saying she'd never come back unless we gave her space. Your mother and I decided it was better to focus our resources and attention on you and Violet. Look to the future, we told ourselves. Stop living in the past."

Will's mouth went dry. He wished his mother's "me-time" would end soon. He and his father were not equipped to deal with this new revelation alone. "So Rose is missing again?" he asked.

"Not *again*. If she's missing, she's always been missing."

Will rubbed his itching eyes. The dust in his father's office was getting to him. "No," he said. "No, she's out there somewhere. She's writing Violet letters."

"I've heard," Douglas said. Will tried not to look surprised. He'd always thought his father was the last to hear about things the rest of the family knew. "Have you read these letters, Will?"

"No."

"No, I haven't read them either."

"Do you think this has something to do with her boyfriend, Damien?"

"I don't know. I don't know anything about Damien. Do you?"

Will pointed to himself. His brows shot up. "Me?"

Douglas kept staring. "Has your mother said anything about him to you?"

"Just that he sounded really nasty when he called here last year. Damien called Mom a bunch of names. He said Rose hated her."

"Yes. I remember how upset she was."

"Well, let's just go through her e-mails," Will said. "Damien must be in there somewhere. We can find him. We can write to him."

Douglas raked his fingers through his hair. "I don't know, Will. I don't think we should go messing around in her e-mails, at least not until we call the police. This time last year, they kept saying, *No foul play. Nothing suspicious*, they told me. Well, what do you call this?" He balled up the sheet of paper where they'd been keeping track of wrong passwords and lobbed it in frustration. "We've lost *a year*. If this Damien is hurting Rose . . . If he took her against her will . . . If he's influencing her . . . Well then, we've given him one whole year to cover his tracks so we can never pin him with *anything*."

There was the far-off sound of his mother's car keys clinking into the crystal bowl on the entrance table, and a weight lifted from Will's chest when he heard her footsteps on the hardwood.

"I wondered where everybody was," Josephine said. Her hair had big, bouncy fresh-from-the-salon curls, and an odd chemical smell that carried. It took a second for Will to fully absorb the change.

"You're blond," he said.

Josephine rolled her eyes lightly and laughed. "That's an over-statement. It's just a slightly different shade. The stylist said women my age always make the mistake of going darker, but actually lighter makes people look younger."

"It's pretty," Will said.

"Thank you, honey," she cooed, leaning down to kiss him. "I'm glad someone thinks so." A throat-clear in Douglas's direction.

Will's father didn't look away from the screen. He blinked once, slow and painful. "Jo, Rose has a year's worth of unopened e-mails."

"What? No." Her face fell. Transfixed by the screen, she moved closer and put one hand on the back of Douglas's chair.

Douglas stood and unholstered his cell phone. "What are you doing?"

Josephine was swirling her middle finger around the laptop touchpad. "Reading her e-mails. I think we need to read her e-mails, don't you?"

"Just wait, Jo. Wait for the police," Douglas said, shooing her away from the keyboard and logging out.

"Okay," she said, trembling. "Okay, you're right. I can see that Damien being behind this. We need to do something. What can I do to help? What if I pull up her credit report?" It was like she kept throwing out questions until one stuck. "That would be a help, wouldn't it? *Finances don't lie*, that's what they kept telling us last year. Would that help, Douglas? Hello? Answer me!"

"Sure, Jo. Fine. That would be great." His words were enthusiastic, but his voice was fat with annoyance that she'd broken
some train of thought.

Cagamosis: an unhappy marriage.

While Douglas stepped into the hallway, Josephine reclaimed his
office chair and typed *credit ratings* into Google.

"What an idiot," she said, of herself. "I should have thought to
do this months ago. Wait here, Will," she said, when the screen
locked on a website advertising "fast" and "secure" three-bureau
reports.

Will didn't know how best to help. His chest felt tight. His
heart wasn't *racing*, so much as hobbling along unevenly, a cripple
trying to run. "Where are you going?" he asked.

"To get Rose's social security card."

She was back a few minutes later. "Oh, honey," she said when
she saw him anxiously fidgeting with a fanged staple remover. "It
will be all right, I promise you. Here, sit down. I won't have you
seizing, on top of everything else."

Will's mother angled the laptop slightly toward her and entered Rose's full name and social security number. As she leaned
over him to type, the salon smell hit him in another heady wave.
This thought occurred to Will: she'd been trying to make herself
more attractive for his father; she was trying desperately to re-
claim one thing from the life she'd had B.C. (*before crazy* in the case
of Violet, *before crime* where it concerned Rose).

"He's not cheating," Will whispered, in case his father was
within earshot. "He's late from work all the time because he's at
AA meetings. The person he's always texting is a guy called Kerry,
his sponsor."

His mother's smile was pure sunshine, the best thing Will had seen all day. Her head tipped back in ecstatic relief. She leaned down and hugged Will's skull with both hands. She peppered his hair with kisses and brushed his bangs out of his eyes. "Shhh," she said, putting a manicured finger to her lips.

Will nodded, understanding that she wanted to let his dad tell her himself.

"So, Will," she said. "Let me tell you about credit scores. Higher is better. Rose . . . Here we go . . . Rose has a seven hundred, which is high. She opened two new cards after she ran away. She's two thousand dollars in debt, but that's not the top of her spending limit."

Will's shoulders clenched. Two thousand dollars sounded like an awful lot. "Is that bad news?" he asked.

"I'd say it's encouraging news. See here? She pays her cards on time and she's still using them."

"So, Damien hasn't hurt her? She's okay?" Last year, during Rose's brief missing-person case, the Hursts had used *okay* as a stand-in for *alive*.

"That's not my place to say, Will. Your sister cut us out of her life. But I'd say, at least according to this, she's not lying dead in a gutter somewhere. Your father overreacted last year, and made our run-of-the-mill family conflict the whole town's business. I'm not going to let him lose his head again. I won't give Rose and that boyfriend the satisfaction." She got an error message and let out a frustrated grunt. "The printer's out of ink. Will, show me how to change the cartridge. Now, please. The police are gonna want to see this."

Violet Hurst

Rose wanted Violet to come live with her. That was the gilded promise, which was so damn dream-come-true, so Publishers Clearing House sweepstakes, it might as well have come with a self-addressed stamped envelope and a message about how changing her life was as simple as ticking a box.

Sounds like you really do hate Mom! Rose had written. Get out of there! Come stay with us instead! I'll help you register for school. I'll help you find a job. Whatever you need, we'll figure it all out. Call me when you get out of the hospital and we'll pick an easy place to meet up. It would be so great, wouldn't it? All the Garfield we want! You'll never have to turn back your watch again!

The last two lines were inside jokes. When they were kids, their mother forbade Garfield comic strips because—direct quote—they "glorified laziness." Also, when Violet was six or seven years old, she'd once turned back the time on her Minnie Mouse wristwatch, thinking it would literally delay six o'clock, when she had to be home for another tense family meal.

At the very end was the lifeline: Rose's phone number. Those ten little digits might as well have been the answer to a combination lock—a big old Master Lock like the one on Violet's old gym locker—and metaphorically speaking, Violet spent a whole year spinning and yanking it, wondering all the while what it would take to get through to the sister who either hated or ignored her. And now, *Open sesame.* The lock had sprung open on its own like some lucky malfunction. All at once, Rose had handed Violet her freedom *and* a (noncompetitive, noncombative) sibling relationship.

Violet was beyond touched. She was thrilled. Rose offering her a place to stay just when she needed one most! But she couldn't help also feeling slightly burned. When she'd opened up in her last letter, she'd wanted some kind of affirmation. She'd been hoping, on some level, that Rose would feel her pain and acknowledge the disparate treatment they'd always had from their mother. *Yes,* she'd wanted Rose to write. *I know you always got it worse than me. I saw that too. I really did. I feel your pain.*

Violet had just stubbed out her cigarette when Edie swung open the patio door. Her eyes were downcast, and she walked with slow, precious movements across the brickface stones. Seeing Violet, her face turned sheepish. "Bum me one of those?" she asked, more to the pack than to Violet herself.

"They're yours."

Edie made a half-assed attempt at a smile. "In that case, give me one?"

Violet had to wield the matches because Edie's left arm was mummified straight down to her limp-looking hand. It was a shocking sight: the long bandage, presumably the long wound. Edie hadn't slit her wrist, she'd slit her whole arm. Just looking at it made Violet's own forearm ache like a cavity.

Violet inhaled the first drag and passed the ciggie to Edie with two fingers. "How are you feeling?" she finally asked.

"Pretty embarrassed, actually."

"If it's any consolation, I think almost everyone here has done their own version. We've all been where you are."

Edie nodded like she wasn't quite convinced. "I've never done it that way before."

"How'd it rate?"

"It was different. It took more out of me. They're always saying, on cop shows and things, how intimate stabbings are. How they take all this passion and anger. I get that now."

A feeling of dread descended on her. She wondered if whoever hurt Will had the gut-level hatred for him that people like she and Edie had for themselves.

"What've you got there?" Edie asked.

"Another letter from my sister."

Edie nodded. "Does she say anything about the other night? You still think she went all *Kill Bill* on your brother?"

"*Kill Will*, you mean? Funny." Violet flipped the envelope over and traced the seal with her finger again. "I don't know. She still won't say a word about Will. She asked if I want to stay with her when I get out of here."

"They're sending you home?"

"Probably. I hope so. Sara-pist is being slippery about the whole thing, blaming paperwork."

Edie ashed thoughtfully. "Moving in with Rose would solve a lot of your problems. At least you wouldn't have to go home to that lying lunatic."

Unless, of course, Rose and Damien turned out to be lunatics too. "It's just a lot to digest. I don't mean to be suspicious. It's just whenever Rose—whenever *anyone*—in my family goes out of their way, there's usually some angle."

"You feel like there's a hidden agenda," Edie said, chewing her lip. "I get that."

"On the other hand, I feel like I have a sister again."

Edie gave her shoulder a supportive squeeze. "You'll figure something out. You have time."

Violet worried the corner of Rose's letter. "I'm not really sure I have much time at all."

WILLIAM HURST

"HERE, DOUGLAS," WILL'S mother said, waving Rose's credit report.

"Great," he answered, looking right through her. "I'll show it to the police when I get to the station."

"Don't just put it in your pocket. *Look* at it. Rose has opened new credit cards! I think that's encouraging, don't you?"

"Fantastic," Douglas said flatly. "I'll be sure they take a look. It has occurred to you that Damien might have opened those, right?"

"You're leaving right this second? Can't it wait until tomorrow?"

"I told them I'd come in tonight."

"What about dinner? You two must be famished."

Will nodded. "I *am*. I'm esurient."

Douglas shot him a look that could maim if not kill. "Just say you're hungry," he said barely under his breath.

"But it means the same thing!" Will's voice was a piglet squeal.

"He's right, Douglas. I mean, really. Just because *you're* not a logophile." Josephine winked at Will and laughed bitterly.

• • •

Even Will could acknowledge it was over the top: the trouble his mother went to, the way she set the table with linen napkins and soup bowls nested in decorative plates.

"Really, Josie," Will's dad said. "There's no time for all this."

"*All this* is just reheated soup. It's in the microwave now. Do you want a glass of wine?" There was a jagged edge to her smile. "Or something else?"

"No, Jo. I just want to get to the station. Are you trying to make me late on purpose? Don't you care about Rose?"

"That's a ridiculous thing to say. Of course I care about Rose. But Will is my priority. If you're so worried, why don't you two put on your shoes to save time? We'll eat, fast as three truck drivers, and then off we go. I want Will *fed*. I have a theory about blood sugar and seizures."

Will's face froze in panic. He hadn't told his mother about his field trip to the head-shrinker's office, about Doc Martin's jackassed theory that Will's disordered nervous system was really just the way his brain's limbic system coped with trauma and fear. When he did, his dad would be in mondo trouble for undermining her.

"Come on, Will," Douglas said.

Will was woozy as he leaned over his Hush Puppies. He felt laden, mulelike, like he was carrying every ounce of nervousness his parents weren't showing.

"Here," Douglas said, tossing his car keys.

Will failed to catch them, and they clattered onto the floor.

"We have to wait for Mom."

"Just go warm up the car."

"I don't know *how*."

Douglas's face was flushed with frustration. "You just slide the key into the hole and turn."

"But what if—What if the car starts to go by mistake?"

"Will, the car isn't going to go anywhere unless you put it into *gear*."

"Oh." Shame bloomed, like a poison flower, in Will's stomach. Maybe home school really *was* failing him.

Will hated the garage at night. It was morgue-level cold, and the fluorescent lights flickered, giving everything a pale, unreal cast. He walked toward his dad's car and tried not to look directly at the fierce scribble of scratches on the driver's door. Reaching for the handle, he caught his lightly warped reflection in the convex window. He thought he saw something—a shadow—move behind him, but when he spun around no one was there. There was nothing other than teetering snow shovels, garden rakes, and a mess of recycling—half-rinsed and stinking—all the behind-closed-doors mess his parents tried to keep out of view. Will slid the key into the ignition, brought the engine growling to life. He opened the garage door on his way back inside.

Back in the dining room, three steaming bowls waited on the table. The soup was cauliflower, and the whole scene looked straight out of the fable of the three little bears, except two of the place settings had glasses of white wine.

Will cast a sideways, raised-eyebrow look at his mother. He was attempting telepathy. *Remember?* he was trying to say. *Remember what I told you in Dad's office about Dad's little problem?*

Josephine just smiled and lifted a spoon. As an afterthought, she asked (commanded, really), "Will, won't you please pass your father the bread?"

Will did as he was told. He dipped into the bowl. He watched the colorless sludge swallow the head of his spoon. "This is terrific," he said, although it wasn't his favorite. He was careful to follow his mother's strict guidelines for eating soup: skim from the front of the bowl to the back, sip from the side. *No, I said, sip! Not slurp!*

"This was in the freezer?" Douglas asked.

Josephine ignored the question. "And why is this so urgent we need to go to the station tonight? Are they going to look at us like we are alarmist fools who could have just called with an update?"

"We're going to the station because I demanded to go," Douglas said. "I want to know the police are taking this seriously. I want to know it's a priority."

Josephine looked at him in disbelief. "And what exactly are we telling the police? That Rose hasn't checked her e-mail?"

"Among other things. Does this taste peculiar to you?" Douglas smacked his lips without relish. His nose wrinkled. "Like dish soap maybe? Were these bowls just washed?"

Will shook his head. He didn't taste anything strange. He took another spoonful and chewed a lump.

Josephine tore a small chunk of baguette in half with brute force. "You're losing your mind, old man. What are the other things?"

"Rose's blow dryer," Will said. "She left it here."

His mother screwed up her brow. "Wait, I don't get it . . . Her hair dryer? Am I missing something, here? Will? *Douglas?* Your sister—our daughter—took her laptop, her phone, her suitcase, her toothbrush. She packed up and left us. She ran out. Didn't we learn anything last year? I mean this . . . This is like déjà vu all over again."

It was unlike her to be redundant, but Will didn't dare pipe up to say déjà vu *implied* all over again. "It was just this stupid thing we heard on the radio," he mumbled with downcast eyes. "Women can't live without their hair dryers. That's what they said."

Josephine's elbow was on the table, her hand fisted around her spoon. "I'm not even going to get started on how sexist that is. And you, Douglas, traipsing around here on a workday, collecting so-called clues. Give me a break. Sherlock Holmes, the sot, and his retarded Watson." She covered her mouth—a coquettish gesture that clashed with her deep, brutal laugh. "Oops, did I say that?"

Cachinnate, a doing word: *to laugh loudly and inappropriately.*

Will helped her clear the plates to prove he wasn't a burden. Alone with her in the kitchen, he waited for her to acknowledge the word she'd called him. When she didn't, Will held up Douglas's full wineglass. "What should I do with this?" he asked.

"Oh, Will," she said, taking it and kissing him hard on the temple. "I can't believe I poured that for him. Muscle memory, I guess. But then once it was poured, I figured I might as well test him. We'll see how serious he is about this whole AA experiment."

The police station wasn't far, but the stretch of state route they took was particularly scary at night. In the backseat, Will sat in the middle and peered out the windshield, on the lookout for road-jumping deer. He said his Hail Marys as they whizzed by four roadside memorials. It was hard to say why this stretch of road inspired so many crashes. Maybe the speed limit was at fault: fifty-five meant sixty-five, and the center line—dotted for miles— meant a lot of people passed at eighty. Or maybe drunk drivers on their way home from Kingston were to blame. Even tonight, motorists drifted toward them, their headlights blinding bright. At the last minute, they honked and veered sharply away.

Josephine leaned over and put a guiding hand on the wheel. "Douglas," she said, gently.

"Wha-aat?" It was a lazy, slack-tongued question the way Will's dad said it.

"Douglas, you're all over the road. Slow down and pull off here."

Douglas took his foot off the accelerator and Will's mom helped guide the car into the empty rail trail parking lot. She un-clicked his seat belt after he slowly slid the gearshift into park.

"What's going on?" Will's dad asked with the same husky breath and slow, draggy vowels.

"You tell me," his mother huffed, unbuckling herself. "Were you drinking before dinner?" She opened her door. Her coat blew open as she strode in front of the car.

His father did seem drunk, especially the way his forehead bumped the door frame when he got out of the car. In the head-lights, Douglas leaned, childlike, against Josephine while she guided him around a pothole in the dirt. A pebble caught the corner of his loafer, and his ankle turned. He caught himself on the hood, clumsy and loose-limbed, his eyes three-quarters shut. Josephine adjusted her grip and helped him regain his balance.

"Mom, is Dad okay?" Will asked after she'd helped Douglas into the passenger seat and was angling the power seat into a steep decline.

"He's fine. Reckless. Selfish, but fine." She slammed the door and returned to the driver's side. Adjusting her seat so it was closer to the steering wheel, she said, "I mean, what kind of person gets blitzed on his way to the police station?"

Will thought back to his father's speech about alcohol hijack-ing the decision-making parts of a person's brain. "An alcoholic, I guess."

"I guess." Her voice dripped with sarcasm. She surfed the radio using Douglas's preset buttons. "The Weight" was playing on two stations simultaneously. The song was one of Will's favorites—the unofficial county anthem, on account of local hero Levon Helm—but it made Josephine shudder with revulsion. She switched over to the AM dial and tuned it to a classical station. The car filled with heavy cello.

Will cast another glance at Douglas. He was sagging and lopsided in the front seat. "What I don't get," he said, "is that Dad didn't drink his wine at dinner. And he wasn't drinking at home with me today."

"Oh, Will, you're so naïve. I remember the days when I let him fool me the way he fools you. I could draw you a treasure map of all the places he hides alcohol in our house." She shifted the car into drive and steered it onto the road in the opposite direction. "We're going to have to bring him home, and go back to the station on our own. I'd say we could let him sleep it off in the parking lot, but if anyone saw him like this . . . in a *police station* no less . . ."

She didn't finish the question, leaving Will to wonder for many dark miles what the answer might be. Would social services come back? Would they take him away? He sank back into his seat and watched the roadside crosses go by. Crux was the Latin word for *cross*. His mother had taught him that. Crux, in English, was pivotal . . . also, puzzling.

In twelve years, Will had seen his father in almost all peaceable variations of sloshed. He'd seen Douglas slurry and accident-prone. He'd once watched his father drunk-dial a phone number for something that promised "five easy payments of forty-nine ninety-nine." And he'd seen, quite often, his father snoring in front of the TV after downing a plus-sized bottle of wine. But Will had never, *ever* seen the flippity-floppity, barely-breathing-type drunk Douglas was at present. It made him want to lean over and check his father's pulse. He tried once, but his seat belt locked and stopped him from leaning forward.

"William," his mom said, warningly. "Seat belt laws. Unless you want to die of internal injuries." She flicked on her high beams and a wall of fog bounced the light back.

Will squinted sharply and held on tight.

Back at home, in the garage, Josephine hustled Will into her car. "Come on," she goaded when she saw him glancing back at Douglas's SUV over his shoulder.

"What about Dad? Shouldn't we bring him inside?"

"No time. And anyway, I couldn't carry him even if I wanted to." She sighed, jaw clenched. "Unless you think you can carry him."

It was a rhetorical question, but Will still shook his head.

"He'll be fine. He'll sleep it off. It's the best thing, I promise."

It didn't seem like the best thing to Will. It was the point in late October where Indian summer rolled directly into wind-chill warnings. According to his mother's dashboard display, the outside temperature was just a few degrees shy of freezing.

Still, his mother was right. There was no conceivable way to heave-ho his father out of the car. He watched the garage door creak down as she backed the car away, and prayed to God that his dad would really be fine when they returned. In spite of everything—the trip to Doc Martin, his dad's persistent pressuring about public school—Will was feeling closer to Douglas than he ever had. *Please, please don't let him overdose or get too cold*, Will thought. *Please don't let him choke on a rerun of his cauliflower soup.*

The police station was located down near the waterfront. Will watched the streetlights reflecting on the surface, forming wavy columns of citrine-colored light. It did something to him to see the nighttime Hudson, so dark and unswimmable. Even in summer it was never a body of water that tempted you to wade in, pants rolled up unfashionably over your knees. It was less a body of water than a tipping ground, a rippling vat of murder weapons, sewage runoff, and PCBs.

The Hursts had tried to avoid talking about it last year, but police had made sure that they knew the deal: actual missing persons were a rare thing around here. Ninety-nine point nine percent of all vanished girls (they were mostly teenaged girls) were found enjoying destructive lifestyles that involved drug debts, the oldest profession, and boyfriends of low-level intelligence. The remaining point-one percent of all cases were usually found, decomposed, downriver from here. For the second time in a year, Will found himself hoping that Rose was safe and sound as opposed to any alternative that put her down in that black sweep of river.

It certainly didn't seem like anyone was expecting them when Will and his mother walked into the station. For thirty minutes, they waited in a shoebox-sized room, while various cops kept doing what Josephine always called "the beverage dance": "Water?" they'd say, sticking their crew-cut heads through the door. And: "We're swamped tonight. Just a few minutes more, we promise. Tea in the meantime?" Every time, Will's mother shook her head politely and addressed them by name. "No thank you, Sergeant Flynn," she said. "We're just fine, Captain Rossi."

"We're just waiting on Detective Donnelly," one of them said. "He's the one that's familiar with your daughter's case."

Josephine nodded. She looked much more worried than she had at home. She twiddled her wedding ring and picked at the hem of the beige dress that was a tasteful echo of her new hair color. "Oh, Will," she said. "Oh, Will, I don't know what I'll do if Rose isn't okay."

"She'll be okay," Will said automatically, putting his hand over her ice-cold one. Though he had no idea if that was true.

Will had been expecting a detective who was something like his old public school principal: someone with a brassy voice and an air of authority that he wore like a big-and-tall suit. But Donnelly was all weary looks and thoughtful pauses. He seemed like someone who had his retirement date marked and circled on his calendar.

"I understand you have some concerns about your daughter," Donnelly said. He had a smell that reminded Will of old books and pine tree air fresheners.

"We're probably overreacting," Josephine said. "It was just my husband—He managed to log in to Rose's old e-mail account, and there were some unread messages."

All the messages were unread, Will thought. Every single one. But it was his mom's rule that children didn't butt in on adult conversation. The back of his throat fizzled. Josephine shot him a look, and he mouthed Excuse me.

"And your husband—" Donnelly started.

"He's still home on the computer. Sleuthing. He wanted to wait until he had more information about her boyfriend, Damien."

"Can you tell me Damien's last name?" Donnelly asked. "It was missing from last year's report."

"Koch," Josephine said. "At least, that was the name he gave me when he called last year. I pulled Rose's credit report too." Josephine slid the sheet across the table. "I can't believe I never thought to do it sooner."

Donnelly said nothing as he studied the piece of paper. "Has Rose had contact with anyone in your family?" he asked.

"She's been corresponding with my younger daughter. For how long, I don't know."

Donnelly nodded, poker-faced.

Josephine touched her neck. "I don't know much about computers, personally. That's unforgivable, I know, especially given my husband's expertise. But I wondered how accurate those inboxes are. I did have a mortifying thought while I was sitting here: Maybe Rose *deletes* her sent e-mails. I'd never forgive myself if we've just come in here and wasted everyone's time."

"You're a mother," Donnelly said. "It's your job to be concerned. So, just to be clear, these e-mails are the only thing that made you worry that your daughter's gone missing again?"

"She left her blow dryer," Josephine said with upturned palms that said she knew how silly it sounded. "Evidently, she left it when she ran away last year. But she took the big things, as you all probably remember." She started the rambling list again: "Her makeup, her computer, her cell phone."

"I remember. There was no signal on her cell phone. We couldn't track it." He tapped a chewed fingernail on the credit report. "According to this, she never paid the balance owed to her provider."

"Oh no," Josephine cupped her mouth with her hands. "Oh no, we missed that. We thought this was good news, didn't we, Will?"

Will sat up taller, like a witness called to testimony. He nodded.

Josephine reached over and smoothed the back of Will's hair in a reassuring way. "We've always assumed Rose changed her number or switched her provider."

"The only inquiries here are for new credit cards."

"Yes. Yes, I saw that."

Donnelly looked down at his notepad. "So," he said. "E-mails, hair dryer, cell phone. Nothing else?"

"Her pregnancy journal," Will said automatically, without thought or foresight. He instantly shrank in horror. He'd spoken without being spoken to. He'd just been sucked in by the ambience of the police station. It had been too easy to imagine himself as a real detective, bringing his police supervisor real clues.

There was a beat.

"I'm sorry, a pregnancy journal?" Donnelly asked. His furry brow bent in a bewildered shape. "Do you have reason to believe your sister is pregnant?"

"No." Will's whole face was blazing. His tongue felt like the sashimi his parents liked to order from the red-lanterned restaurant in town. "I mean, Rose isn't pregnant *now*. She was. A long time ago. Last year."

"So you believe Rose has a baby?"

Will's mother had a displeased look on her face. "No. No, she chose not to have that baby."

"You'll have to excuse me." Donnelly lifted one apologetic shoulder. "I don't have any children myself. A pregnancy journal is . . . ?"

"A nine-month journal," Josephine answered. "A place to track your moods and weight gain."

"Rose wrote about being sad and kind of scared." Will was careful not to look at his mother. "There was a little bit in there about Damien."

"And you brought this journal with you?"

"No." Will's gaze fell to the linoleum. His mind flashed to Douglas at home in the garage. "We . . . I forgot it at home."

"Don't worry, love." To the detective, she added: "It was a meaningless thing. We'd been hoping it would tell us more about Damien. It didn't."

Donnelly nodded. "So the last time you saw Rose . . ."

"In our home," Will's mom answered.

"In your home the morning before she left for school last year? Or in your home the night your son got hurt?" He gestured to Will's splint, and Will fought the urge to cover it self-consciously with his other hand. "It's just—Didn't your other daughter see Rose in your house last week?"

Will looked to his mother, expecting her to ask when and why police had talked to Violet.

Instead, Josephine's face was a mask of cool self-assurance. "Yes," she said, firmly. "Yes, Violet saw Rose that night. As a matter of fact, we *all* did."

Violet Hurst

Violet slept fitfully, in strange contortions, her arms shielding her face and her fingers losing so much circulation that she couldn't feel her clenched fists. Maybe her low-threshold worry about Edie was to blame. Violet was poised for emergency, waiting for the other shoe to drop. She was too attuned to each ordinary whisper, tossing and turning with every footstep and squeaky gurney wheel.

A nightmare woke her three hours too early. She'd dreamed the impossible: that the flashlight darting around her room was coming not from the hospital corridor but from the lawn outside her barred window. When Violet crept over for a closer look, the light hit the pane hard and refracted back over her sister's face. Rose's expression changed, in a flash, from shocked to pleased; she even flashed a Peeping-Tom smile. Violet's whole body wailed from the shock. She woke gasping, sweaty and shivering, the night nurse (the nice one) whispering, "You're safe, honey. You're safe. You're safe. You're safe. Nothing can hurt you here."

Kind as it was, it didn't feel true.

. . .

Later, in therapy, Sara-pist wore a pleased look that bordered on callous. "What was it about this dream that disturbed you so much?"

"I think it was the way she caught me off guard. And the fact that she would intrude on me *here*, when she knew I was hurting. Where she knew it would be embarrassing."

"So it felt like she wanted to connect? Or like she wanted to hurt you?"

"Both. Like hurting me was the only way she could connect."

"We really need to work on these trust issues . . . Do you know what IRT is?" Violet shook her head and pulled her sleeves down over her wrists. "Image reversal therapy. That's where you change how the nightmare ends so it no longer upsets you. If you could give the dream an ending that wasn't scary, what would it be?"

Violet rubbed her hair. It felt like it had grown an inch in just one week without a clipper. "I don't know," she said. "I guess I'd go outside and confront her. I'd tell her I'm trying to work on my shit, and she might consider doing the same, instead of running around playing gotcha."

"That's good." The shrink nodded. "Keep running it over and over in your mind with the new ending."

"But there's a logistical problem with that ending."

"What's that?"

"I *can't* go out and run her off. Because I'm in a locked ward."

The shrink took off her glasses and took a sip from her mug. "Funny thing you mention that," she said.

"You're discharging me?"

"I am," said Sara-pist.

Finally, she could stop Josephine's smear campaign. She could make her escape from Old Stone Way. Violet clenched her fingers. "What does my mother think about all this?"

"She said she's not going to press charges, provided you apologize for what you did to Will."

"Okay." Violet felt helpless and just wrong, having to apologize for something she hadn't done. But it wasn't the end of the world. She could do it. She didn't need validation. *She* knew she didn't hurt Will, and with Rose offering to take her in she had a plan and a place to go, and that was what really mattered.

"Your mom also said she'd work hard to honor the fair-fight contract we've come up with," Sara-pist said. "She's not going to come to you anymore about the ways you've disappointed her in the past. She's gonna try to keep her issues in the here-and-now."

"Great," Violet said, although she didn't believe it for a second.

Violet found Edie in the dayroom, rubbing her eyes and doing a vintage jigsaw puzzle. According to the tattered box, it was a portrait of the astronauts of Apollo 11.

"I think that one's missing pieces," Violet offered.

"Is it? Thank fuck." Edie dropped the piece she was trying to shoehorn into Neil Armstrong's face. "I thought I'd gone stupid or something."

Violet helped her scoop the pieces back into the box. They were curling and yellowed with age. "They're discharging me," she said. "I'm going home."

"Shit," Edie said. "To your parents' house?"

"I've thought about it, and I'm gonna try Rose." Violet gripped her knees where she knelt. Maybe adrenaline was the reason she couldn't stop shivering. She was equal parts liberated and scared.

Edie leaned over the moon and hugged her. "I'll call my roommates," she said. "If it doesn't work out with Rose, I'm sure they won't mind if you stay at our place for a while."

It was tempting. Violet had a flash of the student houses she'd been to once or twice in New Paltz: teacup ashtrays, bowls of comforting rice-based meals, wet towels drying on old radiators, good music, container gardens, tapestries on the walls. But as terrified as she was to see her mother, she couldn't bear the thought of having unfinished business with Will. She couldn't run away and leave him behind, hating her, the same way Rose had left her.

"I've been thinking," Violet said. "About narcissists. How do you get them to leave you alone?"

Edie frowned, ever the damaged scholar of psychology. "Almost impossible," she said, shaking her head. "They almost never give up anyone who's given them narcissistic supply. If you ignore them, they come on stronger. First, with the charm-offensive, and if that doesn't sway you, they'll settle for stalking you."

"So they won't listen to reason."

"Unh-uh. There's really only two ways to deal with them. You can mirror them. You know, flatter them, take their shit, don't set any boundaries. Be a doormat, basically. Or you can limit your contact with them."

"But how can you cut them off if they won't leave you alone?"

"You're talking about your mom?"

"Yeah." Violet eased the decrepit lid onto the puzzle box. "Or whoever."

"Well, you could scare her. If she has a secret—like if she hits your brother, or she claims Rose illegally on her taxes—you could use that to threaten her. It won't take much. Just drop a hint or two. Bluff and say someone, a neighbor or something, knows all about it. Let her imagine the details. Narcissists have paranoid minds anyway, and deep down, they know they fall short of the front they put up."

"So if my mom thinks I have something on her, she'll let me go live with Rose?"

Edie made a small, humming sound. "Maybe." Her brilliant-blue eyes looked unconvinced. "You could try to manipulate her."

Violet shook her head. She had a bad reaction, almost physical, to the thought. She was no ceramics artist where her relationships were concerned; she either cherished them or she smashed them. She had no desire to go sticking her thumbs in people, molding them to her will.

"It's not as bad as it sounds," Edie said. "I just mean, give her so much attention that she practically ODs. Narcissistic supply is like a drug. When they're high on it, they're like toddlers. You can trick them into thinking they're getting their way."

"So you really think if I blow enough smoke up Mom's ass, I can convince her to give me some space?" The irony wasn't lost on Violet. That was exactly the way Rose had broken free: she'd been such an obedient daughter, such a model Hurst, that Josephine had backed off on her overbearing-mother routine, giving Rose enough space to do a runner.

"You might. Just make it look like it's in her best interest. Maybe play it like you can be your mother's mole. You can go live with Rose and report back with useful information. You don't have to deliver on the promise once you're there."

After leaving the dayroom, Violet went to the phone booth and dialed Rose's number. It was still work hours; Rose's phone was off. It rang once, and an automated message introduced Violet to her sister's message box. After the beep, Violet left her cell phone number and the news of her discharge. "Text me sometime today," she said. "Mom or Dad will sign me out of here. I'll go to the farm stand afterward and get my paycheck. After dark, I can meet you tonight, anywhere within walking distance of Old Stone Way. Choose a place, and I'll be there. I know what to do." She paused, then added, "I learned from the best."

WILLIAM HURST

MAYBE THERE IS no truth. That was the anthem of liars everywhere. Will knew that, and still he couldn't stop thinking it. Because his mother's truth was the only available option for him, and her "truth" was an outright fabrication—a bigger L-I-E than the Long Island Expressway.

For another forty minutes, Will sat in that cold, bright police room and swore up and down that he'd seen Rose, jogging down the Hursts' eighteenth-century staircase as if she'd just popped home for a forgotten scarf or textbook.

That was the sickening part: Will wasn't able to tell just one whopper and be done. Each deception called for another one, the same way it had with CPS. Only this deceit was worse. This was perjury: one of last month's spelling words. The flash cards he studied from showed a cartoon man, sweating, one hand slapped down on a stack of Bibles.

On and on Will went with his false oath: "No, I didn't see Rose come in, I only saw her leave." "She was there for thirty seconds, maybe?" "Yes, you're right. Thirty seconds is a long time. Maybe it only felt that long because I was surprised to see her." This was bullshit in Russian-nesting-dolls form, and Donnelly seemed to want to break each sentence open and peer closely inside.

"Did Rose look distressed?" the detective asked. Will shook his head *no*, which was the wrong lie (if lies can be further wrong than they are already) because it had led to Donnelly's inevitable next question: "Why then, if she didn't look distressed, did you think she was in danger or being coerced?"

"Oh." Will grew panicked, and then, in an effort to cover his fear, acted the part of the insolent know-it-all. "It's just that word. When I hear *distress*, I think hurt, or frightened, or grief-stricken. Rose wasn't either. She was more like—"

"She didn't seem like herself," Josephine offered.

"In what way?" Donnelly's pen was poised above his notebook. It unnerved Will, watching his lies gain instant permanence.

Josephine threw out a lifeline. "Will was just thrown by her appearance. It was just makeup, Will. Heavy makeup. And a new hair color. Darker."

Will nodded. His stomach growled audibly.

"And did any of you try to follow Rose?"

Mamihlapinatapai. A naming word. It meant *the wordless, yet meaningful look shared by two people who both desire to initiate something but are both reluctant to start.*

"She ran," Will finally said.

"By the time we made it out the front door, she was already gone. Damien must have been waiting in the car."

"Did you get the license plate number?"

"We didn't *see* the car," Will muttered. "We just assumed."

"Like I said, we're probably just being silly," Josephine said. "If she was honestly in danger . . . If Damien was forcing her to act against her will, she could have called out to us. We were right there. She knew we saw her. She must have known we could help her."

Donnelly scratched his cheek with the pointed cap of his pen. His dark eyes were solemn as a priest's. "Now, this boyfriend, Damien? You're sure this is the man she ran away with? Your other daughter seemed to think Rose had just broken up with her college professor when she ran away."

Josephine got a disapproving look on her face. "I didn't know that."

"It was definitely a Damien Koch who called you on the phone last year?"

"That's the name he gave me," Josephine said again.

"And you're sure it was Rose you saw on the night your other daughter assaulted your son? One hundred percent?"

"Yes," said Will's mother. "Rose didn't hurt Will. Violet hurt Will, but Rose was there."

"She was wearing her white coat," Will added suddenly.

"Ummm," Donnelly said. "It was the same coat she was seen in last year? The one in the surveillance footage from the Metro-North station?"

"Yes, the same one," Josephine said, her eyes tearing up. "That's about the only thing about her that was the same."

Will seized in the car on the way home. It was too much, all that fiction. The story had its own velocity, and by the time Will stepped away from all the lies he'd told, he felt the way he used to feel stepping off the rusted merry-go-round at Lippman Park: he wasn't whirling anymore, but his brain hadn't received the memo. He felt nauseated, dizzy right down to his toes. He curled up in the backseat like a depressed fetus and fell into a thick, gummy sleep.

When Will woke up, every muscle in his body hurt. His mother was yanking his wrist. "Get out," she said. It wasn't a yell, it was worse. It was an ice-cold, overenunciated command—the kind she gave to automated phone systems.

Will suppressed his human urges (no yawning, no groaning) as he stepped out into the garage.

"That-a boy," she said, softening, ruffling the back of his bowl cut. It was a pet owner's gesture. Positive reinforcement. "You did well back there. With a few small exceptions. If it were up to me, I wouldn't have put you through it. But we *had* to go. It would have looked suspicious if we didn't. Blame your fucking father and his goddamn phone call." Her heels clipped the concrete as she walked to Douglas's SUV and wrenched the door handle. "Sober yet?" she asked, as the door swung open. The interior light came on and the passenger seat was empty.

VIOLET HURST

BEFORE VIOLET LEFT the phone booth, she reached into her pocket and pulled out Nick Flores's business card. She dialed the number and felt the same crippling, low-level bashfulness she did wondering if Finch would pick up when she called the Fields' landline.

"Nicholas Flores speaking."

"Nick. It's Violet Hurst."

"Ultra-Violet."

"That's me. I hope you're wearing your shades."

"I am. I am." There was a smile in his voice. "So what's up, U.V.?"

"I'm getting out of here later today, and I've been thinking I'd like to talk a little more about emancipation. You know, how much does it cost? How long does it take? That kind of thing."

"Sure, U.V. We can do that. How about you come see me in the office? What day works for you?"

"I can't come to the office. I'm going out of town for a while."

"Really? Where are you headed?"

"I think I'm gonna go stay with Rose. Have you heard from her yet?"

"Unh-uh." The playfulness went out of Nick's voice. "She hasn't written me back. No phone calls. No e-mails. I looked into that Damien Koch, but no one by that name has an arrest record in the state of New York."

"I don't suppose you could look into Matthew and Francesca Chatsworth? I think Damien is a fake name. Matt was the professor Rose was having an affair with, and Francesca is the wife he's still married to."

"Say whaat? I thought you told me Rose was sheltered."

"Turns out she isn't quite as virtuous as I thought."

"So you think Rose is still seeing this guy?"

"It's a possibility. I just want to know what I'm getting into here. I don't want to go all the way there only to have this aggro professor mad at me for spoiling his weekend trysts."

"Rose told you he's aggressive?"

"No. I'm the one who thinks he's aggressive. We talked on the phone." There was a long pause. "Nick? Are you still there?"

"I'm checking their arrest records."

"You can look it up that fast?"

"You could too, if you were near a computer. It's all public record right there on the Internet. No arrests for Matt. Francesca, though, it says here she got arrested a few years ago for assault."

"Francesca assaulted someone?"

"Uh-huh. Any idea what that was about?"

"No clue. I don't know anything about Francesca." Maybe she should have said anything significant. She knew all the shit on the wedding blog: that Fran thought hyacinths were too fragrant and silk-poly blend dresses made her cringe.

"Well, listen. It was simple assault. Probably Frannie got in some drunken catfight or something. But I want you to be careful, U.V. You know the key to self-defense, don't you?"

"Wear practical shoes?"

"Bear mace. Stuff can take down even the strongest of men. Maybe even a wronged wife like Francesca."

WILLIAM HURST

WILL PACED AROUND the bottom of the staircase and tried to eavesdrop. At first, he heard only his mother's voice: hysterical questions at erratic intervals. It was followed by slamming sounds, the metallic clanging of brass dresser drawer pulls, and a slow tumble like dress shoes falling down from their tree rack. An instant later, Josephine was stomping down the stairs in her stockinged feet.

"Is Dad okay?" Will asked nervously.

The look Josephine shot him was almost as hurtful as the word she'd called him after dinner. And it said the same thing: that Will was mentally deficient. "He's fine," she said, curling her lips as though the word *Dad* had a stench. "Looks like he dragged himself up to bed. He's been sleeping like a baby, while we deal with all the hot water he's dropped us into. Now, Will . . . I need to see that journal." She made finger-quotations around *journal*, as though she'd said *Sasquatch* or *chupacabra*.

"Dad has it."

She leaned against the curved end of the banister. "He does *not* have it. I just checked his coat pockets."

"Then he put it somewhere."

"Somewhere, like *where?*" There it was again, the murdered syntax. The blood slowed in Will's veins.

"I don't know. I didn't see. He didn't tell me."

For a second, Will's mother seemed amused by the staccato answer. She stepped lightly off the bottom stair and hooked an arm around his shoulder, as if she were a Little League coach and Will was a bedraggled pitcher in need of a mound pep talk. "Tell me what it says, Will. Right now. I need to know if I'm going to save this family."

"You're killing the messenger," Will said. Tears were rolling down his face.

"Not everything is about *you*, Will." His mother was groping around the Hursts' junk drawer, her voice like a grimace. "I need to find that diary. I told that detective we'd bring it to him tomorrow. If we don't, it will look—"

"I know, I know," Will sniffed and nodded. "It will look suspicious."

Her head snapped up from the junk drawer's nest of batteries, trash bags, and twine. "Wow, Will. I was going to say *flighty*. Maybe you're against me too. Maybe prep school in London is a bad idea."

"I'm not against you. I just don't know why I had to say I saw Rose."

"I didn't twist your arm. I didn't make you say it. I didn't make you do anything." She averted her eyes again, and some part of her must have known the last part wasn't true. "Are you asking me if I really saw her that night?"

Will held her gaze. There were so many lies he wanted to ask her about—her sham degree, the potentially bull autism diagnosis— but he was too afraid. He didn't know which scared him more: the answers or the thought that asking might make him lose her.

"No, I didn't see Rose that night, but she's here all the time, Will. I just know it. Sometimes I hear things. Doors closing at night. Sometimes my pillow smells like her perfume."

Will noticed a paring knife beside a facedown box on the cutting board. He turned the box over and read the label: *Antihistamines. Liquid Gels.*

When he looked back up, she was watching him with eyes that were tight in the corners. Under the kitchen's downlighting, her newly blond hair gleamed.

"There you go again," she said. "My observant boy. These fall allergies are killing me."

"The journal's not going to be in the kitchen," he said. "It's going to be in a Dad place."

Josephine stood up and smoothed her dress. "I haven't checked his workbench yet," she said. Her face, already young for its age, was suddenly all girlish optimism. "I'll go look in his socket wrench box. Why don't you go back upstairs, check under his pillow? Also, under his side of the mattress? You've got such small, quiet hands. Sometimes I think you ought to be a surgeon."

"But I want to be a writer . . . Why can't we just wait until the morning and ask Dad where he put the journal?"

"Because I'm going to toss and turn all night thinking about it." She stuffed her feet into her quilted slippers and wrapped a throw blanket around her shoulders. She made a swooping motion with her index finger—*get upstairs*—and then marched off to the garage to look under Douglas's chainsaw helmet and Coleman lanterns.

"Will?" she said.

"Yeah."

"I think I've found the perfect prep school for you."

"What's it like?"

"Perfect. Most students go to Oxford or Cambridge when they graduate. Sons of notable figures. No mandatory sports. Ample opportunities for suits, tuxes, and tails."

His parents' bedroom was dark, except for the light in his father's closet. That was all Will saw as he stepped softly into the room: his father's empty hangers swinging from the metal bar, every golf shirt and windowpane sweater he owned in a snarl on the carpet floor.

Douglas was still in his clothes, sleeping in a Jesus posture on the bed: feet together, arms splayed, head rolling awkwardly to one side. His mouth was open, and his chin jutted upward. He looked like he ought to be doing his trademark freight-train snore, only he wasn't. The room was chillingly quiet. *He's dead*, Will thought. But when he moved closer and cupped a hand an inch or two from Douglas's mouth, he felt a soft, slow tickle of an exhale. *Baby's breath*, Will thought, even though he'd never held anything diapered and had little desire to.

He had a thought to care for his drunk dad in some way—to get an extra blanket or put a damp washcloth on his forehead—but none of those seemed quite right. Instead he did as his mom had said: he used one hand to lift the mattress half an inch. He groped along the box spring with the other. Nothing there. He played tooth fairy and slid his hand under his father's pillow. Rose's journal wasn't there either. His father remained as still as roadkill.

Douglas's cell phone was on the nightstand, and Will found himself hoping his father had called Kerry before he'd passed back out.

Maybe he's drunk and sick, Will thought. There were certain medications you weren't supposed to mix with alcohol. He'd once eavesdropped on Violet talking about a girl who had a bad reaction chasing antibiotics with vodkaccinos (bottled frappuccinos with bottom-shelf vodka). Will thought back on his dad's soapy soup and the antihistamine box in the kitchen.

Venenation: poisoning.

He felt an aura like he was going to seize again. He had to crouch down to regain his balance. His chest tightened as his heart skipped a beat. Could his mom have drugged his dad?

Josephine walked in with a water glass in her hand. "Did you find it?" she whispered.

Will shook his head. *You're being paranoid,* he told himself. *You are thinking crazy, despicable thoughts.*

She set the glass down on the nightstand next to where Will knelt. "Your dad will be thirsty," she said. "You can lessen a hangover that way. With lots of water."

Out in the hallway, Will pressed her. He erred on the side of self-effacing. No way he was going to outright accuse her of drugging his dad and hiding evidence. "Sorry, Mom. It's late. My brain's scrambled. I don't understand why we can't just wait until Dad wakes up. Can't *he* bring Rose's journal to the station? You've already been through so much. That long interview . . ." He gave a sympathetic grimace. "All those questions . . ."

She dropped her force field—that four-foot sphere of personal space she guarded so tightly—and stepped toward Will for a hug. "I don't want him finding Rose before we do," she said. "Rose *hates* your father. All those years, all that drinking . . ." She covered her mouth and averted her filled eyes from Will's. "Your father *abused* her. By the time I pieced together what was happening, it was too late. I couldn't protect her. The damage was done."

"That's why Rose keyed Dad's car instead of yours."

A sad smile rippled across her face. "You're such a smart boy. I can't hide anything from you."

"That's why you were scared, I mean, *extra*-scared about Dad having an affair?"

"I worried—" She paused. "I worried he'd reconnected with Rose."

"He tried," Will said. "He was going to hire an investigator to track her down."

"I know. It took me weeks to talk him out of it. I don't think I've fully relaxed since. A part of me worried he'd done it anyway, behind my back."

Will thought back to the night in the kitchen. "That's why after I hurt myself, I had to say Violet did it."

He'd been trying so hard to be a good, helpful boy, washing the crystal pitcher while his sobbing, hysterical mother spooned risotto out of the dishwasher with a silver ladle. But the delicate goosenecked handle was so slippery when wet. After it crashed to the slate floor, sending up a spray of brilliant shards, Will was so horrified with himself that he hadn't thought twice. He'd immediately reached for the largest shard at the same time his mom had closed her fist around his. It wasn't in anger, she'd insisted later. She was just trying to stop him. But Will hadn't known that. Will had seized anyway, and slammed his chin into the corner of the kitchen island. After she'd picked the shards out with tweezers came the long, eastbound ride to the hospital, Will trying not to bleed on the seats, and Josephine saying over and over, *Violet's to blame. You wouldn't have dropped it if she hadn't upset you, screaming like a banshee and waving that knife around. Violet did this to you, Will. Tell the doctor Violet did it.*

She hugged him so hard, his ribs nuzzled his organs. "I know this has been hard on you," she said. "I wasn't lying when I said the hospital was the only safe place for Violet. She won't go anywhere with me. She treats me like I have a forked tongue and horns. I couldn't take any chances. I had to get her away from your father. I have to get us all away from your father."

For the first time, his mom's overprotective streak made sense. Of course, she'd kept Will close. She'd done it to keep Will safe from the predator in their own home.

"What—I mean what did Dad *do* to Rose?"

"Oh, Will, honey. I don't think you have the stomach for it. There's a reason why Rose had to hide her relationships. Why she was so reluctant to date. It made your dad so jealous and, at the same time, he was so fascinated with Rose and her potential sex life. I'd find him drunk as a sailor in the laundry baskets, inspecting Rose's underwear."

Will instinctively put his hands over his ears.

"He hit Rose once. Because she had told him Jason Blake had asked her to the homecoming dance."

Will was shocked. "Rose said she sneezed while she was putting on her dance tights and kneed herself in the face."

His mother shot him a look that said he was dumber than she thought.

"Dad took me to a new doctor today," he said. "He said my epilepsy was some reaction to trauma. He said my autism isn't real."

"Your autism is *real*, Will. As for the trauma, we've *all* had a lot of that. Between Violet's constant outbursts and your father's drunken abuse."

He was searching his mind for something to say—a way to convince her that he really was on her side, even after everything she'd done and made him do—when he glanced out the window of Rose's darkened bedroom and saw the flames curling.

"Mom!" he said. "Mom! Is that fire in our yard?"

"That's our cedar hedge!" she cried.

Running together for the fire extinguisher, Will thought he saw her squelched smile. Rose was here. The idea thrilled her at least as much as it terrified Will.

"Stay in the house," she said. "Your sister might still be out there."

He obeyed, even though he wanted to run outside and scream for Rose, the contemptible coward, to show herself. He watched through a downstairs window while his mother's silhouette sent up clouds of dust. He cracked the window and heard the extinguisher spray. It sounded like *exsibilation*, like the collective hisses of a disapproving audience. When it didn't work, she ran for the garden hose.

Will woke up late the next morning, his eyes bleary from a long night of hunting for Rose's journal. His head spun with fear and a sense of the unreal, remembering how he'd looked under bath mats and swept his hand behind dresser mirrors, hoping, for his mother's sake, to find it taped to the back. When it got late enough at night to be considered early morning, Josephine had dismissed Will from the search. Will had peered in one last time on his dad and felt a sharp jab of hatred. He hated himself for the way he'd let Douglas manipulate him. To think he'd helped his dad crack Rose's e-mail. To think he'd momentarily dropped his guard and warmed to a monster who'd raped or beaten his sister or worse.

He got up and put on the clothes his mother had laid out for him: chinos, a shawl-necked sweater, and a very bold, very prep-school plaid shirt. It meant a big day awaited. Something—he didn't know what—called for business casual.

Downstairs in the kitchen, bacon hissed in the pan. His mother was scraping burnt toast with a paring knife.

Rose's journal was sitting in the dead center of the kitchen island.

"Where was it?" Will asked, smoothing a hand over the lavender cover.

"Bookshelf," she said quietly. "Hiding in plain sight." She brought the knife near her lip in a gesture that said *shhh*.

Will flipped to the third-trimester section, but Rose's post-abortion entries were gone. *Revisionist*, a naming word.

"I tore it out," Josephine said, wobbling poached eggs onto two plates. "I won't have anyone thinking my Rose went crazy. That's not her. That's not who she is."

Will wondered why, then, his mom was okay with people thinking Violet was crazy.

"It's different with Violet," Josephine snapped, and Will felt like he had a fishbowl brain, like she could peer in anytime she wanted and see every thought circling around in there. There was a instant of tense silence. She pushed Will's plate toward him. "Violet's coming home today. We have to eat and go pick her up."

Will felt a sudden rush of blood. His legs went weak with anxiety.

Josephine ate a neat corner off her toast. "Don't look at me like that. I'd keep her there if I could, but the doctors think she's stable and our insurance company wants to send her home. It will be fine."

"No, it won't."

"It will. Let me talk to her." She grabbed his chin and gently lifted his face to look at hers.

"She's going to hate me," he said, looking down at the contrast between his tan loafers and the gray tiles.

"I don't think you have to say anything. No harm, no foul.

That's how I see it. She's not going to have a criminal record. And she needed to be in the hospital anyway. She was hallucinating. She was on *drugs*." When he failed to respond, her tone sharpened. "Will, she's made peace with it all, that's what her doctors said. If you change your story now, it's just going to confuse her. She's still a little fragile and confused. We need to baby her for a week or two."

Will was thrown by his mom's sudden, unexpected tenderness for Violet. He felt his face go pink with envy. "I've been thinking," he said. "Do you think I should change the password on Rose's old e-mail so we don't have to worry about Dad looking through her messages?"

"You know the password?"

Will nodded. He saw his face reflected in the kitchen window. He saw his little prune mouth, his eyes a touch too wide. He was trying to hide the satisfaction he still felt at hacking Rose's account.

"Do it right now," Josephine said. "Before your father wakes up. Make it something we'll remember. Change it to *ChristLove*."

Will tried not to make a face. Moments later, in his mother's office, his father's speech about careless passwords rang in his memory, and he made the O in *Love* a zero. When he got back to the kitchen his eggs were ice cold and rock hard on his plate.

As they were getting ready to go to the hospital, Douglas rolled downstairs. That was really how it looked, like he was trundling: a five-ton construction machine on a wobbly track. His body weight hung off him, and his gray-clammy face looked like something that had been left under a fast-food heat lamp. He was still wearing his clothes from last night. Will might have felt bad for him, if only he didn't know what he knew. Now, when he looked at his dad he saw drunken depravity: loose flesh, sticky breath, ready fists. Just hearing about what he'd done to Rose had made Will feel defiled too.

Douglas picked up the journal, and a vein sprung out of his forehead. "What's going on?" he asked.

Josephine turned her back and sent her plate clattering into the sink. "We're going to pick Violet up from the hospital. That's what's going on. You're welcome to stay here and do whatever you need to do. Call your sponsor, et cetera."

Douglas looked at Will.

Will looked down at his bread crusts.

Douglas stormed to the cabinet and removed a mug. He pulled the coffeepot out of the machine, found it empty, and slammed it back. He looked bewildered and aggressive, like a shaken sleep-walker. All the while, the journal was still in his hand.

Just then Douglas looked out the window. His hand touched the pane and left a mark. He stepped back, aghast. "The hedge," he said. "Jo. What happened to that hedge?"

"I don't know, Douglas."

"The police station—" he started. "Did you tell them about that when you went to the police station? Violet couldn't have done that. She's still in the hospital."

"We went to the police station. Will and I took care of it."

"What did you tell them?" A panicky tone had crept into his voice.

"Everything. The hedge, the e-mails. Well, we didn't have the journal, but we told them about it. You could do everyone a big favor and drive it over there while we're out. That is, if you feel all right to drive." She said this last part slowly, looking at Will in a way that implicated him too.

Will's father slammed the journal down on the counter. "I have not been drinking, Josephine!"

"Oh, right!" she said, with a sarcastic whip of her neck. "Just like you weren't drinking that time you passed out on the Amtrak and woke up in Niagara Falls? Just like you weren't drinking that time you told me—in front of everybody at the IBM Christmas party—to get my *next* husband to pay for Will's piano lessons?"

Will felt her behind him, putting a hand on his shoulder. It was supposed to be a supportive gesture, but he couldn't help thinking she'd literally put him in the middle. He stood there like a stunned human shield. His collar felt wet and he realized he was crying.

Will wondered, did conversations like these happen in kitchens all over town, beneath chalkboard grocery lists: MILK, LIGHTBULBS, EGGS, POPCORN? He used to think they did. He would have *sworn* they did. He'd see other parents in church, pecking each other on the cheek during the part of Mass when everyone exchanged "Peace be with you," and he was dead certain it was their one weekly show of affection. He would have bet his life that every husband in the world was like Douglas, and every wife was like Josephine. But now he wondered. . . . He wondered if every twelve-year-old's mother really did bathe him, call him *stud*, affectionately pinch his butt. He wondered if every father really got slowly pushed out of the family like something old and injured, until, fighting mad, he tore them all to pieces.

Douglas aimed the journal at Will's mother like a gun. "You are the meanest, nastiest, most contemptible bitch I've ever known!" He was all eyeteeth when he shouted, and the word *bitch* left his mouth with a messy spray of spit.

Josephine grabbed Will's hand and gave it a squeeze that said, *Do you see now? Do you see how abusive?*

"A lesser man, Jo . . . A lesser man would beat you half to death."

Will squeezed his mom's hand back twice like a secret code.

Violet Hurst

They arrived with an olive branch. Actually it was a bunch of red gerbera daisies and a foil happy-face balloon. To Violet, the latter seemed cunning and layered with meaning. No question Josephine had chosen it knowing that the same image that read "supportive" to the staff (*How sweet! They want her to be happy!*) had an entirely different message for her daughter: *Smile, little bitch, and pretend everything's fine.*

Violet stood as they approached. An hour after Sara-pist had signed Violet's discharge papers, the staff had finally found the clothes she'd been wearing when she arrived. Her jeans were still mud-and-grass-stained from her tantric romp in the Fields' field, and they felt tighter than they had when she arrived on account of all the bland comfort food.

"Viola." Her mother cupped her cheek, then wrenched her close for a spine-crunching hug that made Violet's skin crawl. "Honey. I can't tell you how much we've missed you. You've really missed your sister, haven't you, Will?"

Will kept his chin aimed at his shoes, but his eyes slowly rose to look at her. He looked like he was afraid Violet would bite him.

"I'm so sorry, Will," Violet said. "I'm still kind of fuzzy on exactly what happened, but I know I never *ever* wanted to hurt you." Out of the corner of her eye, she caught her mother's smile. It was steel-bright, triumphant.

"We appreciate that. Don't we, Will?"

Will nodded. His head was still down; his rag-doll hands still hung at his sides.

"We've been talking, Will and I, and we've decided that if you apologized and if you promised never to do drugs again, then we could both forgive you and welcome you home. So, do you? Promise never to do drugs?"

"I won't take drugs again," Violet said, thinking maybe her mother really was making a liar of her.

"Fantastic. Will, why don't you give your sister a hug. Go on. What was that word you told me the other day? The one that reminded you of Violet? You came to me and said, 'Mom, I miss my favorite . . .'"

"Autotonsorialist."

"Well, go on. Tell Violet what it means."

Will's voice was a near-whisper. "It means a person who cuts their own hair."

Violet waited until she was in the car to power on her cell phone after its weeklong hiatus. Her mother was busy humming along with some dismal and pretentious cello concerto, and Will, in the backseat, was staring at the road with trademark intensity—a look that said if he looked away, even blinked, the car would careen off course. The phone buzzed five times in Violet's palm and the messages told a heavily abridged story of her week:

Message One. Friday night, from Finch: FERN GULLY IN FRENCH=BEST TRIP MOVIE YET!

Message Two. Friday night, from Finch: *YOU ARE CRYSTA. AND I AM THE HUNGRY GOANNA LIZARD IN AMOUR WITH YOU.*

Message Three. Saturday morning, from Imogene: *U OK? WOULD'VE TEXTED BACK SOONER BUT KEPT STARING AT SCREEN, TRYING TO FIGURE OUT WHAT PHONE WAS. JASPER (BAD TRIP) SAID BOMB DETONATER.*

Scrolling through her outgoing messages, Violet realized she'd sent a string of gibberish messages to Imogene and Finch all the way to the hospital. The most lucid read: *SNAPCRAKKAHBOOM!* And: *ROWS GOOD BUT LEFT WAY IDEALLY SUIT !!!!!!!*

Message Four. Saturday morning, from Imogene: *R U AVOIDING US BECAUSE FINCH PROFESSED HIS LOVE? :) HE'S BEEN INTO YOU THIS WHOLE TIME, JUST BEEN STRESSED OVER MOM.*

Message Five. Saturday afternoon, from Imogene: *WTF ARE YOU? DID U GET IN TROUBLE WITH SOCI-JOSIE?*

Violet cast a quick glance at her mom. She couldn't remember when exactly they'd started calling Josephine *Josie the Soci* (the *soci* was short for *sociopath*).

Message Six. From Rose's number: *LET'S MEET AT THE OLD ROSENDALE LITTLE LEAGUE FIELD. WHAT TIME WORKS FOR YOU? MIDNIGHT? 1 A.M.? ARE YOU THINKING YOU'LL SNEAK OUT AFTER BED?*

Violet instinctively hid the phone, afraid her mother would see.

Josephine turned the radio down. Her new blond hair made her look like a factory-defect Soccer Mom Barbie. "So, tell us about the hospital. What was it like? What did you learn there?"

"What did I *learn* there?" As though commitment were a summer internship.

"Yes, Viola." There was her mother's real voice, the sharp one that lurked beneath her public upspeak. "I don't know about your Buddha, but my God gives us the opportunity to *learn* from our mistakes. He teaches us lessons."

Violet fought the urge to beat her head against the window.

Instead, she propped her elbow against it and leaned her cheek into her hand. "Well, let's see . . . I learned a padlock in a sock makes a deadly weapon. I learned that cigarettes are currency. I learned that if you let sugar, bread, and fruit rot in a shampoo bottle for a month, you can get drunk off it."

Her mother raised her voice indignantly. "Oh, it's all so funny, huh? Getting high as a kite, scaring everyone, costing us hundreds if not thousands in medical bills, injuring your brother? By the way, he may have forgiven you, but I'm not there yet. So you'll have to excuse me if I don't see the humor."

"Sorry, Mom. Stupid joke, I guess. I was just trying to lighten the mood." She remembered Edie's words about manipulating narcissists. She had to pretend to sweeten her mother, even as the idea made her flesh crawl. "I learned a lot of things in there."

"For instance?"

"For instance, I'm not sure I want to be Buddhist anymore. It was just a fad, like you said. Peer pressure. I was trying to fit in with the Fields, who are acting weird around me anyway."

"Aha. So you're willing to agree with me about those people now?"

"Yeah. I see now what you mean about their do-nothing life-style."

"And they smell unpleasant."

"Yes, they smell unpleasant."

Her mother cackled and took her hands off the steering wheel long enough to clap her hands in delight.

Edie was right. Her mother was shockingly gullible when it came to compliments and concessions. Violet thought and added: "Stinking or not, I still have to find time to get my homework from Imogene."

Violet hit Reply on Rose's text: 1 A.M. CANNOT COME SOON ENOUGH.

Violet meant it. She was going to have the sister she always should have had—the sister she would've had if their leering mother had left well enough alone. In between all the jealousy and distrust, they had shared small sisterly moments. Violet remembered a weekend when—sick with chicken pox, quarantined in the guest room—she and eleven-year-old Rose outlined each other's spots with a felt-tipped pen. She remembered the way they used to fight giggles over the way three-year-old Will called his Rambo action figure "Rainbow."

"Is that Imogene you're texting? I hope you've told her you're grounded. Because you are. If you think you're going anywhere, you're sadly mistaken."

"It's work," Violet lied. "They've been waiting for me to pick up my paycheck. Can we swing by there now?"

Josephine's expression said this was yet another inconvenience in a string of intolerable annoyances. "I think you're expecting too much of our goodwill and valuable time," she said. "We're studying for the math Regents exam. Will has been working like a Trojan."

Violet glanced back at Will. He sat up defensively like she'd implicated him in something awful.

"No worries. I can bike there. But if I go by bike, I can't bring home the pear tarts Mrs. D has for me." Violet knew her mother loved the pear tarts. Sometimes Josephine replated them and gave them to the priest at Saint Peter's, passing the recipe off as her own.

"Fine," Josephine said. "Just so long as you're quick about it."

As she walked in, she noticed Troy Barnes aiming his iPhone at a cardboard box of potatoes. He had a bandanna around his wrist. His hair was dyed a shade between jet black and purple. "Hey Violet, check this out." He held up a misshapen russet. "It kind of looks like a manatee, doesn't it? I've named it *potato-tee*. What do you think?"

"I think you can do better than that."

"Mana-tato?"

They pinned photos to the bulletin board in the back room: perfectly round avocados, banana slices that looked like electrical outlets, mushrooms that were shaped like human asses. At the end of the season, Mrs. D picked the best one and gave the winning photographer a hundred-dollar bonus.

"It's not as good as the fried chicken cutlet." The fried chicken cutlet was shaped like Africa. "Is Mrs. D around?"

"She's out in the tunnels, I think. Want me to radio her?"

Violet nodded. The tunnels were the unheated greenhouses were they grew kale, lettuce, spinach, carrots, beets, and Swiss chard.

As Troy made his walkie-talkie crackle, he eyed Violet with seemingly fresh interest. Had he heard that she'd gone Planters peanuts? The thought was beyond unbearable. It made the blood drain from her brain.

"Mrs. D?" Troy shouted into the hunk of metal in his palm. His eyes were the same amber brown as the maple syrup they sold. The corners of his mouth curved into a tiny smile.

A crinkling sound from the tiny speaker. "Ye-ess?"

"Your favorite cue ball is here." Troy touched Violet's head like someone petting a cat. His hand lingered on the back of her neck and she felt a warm tingling in every chakra.

Violet whispered teasingly to Troy, "I can put a hat on bald. You can't put a hat on desperate."

That's when it sank in: her friends were the only family she'd ever known, and she was leaving them to go live with a flesh-and-blood relation who felt more like a stranger.

Violet blinked away the thought just as quickly. Wasn't it Sara-pist who said intimacy takes time?

She would need a hostess gift. Possibly she could steal a special vintage from their parents' wine rack. Something with hints of cinnamon, pepper, and sloppy sister bonding. She could picture it already, Rose flushed and tipsy, laughing at Violet's recitation of their mom's favorite sayings: "Go to bed, I'm tired" or "Excuse me for living, but the graveyard's full." She could practically see Rose giving her a "I'm-so-glad-you're-here" hug as she laid out an extra blanket on the sleeper sofa. *I'm glad too*, Violet would say. *You're helping me the way I should have helped you last year. I don't know which to say first: "Thank you" or "Sorry."*

"Rose?" Mrs. D said the word the same way Violet and the rest of the gang mirrored bizarre inquiries from summer tourists: *Sorry, what? Motor oil? Tweezers? Children's backpacks? What would possess you to think we carried that?*

"You think it's a huge mistake?"

"I didn't say that."

"You're looking at me like I'm paying in Canadian quarters."

"Oh honey, it's just—Rose has been away a long time."

"And we weren't close before, I know. But I feel like we have a lot to talk about. I won't be gone forever. I'll try to come back this summer. Maybe I can stay in the dorms?" The dorms were the bunkhouses where the seasonal workers slept on the perimeters of the cornfield.

Mrs. D blew out her lips. "I hope we're still here next summer."

"What do you mean?" Violet was baffled. As far as she could tell, business was as good as ever. "Where else would you be?"

"The sheriff got a tip Dekker's is trafficking prescription drugs."

"*What?*" Violet was gobsmacked. "It has to be a prank . . . Someone's sick, stupid joke."

Mrs. D gave her an intense look. "You haven't heard anything about this?"

"I've been pretty out of the loop for the past week. But I can ask around. I can try to find out more if it helps."

"Don't worry. We'll get through it." She shook her head and smoothed the weathered surface of her desk calendar. "So you're sure your sister is in a good place?"

"Like a doorman building?"

"I'm talking about a good emotional place. You're sure Rose can look after you? People around town still talk about the way she left, about whether she was mixed up with a bad group of people."

"Rose is happy now. And responsible. She's got steady temp work. She's going to help me save some money." The plan Violet had so far went like this: she would be the best houseguest Rose had ever seen. She'd make dinner, clean up, do the grocery shopping and the Laundromat runs. As soon as she got a job, she'd offer to pay rent.

"Gosh, honey. Unless you're a Russian billionaire, I don't think you're gonna save much money living in Manhattan."

"Well, thanks for this." Violet tapped her paycheck. "It's a good start."

Mrs. D looked dubious. "You're still only about two hundred dollars away from being homeless," she said. She bent down and removed a silver cash box from the bottom drawer of her desk. She turned the key and counted out another two hundred in five- and ten-dollar bills. "Here you go."

Violet looked at the bills in disbelief.

"I got kicked out of my house when I was a kid. I've got more advice if you want it." Violet nodded. "Stick to middle-class areas. The rich ones will get you arrested, and the poor ones will get you robbed. It's not safe to sleep in cars. If you have to do it, park in a motel parking lot. While you're at it, pick one with a continental breakfast. Most of the desk clerks aren't paid enough to care if you grab some fruit and cereal."

"Okay." Violet didn't have the heart to tell her she didn't own a car. Josephine had donated Rose's old Honda to the church.

"Hostels can be helpful. Explain your situation to the manager and offer to work for rent. Do you have your birth certificate? Social security card?"

Violet shook her head. "Neither."

"Get them. Take them with you. One more thing—" Mrs. D opened another desk drawer and shuffled through the contents. She pulled out a stack of flyers for other organic farms. "These are WWOOF farms that are looking for workers. Just take them. For options. Check in, okay? Call me on the first of every month. If only so I can give you the gossip."

When Violet emerged from the back room, she saw her mother sniffing the cartoon of milk they had on ice at the coffee bar. "Excuse me," Josephine barked at Troy. "Boy? Hello? Can you come here? Yes, *you*, with the earbuds in. I think this milk is off."

Will was staring into the doughnut display case, as though they were his only friends in the world.

Violet's thoughts went to her sister again. Maybe Rose would have a fresh perspective—new ideas about how to help mother-smothered Will. Violet could help her brother, but only if she helped herself first. She told herself she was leaving, not leaving him for dead.

"What happened to the hedge?" Violet remarked as they pulled into the driveway. The sad, black spindles were all that were left in the middle.

"They caught fire," her mother said.

"How? Was Dad burning leaves or something?"

"Yes," Will said, as sudden as a sneeze. He'd been so quiet the whole ride, Violet had almost forgotten he was in the backseat.

Josephine smiled and shrugged. "You know your father. He hates the leaf-fall time of year."

"Where *is* Dad?" Violet remarked as they pulled into the empty garage. Not that she was entirely ready to see him, especially after all those fights in the hospital. But she needed to act normal, whatever that was.

"I assume he's at a meeting," Josephine said as she brought the car to a stop. "Not a work meeting. An *alcoholics* meeting."

Violet made a small, interested sound, as if this were news to her.

Josephine killed the engine and turned to face Violet with a look of pure disparagement. "You heard me. Your father has quit drinking, and he's working very hard at it. So do us all a favor and try to refrain from the kind of hysterics that drove him to the bottle in the first place."

"I'll do my best," Violet said solemnly. "I really do want to stop being the troublemaker—the family laughingstock."

A double take from Josephine. "Well, I'm glad to hear you say that, Violet. I really am. Recognition is the first step to change."

"I had *a lot* of realizations in the hospital. I realized I'm the one who's been dragging this family down. I mean, *I'm* the reason Rose left in the first place." She gauged her mom's reaction for a minute (she appeared to be buying it) and then continued. "Rose has been writing to me. She *told* me, 'It was like living in a war zone . . . you and Mom fighting all the time. I just couldn't take it anymore!'"

Josephine smiled smugly, "So let me get this straight. You're apologizing to me?"

A pit opened in Violet's stomach and she tasted bile. "I guess I am, yeah. Mom, I'm really sorry."

Josephine leaned over the gearshift and leaned in for another hug. Violet tried not to tense up. She tried to lean into it and imagine she was elsewhere. In Sheep Meadow, maybe, on a warm spring day, sipping coffee from a paper deli cup with Rose.

The bathroom had the only locking door in the Hurst house, and thus offered at least the illusion of privacy. Illusion because Josephine liked to come knocking the second you got the shampoo in your hair, demanding something from the vanity drawers that just couldn't wait.

Violet turned the shower on and spent the next twenty minutes plotting. She was aching to pack, yet she knew she'd have to wait until her snooping mother went to bed. Even then she could only take what would fit in her schoolbag: a couple changes of clothes, nothing too heavy or oversized that she couldn't manage it on the two-mile bike to the baseball field. She had her social security card—she'd found it in her mother's jewelry box—but the birth certificate was a different matter. Violet didn't have a clue where Josephine kept the family admin files.

She wanted to see Imogene too, even though she wasn't sure if the feeling was mutual. Violet sat on the toilet lid, wiped the steam off her cell phone, and composed a ridiculous message asking her friend if she could drop by, return Beryl's copy of *The Celestine Prophecy*, and say good-bye before she ran away to live with Rose. She cringed as she pressed the Send button. Violet knew full well it sounded like the kind of off-the-wall claim a compulsive liar would make, but it *was* the truth and she felt powerless against it.

As she was waiting for Imogene to respond, her phone

hummed with a message from Rose: ONE O'CLOCK IT IS. SEE YOU
THERE! GOOD LUCK SNEAKING OUT! :)

Hot on its heels came Imogene's reply. Three words, urgent or
pissed off or both: COME OVER NOW.

Violet made it to the Fields' house by saying again that she had to
pick up the homework she'd missed. Josephine pushed out her
lips in a way that said she smelled bullshit. But Violet's speech in
the car had obviously earned her a few extra brownie points, and
ultimately her mother let her cruise off on her bike with a hand-
on-heart promise to be home by dinner.

When Violet got to the Fields' house she was relieved to find
Imogene and Finch alone and unsupervised. They were in the
kitchen, making dill weed sandwiches. It was a Field family favorite—a mishmash of cucumber and raw garlic cloves slathered
in vegan mayonnaise.

"Where's Beryl?" Violet asked, even though she was relieved
she didn't have to explain her plan to another adult that day.
Whereas Mrs. D had cautiously condoned running away, Beryl
was far more likely to urge a family-healing, talk-it-out approach.

"Omega Institute," Finch said. His fingers were in a forty-
dollar jar of the pink Himalayan sea salt Beryl bought for its healing benefits.

"What's the lecture?"

Finch shrugged. "It's some class in Kundalini awakening, I
think."

"No," Imogene said with unnecessary force. "It's a class in
shamanic empowerment. Some bitch from Woodstock told Mom
she was sick because she lost her power animal."

"Oh yeah," Finch said, as though suddenly remembering.

"She said Mom's power animal was a raven." He laughed and halved his sandwich with a knife.

Imogene's face was hard. "*And* she convinced Mom she had cancer because she'd lost her life force. What did she call it?"

"Soul loss," Finch said, chewing. "Right. Some dark energy—the *cancer energy*—moved in and filled the space where Mom's soul used to be. What a bitch, right?"

Imogene mussed the pink side of her rainbowed hair in frustration. "So anyway, I'm dealing with that, and then I saw your message about moving in with *Rose*."

"I know it's kind of . . . unexpected."

"Unexpected? It's fucking random!" She glanced at Finch, who was shaking his head again. "I'm sorry, but it is! You don't want to live at home with Josie the Soci, I get that. But you can stay *here*! You don't have to go running off in the middle of the night like you fucking robbed a bank! You haven't done anything wrong. We believe you, don't we?" Finch nodded. "Totally."

Imogene fiddled with one of her oversized rings. "I'm so sorry about what I said at the hospital. We should have considered the source." She meant Josephine.

"Absolutely," Finch said. "In a normal situation we would have considered the source."

"It's just we didn't know what to think. You were in that place . . ." Imogene was sputtering. She had a tiny glob of vegannaise on her lip.

Violet hugged her. "I appreciate it. I do. But I can't live with you. You know my mom would be over here in a second, screaming at Beryl, blaming your mom for turning me against her. It would be gross, and messy, and I won't put your mom through that. Especially not now. Not when she's dealing with breast-groping shamans."

The sound Imogene made was equal thirds laugh, spit, sob.

"You *can't* leave," she said. "You can't. You're my unbiological sister. And you're Finch's soulmate!"

This line of teasing made them both blush.

"You're going to come visit me, idiot. Next weekend, maybe. We can go to the natural history museum."

Imogene sniffled and wiped her face on the arm of her sweater. "Only if we can get stoned and hang out under the blue whale."

"Deal."

"Call me when you're with Rose? No matter how late it is?"

"I will."

"Do you think Rose is going to be different?"

"I think so. At least, she *seems* different. In a good way. Rose is on my side. And I really need that right now."

"We're on your side too."

"I know you are. But Rose has been where I am. She understands what this is like."

Imogene nodded sadly. "That's a good thing, I guess. Anyway, don't forget to call me."

Back at home, Will was setting the table for what looked to be a no-punches-pulled vegetarian meal. Violet didn't trust it at first. She inspected and sniffed. She lifted the top on her mother's beloved soup terrine and spied something orange and vegetal (pumpkin soup? sweet potato?). In the kitchen, she'd caught a glimpse of acorn squash, halved and stuffed with some combination of white beans and chard. Only she was aware of the irony: her homecoming dinner was secretly her farewell meal. And just as Violet had decided to leave, it was beginning to seem as though peaceful coexistence might be possible.

She felt giddy and reckless. "So, Mom," she said. "I'm seeing a conspicuous lack of bacon."

Josephine jutted her chin. "Well, I still don't buy all that righteous baloney about not eating food with a face. But we could all stand to be a little healthier. I'll give you that." She untied her apron and added, "Not that you will *ever* see me put my lips on that meat substitute you like—the one that looks like a parboiled hot-water bottle and gives you that hideous breath."

Violet nearly laughed. Things that would ordinarily piss her off just seemed funnier the closer one a.m. got. It was like being stoned, only not, and she suddenly understood Edie's beatific smile on the night of her birthday. With one a.m. in sight, nothing, nothing registered on Violet's give-a-fuck-o-meter.

"Violet!" Douglas was home from his guys' night with Bill W. He called down from the second-floor landing. "Violet! Can you come here?!"

And that was another thing that would have bothered her before. The way her father spent the whole of their family life hollering from a distance. He hadn't seen her since she'd come home from the hospital. Couldn't he just come downstairs if he wanted to welcome her home? Why was he like a man trapped on a high mountaintop, calling down through the mist?

Violet found him in her parents' bedroom. "You beckoned, sire?" She was bracing herself for another heart-to-heart or its chemically dependent equivalent: liver-to-liver.

Turned out she was giving him too much credit. There was no *How are you feeling?* No *Welcome home.* "I need to see Rose's letters," Douglas said. "The envelopes too."

"Why? Seriously Dad, what does it matter? Did you ever consider that they're private?" She wanted to ask if it had ever occurred to him that she, like everyone, had personal boundaries. This, in spite of her parents' near-constant invasions. But then she reminded herself: *I'll never have another conversation like this again after one a.m. One a.m., one a.m.* She'd been repeating it so often it sounded like a second heartbeat. "You're not reading them. They're mine."

"Violet, there are too many secrets in this family."

"That's not my fault! I'm not the one who keeps secrets. I'm the one who spills them, and all I do is get in trouble for it."

Her father looked at her like she was speaking in tongues.

"I'll tell you what. I'll give you her addresses. Just let me grab a piece of paper."

Violet wandered into her mother's office on the hunt for something to write on. Goya's "Drowning Dog" was open on the desk. Staring down at the picture with the peculiar mental clarity that leaving gave her—it wasn't hindsight exactly, but some premonition of it—Violet could see that her mom was a lot like Goya's Fido. Josephine was constantly treading water. Josephine was forever over her head where other humans were concerned. Maybe she expected people to abandon her, and thus pushed them until they did. Maybe, like Goya's dog, Josephine felt so inadequate that she held her head up even higher. Yes, her mother had lied about her, possibly framed her, tried to ruin her friendships, tried to ruin her life, but even with the hospital bracelet still sliding up and down her wrist, Violet felt almost sorry for her.

She closed the book, thinking, *Whatever's wrong with you, I didn't cause it. I can't cure it.* Josephine wasn't just any drowning dog, she was a drowning pit bull, and Violet was dead certain she'd eat the face off anyone who tried to save her.

Violet reached for the piece of scrap paper on the corner of the desk. It looked like an old homeschool worksheet, something no one would miss. She flipped it over and copied the addresses (both town and country) onto the back, and gave the letters to her father as per his request-slash-demand. It wasn't until she was sitting at dinner, chewing her beans, that she realized what it might mean for her and Rose.

. . .

During dinner, Violet could feel Will sneaking wounded glances at her as he balanced his spoon, awkwardly, in his nondominant hand.

"How about soup in a mug?" she whispered. "Will, do you want me to get you a mug?"

"Aw, your sister's so concerned for you," Josephine said through a sip of ice water. If she was mocking, her voice didn't let on. The butt of her glass smacked the table. "So you got your paycheck then, Viola?"

"I did, Mother. Thank you."

"And Doreen wasn't at all bothered by your little trip to the hospital?" Doreen was Mrs. D's first name. *Double D,* Mrs. D joked. *It's a wonder I made it through middle school.*

Violet licked her spoon. "Mrs. D was really understanding about it all."

"That's lucky. I would feel *so* badly if anything jeopardized your job there. We all know how much you get out of it."

Douglas looked up from his chard.

Josephine lifted her fork and knife. Her sharp glare clashed with the casual tilt of her head. "Fulfilling work, isn't it?"

"Yep," Violet said obligingly.

"Some might say, the work is so good it's practically *addictive.*"

Violet rolled her eyes. "I guess so. Dad, could you pass the water? Is that a new pitcher?"

"Don't skirt the issue, Viola."

"*What* issue, Mom? Dad. Water. Please."

"The issue is: You, trading prescriptions with that pack of losers. I've read your diary, Viola. The *pharm* stand? With a P.H.?"

The kitchen phone trilled at her mother's kitchen desk.

"It was *you* wasn't it? You called the police on Mrs. D." Violet's head was pealing in time with the portable phone. "You're trying to ruin her business, her livelihood, because you're jealous that I like her better than you?"

Josephine tossed her lapped-napkin onto the table. "William, get the phone. Douglas, back me up here."

"If there are drugs there, Violet . . . And minors . . ."

"Mrs. D doesn't sell drugs, Dad! She sells beetroot!"

"Good evening, Hurst residence. William speaking." His usually wide eyes popped a millimeter more. "My *sister*?"

"Damn it, Viola, what did I say about telling your friends you're grounded?" Josephine crossed the kitchen and pried the phone from Will's hand. "This is Viola's mother. With whom do I have the pleasure of speaking?"

Will muddled to his chair and stared at his plate.

"Excuse me? You *know*. You know what?" Josephine turned her back to the table. "I'm warning you— You don't know who you're dealing with. How dare you—"

Douglas's fork clattered to the floor as he shoved back his chair. "Who is it, Jo? Is that Rose?"

"She's gone now, Douglas. Everything's fine. She hung up."

Violet felt her jaw clench. "Who was it?"

"A friend of yours, evidently."

"What friend?"

"Francesca-someone?"

A heavy quiet ensued.

Violet crossed her arms.

"She said she knows *all about* your sister. What, exactly, does she think she knows about Rose?"

"Beats me."

"Don't lie to me, Viola. This is a family matter. It concerns me. What have you said to this person?"

"None of your business."

"Who is this Francesca? Why haven't I met her before?"

"She's a friend." Violet shrugged and rolled a bean across her plate.

"What have we talked about all week, Violet?" Douglas jumped in. "About the dangers of keeping secrets? If this Francesca has information about Rose—"

"Violet always does this!" Will shouted, lifting his acorn squash and smashing it bean-side down into his plate. There were tears of pent-up frustration in his eyes. "Violet only cares about herself!"

"Viola, go to your room," Josephine ordered. "I won't have you upsetting Will."

"I haven't done anything to Will! I mean, what have I done to Will? Dad, a little help here?"

"Violet, what did you learn in meetings, over and over, this week? You're only as sick as your secrets."

"God, Dad! This isn't about your fucking disease!"

"Wow, Viola," Josephine said with sudden composure. "We *sure have* missed you. We've certainly missed *all of this*. Go to your room. Get out of here now. Don't even bother with your plate. I can't even look at you."

Violet went to bed at nine, and spent the following three hours with her eyes glued open, her mind running laps as she watched the splintered numbers on her bedside alarm clock. She heard her mother speaking in low, frustrated tones as she flossed Will's teeth. Violet kept waiting for someone to shine a light inside her room and check that she was still breathing, they way they had in the hospital, but she was all alone with her second-guessing and mounting fear.

At thirty minutes to one, she crept downstairs through the

darkened house and stole her father's headlamp. Theft didn't matter now. Nothing mattered now. Whatever happened tonight, Violet was snipping family ties. Violet had always thought her mother's rejection was a sentence close to death, but now it seemed like a lucky break. She didn't share her family's mass psychosis or magical thinking. She was free to seek answers and she wanted to find them, deranged as the truth was likely to be.

In a way, she had the Dekkers to thank. Mrs. D had taught Violet the three Ds of pruning: "Cut off everything that's diseased, dead, or damaged." And the Hursts were all three. Violet didn't have any hope for straightening out as long as they were bearing down on her.

Violet's bike caught air as she took the steep turn down into the Little League fields, and for a second she worried that she was going to lose control, skid on pebbles, go crashing sideways into the boarded-up hot dog stands where she'd loitered at many of Will's old T-ball games. But she didn't. Her tires caught and gripped, and she cruised on her brakes down past the baseball diamonds to where the rec fields met the creek.

The night was clear, the full moon starting to wane, and Violet's hands were stiff from the cold. She blew on her fingertips as she dismounted and went to light the last of Edie's cigarettes. According to the time on her cell phone, she was still ten minutes early, so she turned off her headlamp and followed the sound of gushing water into the sparse woods.

The creek was pumping high on account of all the rainfall. The current completely engulfed the rocks where, in the summer, she and Imogene liked to read and smoke trees, Finch usually farther downstream twirling around on a raft and getting what he always called an "inner tube tan," where every part of him sunburned but his butt and the backs of his legs. She tried to console herself with the thought that she hadn't seen the last of her friends.

Somehow, some way, there'd be lots more summers of creek swimming, tangled hair, geeky river shoes. She didn't have to give up growing things and working the land: having dirt under her nails and that particularly satisfying deep muscle ache that came from pulling weeds and lifting shovels.

A dog barked high up on the hill on the opposite bank, and Violet started from the sound. The pit in her stomach was growing, and when she looked down at her phone, it was two minutes past one. Her anxiety had changed. Now, instead of fearing what would happen, she was worried that she might get stood up. What if no one came? What if she stood there for hours in the frigid cold, only to ride home? What if she was always left wondering where Rose really was?

The dog broke into another fit of rabid barking, and Violet saw headlights through the trees. She stomped out her cigarette and walked quietly toward them, hoping to maintain her distance and get a view of the car. But she didn't have to. She heard the running engine, and then the sound of the car stereo. It was a song Violet knew well: the fifteenth string quartet of Dmitri Shostakovich. As she got closer, she saw her mother's face under the interior light. She was shoving Violet's bike into the back of her car.

Violet, soft-footed in her Converse sneakers, was able to sneak up from the rear and yank the back tire.

The handlebars came sailing backward into Josephine's torso, and for a moment she was wedged between the bike and the open car door. Violet pulled harder and the bike careened into the dirt on its side, the brake lever loudly scratching the side of the car as it fell.

For a fraction of a second, her mother looked frightened, but then her face sprang back into the same expressionless mask as always. It was a face that never changed, not with age or wisdom and certainly not with concern.

"I know what you have planned, Violet. And I can't allow you to do it." Her voice was as calm, cool, and controlling as it had ever been. "We can repair our relationship. Today made me realize that. We had a good day today, didn't we? Didn't today prove we can talk, laugh, and enjoy each other's company?"

Violet wanted to say she'd never seen her mother laugh unless it was at someone else's expense. Josephine never talked with anyone, she talked *at* them or she forced words into their mouths like ball gags; she found a way to make people say what she wanted to hear. "I don't want a relationship, Mom."

"You can't live with Rose, Violet. You just can't."

It was like her mother had set up the shot, and all Violet had to do was bring the whole game crashing down. It was the moment Violet had been both dreading and obsessing about, ever since she found the piece of paper on her mother's desk. Every muscle in her body clenched. She felt a shiver, like an electric current pulse through the bone-cold autumn air, and it took her a minute to realize it was her own primal scream. "No, I *can't* go live with her!" She was shrieking. "I can't go live with her! Can I?! And we both know why that is!"

"I don't have the faintest clue what you're talking about. Have you gone crazy again, crazy girl? Cuckoo?" She rolled her eyes and twirled her index finger. "Get in the car now. We're going home."

Violet's hand tightened around the cell phone in her pocket. "I'm not going anywhere with you."

She moved closer, and Violet instinctively backed away. "Violet, I am your mother. And you will do as I say." Violet pressed the call button on her cell phone and held it to her ear. "Violet, put that phone away. I'm warning you. Who are you calling? I asked you a question."

Violet put a hand up. *Just wait.* When the line began to ring, she said, with dripping sarcasm, "I'm calling Rose. Let's wait and see what happens when I call Rose." For a second, there was silence and Violet thought she had it all wrong. She thought maybe she *was* crazy, paranoid, schizo/bipolar. She was almost ready to let her mother load her bike back into the car, when she heard the small ring in the front seat.

Her mother stepped in front of her as she moved for the passenger door. "What do you think you're doing? Answer me. Violet? I am talking to you!"

But Violet just shoved her aside and made a grab for the handle. Inside, she followed the sound and slammed the glove compartment open. Inside was a cell phone. Cheap. Prepaid, probably. Violet held it up inches from her mother's face. Her anger was as pure and electric as any drug high. "Wasn't it bad enough?!" she screamed. "Wasn't it bad enough you came between me and Rose while she was here?! Did you really have to keep doing it after Rose was gone?!"

Her mother's face went smug, and Violet knew she was about to break into the overenunciated near-whisper she always used when she was actually in a blind rage. "What makes you think Rose is gone? Aren't you the one who said you saw her the other night?"

Violet waved the cell phone again, and Josephine tried to grab it from her hand. They ended up bent over and grappling over the cheap piece of plastic. The keys bleeped repeatedly under their fingers, and Violet couldn't help thinking her mother didn't know how to set the thing to silent mode. Josephine was tech-stupid. The snail mail was case in point.

In one fast vicious movement, her mother's fingers were in Violet's face, clawing her left eye with her freshly manicured tips. The pain brought glittering red stars, bad as any acid trip, to Violet's eyes. It was instinctive: Violet let go of the phone and clutched her stinging lower eyelid, at which point Josephine took off running into the woods.

Violet followed her. She pointed herself in the direction of snapping branches and swooshing leaves and ran as fast and quiet as a fox. She was better in the woods. She was like her namesake that way. Whereas her mother was proudly prissy, divorced from everything outside herself. All of nature, all the world was Josephine's blind spot.

She found her mother sitting on a downed log down by the water, legs crossed girlishly at the ankles, as though she were waiting for a lover to show.

"Where's the phone?" Violet asked sharply.

Josephine turned around to face the sound of her voice. "Wanna guess?" she asked with the lilting, impish voice that made Violet sick. To think she'd let her mother convince her for all those years that she was a problem child. If anyone was the enfant terrible, it was Josephine.

"You didn't. Tell me you didn't really throw it in the creek."

Her mother threw up her hands. "Whoopsie."

Violet tried to tell herself it didn't matter. She still had "Rose's" letters. And Violet still had the piece of paper she'd found on her mother's desk. At first she'd thought it was a homeschool exercise. But those letters . . . Violet had seen so much of that anal-retentive handwriting recently. It only took her a few moments to realize it was a handwriting key. Josephine had used something—probably Rose's old school notebooks—to trace the shape and style of every letter of the alphabet as rendered by Violet's sister.

Violet's own phone was in her hand. "I know it was you who's been writing me, Mother."

"Oh, will you just . . ." Her mother looked up at the moon and made a grunting sound like Violet was spoiling the scenery. "If you know so much, why did you come here in the first place?"

"I came to confront you. Like I would really have this conversation at home with Dad and Will jumping in. As if I need you all ganging up on me the way you did at dinner."

"They were *defending* me. Because I'm right, Viola. Because you're the one who needs to be put in your place."

"They don't love you, they're afraid of you! I was excited to see Rose! Don't you get that?" Violet, who hated and feared her mother more than just about anything, had never suspected Josephine was as heartless and conniving as this, not when she ran her fingers over that first wax seal, not when she drafted all those painstaking replies. Deep down, deeper than anything, she'd honestly believed her sister missed her. She'd believed it through giving her notice at work. She'd believed it through packing her backpack and saying goodbye to the only people in the free world who gave a shit about her. "Why the fuck did you start writing to me in the first place? Why *now*?"

"Because of what you wrote in your diary."

Violet gritted her teeth in frustration. "Why are you still reading my diary?!"

"Oh Viola, stop playacting. You and I both know you *want* me to read your diary. After we argue, you write things like, 'I feel so bad for the way I treated Mom' and leave it out in plain sight for me to read."

Now was not the time to argue that under her mattress was not in plain sight. Neither were any of the other hiding places Violet had tried: in her pillowcase, in her sock drawer, in a box of Lightdays sanitary napkins.

"So what did I write that was worth *all of this*?"

"All those things about me being overbearing. You said it probably made Rose want to kill herself. You said it was why you were starving yourself."

Violet remembered the entry now. She'd been writing about

sallekhana, saying her only reservation about it was the thought that her mom might be the one who found her dead in her sleep. *I can't imagine her crying over me*, Violet had written. *More likely she'd redress me in an outfit she liked. That, or she'd slap me a dozen times, knowing I couldn't tell.*

"You were so insensitive," Josephine said. "So vicious. I felt like you needed reminding . . . Rose loved me. Even when we didn't get along, she loved me. She was never like you."

It took Violet a second. She had been thinking her mother had sent her to Fallkill because of the way she'd shouted, *Rose is here! Did you see her? I saw her!* And then it hit her, one word with the force of a freight train.

"Suicide. The other night, in the kitchen . . . I said the word *suicide*." Of course, Violet had been thinking about her own when she said it, and her mother, ever the narcissist, had put the word into a context that was meaningful to her.

"Yes."

"And you had to make it look like Rose was still alive because you hid her suicide from us." Violet took a deep breath. Her cell phone trembled in her hand. "Rose's good-bye letter was a suicide note, wasn't it?"

Josephine had turned away to face the water.

"Hello? Earth to Mother? Answer me. It was a suicide note, wasn't it?"

"Shhh," Josephine hissed. "Keep your voice down."

"What? Who's going to hear us? The ragweed? The fucking deer? Was Dad in on this, too?"

Her mother said nothing. So Douglas didn't know. It would never occur to Josephine to think of anyone else. She'd never considered that the rest of the family might want to say good-bye and grieve. She'd never thought they'd need closure.

"I just don't understand. Why would you do that?" Violet

moved closer, though every muscle in her body urged her to run the other way. She had to lure her mother the way Edie had said. If she wanted any answers, she'd have to flatter and feign concern for the monster—who was sitting in front of her, even as she wanted to plunge a stake through her heart or scream like a little lost kid for police. Violet tried to keep her voice even. "I mean, everything else"—she wanted to say *legality*—"aside, hasn't it been hard on you? Dealing with that kind of tragedy alone? I could have helped you. Other people too."

"Oh, Violet, how stupid are you? Don't you *get* it? I won't allow people to think of her that way."

Violet could barely breathe. Her voice was shaking. "I hear you, Mom. But you can't control other people's perceptions any more than you could control Rose. People have minds of their own. Life isn't some big play where you get to direct, and orchestrate, and play set designer."

Josephine howled. "I won't have this whole town thinking your sister was this mopey weakling! Rose wasn't a sad sap! Your sister was a star! She had all the talent in the world, even if she chose to throw it away!" Violet put a hand on her mother's brittle back. "You'll understand when you're my age. I did her a favor. You and your brother too. When people hear the name Hurst, they think of the beautiful little girl who played Sandy in *Grease*. Not some tortured little beatnik."

"It's okay, Mom," she said. "We can talk this out. Just breathe. Relax. Let go."

"Oh Violet, I really don't need your hippie shit right now."

Violet was stung, but not daunted. She thought of Goya's dog. "I know you feel like you're drowning right now. But you're not alone. I'm here." She remembered what Edie said about narcissistic supply. *It's like a drug. When they're high on it, you can trick them into thinking they're getting their way.* "I can help you. But first, I've got to understand. My mind works slower than yours. Start at the beginning. Start with Rose's letter."

"It was on the front seat, when I found her." Josephine's voice was high and pinched.

"Where did you find her?"

"In the garage. With the car running." She sounded put out, as if Violet already knew all this and was wasting her time with unnecessary questions.

"The neighbors," Violet said with a sudden rush of understanding. "They said our garage door was open all day. You were airing it out."

"I told the police Rose must have left the door open."

"I remember," Violet said. Her head was rushing in time with the creek, but she tried to make her voice reassuring. "So the note . . ."

"I couldn't read it. I was so angry at her, I couldn't even bear to touch it. I wouldn't give her the satisfaction. It just sat on the seat beside me while I drove Rose's car to the station. The whole way, I just kept thinking Rose had no right to leave me. I could never replace her. Your sister was irreplaceable."

Violet swallowed hard. Her mother was talking about Rose as if she were an object, a priceless object, but still . . . "You're not alone," she repeated. "People love you. Will loves you. You're his whole world."

A brittle little laugh. "I always knew Rose would leave me the way my mother did. Rose even looked like my mother. Rose looked at me every single day with those eyes—my mother's big blue eyes—and I thought one day you're going to realize I'm not the perfect woman you think I am. And when you do, you'll toss me aside like I'm nothing. Like I'm garbage."

The image made Violet shiver uncontrollably. Her mother mostly accused people of wrongdoings she committed herself: Will was "sick." Violet was "crazy." And now, Rose had "discarded" Josephine, when clearly, criminally, it had been the other way around.

"So you were the one who packed Rose's suitcase? You took her computer and turned off her cell phone?" Violet's voice wavered. "You paid for parking and a train ticket on Rose's credit card?"

Silence.

"You lied to the police when you said Rose called you from her boyfriend's house."

"I should think that's obvious."

"There is no Damien. You made up that call. You made up that name." It figured that her mother would choose something more dramatic than Joe or Mike. Even Koch had prestige; it was a hundred-billion-dollar name.

"You were the one who unenrolled Rose from school?"

"I forged her resignation letter. I had to. Your father had reported her missing. He'd done it without even consulting me first! Can you imagine? He left me no other option; I had to make it look like Rose ran away. I took out new credit cards in her name. I figured everyone would back off once they saw her credit report." Even in the dark, Violet was almost positive her mother smiled. "I know what you're thinking, you with your Buddhist ethics. I used the cards for theater tickets, mostly. I bought and did things Rose would have enjoyed. It was a tribute to her. I gave her the life she should have had. The one she would have wanted."

Violet couldn't hold back any longer. "You gave her the life you wanted for her." She shook her head. There was something she still didn't get. "But there was security footage of Rose at the

MetroNorth station. You said the police showed it to you and Dad." The thought of her mom reviewing the tapes brought a sudden, sick rush to her stomach.

"Oh, Violet." The condescension had crept into Josephine's voice again. "Those cameras are hung so high, and they only record one second out of every four."

Violet put a hand to her mouth and spoke through it. "You wore her clothes. Her *shoes*, even. You pulled her suitcase."

"That white down coat." Nostalgia clung to her mother's voice. "It smelled so strongly of Rose's perfume it made me cry. You remember that perfume? All the vanilla? Your sister used to smell like this little sugar cookie. And when I pulled the hood over my head, I had a glimmer of what it must have felt like to be Rose—women rubbernecking, men drooling."

More likely, people had been rubbernecking at her age-inappropriate clothes. "Okay, so you got on the train in Poughkeepsie disguised as Rose. How did you make it home?" The train to New York City was an hour and a half each way, and Josephine had been back at Old Stone Way when the bus dropped Will and Violet home from school.

"Use your *brain*, Violet. I didn't go the whole way. I got off in Beacon and called a cab."

"So where does Rose fit into all this, Mom?"

"What do you mean, where does she fit into it?"

"I mean where is she?" She couldn't bring herself to say it, but Josephine's silence demanded she say it: "Where is her *body*, mother? What the fuck did you do with Rose's body?"

"She's somewhere that brought her pleasure. That's all you need to know."

It was too much. "You don't get to decide what I know! I know you don't get that, and I have compassion for you, I do. I get that you had a tough childhood, and your brain didn't cook right . . ."

Josephine rose and took a step toward her. "Violet, I'm warning you. I won't accept being spoken to that way."

"Just because you brought Rose into the world doesn't make her your real estate! She was my sister! She was a human being! Not a puppet! And the second she stopped playing along, you did everything you could think of to destroy her! Rose did what she did because she was a good girl. She did it because she knew, deep down, that you wanted her to. She might have killed herself, but the blood is on your hands!"

"That's ridiculous. I wanted your sister to be happy. That's what all mothers want for their children."

Violet turned the voice recorder off on her phone. "Some mothers. Not you. Those are empty words to you. Greeting-card words. Something you picked up from one of the other moms at the PTA and kept repeating because it sounded right. You don't have the first idea who your children are. And you don't even want to know us."

"I love my children, Violet! Even you! I may not like you, but I still love you!"

"You love the images you picked out for us. You love Will when he's playing the good boy because he fits into some fake-ass idealized version of your life. And you love me when I'm playing the bad girl because you can project all the twisted parts of yourself onto me. You don't give a shit about anyone's happiness but your own. And the irony is, you'll never be happy!"

For a second, Josephine's beauty-pageant posture collapsed. "I am your elder, Violet! How dare you say that to me?!"

"It's true! You won't ever be happy because you don't live in the world of other people. You can't connect with anyone. You don't feel empathy. Tell me, Mom, why did you really pose as Rose and ask me to meet you here?"

Josephine shook her head.

"Come on! Why did you send me that note in the hospital once you realized they weren't going to keep me there for the rest of my natural-born life? *Hi, it's me Rose. I love you. Come live with me.* You were going to help me get lost, good and permanent, weren't you? Rose was a good girl. Once she felt how much you despised her, she killed herself for you. But not me. Not no-good Violet." She spread her arms. *Here I am.* "If you want me gone, you're gonna have to do it yourself, Mother. With your own two hands."

"I don't have the first idea what you're talking about."

"Oh, just fucking *own* it for once in your life! You made it impossible for me to know Rose. And now I never will." Rose was gone. That revelation, still sinking in, brought a rip of fresh pain.

Josephine stepped toward her. "So, Viola . . . We need to talk about what happens next. . . ."

Violet shook her head. "I'm not keeping this secret."

Josephine reached out, gently, and touched the new growth on Violet's scalp. "You *know* now, Viola. And what do I always say? I don't burden you with unnecessary information. . . ."

The next second, her mother had hooked a foot around her ankle, and Violet was falling flat on her back, feet scrabbling, not getting any traction against the heavy leaf-fall and creek-washed pebbles. It happened so fast, and yet Violet experienced it all frame by frame: she gasped for air, clawing her mother's hands as they closed tighter around her neck. The dog was still barking. Headlights flashed somewhere in the far distance. And there was Josephine straddling her hips, riding her in a way that was almost incestuous as she tried to wring every last breath out of her. Violet, who barely remembered a word from the King James Bible, had a spasm-thought of Job. *He (or rather She) who giveth life can taketh away.* Violet knew without a shadow of a doubt that her mother was thinking the same thing as she mashed her windpipe. Buddhism, Jainism, Catholicism, whatever. In the end, it didn't matter. The only God Josephine let people worship was her.

Violet scooted her butt. She twisted and threw her hips. She wanted to scream, but she was too focused on the pressure behind her eyeballs and the immense underwater silence in her head. Blood pooled in her face. She blacked out and abruptly faded back in. It wasn't like people said. There was no white light. Violet didn't see her life flash before her eyes. She had only one supersalient thought: she did not want her final, dying image to be her mother's face. It was worth living for that reason alone.

William Hurst

It was the first command decision Will had made in years. He hadn't asked permission. He hadn't consulted with his mother first. When he saw the stamp rolling around in his mother's sewing box, he'd shoved it in his pocket the very second his head had stopped spinning with shock. He'd taken the stick of pink wax too and even realized with horror that he'd been with his mother when she bought it at the classy stationery store in Manhattan. She'd claimed it was a candle at the time, and Will had been too bored to pay closer attention. They'd been so close to Union Square, and Will had been watching the skater boys through the storefront window; they'd been mesmerizing, wearing the kind of tight low-slung jeans that Josephine forbade, tossing their flippy hair, doing boardslides and pop shove-its and landing on their appealingly feminine faces as if the pain were nothing.

As he stood at his mom's desk, the past couple of months took on a whole new meaning. It was like the moment when you finally see the flip side of an optical illusion. Holding the treble clef in his palm was like seeing a vase come into shape where two chinless faces used to be. Will understood, at long last, why his mother—who was so quick to read Violet's diary—had brought "Rose's" letter to the hospital without steaming the envelope open first. He realized why, even as they were dressed in their opera best, Josephine had needed to drop outgoing mail in a blue sidewalk mailbox. Even his mom's disappearance in Newburgh was suddenly accounted for. There had been a UPS store in the same shopping plaza. His mom was using "Rose," someone Violet trusted, to spill the beans about their father's abuse. If Violet knew who she was really corresponding with, she'd never trust their mother again. If Violet found the wax seal set, she'd ruin London for everyone.

And so, just like that, Will flushed them both down the toilet, even though he'd been warned a million times that anything other than toilet paper was bad for the septic. His mother wouldn't mind. Will was sure of it. She was likely to thank him, even call him her hero.

But his mother had been irritated at bedtime. It wasn't rage, exactly, and it wasn't directed at him. It was just the low-level, distracted anger that she got from time to time, where her pupils seemed to dilate and she didn't seem to hear a dang word he said. She'd found a string of tiny infractions to tell Will off about: dirty tissues in his pockets, crust behind his ears. When he tried to ask her about Rose's letters, when she scolded him for the way he said "ask." ("Ask! Not ax! We're not chopping firewood! I swear Will, I am this close to sending you to a speech therapist!") And so Will had given up asking. She'd brushed Will's hair so hard that the wooden head of the brush kept knocking his skull. When she wrenched his pajama shirt over his head, she'd half-strangled him by accident in the process.

Will had gone to bed with self-hatred that cut deep. He'd lain awake long after the house had gone silent, softly practicing his diction, stressing out about the Regents exam, hating his weak disgusting parts—the needy little boy locked away inside him.

Finally, at some ungodly hour of the night, Will had done the only thing that helped when he felt that way. He'd softly closed his bedroom door, leaned his head against it, risen on tiptoe and slid both hands under the elastic band of his pajama pants.

Cacoethes: a bad habit or insatiable urge.

His breath was quiet, his hands unforgiving and desperate. He thought of skater boys, prep school boys, he thought of old men, adults like Dr. Martin and Mr. Razz. He even pictured Jake Greenberg who, in teasing him, had made a certain motion with his hands—a gesture that had first given Will this idea. Will had to do it this way, always the same way, leaning against the door that didn't lock, the door that meant his mother could walk in at any time. But it was more than that. . . . Standing up, the door against his forehead, anchoring him, was the only way it felt right. Will fell into a heavy trance and he vowed, same as always, that this was the last time. Almost there, he promised himself he would never again succumb to this bizarre bedtime ritual. And then it came: the strong, righteous shudder and one bright, blissful second that blew his mind blank. He couldn't think of anything at all, let alone how unacceptable he was, how ill-equipped he was to live in this world.

The inner calm didn't last. It never did. Will pulled his hand away wet—something that had never happened before—and waddled back to bed, feeling more immoral and unnatural than ever before. Boiling with shame, he balled up his briefs, hid them under his bed, and got another pair, certain he'd betrayed both God and his mother.

It was still dark when Will woke. Engines grumbled in the driveway. Blue-and-white lights were flashing through his gingham curtains. Feet pounded the stairs, and his father was calling his name, sniffing Will out like a predator.

Will sat upright in bed, his bent knees making a teepee of his bulldozer sheets. His first instinct was to think about places where he could hide. In the closet. Under the bed next to the tighty-whities he'd planned to de-goo in the morning. Will's stoplight alarm clock said 4:02 a.m. He didn't know if he was still dreaming, whether his father's voice was a night terror. Will just sat, still as death, frozen in fear and guilt. He didn't know what to be scared of or what he'd done wrong, but those felt like the only two emotions Will had to pick from.

The door flew open, and suddenly his father was standing over him, ripping back Will's striped duvet, patting Will's chest, snatching him forward off his small altar of pillows, shaking him too hard with his big, gruff hands, his face too close, his breath too meaty and hot, asking Will intrusive, aggressive questions like *Are you okay?* Every time Will squealed and shoved him away, there were more questions. Prodding begat pawing.

"Mom!" Will screamed, hurling himself out of bed. "Mom! Mom!" Will ran down the hallway to his parents' bedroom and hollered his throat raw for her.

Douglas was hot on Will's heels, dropping his hands down onto Will's shoulders. "Will, is your mother *here?* This is important. Talk to me."

Every time he spun Will to face him, Will twisted the other way. "Get off me! Don't touch me!" Will realized he was wailing. And then there was a policeman mounting the stairs, square-shouldered, cinch-waisted, the only person in the whole world who could save Will at that moment. "Get him off me!" Will pleaded.

Will felt mutinous, inconsolable as he broke every unspoken commandment in the Hurst family rule book. He cried like a child and pleaded for help. Will knew it was embarrassing the way he went barreling toward that cop. It wasn't nice. It wasn't respectable, but Will was too spooked and confused to care. He begged for help. He scream-detailed everything his mother had told him about Douglas's abuses. "I want my mom! I want my mom!" he told the officer.

And then Will heard the words that hit him like a bullet hole to the stomach: "We're looking for your mom, buddy. I promise you we are. The trouble is, we don't know where to find her right now."

VIOLET HURST

SHE CAME TO at the sound of Josephine's voice. "Yes," she thought she heard her mom saying at some distance. "Once I realized what was happening, I was concerned too."

The moon wavered in the sky as Violet focused her eyes. She sipped a small lungful of near-frozen night air. Her throat hurt so badly she could barely swallow, and her legs were so limp she could barely bend her knees. She strained her ears. There were more running engines. Other voices said things Violet couldn't make out.

Then came her mother's voice, too loud. "I don't know what's gotten into that child. Sneaking out alone to meet Lord knows who. [inaudible] You'd think I'd taught her nothing."

In conversations outside their family, Josephine always spoke one notch louder than normal people. It was only her mom's appearance—the twill jackets and bleached white teeth, the meticulous grooming and TV news anchor hair—that lent her some illusion of sanity. *The voice doesn't lie*, Violet thought, as she sprawled in the dirt. And her mother's steeply-pitched voice was *Grey Gardens*. If only people closed their eyes when Josephine spoke, maybe then they'd hear it: cat-woman crazy, fueled by sadism and bottomless need.

Violet heaved herself onto one elbow, bones zinging. She realized swallowing wasn't the only issue. It hurt to inhale. Breathless as she was, each gasp brought hot pain. It felt like someone shoving a cleat down her throat. She rolled over, teeth chattering, and puked lukewarm soup onto the pebbled ground.

Violet probably should have been scared, but her only thought was to get to whoever her mom was talking to before she sent them away. Cautiously, she pushed herself up to a position that approximated standing. Her heart was pulsing. Through clumped trees, she could see headlights, four of them, like eyes staring off into the middle distance, exhaust rising around them. Violet held the gaze of those cars while she staggered headlong back through the woods, feet flopping through leaves littered with trash. Her ankles turned on tree roots, hidden rocks, crushed cans. Each fresh breath choked her.

It was claustrophobic pain, the kind that held her inside it instead of vice versa. Still, she focused on the voices and the engines, the headlights in the distance. The conversation had died down, and Violet could hear car doors closing. She quickened her step, starfishing her hands against tree trunks for balance. As long as there were four headlights—not two—she wasn't alone with her mother. As long as there were four, she wasn't alone in the woods, in the world.

A car door swung open and music, Van Morrison, pooled into the parking lot.

"Violet?!" It was Imogené, running wild-eyed toward her through the pale exhaust.

Josephine was coming at Violet too. Her public face was back in place. She had her hands clasped over her mouth. "Violet! Honey, thank God! We were so worried!" Her eyebrows were twitching around, trying to strike some expression that might pass for maternal concern, but her panicked eyes didn't know where to look. They kept sliding back toward Imogene. Josephine, ever the performance artist, trying to get a read on her audience.

How hard Violet tried to say, *I'm not going anywhere with you.* All she could manage was a painful wheeze. She just kept propelling herself forward, toward Imogene, even as Josephine started pulling on her jacket, trying to usher her into her red sedan.

"Get in the car," Josephine said. "Come on, let's get you home! Then we'll talk about the trouble you're in!"

But Imogene saw something, Violet's tattered eye, or the vomit on her jeans, or the expression on her face. Something. "Oh my God," she gasped. "Oh my God, Violet. What did Rose do to you?"

"Thank you, Genie. I have this covered. Viola, get in my car now."

It took so long for Violet to make herself understood. Shaking her head NoNONO. Desperately pulling her mother's hands off her, only to have Josephine latch on again, holding tighter than ever with spidery fingers that made Violet's flesh crawl.

Imogene had a scared, polite look on her face: "Mrs. Hurst, I don't think she wants to—"

Josephine tightened her death grip on Violet's wrist. "This doesn't concern you, Genie. Stop speaking for my daughter. As a matter of fact, stop talking to my daughter, period. We wouldn't even be out here if it weren't for you."

Imogene, mouth gaping, put a hand to her sternum. *"Me?"*

"Yes. You and your brother and your bad influence. The marijuana. And the sex and the sacrilege. It's unseemly! If I were your mother—"

"You're not her mother, Josephine."

Violet looked up, light-headed, and saw Beryl Field. She was standing between the parked cars, pashmina knotted around her head, earrings softly swinging, headlights blazing through the big holes of her crocheted poncho.

"I think it's probably best if Violet spends the night with us," Beryl said, flat and definitive. "Come on, honey. Imogene, please help Violet put her bike in our car."

A shiver shook Violet's spine. She threw a side eye at Josephine. She was prepared for more moralizing, waiting for her mother to launch into her well-worn diatribe—the one she always uttered in private about Rolf and Beryl's spineless, indulgent parenting. Instead, she walked with measured steps to her car. Before she pulled away into the huge black night, her rear wheels sending up a faint waft of dust, she turned back once to say: "What's your prognosis these days, Beryl? I'd tell you drop dead. But Violet tells me you're nearly there."

Beryl drove straight to the Kingston emergency room. Imogene sat in the backseat, crying and holding Violet's hand as she quietly, literally, coughed up the story of the past week, along with everything her mother had confessed to at the creek. She was shell-shocked at least three times over, but the details spewed out anyway. She couldn't keep them to herself. She had to talk about things before Josephine found a way to put a spin on them, before the crazy could be rationalized away.

"I almost didn't come!" Imogene kept saying. "But I got worried when you never called me. The whole ride over, I just kept saying, I know this is stupid. I know I'm thinking crazy. Didn't I, Mom? But I wasn't thinking crazy enough. What would have happened if we hadn't come?"

Beryl kept the journey short, the music cheerful and low-volume. She put her foot down and drove fast through the tiny, one-way streets of Kingston. Dark ivy and old stone houses sucked up the headlights, and Beryl flashed on her high beams. She let the girls have their moment, and only let on how freaked out she was once, when she shuddered horribly at a four-way stop, Violet telling them about the way Josephine had dressed in Rose's clothes.

"She must have been sick with grief," Beryl whispered. "Temporarily mad."

It was a mistake, attributing normal human emotions to Josephine. But Violet didn't blame her. Beryl was an empath, and she mothered the same way she lived—trying to put herself in other people's shoes, trying to experience the world as her children and their friends and their friends' families did. Violet's mother was the opposite. If anyone refused to accept Josephine's fantasy as their reality, Josephine rejected them, hurt them, or hid them from view. Stuffed with the full-time narcissistic supply Will gave her, she must have felt bold and invincible. She'd probably imagined she'd never get caught.

"Not a chance," Imogene laughed through a sob. "Josephine is *permanently* mad."

Beryl shushed her. "Violet, honey, I'm sure she can get help. Therapy. Something."

Violet nodded noncommittally, but she wasn't so sure. Beryl had cancer. Beryl knew she was sick. She did research, she listened to medical professionals, and she actively, desperately wanted to get well. Josephine, on the other hand, wouldn't entertain for a second that she was hurting herself or the rest of the Hursts. Called out by a court of law, Violet knew her mom would swear up and down that she was no more controlling or manipulative than any other woman on the planet. If a therapist tried to help Josephine, she would intimidate and shame them until they felt worse than she did, until they were too broken to look down on her. Being cured first required admitting you were ill, and

Violet knew Josephine would never, ever do that. Her mother would much rather go on pretending she was flawless and edit out anything (or anyone) that proved otherwise.

At the hospital, they photographed and fingerprinted the purpled-yellowed bruises that wreathed Violet's neck. They patched her tattered lower lid and cheekbone. The doctor shined a light in her eyes and down her throat, and asked if they felt painful. It all felt painful. But nothing hurt more than the knowledge that Rose was dead and still lost, her body in some sick, secret spot of her mother's choosing.

Violet let her friends take care of her, even though her mind and body fought her every second of the way. Imogene sat beside Violet in the hospital bed, one arm around her and the other controlling the bedside TV remote, conscientiously avoiding channels and emotional triggers the same way they'd done for Edie in the hospital (no reality court shows, no talk shows that trafficked in toothless family dysfunction). When the cafeteria opened, Beryl brought them hot coffees and big, oily Danishes that tasted of nothing but lard. She wrapped them up in the patchwork quilt she kept in the trunk of her car for summer picnics and winter roadside emergencies and sat in the corner blowing on a paper cup of green tea, never once letting on if she was dismayed to be back in a hospital so soon after her lumpectomy. Violet lay back and tried to avoid the ever-present voice in her head, the one that incessantly told her: *If you need help, don't ask for it. Do it yourself. Do everything yourself.*

Finch was the angry one. He drove to the hospital in the Fields' VW Vanagon and immediately began pacing around the cold, neutral room, raging at no one in particular, pulling aside the doctor and the cop, demanding more answers in a manner that was flattering and spouselike if not entirely helpful. He just didn't get it. It just didn't fit into the science of humanity. That was what he kept saying over and over: "A mother attacking her own kid! That's logical, maybe, in the American South during slavery. Save your daughter from the horrors that you were forced to endure—I get that. *That* is some Toni Morrison shit. But Josephine wasn't trying to spare Violet from a lifetime of rape and poverty. She is a privileged white woman living in the modern first world!"

"It's not logical to us," Imogene said. "Wherever Josie is, it makes sense to her. The psychologist on call told us it was probably the culmination of long-standing patterns."

Actually, she'd said long-standing patterns of relational dysfunction. Violet had hated every second of her psych evaluation. Another therapist in a week jam-packed with mental health professionals. This one had stayed too long and sat too close to the bed, with her understanding brown eyes that willed Violet to cry. But Violet hadn't cried, not once. She'd still felt like she was down in a deep old well, and everyone else was calling down to her from the surface. They avoided sharp sudden movements and mouthed reassuring things. They thrust statements and medical forms at her. They filled dark vials with her blood. It took all the energy Violet had to respond, sign her name on the line, thrust her inner elbow out for the needle.

Finch left after Beryl asked him to drive home and make up the guest room for Violet, at which point a woman from CPS, Trina Williams, came in. She claimed to be a colleague of Nicholas Flores, and when Violet asked why Nick didn't come himself, she said something poignant about some things being easier to discuss in female company. What followed was a whole arsenal of questions about Douglas: Was he an alcoholic? Did he ever hit any of the Hurst children? Was it true that he took an unhealthy interest with Rose's sexuality? She asked the questions apologetically, and her kind brown eyes said she knew Violet would rather be thinking about anything else. Violet answered truthfully: *Yes an alcoholic, but a recovering one. No, no hitting. It was their mother that used to scrutinize Rose's underwear.*

The morning sun was exploding through the window, lighting it up all pink and orange like the stained glass Violet had stared at in church so many times growing up. And Violet could not stop thinking of places her mother might have dumped Rose. That was how she thought about it: *dumped* or even *chucked away*, like trash lobbed out a car window at high speed. No doubt her mother would have argued some figment like she'd laid Rose to rest. But wherever Rose was, there was no chance it was the tranquil place she'd envisioned when she put the key into her car's ignition that final time. She wasn't resting, she was rotting in an unmarked grave, or else she'd already been eaten and composted by a family of black bears. That was the unpleasant truth of it. There was no death certificate. No burial records. There were three passable elements out of the four—earth, fire, water—and Josephine must have picked one and run with it.

A few hours before discharge—Violet's toxicology results came back clean—Detective Donnelly came by. He apologized. Last night was all his fault, he'd said. He'd been planning to get in touch. Douglas had shown up at the station yesterday afternoon with a diary he said proved Josephine had been harassing Rose, but when police reviewed it, they'd found a number of pages had been ripped out. Violet's father had said he'd always had a nagging feeling about last year's surveillance tape from the train station. There had been something of a stiffness missing from Rose's gait. He thought, at first, freedom had relaxed her a bit, but ever since he'd quit drinking he'd been asking more questions and paying closer attention to the timing of things. Rose went missing from the family photos shortly after he'd first suggested trying to track

Rose down through a private investigator. His car was keyed, supposedly by Rose, around the same time Josephine began accusing him of having affairs. Once Rose "resurfaced," Douglas noticed Josephine started treating her like the family dog; if something was missing, "Rose" took it for collateral; if something broke inexplicably, "Rose" did it in a vengeful rage.

In light of his conversations with Douglas, Donnelly had driven down Rose's old missing-person flyer to Newburgh, where the UPS store manager had said he'd never seen Rose in his life. According to one of the clerks, the owner of the box was a middle-aged brunette who tended to talk on her cell phone and bitch about the prices as though he were personally trying to rip her off. "I considered your mother," Donnelly told Violet. "But I knew her as a blonde. When she last came to our station, your mother was blond."

"Her letters came so regularly," Violet said. "When I wrote her, she got back almost immediately."

"It's a service they have. Whenever an envelope arrived for her, the store called the number she included in her letter to you."

"That number went to a disposable, I think," Violet said. "She threw it in the creek."

"I'm sorry to interrupt," Beryl said. "Do you have Josephine in custody?"

Donnelly nodded. "She went back to Old Stone Way early this afternoon. She'd spent the morning shopping in Rhinebeck. Said if she was going to be arrested, she wanted to be wearing a new a dress. She'd even been to the beautician. She told the mug shot photographer she'd had her makeup professionally applied. Excuse me if I say that gave the boys a laugh. They've been calling her *Maybelline*. You know, *Maybe she's born with it . . .* "

Violet was too tired to smile. "Whatever it is, she was definitely born with it." But the second she said it, she wondered if it was true. Was it abuse or genetics that made her mother the way she was? Maybe Josephine's genes were the match and her own mother's abuse was the thing that struck it. Whatever the cause, Violet couldn't do much but stand back and watch the flames twirl.

At the very least, Violet was more certain than ever that she wasn't her mother. No matter what horrors happened in her life, nothing short of a brain transplant could make her see the world the way Josephine did.

WILLIAM HURST

HERE ARE THE things Will made dead certain the prosecutor couldn't charge his mother with:

Manslaughter 2 (class C felony) for intentionally causing Rose to commit suicide. There was still Violet's testimony, in which she claimed their mother had accosted Rose with a photo of a dismembered baby in all its burgundy gore. But Josephine's defense lawyer—a gorgeous, if paunchy, silver-haired fox, who professed his love for her the second their trial was over—was quick to remind the jury that Violet was a druggie who regularly saw things that didn't exist: Aztecs, Hindu symbols, messages from the mystical "beyond." During the trial, he brought up what he called Violet's "schizophrenic breakdown." He pulled out her junior-class yearbook and pointed to a picture of Imogene and Violet, above the caption: Psychonauts. Will's mother had destroyed the latter portions of Rose's pregnancy journal herself, and Will swore on God's holy Bible that he'd never read anything along the lines of the incriminating passages his father had described. Technically speaking, it was a false, purposefully misleading statement. But Will was pretty certain God placed a much higher priority on honoring one's mother. Will still had it in his heart: ChristLove.

As soon as it was safe, Will had logged in to Rose's e-mail and wiped her whole history clean. In-box, outbox, everything.

Identity theft and criminal possession of stolen property (class E felony and class A misdemeanor) for possessing and using credit cards in Rose's name. Before Will left for the police station early that morning, he'd dressed in the clothes his mother had left out for him. It was casual for a change. A sweatshirt with submarine appliqués and a pair of cuffed jeans. Sliding them over his hips, he'd felt something stiff and rectangular in the pocket. Credit cards. Four of them in Rosette P. Hurst's name. Sure, Josephine might have put them there to frame him; in one moment of sacrilegious thinking the thought had crossed Will's mind. But he liked to think she'd left them there because she trusted him, and she knew he would do the right thing if everything were to go wrong. With a policeman waiting outside the Hursts' one locking door, Will had chopped them up over the toilet with the same razor-sharp scissors his mother used to trim his hair. Gone forever in a couple stuttering flushes. (*Sorry for the holdup, officer! My nervous stomach goes crazy when I'm alone with my monstrous father!*) There were no incriminating goods. Will's mother had used the cards entirely on museums, haircuts, and lunches at the 21 Club. She'd bought tickets to *Come Back Little Sheba* and *Legally Blonde: The Musical*.

Here were the charges Josephine couldn't escape:

Criminal obstruction of breathing (class D violent felony) for strangling Violet. The prosecutor tried to argue attempted murder on the grounds that Josephine had lured Violet to the rec fields for exactly that purpose, and claimed Will's mother would have completed the act if only Imogene hadn't interrupted. But the silver fox assured them no jury on the planet would convict her of that. He was right. They didn't. Not even when the plane tickets came to light; Josephine had bought herself and Will two first-class tickets (not to London, but to Croatia, where the cost of living was cheap and the United States had no extradition agreement). One of the jurors was even quoted saying, every mother feels the occasional urge to wring her teenage daughter's neck. Josephine got two years for cutting off breathing and blood circulation, and she's likely to be out much sooner.

Obstruction of justice (class A misdemeanor) for covering up Rose's suicide. Will's mother's confession—voice-recorded on Violet's Android phone—was inadmissible in court. And even though Josephine told more or less the same thing to police, there was simply no legal precedent. They tried to nab her for digging an illegal grave. But the cadaver dogs found Rose's remains on the Hursts' property, exactly where Josephine told them they would. Will's mother hadn't dug anything. She'd lowered Rose down into one of the deep fissures in the bedrock in the woods just beyond the backyard (the Hursts' property literally put the "ridge" in Stone Ridge). After Rose had transferred to geology, she'd been fascinated by them: these deep twelve-foot-by-twelve-foot cracks in the ground, made from years of ice expansion, the slit-openings not more than two feet wide in some places. Josephine argued that it was a natural burial, green, and she would have thought Violet would have appreciated that. Still, something of the details—the tarp, the wheelbarrow—put everyone off. "It was the way you'd bury a dog," the prosecutor spat. "Not the way you'd honor a human being, a beautiful young woman and unique individual." That last part had made Will's mother lift her chin and smile through her tears.

Secretly, Will thought he would have liked to see Rose preserved. In the funeral of his dreams, his sister would have been laid out in a glass casket, perfect as a fairy-tale princess or a boxed prom corsage.

Douglas, on the other hand, had Rose exhumed and cremated. Her memorial service, packed though it was with the friends she'd thought had forsaken them, featured mangy combinations of cheap flowers—sunflowers and cosmos in sad little Ball jars. The photo that he chose to blow up was a snapshot of Rose in full hiking regalia, her nose sunburned and peeling.

Will sat in the pews and thought how much better his mother would have done it. There would have been pink satin, white peonies (roses were too obvious), a soft-lit Vaseline-lensed head-shot, and something from Elgar's *Enigma Variations*. "Nimrod," probably.

But it was Douglas and Violet's deal. So instead there was a candlelight vigil and a folk version of "This Little Light of Mine," as rendered by a few flanneled idiots who couldn't be bothered to shave for the occasion. Will, on the other hand, was smooth as a Ken doll. Sweaty peach fuzz gone from his upper lip. The silver fox had given Will a lesson just before the trial and even confided the secret to shaving around your Adam's apple (swallow and hold). The advice turned out to be similar to other lessons the boys in Will's boarding school were teaching him; turns out "swallow and hold" also applied, more or less, to marijuana smoke and shots of Jameson.

That's right. Will had made it to boarding school after all.

The idea had come to him during those first few months when it had seemed like things couldn't possibly get worse. Douglas had just served Josephine with divorce papers. Josephine was awaiting her trial in jail. Violet was living with the Fields because she could, because she could shit on her own doorstep and then breeze on to her next location—the whole world was Violet's commode. CPS had claimed to take Will's claims against his father seriously, but the case was hard to prove without Violet's collaboration, and ultimately, custody was restored after a few short weeks in foster care for Will and a few laughable parenting classes for Douglas.

Will's foster home had been so dull and consistent it made his head swarm. There were no dramatic exits, no outpourings of rage or devotion. Will had an almost-allergic reaction to the tranquillity. He stayed out at a farmhouse in Pallenville, where there were acres upon acres of nothing, just zagging squirrel tracks on white fields and bronze sprays of deer piss in the stale snow. Will's barren foster parents, Sally and Larry, had no cable and no reading material save for the Lehman's catalog and a survivalist magazine called *Pioneer Living*. It had made Will stir-crazy, short-tempered, and concupiscent.

What's worse, Larry and Sally had been *too* kind. They were the kind of understanding that made Will feel boxed in and made his fellow foster brothers up the ante on their attitude problems. The boys Will lived with, Carson and Bodean, would destroy their clothes explicitly so Sally would buy the brands and styles they wanted (mostly camo-colored ensembles from Gander Mountain). They would demand to go to the ER if their stomachs hurt, just for the hell of it, just because they knew the law required Larry to take them.

Will had called up Bodean after CPS had sent him back to Old Stone Way, after he'd spent four long days feeling like a heretic, living with the man, Douglas, who'd talked slanderous trash about his mother to the press, calling her a "master of manipulation" and "the human equivalent of a burning building."

Will had needed Bodean's help. Will had needed Bo to hit him in the face as hard as he could. Will fantasized about that punch for weeks until they could finally meet up at Forsyth Park and make it happen. The blow, when it came, did the job in more ways than Will had ever imagined. It left him with a juicy black eye and a lust for pain. Will had gone home that night and informed Douglas that he had one week to cut a tuition check to a year-round, coeducational boarding school on the Massachusetts border. Otherwise, Will said, he would tell CPS his father had given him the shiner. He threatened to hurt himself all day, every day and blame it on Douglas, unless his dad sent him to live in the foothills of the Berkshires. At the time of the dramatic confrontation, Will had actually held the CPS complaint number in one hand and the school brochure in the other. *Eenie, meenie*, he'd told Douglas. *Take your pick.* If Will's father had even bothered to peruse the latter before agreeing to it, he would have seen lustrous foliage, boys in lacrosse shorts, snowy towers, brick arches, and the great-looking offspring of the power elite.

Will wore his uniform (red tie, blue blazer) to Rose's ceremony, and he could feel Violet's eyes boring into his school crest. She had been hounding Will for weeks, sending him letters very similar to the ones "Rose" had sent her, trying to get him to stop being furious with her for pressing charges, living at Imogene's house, doing what she, quote, "needed to do" in order to live a "peaceful and productive life." Will never responded, but he liked being pursued, and he took some solace in the fact that he wasn't the only one who struggled with peace and quiet. Just like him, Violet seemed addicted to family showdowns and tear-jerkers. Unlike Will, she didn't have the petty jealousies and backstabbings of boarding school to keep her appetite for drama sated.

Before Rose's ceremony, Violet had cornered Will by an edible arrangement and tried to make him see all the ways Josephine had come between them.

"I want to try to relate to each other directly," Violet had said. "Without Mom coming in between us. I'd like to think we can go to one another. . . . You know, just you and me. No pretending. No script. No more inauthentic representations of ourselves."

In response, Will just smirked and asked how her xerophagy was going. Violet didn't get it and Will didn't give her the satisfaction of a definition (diet of bread and water). She'd torched his family, burned it like every other bridge she'd ever crossed. And who knew if the word even applied anymore? Violet's messy bob haircut made her look rounder in the face. Chipmunk-cheeked. Oil, sugars, flour: all vegan.

Will's only input to Rose's memorial was the poem he selected to read. He picked Victor Daley's "In Memory of an Actress," and recited it with all the polish he'd once brought to his one-boy Edgar Allan Poe show:

> Say little: where she lies, so let her rest:
> What cares she now for Fame, and what for Art?
> What for applause? She has played out her part.
> Her hands are folded calmly on her breast,
> God knows the best!

Mourning Rose felt a little bit like mourning a celebrity. He was moved by the collective grief, the community outpouring, but he didn't know her well enough to feel deeply moved on a personal level. Rose had been a princess, but not one of the people. To Will, she was so privileged, so glamorous, and so very old that she'd never seemed fully human. As the years passed and Will entered his late teens, he'd come to see her like one of those passé symbols of good times everyone liked to talk about. Rose was like an SUV or a zero-down mortgage. She'd been their status symbol, something attractive but unsustainable, something the Hursts had paid heavily for.

After the memorial service, Will visited his mother in her orange jumpsuit and they gossiped like two bitchy soap opera vamps. She updated him on the divorce and her late-in-life romance, and he gave her a professional-grade manicure (cuticles, base coat).

Chirocosmetics: the art of manicure.

As always, they talked about London. (Josephine: "The British value eccentrics like you and me.") They were still moving there, she promised, once her release date arrived, and their life abroad would be all the better with her alimony money when it came. They would rent a place in Marylebone. She'd buy Will a tailor-made suit made of fine English fabrics. She'd send him to Fortnum & Mason, where they sold butter biscuits made of crystallized French violets and rose petals. "What about William cookies?" he'd joked, but she didn't get it. She just looked at him like he'd belched without excusing himself, and asked to see the printouts of her latest newspaper and Internet mentions.

Her mug shot pleased her, even if the headlines didn't.

Still, she grabbed his hand and said, "Will, never forget what I'm about to tell you. Promise?"

He promised.

"It's better to be hated than it is to be ignored."

He believed her. Mostly, when he called or visited, they talked about Violet. How selfish Violet was. How Violet had wronged Josephine. How Violet had defamed Rose and her memory. Josephine never asked Will about his seizures, which he'd apparently outgrown, or about his maybe-maybe-not Asperger's syndrome. If she ever did, Will liked to think he might confide in her about his struggling academics—the way he was at least two grades behind in science, geography, and math—about the way boys sometimes shoved him in the hallways and called him *faggot* and *pervert*, about the way he'd finally had blah, awkward girl-sex with a Korean exchange student to try to prove them wrong. He liked to think she would reassure him like a woman on a sitcom or a Mother's Day card: that she'd tell him to be himself, to surround himself with people who didn't just put up with the way he was but actually loved him because of it. Once, when Will was crying on the shower floor—crying because the closeted, conservative WASP he was in love with had thrown a flying fist in his ribs—he imagined his mother cradling him, telling him his life would unfold in a brilliantly beautiful way. Because he was worth it. Because he was special.

These days, Will's head swam with unusual words:

Gorsoon: a boy servant.

Teen: a homonym, which could mean either young person or injury; grief.

Hiraeth: grief for lost places. Homesickness for a home you can't return to. A home that maybe never was.

But William Hurst's favorite word, hands down, was still *eel-logofusciouhipoppokunurious.* It meant *good.* Will didn't expect other people to understand it, this complicated word for such a seemingly simple thing. But to Will, *good* was precisely that complicated. *Good job. Good boy. Good point. Good heart.* Those were the kinds of words he'd been waiting to hear all his life. They never came, but Will never stopped waiting for them; he just kept throwing all his strange, clever words at the world, hoping that one day they would.

Violet Hurst

To begin with, the media interest seemed like poetic justice. It gave Violet a secret thrill to see her mother—the woman who'd committed a pick 'n' mix of heinous crimes because her self-worth was so dependent on outside opinion—mentioned on *Anderson Cooper 360* and written up in the Strange Crime section of *The Huffington Post*, where the reader comments included:

Mother of the Year Award goes to . . . #sarcasm.

Articles like this one make me think the U.S. needs to institute the old Chinese practice of issuing birth permits before allowing reproduction.

And, *Karma's a bitch!*

But in the end, karma wasn't a bitch. Violet only had to watch her mother's manifold TV interviews from the courthouse steps to realize Josephine was flattered by the attention instead of shamed by it. Violet's mother didn't recognize the difference between fame and infamy. It was Violet who carried her mother's shame. She was the one who had to go back to Stone Ridge High School and hear the whispers as she walked by.

She'd only planned on staying with the Fields for a couple of weeks, but it turns out they needed her just as much as she needed them. Violet's anger and sarcasm had a place and purpose at the

Fields' house, especially with Beryl, who had decided to take a new, Western-thinking "fuck cancer" approach. Beryl's new motto was: chemo, not sea kelp. At the girls' suggestion, she named her boobs Knuckle and Knobby and charted their progress, forcing them to compete with one another in order to be healthy again. When they failed to improve at the same pace, Violet, Imogene, and Finch would take turns berating them in low, authoritative voices: *Listen up, cancer, we're not mad. We're just disappointed.*

Come March break, Rolf sent the three of them to apprentice at a permaculture farm site in Hawaii, while he and Beryl got some rest and relaxation at the Mauna Lani Bay Hotel. Imogene, in particular, didn't want to leave Beryl, not even for a few weeks, a day, a second; she considered it lost time, precious mother-hours she might never get back. But once they were there, sleeping in the open air at thirteen hundred feet, the subtropical forest teeming with feral pigs and night-chirping coqui frogs, they could all three agree it was exactly the change of scenery that they needed. There is no time for quarter-life crises when you are mulching coconut hulls, boiling taro root, and doing your business in the dank, rank composting toilet.

Violet faced her camping hammock west because she'd read in one of Beryl's New Age books that it was the direction of endings. "What do you need to finish?" the author wrote. "To whom do you need to say good-bye?" The Hawaiian sunset was all cotton-candy pinks and good-weather clouds, but something raged blacker than ever in Violet's chest. There were too many things she needed to say "so long" to and couldn't.

She couldn't say good-bye to Rose, the sister she'd known better than she ever thought. She kept going over the past couple years in her head, kept trying to imagine places—various moments in time where she could have built a bridge, done or said something that could have united the two of them over the dividing presence of their mother. (Josephine. Ugh, Josephine: dirty, and powerful, and quick-moving as the Hudson.) Violet kept having flashes of Rose with a telltale palm over her lower belly. She kept picturing Rose highlighting her latest script at the dining room table. What if Violet had gone with her to Planned Parenthood? What if Violet had offered to help her run lines? Each scenario seemed cheap and implausible. But it was impossible to stop brainstorming ways that it might have been different. Her brain kept envisioning alternate realities where Rose was alive, and she and Violet could feel close in each other's presence, a place where closeness wasn't painful or treasonous.

Violet couldn't stop feeling guilty about Douglas either. Douglas, financially drained, extorted by Will, pacing around the big, lonely, historically significant house he couldn't sell until the divorce was finalized. Violet went over most Sundays and let him cook her something from Ottolenghi. He was watching too much Food Network, checking out cookbooks from the Stone Ridge library in stacks and splattering them with soy sauce and oil. His sobriety seemed to be going well, even in spite of his shit-ton of stresses, but Violet founded him much too exhausting to live with full-time. He spent too much time convincing her that he was coping, and too little asking whether she was. His gaze was needy, childlike. Sometimes he looked at Violet as though she were his mother. Others, he lavished her with strangely chosen compliments as though she were his wife. Violet had heard rumors that he was getting friendly with the spin-class teacher at his gym—a tanorexic, sports-braed woman with echoes of Josephine in her willful black eyes. When Violet woke up nights, dreaming about her mother's hands around her neck, she often stayed up worrying about the woman Douglas would choose when he remarried. Violet never doubted for a second that he *would* remarry and quite quickly at that. Even as he quit drinking, he was a man who clung rigidly to the familiar. He didn't want bonding, he wanted bondage.

You'd think Will would have been the easiest Hurst for Violet to let go of, but as it turned out, he was the hardest. In Will, she saw something of the children both her parents must have been. She wanted to give him a close, trusting, respectful relationship. It was only after Rose's funeral that she realized closeness panicked Will. Trust pained him to the point of torture. Her brother didn't *want* to be loved; to him, love felt like a gunnysack over the head. Will wanted more than anything to stick to the script he'd been born with and try out all the parts. Will would go his whole life rotating through the Hurst cast of characters—alternately playing the abuser, the victim, the bystander, and the hero—but he'd never, ever exit the theater. Sometimes, in sunnier moods, Violet held out hope for him. Maybe one day, down the road, Will would meet a decent boyfriend or a patient shrink—someone who'd free him from his mother's death-grip one small inch at a time.

Not that Violet was a cured woman. In Hawaii, she realized she couldn't play. Not the way other people did. Sure, she could dig trenches and weave palm leaves until her hands were stiff and covered with sores. Yes, she could drink 'shroom tea with honey and swim in a warm, trippy metaphysical sea. But she couldn't bang on the vibraphone or patty-cake bongos with her fellow interns. Not sober and not for the hell of it. When one of the cooperative members' babies—blond, gender indeterminate, topless in a pair of homemade overalls—came to Violet with a plastic pony, Violet's first instinct wasn't to snort and whinny, it was to fight tears. She wasn't shell-shocked. This wasn't the fallout from two terrible years and the fact that her mother had tried to wring her neck like a rag. Violet, beneath all her glibness and occasional drug-giddiness, realized she couldn't have innocent fun.

In Hawaii, Violet was confronted by this small pickle: she was apologetic about wanting to live for her own enjoyment. She felt really guilty about having her own identity, and doubly fucking terrified when she experienced something beautiful or even pleasant, accustomed as she was to her mother ruining it, usurping it, or passing it off as inconsequential.

Maybe, someday, some gifted acupuncturist or Reiki healer could dislodge, in one go, all the Josephine-shaped shrapnel that was embedded in Violet: her shame, her underachieving, her willingness to absorb the kind of physical and emotional pain that most people wouldn't accept in their lives. In the meantime, she decided she would just keep following the bittersweet terror that told her when she was on to something. Not anything quite so profound as "growth" or "healing," just a little bit of childhood unease replaced by a small gush of gratitude for the tiny moments when she could live in the moment and be herself.

Late one night after laying down mulch, Finch kissed her in the wood-burning hot tub. It was a good kiss, deep and spine-tingling, and she surprised both of them by sobbing like he'd punched her in the throat. Finch just gently pulled her head to his chest and laughed, "Good for you then, was it?" It *was* good for her, first reaction aside. It was good, and terrifying and a fantastically long time in the making.

The night before they left the farm, they watched a wild boar giving birth to a litter. Three boys and three girls. Striped and fawn colored, like mini-deer or giant chipmunks. Each one crashed, skull first, into the world and lay stunned in the dirt until their minutes-older siblings gave them a sniffing nudge. Then, squealing, still tethered by umbilical cords, they walked, working hard to get their hind legs under them. Maybe it was stupid to be moved by a species of the pig genus, but Violet and her friends were. It was an intense birth, gory as a tragedy. It left them awed.

Afterward, Finch got wasted on rum. Imogene cried so hard her face still looked mangled the next day. One of the other drunkish interns kept saying, "Wouldn't it be amazing? To come into the world and immediately be able to stand on your own feet?" It *was* amazing, and even Violet could see that was exactly what she'd done. She had walked away from the first and most dire of her life's disasters. Her birth. Her mother. The dynamics of her family and her childhood. She'd survived, and now it was her job to do more—to really *live* where she'd once just tried to endure from one day to the next. To be honest, it felt more daunting than exciting. It had been easy to make Josephine happy (or unhappy). Fighting for her own happiness was far less straightforward. She hardly knew where to begin.

Violet surprised herself by getting into art school, even if Douglas, who was drained from Will's private school expenses, couldn't afford to send her. Instead, she took a year off and saved up, working full-time at Dekker's.

It turned out to be exactly the kind of hands-on, knackering work she needed. Mrs. D spared her the cash register and the tourists, and instead let her do some of the heavier farmwork. Lugging hoses. Heaving old car tires onto the plastic sheet of the silage clamp. It kept her away from the farm stand, where Josephine's new defense-lawyer boyfriend tended to linger in the parking lot (sunglasses, convertible) and spy on her. She couldn't imagine what he possibly reported back: *Violet refilled the microgreen bin, then restocked the frozen quiches.* Juicy. Or maybe it *was* juicy. Even from the confines of her eight-by-eight cell, Violet's mother probably felt affirmed by the fact that Violet wasn't in college. It was still too easy to conjure Josephine's voice: *See? I told you Violet was a screwup. No discipline. Not smart enough. Of course, she'd forgo a higher education.*

Those were exactly the kind of thoughts Violet couldn't have out in the fields, with her joints creaking and the bridge of her nose turning red. It was impossible to be in her head when she was doing that kind of work. All the hauling and digging burned off some of the remaining panic (over her mother), anger (at Will), and frustration (with her dad).

Not that Violet's Dekker's life was all unskilled labor. Mrs. D took her under her wing, bringing her to meetings of the Local Growers Association and asking her to paint the Dekker's sign, weekly, with the crop of the moment. The final product was always dark, but usually funny: a Thumbelina-sized woman struggling to carry an ear of corn, a boy with an apple on his head like he was about to be shot. She even convinced Mrs. D to open up the farm stand as a flea market in the winter months. It wasn't hugely profitable, but it gave the community a little lift during those last lonely weeks before the ground thawed and the seed catalogs arrived in the mail.

After Finch and Imogene left for college, Beryl let her stay rent-free in the Fields' guest cottage. She managed to buy a car from one of the Dekker's meat suppliers. A truck, actually. An ugly but well-maintained pickup with at least a jillion miles that she planned to drive until the valves melted. Mostly, she drove it to visit Imogene at Hampshire College and Finch at Wesleyan. Both had yearned for UVM but decided to stay closer to home, or rather, closer to Beryl, and Violet could drive to each school in just about two hours.

Violet and Edie still spoke. She was back at Vassar, finishing up her last few credits in some sort of theory class that had her writing papers on neoliberal societies with postclassist philosophies. Her fellow students overused the phrase *social construct* in a way that drove her crazy.

"Today someone raised their hand and said depression is a social construct," Edie wrote in one of her near-weekly e-mails. "I swear, Violet. It took everything I had not to flip the table. I shouldn't take it personally, I know. They think ketchup is a social construct. They think pants are a social construct. But it still makes me feel so fucking judged and lonely."

One Martin Luther King, Jr. weekend, Violet went down to Poughkeepsie and spent the weekend with her. Edie had been at Fallkill longer than expected, and her old housemates had been forced to fill her room with someone else. So Edie was back in the residence halls, rooming with a girl (not of her picking) who wore too much red lipstick, drank water from a Bordeaux glass, and talked about little but her "heteroflexibility." Or, more specifically, whether wanting to sleep with her boyfriend's friend meant she was at the end of a monogamous relationship or the beginning of a polyamorous one.

By that time, Violet didn't feel as out of place on a college campus. It wasn't like those first few times she'd visited Imogene and Finch, when she couldn't get past all the acronyms people used to describe the buildings and dining halls: ASH, CFF, MDB. She wasn't as floored by tales of library sex and repulsed by the smells of damp laundry and cheap watery beer.

Edie hadn't had any episodes on her latest cocktail of medications, but she still didn't seem entirely at ease. It was a bit like she'd driven the black dog of depression over the Pennsylvania border and abandoned it in a field. It was gone, but still out there . . . somewhere. Edie just kept waiting to hear it scratching at her door, filthier and more ravenous than ever.

"I feel the same way about my mother," Violet had confessed.

Back when Josephine first began her jail sentence, she'd sent Violet a short letter saying she really wanted to "rebuild their relationship." The other inmates were sick of hearing her weeping, she said. She said she felt like she had lost not one daughter, but two. Violet had let the letter sit for a week or two, trying to decide whether it was merely words—the same kind of seduction story an abusive husband would give. *I'm sorry, baby. You mean so much to me. I swear to you it will never happen again.* Only Josephine hadn't even admitted any guilt. She hadn't, in fact, said she was sorry at all.

Violet had been composing her reply, ready to give her mom the benefit of the doubt, when a follow-up letter arrived. In it, Josephine accused Violet of using everything that happened with Rose as an "excuse" to "terminate" their "relationship." She said Violet had always been difficult: a colicky baby, a defiant child, a narrow-minded young adult, rejecting and all but impossible to love.

Violet *did* write a rebuttal to that one. She was halfway to the post office before she realized her folly. If Josephine couldn't use false promises to rope Violet back in, she'd use insults in the hope Violet would come running to defend herself. Violet didn't jump to the challenge. Instead, she tore up the unsent envelope.

Eventually, Josephine's boyfriend started sending gifts to Violet at the Fields' address. A big fleecy bathrobe (the note read: *Mommy wants to make sure you are keeping warm*). A necklace with an H-shaped pendant (for Hurst) with a note that read: *From your loving mother, thinking of you on your birthday.* Violet donated the robe to the Tibetan Center's thrift shop. She marked the necklace "return to sender."

Finally, Josephine sent Beryl a scathing letter accusing her of turning Violet against her own flesh and blood. Violet managed to persuade Beryl not to respond. "It's counterproductive to all of us," Violet told her. "Instead of helping me let her go, it will just start the cycle all over again and make me hate her more." In the months since, there had been an eerie silence from Josephine's camp. It felt peaceful, but ephemeral. Violet got the sense that her mother wasn't done yet.

That MLK weekend, Edie gave Violet a road map to no contact as they drank honey drip coffee in her favorite Vassar-adjacent coffee shop:

"In another year, you'll get to the place where your mom simply won't exist to you. You might be able to put words to some of your own coping mechanisms and self-defeating behaviors. You'll probably wild out a bit. Tattoos, casual sex. Don't go crazy. After two years, you should be able to see yourself outside your family context. The grieving period will be winding down. You'll be heavy in the process of unlearning things she taught you: fucked-up things you say and think but may not believe deep down. After three years, you should be able to pick men you trust, not just megadouches who trigger family stuff. After four years, you'll realize taking care of people feels good, but you're not Atlas. You don't need to hold up the world. You don't need to attend everyone's life crises. After five years, you'll probably still have problems with intimacy, but you won't be compelled to fling yourself headfirst into relationships you know you don't want."

Violet nodded, even though things were going well with Finch. They were talking seriously about Violet moving to Middletown next year. He kept encouraging her to apply to the art department with a series she'd been working on. They were 3D charcoal drawings that she then photographed. If she drew a tarantula, she snapped her fingers picking it up. If she drew dominoes falling down, she clicked a photo of her hand knocking the first one over.

"When do I get to feel good?" Violet asked. "Or at least neutral?"

Edie thought for a minute. She looked older than she had in the hospital, little threads of premature gray in her dark hair. "Five to ten years, maybe? Or maybe, by then, it's just that you're too tired and battered. You don't have the energy to be self-destructive."

Sometimes Violet looked back with nostalgia on the drug-recovery program she did in the hospital. She wished addiction were her problem. Giving up family, even an abusive family, felt even harder than kicking a drug habit. "Anything else I should know?" she asked.

"It helps to know older women," Edie said. "Neighbors. Mentors. Don't run away from women who offer you momlike kindness. Just don't get all your mothering from just one place. That's when things go terribly wrong."

By the time Beryl lost her fight to cancer, Violet had already grieved Josephine as though she were dead. She'd done the angry thing. The heartbroken thing. The socially awkward thing where she felt ungainly and inept: her conversations were awkward, even her greetings felt weird. She'd come to terms with the fact that she'd never have a mother who could celebrate at her wedding or the birth of her first child. She'd accepted not having a biological mom she could call for advice when things weren't going well, when a layoff happened, when the car broke down. Even if Josephine had been in Violet's life, she couldn't have done any of those things. Josephine wouldn't allow anyone to be happy unless she was the source of their happiness. If Violet had been riding high, Josephine would have been ratty and envious. If Violet had been feeling low, Josephine would have kicked her while she was down. Violet missed the idea of mother (mother in general) far more than she missed mother-specific.

Beryl was different. When Beryl died, Violet missed a million little highly specialized things. She missed the way, when you couldn't figure something out in the kitchen, Beryl had a way of showing you how without making you feel stupid: roll out the sticky dough between sheets of wax paper, smash the garlic clove with one fist and the side of the knife. She missed the way, even after Violet moved out of the guest cottage, Beryl found excuses to visit and call: to tell Violet about the funny thing that happened to her when she was shopping for mattresses, to make sure Violet had power in the torrential snowstorm. Violet missed the way Beryl looked so deep into your eyes when you told her something: *I'm with you*, that sweet gaze said. *Even if I don't agree, I'm here. I'm engaged. I want to understand.*

In those first tender months after Rose's funeral, Beryl had told her: "I know things feel messy right now. It probably feels like life has just chucked all these ingredients at you. Flour's hanging in the air. Milk is dripping down off the counter. But everything you're going through . . . You're going to turn it all into great pancakes someday."

The last time Violet visited her in the hospice, Beryl had looked up from her pillow and said, "Get the syrup. I smell pancakes." The nurses thought she was talking nonsense, but Violet knew what she meant. Violet's life felt like a guilty pleasure. Something she'd stolen. It was the one gift her mother had never intended for her. Josephine had birthed Violet for Josephine.

But Violet was going to live for herself.

Acknowledgments

As Violet would say, I must have been an exceptionally good person in a past life to know such inspiring women in this one.

Thank you, first and foremost, to my editor Alexis Washam for being my patient teacher and my sister in darkness. I've never loved writing more than I have with your contagious energy and warm, incisive guidance on the other end of the line. Also, my husband's pet name for me is "Spoiler Alert," so without you, this would have been a far less suspenseful book. Hopefully, all that clue-slashing hasn't left you carpal tunneled.

Thank you to my agent Amanda Urban for reading and re-reading and re-re-re-reading, always with trademark frankness and kindness.

Thank you Josie Freedman, also at ICM, for loving Will as much as I do. What's more, at the exact second I was doing my best Munch scream, you called with all the answers I could have possibly asked for.

Molly Stern, Crown's Publisher, I can't even begin to put ten years' worth of gratitude into words. In the trippy Oz of my adult life, you've been my Glinda the Good. You sent me down this book's path long ago (probably without realizing it), and I'm so thankful you gave me the opportunity to *realize* it.

Other jewels in the Crown: Sarah Bedingfield, Sarah Breivogel, Lauren Kuhn, Rachel Meier, Jessica Prudhomme, and Jay Sones.

Thank you to everyone in the Mother-Motherland: Martha Frankel and her perennially awesome Woodstock Writers' Festival; Barbara Cole; Cassandra Mahoney, Robin Shornstein; Woodstock Day School; the Mid-Hudson Library System; and The Golden Notebook, the coolest bookstore in Woodstock.

Also, on the subject of booksellers, I owe a huge debt of gratitude to Miwa Messer and Barnes and Noble's Discover Great New Writers Program, who have been my friends and cheerleaders ever since I was, well . . . a drunken cheerleader.

Thank you to Christie Lafranchi, Devon Banks, Corvette Hunt, Mary Karr, Joan and David Lehmann, and the great many Hamiltons (especially Carol, for always being there to talk female-noir with me and remind me, in British-fashion, to keep calm and type on).

Speaking of British allies, I owe a great deal of gratitude to Kim Young at HarperCollins UK for help in this book's final inning.

Thank you, above all, to my husband, Eamon Hamilton, and my three children for being my anti-Hursts. You are family like I never knew it could be.

MOTHER, MOTHER

ESSAYS,
READER'S GUIDES,
AND MORE

A Reader's Guide

Everything is just perfect in the Hurst household . . .
or that's what Josephine Hurst would like people to
think. In truth, Josephine knows better than anyone that her family is falling apart: her husband,
Douglas, is an alcoholic and possible adulterer; her
sheltered son, William, suffers from stress-induced
seizures; daughter Violet is using drugs and delib-
erately starving herself; and casting a shadow over
all is the absence of her eldest child, Rose. Josephine
is determined to bring it all into line—or at least to
make everything appear picture perfect to the outside world, no matter what the consequences to the
damaged souls in her own home. But when she has
deceived and manipulated and still has not regained
control, Josephine's methods turn from damaging to
truly terrifying—and her children's very lives hang
in the balance.

Seen through the lenses of her two remaining
children, the novel tells the story of a family spiral-
ing into crisis as the lies they've lived with begin to

crumble, and the truths they uncover threaten to tear them apart.

In order to provide reading groups with the most informed and thought-provoking questions possible, it is necessary to reveal important aspects of the plot of this novel. If you have not finished reading *Mother, Mother*, we respectfully suggest that you wait before reviewing this guide.

QUESTIONS FOR DISCUSSION

1. With Violet's drug use and Josephine's manipulation influencing their perception of events, neither William nor Violet is completely reliable as a narrator. Did you consider one of them to be more trustworthy than the other? Were there other characters you would have liked to hear from as narrators?

2. Were you optimistic about Violet's reunion with Rose? How did you envision their life together playing out?

3. Violet assumes that from their birth, Josephine never felt real love toward any of her children. Do you think that is true? Do you think it is possible for a parent to love his or her children and still behave in the ways Josephine did?

4. What do you imagine Josephine's childhood was like? Do you think there is any truth to her assertion that her own upbringing was more painful than the one she is giving her children?

5. What do you think of Douglas's role in the story? Does he share the blame for the state of his fam-

ily? Do you think Josephine truly suspects him of having an affair, or is this part of her manipulation of William?

6. The hospital staff knows that Violet has used drugs and attempted to starve herself to death, and it is suspected that she violently injured her own brother—still, the theme of her treatment seems to be a supposed compulsion for lying. Why do you think this is? Why does her doctor insist she address it?

7. How does Violet compare to the friends she makes in the hospital? Do you think she belongs there? What kinds of insights does Edie bring to Violet's situation, and how are they helpful or harmful?

8. Was William's misdiagnosis a deliberate scheme by Josephine? Do you think that, in her mind, she was truly trying to do right by him?

9. What role do you think that Josephine's own childhood plays in the way she treats her family? Does this excuse her behavior?

10. Violet predicts that William will never be fully free of his mother's influence. How do you envision Josephine's influence playing out in his adult life? How do you think Violet herself will feel the effects of Josephine's cruelty in future relationships?

11. What effect do you think Josephine's parenting had on the relationship between Violet and Rose? Was there ever a chance that they could've become close, before Rose disappeared?

12. Do the Hursts remind you of any families that

you know? How effectively do you think they hide their dysfunction from the rest of the world? How common do you think that is?

13. Are there any good parents represented in the book? What specifically differentiates them from the Hursts?

14. At the end of the book, Violet identifies the Hursts as the characters they have played: abuser, victim, bystander, hero. Which Hurst do you think she has in mind for each role? Do you agree with her characterizations?

An Essay from Koren Zailckas:
An Expectant Mother

"It's so hard to be creative in two ways at once," gripes Roxy, the pregnant poet, in Diane Johnson's novel *Le Divorce*.

As the mother of three children, I cosign that complaint.

Don't get me wrong, I know a lot of expecting, working mothers who have it worse. My girlfriends have managed, somehow, to conduct board meetings while they choke down morning sickness. I know others who've waited tables, punched registers, and paced hospital corridors all day long on swollen feet—their backs spasming all the while and their little bundles slam-dancing in their beach-ball stomachs.

By comparison it seems pretty wussy to grumble about being a pregnant writer. I mean, come on . . . . At the very least, I was spared the horrors of maternity pantyhose. Instead, I got to spend each working day in my husband's hooded sweatshirt with a rubbish bin balanced between my knees and saltine crumbs scattered across my keyboard.

Even so, another baby was the farthest thing from my mind when I was confronted with the pink positive sign of a home pregnancy test.

At the time, I was deep in the first draft of my first novel *Mother, Mother*—a thriller about a frighteningly dysfunctional family—and I was so entranced by the work, it didn't even occur to me that I might be pregnant until I looked like I was smuggling a small watermelon under my shirt. When I vomited in my lap on the Interstate, I convinced myself I had food poisoning. Faced with chronic headaches and exhaustion, I entertained thoughts of cancer.

Call it repression or selective stupidity. But as the mother of two toddlers, I was already creeped out by how easy it was to channel *Mother, Mother*'s controlling Josephine—a woman so engulfing she flosses her twelve-year-old son's teeth. At that time, being pregnant with a third child seemed like the ultimate "Help, I'm becoming my mother!" moment.

"I need a favor," I finally told my husband. "Will you go into the downstairs bathroom and tell me what the pregnancy test on the counter says?" I didn't want to be the one to know the news first. What if I ended up with two daughters and one son, just like Josephine? And what if, once I finished the book, I found I couldn't turn off Josephine's emotionally needy, secretly mean voice?

Through the closed bathroom door, I heard my husband's laughter.

"We are, aren't we?" I said, fighting tears. I felt almost as though Josephine had impregnated me. Like she was throwing another obstacle in my way, making it harder for me to expose the Hursts' secrets.

My husband wrapped his arms around me. "Number three," he said, smiling. "I think it's brilliant."

In the end, having a third baby *was* brilliant. Not only did our little girl round out our family, she was an unexpected muse. Born with a big voice and Bindi-shaped birthmark, it was easy to imagine her one day being as courageous and spiritual as *Mother, Mother*'s Violet.

Lying in a hospital bed, cuddling my newborn, I accepted once and for all that I wasn't Josephine or my mother, whose patterns of borderline personality disorder had loosely inspired the character.

Some readers may think Jo is over the top. But in some aspects, she's even more subtle than the mother I knew. Whereas Jo still flosses twelve-year-old Will's teeth, mine was fighting to shower me at the same age (other daily intrusions included reading my diary no matter where I hid it and coming into my room at night like something out of *Black Swan*). I vividly remember one morning when I woke to find a pair of sewing scissors under my pillow, exactly the same way Will does, and suspected my mother put them there for reasons I couldn't (or didn't want to) guess. And just like Will, my childhood was riddled with dissociative fainting spells; I used to wilt like a daisy—never at school or while playing with friends, only when I was alone with my mom.

In truth, *Mother, Mother* was born of post-traumatic stress disorder, a condition that worsened after I became a mother myself. In relating to my kids, I found myself having daily, vivid flashbacks of what I'd lived through at their age. But my newborn daughter also helped me remember why I'd embarked on *Mother, Mother* to begin with: so I could bring some of my own childhood traumas into consciousness, therefore lessening the likelihood I'd repeat them with the beautiful, hilarious, loving, and insightful little people who stood before me, wielding fairy wands and trailing superhero capes, demanding I cut the crusts off their sandwiches.

One day, when my daughter is much older, I hope to tell her all the ways she helped me with this book. She went through the process with me, keeping me anchored to the present, reminding me that there was life outside of my childhood memories and their fictional reincarnation, the Hursts. Her every hiccup reminded me that I wasn't as vulnerable and dependent at Josephine's children. Her every kick was a gentle nudge, telling me that I was an adult and a mother—I was creating a healthier family of my own.

What's more, my little one kept me on my target date. I'd already edited one book, with my first daughter in a sling around my chest, and I didn't want to do it again. Goodness knows, writers are great at skirting deadlines. But a baby's due date is one deadline that can't be pushed back.

A Conversation with Koren Zailckas

Q. How close do you feel to the character of Violet—was she based on your teenage self? Do you feel that Violet has an eating disorder, or is she just trying to find a way of coping in an impossible situation? Are Eastern religions something you are or were interested in?

A. I definitely relate to Violet as the family black sheep and as someone who self-medicates in order to cope with that role. I remember that moment in my adolescence when I stopped trying the way Violet has when we meet her: I'd stopped trying in school, stopped trying to get along at home, stopped trying to make anyone think I was anything but a disappointment or an imposition. I wasn't aware of my deeper motivations at the time—much as Violet doesn't realize hers—but self-sabotaging was damn near angelic. Being "bad" was an attempt to please an unappeasable parent. It was almost the most obedient thing I could do.

Also, much as Violet uses drugs, I did a lot of binge drinking in an effort to numb out anxiety, family pain, PTSD. I didn't quite realize it when I wrote my memoir, *Smashed*, but binge drinking was a subconscious effort to kill myself in a way that could pass for accidental and socially acceptable (at least for a teenager and college student). A dysfunctional family can feel like a life sentence, and I just couldn't envision any other way out.

I think that doomed feeling probably inspired Violet's sallekhana. She's definitely toying around with eating disorders (a lot of children of narcissistic parents do). But I think, for Violet, it's more about self-abandonment. The Hursts treat her, almost, like she doesn't have a right to be there at all, and so she's trying to make her outsides match her insides. The goal really is death. Even if sallekhana, in Violet's case, has an element of teenage angst.

I went through a period, after *Smashed*, when I was drawn to Eastern religions. I bought books by Pema Chödrön. I spent a week, cross-legged and close-eyed, at a Buddhist center. The idea of forgiveness appealed—that you could just meditate, be your better self, and rise above all the family dysfunction. As it turns out, that's not a very effective way to deal with childhood trauma. In fact, neither is getting angry. You have to grieve a bit. And you have to give testimony. Maybe that's with a therapist or a friend, maybe it's in a notebook that you alone read. But, in the telling, a story of helplessness becomes one of resilience and strength.

Q. Rose haunts this book from the very beginning, yet her personality feels diffuse and unknowable—both of her siblings often note that although they grew up with Rose, they never quite understood their sister, and that she was always changing. What was it like to write a character whose defining quality was her absence?

A. Writing Rose was frightening. Especially as a fiction rookie. It felt like doing fiction "wrong." Because novels—at least the ones I love and hold dear—all have really finely drawn characters with a host of personality quirks.

But people like Rose are common, especially in the context of dysfunctional families. They're dissociative, occasionally very shell-shocked and blank. They are the children who, psychologically speaking, had to shrink down and make themselves small in order to accommodate their larger-than-life caregivers. They haven't been allowed to take center stage in anything, including their own emotions and thought processes.

The irony with Rose is: she's an actress, and her mother often thrusts her into the spotlight. By the time we meet the Hursts, Josephine has spent a long time objectifying Rose on the surface, even as she dismisses her on a deeper, almost atomic, level.

Obviously, this is really confusing for Rose. She's been so engulfed by her mother for so long. She hasn't been allowed an inch of space in which to figure out who she is and what she wants out of life. It seemed only natural that Will and Violet should struggle to define their older sister because Rose hasn't had the freedom to do as much for herself.

Q. The three Hurst children's reactions to their upbringing are very different: self-destruction, healing, and imitation. Do you think these are the three most common reactions to an abusive childhood? Do you believe a child's nature affects how he or she reacts to abuse? Given your own experiences as a kid, do you feel you could have ended up like Rose or Will if circumstances had been different?

A. I suppose the honest answer is: I don't know. I don't know why we all react to trauma differently. Probably birth order has something to do with it, as well as genetic factors. Personality-disordered parents, especially borderline mothers, have a real psychological imperative to make one child the golden child and another kid their scapegoat—that way, they can project their own aspirations and grandiosity onto one child, and their undesirable "bad" qualities onto another. I think you can see that in the way Josephine picks out roles for her children: "The Performer" (Rose); "The Creature of High Intelligence" (Will); "The Needy One" (Will, again); "The Saboteur" (Violet). Really, these are things Jo aspires to, or else they're the parts of herself she isn't willing to face.

Over time, some kids like Will and Rose will take those pigeonholes on as their identity, while others like Violet will choose to step away and reevaluate who they really are deep down. Violet also has a wider support network. She has empathetic, maternal figures in her life, women like Mrs. Field and Mrs. Dekker. These women have taught her how healthy, reciprocal love looks and feels.

I shudder to think I might have ended up like Rose or Will, but that's probably not too far off from the truth. In order for change to happen, you have to reach a point where your love outweighs your fear. I think that happened for me in my midtwenties. I finally let myself imagine a future outside of my role in my family. I realized I really wanted to build a healthy family of my own, and in order to do that I had to be willing to address the past. You can't change how you relate to trauma if you can't bring yourself to look squarely at it.

Do you believe that personality disorders can always be diagnosed? We see a lot of psychotherapists in *Mother, Mother*—do you put any stock in their findings?
A. I definitely believe in therapy, especially for people who have anxiety, post-traumatic stress, difficult childhoods. The process, when it works, is simply about bringing the painful past into mindfulness.

You don't forget a bad childhood simply because you try to push it out of your mind. On the contrary, it only makes you more likely to accidentally reenact the abuse—the things that seem too terrible to fully remember, let alone say. You pick a dangerous partner because he or she reminds you of your punishing parent. You find it hard to be empathetic to others because you were never taught how to have compassion for yourself.

A lot of childhood trauma has a static, wordless quality. You keep it to yourself, and it looms huge in your consciousness. But once you talk about it, give it language, you can begin to change the way you relate to it.

Through storytelling, an experience of fear and hopelessness transforms into a story about human resilience and triumph in the face of adversity. It changes the way you relate to yourself and transforms the way you interact with others. Many of us think, "If anyone knew what I've been through, they'd think I'm a freak. They'd want nothing to do with me." Maybe an abuser even planted that message. But when we talk about trauma, we realize what seems shameful is actually very common. The experiences that once felt so alienating become a source of connection to other people. You give testimony, and droves of people come forward and say, "That happened to me too!"